Praise for Tiffany Reisz's *The Bourbon Thief*

"A dark, twisty tale of love, lust, betrayal, and murder…this novel is not one to be missed."

—*Bustle*

"I loved [Reisz's] Original Sinners series, and this book looks like an epic to delve into on a long, lazy afternoon. Her prose is quite beautiful, and she can weave a wonderful tight story."
—*New York Times* and *USA TODAY* bestselling author Jennifer Probst

"*The Bourbon Thief* isn't just good, it's exceptional. The story captured my imagination; the characters captured my heart."

—*Literati Literature Lovers*

"Reisz fills the narrative with rich historic details; memorable, if vile, characters; and enough surprises to keep the plot moving and readers hooked until the final drop of bourbon is spilled."

—*Booklist*

"Beautifully written and delightfully insane…Reisz vividly captures the American South with a brutal honesty that only enhances the dark material."

—*RT Book Reviews*, Top Pick

"Impossible to stop reading."

—*Heroes and Heartbreakers*

"*The Bourbon Thief* is the sort of book that knocks you off your feet, steals your sanity and keeps you up all night reading! Fair warning—this is definitely a nontraditional love story… Not for the faint of heart!"
—*RT Book Reviews*

"Prepare yourself for soap-operatic level twists, and also to ignore everything else in your life as you race to the end of this eyebrow-raising tale."

—*RT Book Reviews*

Also by Tiffany Reisz

THE BOURBON THIEF

The Original Sinners series

The White Years

*

THE QUEEN
THE VIRGIN
THE KING
THE SAINT

The Red Years

*

THE MISTRESS
THE PRINCE
THE ANGEL
THE SIREN

For a complete list of books by Tiffany Reisz,
please visit www.tiffanyreisz.com.

THE NIGHT MARK

TIFFANY REISZ

MIRA

Recycling programs
for this product may
not exist in your area.

ISBN-13: 978-0-7783-2855-1

The Night Mark

Copyright © 2017 by Tiffany Reisz

For questions and comments about the quality of this book, please contact us at
CustomerService@Harlequin.com.

www.MIRABooks.com

Printed in U.S.A.

To the men and women who tended the world's lighthouses and to everyone who ever kept a light shining in the dark...

THE

NIGHT

MARK

Faye closed her eyes and thought of *Casablanca*.

Easy to do since she'd been watching it earlier that day. She'd also watched it the week before and the month before that. In the past four years, she'd watched it at least ten times, definitely more, but ten was all she would admit to if asked. And her husband had asked when he'd come home from work and found her watching it.

"Again?" Hagen had asked.

"It's a classic" was all Faye had said.

Now, hours later, as Hagen kissed the back of her neck, her thoughts returned to *Casablanca*. It was nine o'clock on Friday night, the one hour of the week they usually made the effort to show up for their marriage. But she hadn't felt well all day—tired, aching—and all she wanted to do was close her eyes and go to sleep. Since she couldn't sleep, she dreamed of Rick and Ilsa and Morocco while Hagen did his best to pretend theirs was a real marriage.

Faye was far more concerned about Bogie's Rick than Hagen. Had Rick ever found someone else to love or had he made a monk of himself, living in celibate devotion to his beloved Ilsa for the rest of his life? Or maybe he'd died shortly after Ilsa got on that plane, killed by fascists or Nazis on his way to Brazzaville with Louis. Faye hoped he had died. Better that than live for decades still in love with a woman he could never have again.

Whoever first said it was better to have loved and lost than never to have loved at all had neither loved nor ever lost.

But Faye had. She'd loved and she'd lost and as she lay in the bed of a man who didn't love her any more than she loved him, she would have sold her soul to not have done either.

"Faye?" Hagen said in her ear. He'd been nice to her today, so she opened her eyes.

"Yes?"

"Your phone's beeping."

She reached for the phone on the bedside table and saw she had a text message.

Check your email asap

It was from Richard, her friend who owned the only decent camera store in Columbia, South Carolina. There was no good reason he would be emailing or texting her on a Friday night that she could think of and many bad reasons.

"Emergency text. I'll be right back," she told Hagen who immediately rolled onto his back and stared up at the ceiling, silently seething—as usual. Why did she even bother lying? He was always angry at her these days. She looked at him, looked at him longer than she meant to, longer than she had in a very long time. Wives of her husband's coworkers called Hagen a "catch." That he was handsome—brown hair, brown eyes, good body—was merely the smallest part of the equation. He was a good provider. That was what one of her neighbor ladies had called him, and here in the South, where men were still expected to be breadwinners, patriarchs and kings of the castle, that was the trump card. It didn't matter that Hagen spent every free moment outside work golfing with his buddies, that he rarely spoke to her except to criticize how she'd spent her days and that the sole reason he was trying to have sex with her was so they could pretend they were happy together when they both knew better.

Faye shut the bathroom door and read her email.

Hey, Faye—I just had to cancel some work. Got too busy with weddings. If you're interested, I'll give them your name. The ladies of the Lowcountry Preservation Society need a photographer for their annual "Journey through Time" fund-raising calendar: $10,000 for 100 exclusives. Landscapes, beach scenes, historical houses, ladies in dresses, the usual old-timey tourist shit. Due date August 1. Yes or no?

Work.

A job offer.

She hadn't expected that. She hadn't taken on a professional photography assignment in almost four years. Last week she'd stopped by Richard's camera shop to buy a replacement lens cap for her Nikon. It had fallen off during a walk two weeks ago and rolled into a gutter. She'd mentioned to Richard she missed going out on assignments. He'd told her to help him with his summer wedding load, and she'd simply smiled at him and said, "No, thanks. I don't do weddings."

But this job wasn't a wedding.

Faye knew she'd been in the bathroom long enough she was risking a fight, and though she wasn't scared of getting in a fight with Hagen, she was just too tired for it tonight. Out of guilt she made herself try to go. When she did, she discovered exactly why she'd been feeling so tired and miserable and aching all day.

To stall for time, Faye washed her hands. She washed them till they went pruny and then kept washing them. She washed them for so long she forgot why she was washing them. Once she'd read a phrase in a book—the valley of tears. She didn't know where she'd read it, but she guessed the Bible. This was the moment she should go into that valley and find her tears. She wanted them. She needed them. In her heart she wandered through brambles and thorns and down a steep ravine and into the valley. At the bottom she found a river, where all her tears were supposed to be. The riverbed was dry. She had no more tears left.

She heard a soft knock on the bathroom door and started.

"Faye?"

"Yes?"

"It's been ten minutes." His voice was testy, impatient, his usual tone with her these days. All day every day.

Faye dried her hands and opened the door.

"Sorry," she said.

He nodded and turned around. "I'm going back to bed. Hurry up, okay?"

Faye didn't want to hurt Hagen; she truly didn't. She didn't want to hurt anyone, but there was no way to say it that wouldn't hurt him.

So she hurt him.

"I'm bleeding."

He stopped. His broad, powerful shoulders slumped and

the air seemed to go out of his body like a balloon with a pinprick in it.

Slowly, he turned around.

"I'll call Dr. Melzer."

"Don't call anybody."

"But—"

"Don't." She couldn't face any more doctors. She couldn't face more pity, more sympathy, more tests, more shots, more touching parts of her she never wanted touched again.

He started toward her and she took a step back.

"Please don't touch me," she said. If she thought for one second he would hold her to comfort her, she might have let him. But he didn't want to comfort her. Hagen wanted her to comfort him, and that she couldn't do. She had nothing to give him.

"Faye?"

"I think I should just go to bed."

His eyes looked black in the low light of the hallway. Her toes were cold on the hard bamboo floor. Where were her woolen socks? Hagen always kept the house so cold.

"You're having another miscarriage, and you're going to bed." Hagen wasn't asking her a question. He was registering his disgust with her.

"You have to be pregnant to have a miscarriage. It didn't take," she said. Hagen had begged, practically demanded, she try one more IUI procedure, and she'd agreed to it when he'd called it their "Hail Mary." Well, they'd hailed Mary and Mary hadn't hailed back.

"Do you have a fever?"

"No."

"How heavy are you bleeding? Maybe it's still—"

"It's over, Hagen. It's just… It's all over."

Somewhere in the valley, the tiniest trickle of water appeared in the riverbed, the tiniest trickle of water appeared on her face. She wiped it off immediately.

"Faye...please."

"Don't worry about me."

"Don't worry about you? You tell me you're losing the baby, and I'm not supposed to worry about you?"

She returned to the bedroom, Hagen following her. The bedroom. Their bedroom. Their ridiculous bedroom. Hagen had picked out all the furniture. It looked like something from the Biltmore—king-size iron bed; chocolate-colored walls; brick fireplace; oversize espresso leather armchairs, artfully distressed, of course; gilt-frame landscape paintings on the wall picked out by the decorator by artists neither of them could name. It was a showroom more than a bedroom. *Look how much money we have. Look at how sexy we are. Look at how glamorous our marriage is.* She hated everything about the room except for the pillow-top mattress. Sleeping was her favorite pastime these days. She took her mattresses seriously.

"I wasn't pregnant. It didn't work. And even if I was, it's not like you can do anything about it," she said, climbing back into bed. She reached for her book. It would make a fine shield between them.

"What are you doing?"

"Reading."

"You're reading. While having a miscarriage."

"I got my period. It is what it is."

"You don't care, do you? You don't care that this is happening?"

"I can't care," she said.

"Why can't you care?"

"Because if I let myself care about anything that happens to me, I wouldn't be able to get out of bed."

"You don't get out of bed anyway."

She sighed and met his gaze. He was looking at her, eyes boring into her. Did he see her at all? Or did he just see what he wanted to see? Pretty brunette with violet eyes and good breasts. Quiet, biddable when necessary, like when he trotted her out for company functions and she painted on a smile and wore it until her cheeks hurt.

"Oh," she said. "Good point."

"Do you care at all?"

"Please leave me alone, Hagen. Please don't make me have this conversation now. I was washing blood off my hands five minutes ago. If you won't let me read, then let me sleep."

"Sleep? I called you at noon, and you were still in bed."

"It's almost impressive, isn't it? Give the lady a prize, right?"

"Don't say that."

"What?"

"Don't bring Will into this."

"Oh, yeah, I forgot I'm supposed to pretend he never existed. I'm sorry."

Hagen stopped at the edge of the bed. Faye tried to rest her head back but the stupid iron headboard might as well have been a wall of nails.

"You know what your problem is?" Hagen asked.

"Yes," she said, because she did, but Hagen went on as if he hadn't heard her.

"You want to live in the past. You watch old movies. You haven't read a book written after 1950 in four years. You listen to Frank Sinatra and Ethel Merman all day long like a goddamn ghost in my house."

"That's not true."

"It's not? Really?"

"I got this book yesterday, and it was written two years ago."

Hagen plucked it out of her hands and read the title in as cold and cruel a voice as any man had ever read a book title.

"*The Bride of Boston; A Jazz Age Mystery.* Who the hell is the bride of Boston?"

"A girl who disappeared in 1921," Faye said. "Vanished into thin air. But it has a happy ending."

"Oh, yeah? What's the happy ending?"

Faye smiled. "She was never seen again."

Hagen threw the book across the room.

"Jesus Christ, Faye, what the hell is wrong with you? Women would kill to be in your place."

She rolled onto her side and into the fetal position. Tears leaked from the corners of her eyes onto the pillow. She willed them away, willed Hagen away, willed the world away. But they didn't go away because her Will was gone.

Hagen must have seen he'd gone too far. He knelt by the bed so they could look each other eye to eye. As he reached out his hand she flinched, fearful he'd strike her even though he never had before.

"Faye."

"Will never threw anything but baseballs," she whispered to herself.

"You can't live in the past. It's not living. The past is dead," he said, his hand on her face. It did nothing to comfort her.

"Everything I love is dead."

"Don't say that." Hagen spoke through gritted teeth. He

had such nice straight white teeth. "Don't say stupid stuff like that. It's melodrama."

"I'm a melodrama queen."

"I believe it. Do you think you're the only person who has ever lost anybody? Everybody loses somebody eventually."

"But not everybody loses Will."

"I lost Will, too. Goddamn it, Faye, he's dead. And I'm not and you're not. You have a husband who loves you very much—"

This is the most you've talked to me in six months.

"You live in a mansion."

I hate this house. It feels like a prison. Everything's made of iron and it's turning me to iron.

"We have all the money we could ever need or ever want."

Your money, not mine.

"You don't even have to work."

"I miss working." She said that out loud because Richard's email had reminded her how much she missed working and how much she resented Hagen telling her she shouldn't. "But you don't want me to work. It makes you look bad in front of your boss because he's a chauvinist."

"He's old-fashioned. That's all."

"And you say I live in the past."

Hagen turned his back to her. Who could blame him? Why he hadn't dropped her yet she didn't know. Masochism maybe? Heroism? Maybe he wanted to save her. Maybe he was too embarrassed to admit he couldn't.

And the truth was he had a point. She did live in the past. She hadn't watched a movie made after 1950 in four years. Today she'd watched *Casablanca* while lying in their bed. They were all dead—Rick and Ilsa and Sam who never did play it again. A DVD of *The Maltese Falcon* sat on top of the television, waiting to be watched for the tenth or twelfth time; she couldn't remember. Bogie was dead. Hammett was dead. And the Maltese Falcon never did get found, did it? People searched for it, fought for it, died for it, and in the end it was nothing but a hoax, lead where there should have been gold.

"Okay," she said.

He narrowed his eyes at her.

"Okay, what?"

"I'll stop living in the past."

"You will?" He sounded skeptical, as if she'd agreed just to shut him up.

She climbed out of bed and walked to the closet. From the top shelf she pulled a battered silver suitcase—eighty dollars from Target—with a peeling Boston Red Sox sticker on the side. A relic from her old life. She'd carry it into the new one.

"Faye?"

"I'm going to New Hampshire to stay with Aunt Kate and Mom. Then we can file there."

"File?"

"For divorce," she said.

Hagen laughed.

"You're filing for divorce. In New Hampshire."

"New Hampshire—famous for maple syrup and quickie divorces. I need to see Mom anyway. Not that she'll see me, you know. She doesn't remember anything that happened after 1980. She thinks there are just the two *Star Wars* movies. I'm not going to tell her any different. I must get my living-in-the-past tendencies from her."

"She has dementia. She has an excuse. You don't."

"You're right. I don't have an excuse to live in the past,

so I won't live in the past anymore. I will move on with my life and into the big bright future. I can't wait to see what this beautiful world we live in has to offer me—can you?"

Her anger gave her a rush of energy like she hadn't felt in years. She stuffed clothes and socks and shoes and underwear into the suitcase, haphazardly but with purpose. Hagen watched her with bemusement at first, a look that slowly turned to realization as she slipped on her jeans. She wasn't kidding.

She snatched her book off the floor and flattened the pages Hagen had crushed by throwing it across the room. She found her purse and her charger. She grabbed her phone. And as soon as it was in her hand, she felt it buzz with a text message.

Faye—forgot to tell you that they need an answer by tomorrow. If you want the job, let me know soon as you can.

"You're actually leaving," Hagen said, and she heard the first note of sincerity in his voice all evening. They were an ironic couple, never saying what they meant. Irony had failed them tonight.

"You want children, and I can't give them to you."

"We can try IVF. We can adopt. We can—"

"I don't want to try IVF, Hagen. I don't want to adopt. I don't want…"

"What do you want?"

What did she want? She looked at her handsome husband with the good job that paid all the bills and took all her worries away. He could give her everything she was supposed to want.

"I don't want to die here," Faye said.

It wasn't the dying that bothered her in that statement. It was the *here*. She didn't want to die *here* in this cold, cold house with this cold, cold husband she slept with in a bed made of cold, cold iron.

"And I will die here if I stay," she said with cold iron finality.

The look on his face said he believed her even if he wasn't willing to admit it. She waited. He didn't say anything more.

She paused at the bedroom door. She'd stay at a hotel tonight, then fly to her aunt's house in Portsmouth tomorrow. She'd file for divorce there and let Hagen have everything. There would be nothing for the lawyers to fight over as long as she didn't ask for anything. She'd be divorced by June 5, her thirtieth birthday. Ah, June—a great month for weddings, a better month for divorces. Widowed and divorced, two miscarriages and two failed IUI treatments, all before she turned thirty.

Give the lady a prize.

"You won't contest the divorce?" Faye asked.

"No," Hagen said.

Faye nodded.

"For what it's worth," Faye said, "I wish…"

Her throat tightened to the point of pain.

"What, Faye? What?"

"I wish I'd never married you. For your sake. Not mine."

She looked at him, and he looked at her. She wondered if they'd ever see each other again. And she waited for her tears to come but they were gone, the valley dry again.

"Yeah, well," he said, "you're not the only one."

And that was it. He didn't weep. He didn't scream. He didn't argue. He didn't beg. And when she picked up her suitcase and left Hagen alone in the bedroom, he didn't follow her. It was over.

She put the suitcase in the trunk of her Prius—a gift from Hagen that he would probably demand she give back—and hit the button to open the garage. Before she backed out, she pulled her phone from her jeans pocket.

She reread Richard's email. Sounded like a big project, this fund-raiser calendar thing. Landscapes, houses, ladies in dresses… She hadn't worked a big job like that since getting married. She hadn't done much of anything since getting married. But she'd need the money. And she'd need the distraction.

Faye hit Reply and typed her answer.

Richard—I just left husband.
In other words, I'll take the job.

2

Faye made the divorce easy on Hagen and he stayed true to his word and made it easy on her. Faye asked for nothing but the Prius and the twelve thousand dollars she'd had in her bank account on their wedding day. He handed over the car keys and wrote her a check. And that was that. He got the house, the other car, the boat, the money and the all-important bragging rights. She'd left town, which gave him the freedom to conjure up any story he wanted. He could tell the world she'd cheated on him with every man alive if he so desired to play the cuckold. He could say she'd refused marriage counseling if he wanted to play the martyr. Or he could tell them the truth—that he wanted babies and her body clearly wasn't on board with this program. She'd lost Will's baby. She'd lost Hagen's. And the two insemination attempts had failed.

Three strikes was an out, but four balls was a walk.

Faye walked.

It was easier to do than she'd thought it would be. Hagen hadn't put up a real fight. Knowing him, he'd probably been secretly relieved. The past four years she'd slowly lost touch with the world until everything had started to take on the feel of a TV show, a soap opera that played in the background. Occasionally, she'd watch, but never got too invested. Finally, she'd simply switched off the television. *The Faye and Hagen Show* was over. No big loss. The show only had two viewers and neither of them liked the stars.

A couple months on the coast would do her good. The saltwater cure, right? Wasn't that what the writer Isak Dinesen had said? "The cure for anything is salt water—sweat, tears, or the sea." Faye should get more than enough of all three photographing the Sea Islands in the middle of summer.

As soon as she'd packed her bags and drove away from Hagen's house for the final time, Faye hit the road. In summer tourist-season traffic, the drive from Columbia to Beaufort took nearly four hours. Who were all these people lined up in car after car heading to the coast? What did they want? What did they think they'd find there? Faye wanted to work, that was all. She wanted to do well with this assignment since one good job led to another and then another. Life stretched out before her from now until her death, her work like the centerline of the highway and if she kept her eye on that line maybe, just maybe, she might not careen off the edge of the road.

Faye took the exit to Beaufort, the heart of what was known as Lowcountry in South Carolina. It felt like its own country as the terrain turned flatter and greener and swampier the deeper she drove into. After the exit, she passed a huge hand-painted sign off to her right. Lowcountry Is God's Country, it read in big black letters. Interesting. If she were God she'd pick the Isle of Skye in Scotland maybe.

Kenya. Venice. But Lowcountry? Seemed an odd choice. She wondered what being "God's country" entailed, and then she passed four different churches, four different denominations, and all in a quarter-mile stretch. Clearly God owned a whole lot of real estate around here.

Faye made it to Beaufort by dinnertime. Needing to conserve her money, Faye had rented a room in Beaufort. Just one room in someone else's home. She wouldn't have a private bathroom, a situation Hagen would have found an unacceptable affront to his dignity, but Faye found she didn't mind, not at all. Now that she didn't have to think of anyone's needs but her own, she'd discovered just how little she needed.

The house was on Church Street, a faded Southern Gothic Revival river cottage, a revival someone had forgotten to revive. White paint in need of power washing, three tiers of verandas missing a baluster or five, Spanish moss and ivy competing for ownership of the trees… Faye liked it immediately. It was owned by Miss Lizzie, a woman who rented the rooms out mostly to college kids attending the University of South Carolina's Beaufort campus. So few students attended classes in the summer, however, that Faye had ended up with what Miss Lizzie said was the best room in the house.

Faye's hopes were not high, but Miss Lizzie, an older black woman with a spray of pure white hair around her head like an icon's nimbus, welcomed her into the house with a wide smile that seemed genuine. Faye did her best to match it. The third-floor room she'd been given surpassed Faye's low expectations by a large margin.

"Here you go," Miss Lizzie said. "I keep this as my guest room. No kids up here. I'd hate to put a grown woman like you in the same hall as my college boys. They get a little rowdy. You'll like it up here if you don't mind the stairs. My sister stays here when she visits but she's not coming round again until October. Too hot for her."

"It's beautiful," Faye said, wearing a smile she didn't have to fake. She hadn't been impressed by anything in a long time, but this room spoke to her in its spareness. The floors were hardwood, a deep cherry stain polished to a high shine so that in the evening sunlight she could see every last rut and groove on the floor, elegant as an artist's brushstrokes. The wounds gave it character and beauty. The bed was a four-poster, narrow, like something she'd seen in preserved historic homes. It bore an ivory canopy on top and ivory bed curtains; an ivory bedspread with a double-wedding-ring Amish quilt in a shade of dark and light blue was folded at the bottom. In case she got cold, Miss Lizzie said. South Carolina in June and July? Faye was fairly certain she wouldn't have to worry about catching a chill.

"Closet over there," Miss Lizzie said, pointing at a buttercream-yellow door. "Dresser there. These doors lead to the balcony," she said, indicating a set of French doors. "No screen doors, so try not to let the mosquitoes in."

"Are you Catholic?" Faye asked.

"Of course not. I go to Grace Chapel. It's AME." The tone of denial Miss Lizzie employed made it sound as if Faye had asked her if she were a government spy hiding out on foreign soil. Then again, that was what many people once thought of Catholics in the United States.

"I saw the prie-dieu." Faye pointed at the carved wooden kneeler by the bed. A ceramic gray tabby cat sat on top of it next to a lamp. "That's why I ask."

"The what? I thought that was some kind of step stool or side table."

"It's for praying. Private prayer. You kneel on this bottom step here and maybe rest your prayer book on the top part."

"You're of the Catholic faith?" Miss Lizzie asked, touching her chest as if to clutch at nonexistent pearls.

"No, but I'm a photographer. I did a photo shoot of Catholic churches for a book once."

"I see. You here to photograph things?"

"For a calendar. A fund-raiser."

"Well, that's nice, then. Who doesn't need funds these days?"

Faye laughed. "Anyway, it's very pretty." Faye touched the prie-dieu. It was simply carved but sturdy stained rosewood. The wood was lighter where the knee would go on the bottom board as if someone had prayed on it many times. Were his prayers answered? Why did Faye assume it was a he?

"It's from the lighthouse, the old one," Miss Lizzie said.

"Lighthouse? The one on Hunting Island?"

She shook her head. "Not that one. North of Hunting Island, there's another island. Bride Island."

"Bride Island? That wasn't in my guidebook."

"Only locals call it that. And it wouldn't be in the guidebook. It's private. Rich black lady owns it," Miss Lizzie said with quiet pride. "Paris Shelby."

"Any idea if Ms. Shelby allows visitors on the island?"

It sounded promising, an old lighthouse on a private island. Maybe it hadn't already been photographed to death. Perfect subject for a preservation society calendar.

"I wouldn't know. And Mrs. Shelby hasn't been around much this summer."

"Thank you anyway. Maybe I can find a way out there."

"Here's your key," Miss Lizzie said, handing her a silver key on a brass ring. "Now, you remember this isn't a hotel. I won't be changing your sheets or bringing you breakfast. That's your job."

"I don't need much of anything, I promise."

"You can use the kitchen. We let the kids use it as long as they clean it up, so you can use it, too. The top shelf in the fridge is yours. I cleaned it off."

"I appreciate it. I'm only here to work this summer. I'll stay out of your hair."

"My hair thanks you kindly," Miss Lizzie said with a debutante's coy smile. "There's not much left of it to get into anyway." She patted the wispy curls back into place and left Faye alone in her new home.

Faye set her suitcase on the luggage rack and her equipment case on the bed. A fine room. Perfect for her needs. She'd live the simple life this summer—no television, no movies, no surround-sound speakers and five remote controls only Hagen knew how to work. She'd sleep and she'd eat and she'd work, and when she wasn't working she would walk or read or do nothing at all.

She lay on the bed, staring up at the canopy and planning her itinerary for tomorrow. A drive around the islands to scout locations and maybe a few pictures if the light was right. No time to waste. She was no one's wife anymore. If she didn't work, she didn't eat. She should have been afraid, but she wasn't. Supposedly she'd lost "everything" in the divorce and had been left with almost nothing. Turned out almost nothing was exactly what she wanted.

With help from a sleeping pill, Faye slept well that first night in her new room. In the early dawn hours, when the sun had just begun to peek into the room, she woke up and felt the strangest sensation, a sensation she hadn't felt in more than four years.

Hope.

Hope for what, she didn't know, but she knew it was hope because it got her out of bed before six o'clock. She knew there was something out there she wanted and something told her if she chased it, she just might catch it. She put on her bathrobe and opened the French doors, but froze when she saw the visitor perched on the wooden railing of the little balcony.

She wasn't sure what it was—a heron or a crane or an egret—but it was a big damn bird, that was for certain. Two feet tall, white body, blue-black head and a long bill, sharp as a knife. Faye considered retreating but stayed riveted in place, staring.

"Have we met before?" she asked the bird. Its only reply was to turn its head rapidly toward the sun. She wasn't sure if that was a yes or a no.

"Wait a second… I remember you."

Faye recalled a cold morning on the Newport pier, a morning she would never forget, though she might want to. She'd gone at sunrise, early so no one would see her and try to stop her. On that winter morning, she'd found herself the sole visitor on that lonely pier, a sorrowful sight in her gray trench coat and Will's ashes so terribly heavy in her hands. As she walked to the end she was tempted to keep walking. What was that old insult? Take a long walk off a short pier? Yes, that was exactly what she'd wanted to do. But then a large white bird with a black head had landed on a boat tie-up, startling her with its size and sudden appearance. They'd eyed each other for a few seconds before Faye had continued walking toward the end of the pier. She'd fully expected the bird to take off as she neared it, but it hadn't. It stayed while she knelt on weathered gray wood and poured the ashes into the water and it stayed when she stood up again. It flew off only as she started to walk toward land. For a second—a foolish stupid second—she'd thought the bird was watching over her, making sure she didn't take that long walk off that short pier.

"What are you?" Faye asked the bird, not expecting an answer. The bird merely shook its wings in reply, and Faye sensed it readying to take off.

"Hold on. Stay there one second, big bird. I want to get my camera. Just a camera. Don't be scared." Faye backed into the room, trying her hardest not to make the floor squeak under her feet. From her leather camera bag, she pulled out her Nikon. Carefully, she crept to the doors, but the moment she lifted the camera to her eye, the bird launched itself off the balcony. The one shot she captured was a blur of white in the distance. Faye laughed. Well, there was a very good reason she hadn't gone into nature photography.

After an early breakfast of cereal and tea, she found Miss Lizzie weeding her garden out back. Faye sidestepped a discard pile of murdered plants. Discerning what was weed and what was garden took better vision than Faye's twenty-twenty, and she wasn't sure Miss Lizzie could tell the difference, either. Faye asked her if she knew anyone with a boat. Miss Lizzie suggested she talk to Ty Lewis in Room 2 on the first floor. He was a marine biology student doing some project on the islands over the summer. He went out on a boat often, Miss Lizzie said. Even if he couldn't take her out he could probably point her in the direction of someone who could.

When she returned to the kitchen she found her man.

Had to be him. He wore a T-shirt—a shark and octopus locked in battle on the front with the words *The Struggle is Real* underneath. He had dark brown skin inked with dozens of black tattoos up and down both arms—fish, it looked like, lots and lots of fish—and half a dozen silver piercings: eyebrow, both ears, nose and lip, plus a bonus upper-ear piercing. He had dreadlocks pulled back in a ponytail. He was also handsome enough Faye had to remind herself she was thirty, not twenty.

Twice she reminded herself of that fact.

"Are you Ty?" she asked, pulling a mason jar—Miss Lizzie's version of iced tea glasses—from the cabinet.

"I am if you're asking." He gave her an appraising look and the appraisal came in high.

"I'm asking," she said. "Faye Barlow. And don't flirt with an old lady. Our hearts can't take that much excitement."

"If you're old, I'm Drake. What can I do for you?"

"I heard you have a boat? Or access to a boat?"

"I might have access to a boat," he said between bites of scrambled eggs and sausage. He sat on the counter, not at the table. When was the last time she'd sat on a kitchen counter? High school?

"Would you let me pay you to take me out somewhere on your boat? I need to take some pictures of a lighthouse."

"You can drive to the lighthouse. Best beach in the state. Don't tell anybody that, though. I wanna keep the tourists at Myrtle Beach, where they belong."

"Miss Lizzie said there's another lighthouse, one on some place called Bride Island. Do you know it?"

"I know it. Hard to get near it, though. There's a sandbar in the way."

"Guess that's why they needed a lighthouse. Can you get into the area at all? I have a long-range lens on my camera."

"I can probably do that."

"Today? Tomorrow?"

"This evening? Five?" He hopped off the counter and poured himself a massive glass of orange juice, so big it made her teeth hurt and her blood sugar spike just looking at it. Did college kids know that their days of eating and drinking like that were numbered? She wanted to tell him, then decided to spare him the awful truth that time was a thief, and a metabolism like his would be the first thing it stole.

"What's the charge?"

"Dinner. With me. You know, after we get back from the boat."

"You're too young for me, and I've been divorced for about—" she pretended to check her watch "—ten days."

"You celebrate the divorce yet?"

"Is that a thing people do? Celebrate the painful dissolution of a marriage?"

"Who wanted the divorce?"

"I did."

"You love him?"

"No."

"Like him?"

"No, but he didn't like me, either."

"You have kids?"

"No."

"Good in bed?"

"Fair to middling," Faye said, shrugging.

Ty laughed. "Then hell, yeah, it's a thing to celebrate."

"I will have an age-appropriate celebration. You're too young for me."

He looked at her, tight-lipped and disapproving. "I'm twenty-two."

"I'm thirty."

"Thirty? Oh, my God, Becky, where were you when JFK was shot?" he asked in a Valley girl voice.

She glared at him.

"You flirt weird. Did you learn this in one of those men's magazines with a woman in a metallic bikini on the cover?"

"Possibly. Is it working?"

Faye sighed. "It's working. But just dinner. I'm not sleeping with you. I'm supposed to be sad."

"Are you sad?" he asked, stepping up to her and looking her right in the eyes. She couldn't remember if Hagen had looked her in the eyes the entire last year of their marriage. She'd forgotten how scary it was to be seen.

"Yes," she said.

"Because of the divorce."

"No, not that."

"Then why?"

Faye smiled. "Who knows?" A rhetorical question. She knew why she was sad, but Ty didn't need to know.

"We'll go to the ocean today," he said. "It knows things. Maybe it can help you."

Okay.

So.

Faye had a date with a twenty-two-year-old college student. That was unexpected. Probably a very bad idea, as well. Maybe a terrible idea. Then again, he did have a boat. And he was cute. And she was single again.

And… For a split second while flirting with Ty, Faye had been almost okay. The saltwater cure seemed to be working already. And for a woman who'd been in mourning for four straight years, Faye knew "almost okay" was as good as it was probably ever going to get.

But she would take it.

Ty had the boat, but Faye had the car. Unless she wanted to ride twenty miles on the back of Ty's scooter, she would be driving herself on her own date. It was nice. She felt very modern. Old but modern.

Ten minutes into the drive to the dock on Saint Helena Island, Faye pulled over in a church parking lot and gave Ty the keys.

"You want me to drive?" he asked, cocking his pierced eyebrow at her.

"I can't drive and location scout at the same time without getting us in a wreck. I assume you can drive?"

"I have my learner's permit," he said, taking the keys.

"You're cute."

"The goddamn cutest," he said as he opened the door and got behind the wheel.

As Ty drove, Faye stared out the window and jotted the occasional note on her steno pad. She should take pics of the old Penn School. The trees surrounding it were some of the most photogenic she'd ever seen. She also noted a crumbling ruin of a church that would make for a beautiful shot, maybe even the cover of the calendar. Thankfully Ty didn't pester her with small talk as he drove them to the boat. He pointed out interesting scenery here and there—that road took her down to the old fort, this road took her to a converted plantation house… Useful things. Helpful things. She made notes of them all.

They arrived at the dock, and Faye nodded her approval at the boat. It looked adequately seaworthy, some kind of speedy fishing boat converted into a research vessel. It had a blue-and-white hull with the words *CCU Marine Science* painted on the bow and the number four on the stern.

"You won't get in trouble for taking me out on your school's boat, will you?" she asked.

"It's mine for the summer. As long as I give it back in one piece with a full tank of gas, and I get my work done, they don't care what I do with it."

"What are you working on this summer?" Faye asked as Ty took her hand to steady her on the wobbling boat ramp. Inside the boat she sat on the battered white vinyl seat, mindful of the box of instruments on the floor as Ty settled in behind the wheel.

"Beach pollution mostly," he said, as he steered the boat away from the dock. "The effects of pollution on coastal wildlife, the fish especially. I'm taking water samples all summer up and down the coast."

"Are these beaches polluted?" she asked. "They look clean to me."

"Think about rain," Ty said. "Think about a rainstorm in your town. Water comes down and washes everything clean, right? What sort of stuff gets washed away in a rainstorm?"

"Bird shit," she said.

"Squirrel shit."

"Bat shit," she said, and they both laughed.

"Oil from your car on the street. All that gets washed into the gutter, which goes into the sewer. Where does that sewer go?"

"Please don't tell me the ocean."

"Goes right to the ocean. Decades ago they built these drainage pipes from the cities, and those pipes empty into the ocean near the beaches. That's why you shouldn't swim around here after a rainstorm. Like swimming in a sewer."

"That's disgusting."

"It is what it is," he said with a shrug. "People want to pretend all that shit magically disappears into the gutter and is never seen again. But it's gotta go somewhere, right?" He started the engine and eased the boat toward open water, steering it neatly between two sailboats, one with the elegant name *Silver Girl* and the other with the less-than-elegant name *The Wet Dream*.

The boat bounced hard as it skimmed over the top of a large wake left by a fifty-foot yacht. But Ty seemed imperturbable at the helm. He drove with a focused calm, intent without intensity—a true expert. She liked experts. The world needed more people who were good at their jobs.

"So why marine biology?" Faye asked, shouting over the steady hum of the engine.

"Grew up near Myrtle Beach, watched sea turtles hatching when I was a kid and fell in love. That's all I'm trying to do—keep these beaches for the turtles. Don't give a shit about the people."

"That's not very nice."

"People are why we're in this mess. Last year I pulled ten plastic bags, two Coke cans, half a nylon fishnet, and a goddamn pink Croc shoe, size six, out of the stomach of a shark. You know what we say about that down here?"

"What do we say about that down here?"

"That ain't right. That's what you say. You try it."

Faye put on her thickest faux Southern accent. "That ain't right."

"Not bad. I took pics of all that mess, made signs and hung them up on every beach from here to Savannah."

"You must make lots of friends that way."

Ty snorted a laugh. "Yeah, they aren't too happy with us when we tell everybody their fun summer vacations are killing the wildlife. They think we're scaring off tourists. We are, but we're not doing it to be assholes. We're doing it to wake people up."

"Are you waking them up?"

"All we can do is ring the alarm. Most people aren't going to start paying attention until they have dirty ocean water on their doorstep. Bad as it is, I admit I'm gonna laugh when those rich white boys are playing golf in three feet of seawater."

"My ex-husband was one of those rich white boys. He loved coming down here to golf with his buddies."

"Sorry," he said, looking awkward.

"I'm not." She winked at him.

Ty smiled and hit the gas. Coming here had been a good idea. She should thank Richard for sending her the job. This job was just what she needed—work. Real work. Meaningful work. Plus sand, surf, seafood and a chance to be her old self again. She knew the old Faye, the Faye who'd existed before the miscarriages and the failed marriage... The old Faye wasn't sad like the new Faye. The old Faye felt things, felt them deeply. The old Faye fought for things, too, didn't give up or give in. And the old Faye would definitely go on a date with Ty. Absolutely.

Ty glanced at her out of the corner of his eye. A college boy had just checked her out.

Maybe the old Faye and the new Faye had something in common.

"Is that it?" Faye asked, pointing to the top of a lighthouse peeking out from the tree canopy.

"That's Hunting Island. Pretty lighthouse. You can climb it for two dollars."

"I think I can cover that. I'll go tomorrow. Today I want to see Bride Island's lighthouse."

"We're a couple miles out from there still. The lighthouse is on the north beach. You can see it a lot better than the Hunting Island lighthouse. It was never moved so it's right on the water."

"What do you mean it was never moved?" Faye asked, pausing to dig a strand of hair out of her mouth. She'd forgotten how windy it got on a boat.

"You see that long spit of sand there?" Ty pointed to what looked like a yellow cat's tail lounging a few hundred yards out into the water.

"I see it."

"That used to be land. And that's where the Hunting Island lighthouse stood. Built in the 1870s, but they had to move just a few years later. The land had eroded that much already. Going, gone, almost gone..."

"It's really all going away, isn't it? The coast?"

"Let's just say you won't catch me buying a beach house."

"It's too bad. I always feel like a better person when I'm on the water." The air smelled cleaner here. The water seemed purer. She wanted to strip off her clothes and dive off the side of the boat and let the water baptize her a free woman.

"The ocean is big," Ty said. "And we aren't. It's good to be humbled every now and then."

"You ever go through a divorce?" she asked.

"Not yet."

"Trust me, I know from humble."

"You don't seem humbled," Ty said.

"What do I seem like?"

"Like a woman who just got out of jail."

Faye grinned and was about to ask him what a woman just out of jail ought to do first when Ty raised his arm and pointed.

"There it is," Ty said, and Faye looked up from the dancing blue water to the island on their port side.

"That's Bride Island?"

"That's it."

Faye studied it, not sure what she was looking for except something to justify the trip out here. From this distance, about five hundred yards from shore according to Ty, it looked like Hunting Island. White sandy beach, a line of ocean debris where the tide met the shore and a thick forest of trees. Faye picked up the binoculars and studied the trees. She saw no palms or palmettos, no pines, no evergreens at all.

"Are those live oaks?"

"I don't think they're dead oaks," Ty said.

"You know what I mean."

"They're white oaks. Lady who owns the island owns a bourbon distillery in Kentucky. They get the trees for the bourbon barrels from here."

"White oak? Interesting. Naturally occurring or did the owner plant them?"

"You know anything about Bride Island?" Ty asked, slowing the boat.

"Not a thing except I couldn't find it on the guidebook map."

"It's just Seaport Island on the maps," he said. "But call it Bride Island if you want to sound like a local."

Ty turned off the boat and let it bob gently in the water.

"Where'd the name come from?" Faye asked.

"Some rich planter came over from France in 1820 or something. He sent home for a girl to marry and they shipped her over here, got her in the rowboat to bring her in. They say it was love at first sight. She was so beautiful he waded right into the water to meet her boat. And when she saw him coming for her, she got out of the boat in her fancy dress and eight hundred skirts underneath and waded out to meet him. But the water weighed her down so hard, she started to go under, and he picked her right out of the water and carried his bride to shore. So it's Bride Island."

"Romantic," Faye said. "Minus the almost drowning. Don't swim in big dresses."

"Gets more romantic. Their kid fell out of a tree and broke his neck. The bride drowned herself. And the husband went crazy and committed suicide by burning the house down with him inside it. But he was a slave owner so you know what we say to that?"

"That ain't right?" Faye asked.

"Nope. We say this." Ty raised his hand and defiantly flipped off the island. Faye smiled. She appreciated the sentiment. "Legend is, if a girl swims naked in those waters, she'll find her true love right after. But don't do that. Lotta girls have drowned out here. Only man they meet is Jesus."

"I'll make a note not to do that, then."

"You don't want to find your true love?" he teased. "Or drown trying?"

"I just got divorced."

Ty shrugged. "Nobody wants to be alone."

"I do. I'm never getting married again—that's for sure."

"You say that now..."

Faye shook her head, tried not to smile. Had she been this sure of herself at twenty-two? Probably. She wouldn't tell him he'd be awash with self-doubt by thirty. Maybe he was one of the lucky ones blessed with eternal certainty of purpose. Once she thought she knew it all, too. All Faye knew now was that she knew nothing except what she'd told Ty—she never wanted to be anyone's wife ever again.

While pretty and picturesque, Faye didn't see anything on the south shore of the island worth photographing. No houses, no landmarks, no rock formations or wildlife. Only sand and grass and trees. Ty started the boat back up, and they made their way around a bend to the north shore of the island.

And there it was.

Faye stood up and gripped the gunwale, camera momentarily forgotten.

The lighthouse appeared like something from a dream or a painting of a dream. Solid white and shimmering wet after a recent rain, it shone like a pillar of pure moonstone. The roof of the lighthouse was black and glinting and below it the widow's walk around the lantern room was like an iron choker. The glass panels surrounding the lantern room looked intact, and in the evening sunlight they winked and flashed, casting the illusion that the beacon inside still burned. True, the paint was peeling and the stone facade chipped and cracked, but it was magnificent, dignified and elegant, like an English stage actor who'd played Hamlet in his youth and in his later years strode the boards as Lear. Once a mad prince, now a mad king.

"You like it?" Ty asked.

"I love it," she breathed.

"It's not bad," Ty said. "Only one on the East Coast with a solid white day mark."

"Day mark?" Faye repeated.

"Lighthouses have a day mark and a night mark. The day mark is what they call the paint job," Ty said. "Some lighthouses have wild paint jobs. I've seen candy stripes and diamond patterns, red stripes and black stripes."

"And the night mark?"

"The night mark is the pattern the light flashed. Some lighthouses had a steady beam. Some lights flashed. That's how navigators told lighthouses apart. Every part of a lighthouse had a use. You have electronics and radar and sonar and GPS on boats now. Imagine trying to get from here to Maine without any of that."

"I couldn't get from Columbia to Beaufort without my GPS."

"Yeah, I'd last three days if that before I ran into a sandbar or reef. Lighthouses saved a shit ton of lives." Ty narrowed his eyes at the lighthouse and shook his head. "Probably won't last much longer before it falls into the ocean."

"I'll make it immortal," Faye said, pulling her camera out of her bag. She lifted it to her eye and got off a few dozen shots as quickly as she could. Despite sitting on the very edge of the water, the lighthouse looked secure enough to climb if she could find a way to it. It sat on a base of rock four feet or more above the sand. Behind it she saw another line of rock.

"What's back there?" Faye asked, pointing at the rocks.

"Probably where the keeper's cottage stood," Ty said, squinting at the shore. "It was a nice job if you could get it. You get a house and you go to work ten feet from your back door. The beach is your front lawn. Of course, you have to climb about a million stairs a day. And there's nobody else for miles around if you get hurt or get sick. And when the hurricane hits, you got nowhere to go except inside the lighthouse."

"That sounds like my dream job," Faye said. "I'd take pictures of the beach every single day and watch it change through the seasons. And I'd have killer quads climbing those stairs three and four times a day."

"Sounds boring as shit to me," Ty said.

"Maybe I was a lighthouse keeper in my past life."

"Maybe you were boring as shit in your past life."

"Distinct possibility," she said, getting off a couple more shots as they rounded the island's northern shore.

"It's a shame the lighthouse is locked away on a private island. It should be open to the public."

"What? You want tourists climbing up and down it every day, putting their gum on the steps and tossing their Coke bottles off the top?"

"Maybe not. But I want to climb it," Faye said. She didn't want to climb it. She needed to climb it.

"I'm sure there's a way. Just not from here. You can't see it from here, but there's one nasty sandbar under the water by the pier."

"It's okay. I'll find a way out there. I'll sweet-talk anyone I need to."

Near the base of the lighthouse, Faye noticed the remnants of an old pier, thick, rotting wood pillars poking out of the water like a hundred tiny islands. At the last pillar where the pier had once ended, Faye saw a bird land—a white bird with a long bill and a blue-black head.

"Ty? Do you know what that is?" She pointed at the bird. Ty narrowed his eyes. She handed him the binoculars and he peered through them. He laughed.

"Somebody must be having a baby," he said.

"What is it?"

"A stork. A wood stork."

"Do you see wood storks around here often?" she asked.

"Never seen one out here. Not too many of them around anywhere."

"I swear to God that very same bird or its identical twin was perched on my balcony at six o'clock this morning. Bizarre." She didn't tell Ty about seeing a bird just like it when she'd scattered Will's ashes. She liked Ty and didn't want him thinking she was imagining things like birds stalking her.

"You sure you aren't pregnant?" Ty asked.

"If I were, I'd still be married."

"Just checking. I mean, you know how storks are."

Faye stared across the water at the stork. It turned its large head and seemed to stare back at her.

"I had this baby book once," Faye said. "Don't ask me why, doesn't matter. But it had a whole chapter on the stork symbol. Supposedly in Egyptian mythology, the stork was the symbol of 'ba' or the soul. While a person slept, their soul would fly in the form of a stork and come back to him. They could even carry the souls of the dead back to the body. I think. Read it a long time ago."

"That stork is carrying some dead guy's soul? I like babies better. Long as it's not my baby."

"Can you kill the engine? I don't want to scare it away."

Ty cut the engine and peered through the binoculars

again. Faye lifted her camera to her eye but took no pictures. She was waiting. She sensed the second her shutter snapped the bird would fly off, and she would lose the shot. She had to get it right the first time.

The boat bobbed in the water, drifting ever closer to the pier. The shot lined up the way she wanted—the lighthouse filled the background, the pillar and the stork were left of center and the trees formed a frame on either side.

One…two…three…

Faye clicked the shutter and got off as many shots as she could in quick succession. Her instincts had been right. As soon as the clicking reverberated over the water, the bird took off. Faye couldn't have planned it better. The wood stork soared into the sky, heading straight toward the sun fearless as Icarus, and she captured every last beat of its wings.

"Perfect," she said, flipping the camera over. She scrolled through the pictures, creating a sort of flipbook as the bird tensed, stretched its wings and then launched itself into the sky. She scrolled backward and set the stork back down onto the pier like magic.

"Damn," Ty said, glancing over Faye's shoulder. "You're good." His shoulder butted against hers, and he seemed genuinely impressed by her work.

"I'm not bad."

"You make much money doing this?" he asked.

"I didn't become a photographer for the money. Nobody does, I promise."

"Why'd you do it, then?"

"When I was younger, I thought I wanted to be a photojournalist. A modern Dorothea Lange."

"Who?"

"You've seen her pictures. She took photographs of migrant workers during the Great Depression. People in bread lines, starving people, people driving across the country to get jobs picking fruit in California. When those pictures were published, it woke the country up. FDR's New Deal might not have happened without her pictures. Before her the poor were seen as defective, as inferior. She took beautiful pictures of poor people, dignified pictures. People saw themselves in the suffering. They saw the humanity. One photographer, one woman, in the right place and the right time could change the world."

"You gonna change the world?"

"That was the plan. Once upon a time. But every college kid thinks they can save the world." She grinned at him, and he rolled his eyes. "But it's a hard gig to get into, the changing-the-world gig. I settled for working at a tiny newspaper in Rhode Island out of college. Newspaper jobs are nearly impossible to get now. Good thing my ex-husband had money or I might have starved. Or worse, had to get a real job."

She joked about it, but the truth was, she regretted letting Hagen's money keep her at home when what she should have done was go back to work doing what she loved. But when they'd gotten married she'd been in no shape to save the world. She could barely get out of bed the morning of their wedding. So what was stopping her now?

"Dorothea Lange took pictures of people suffering from the Great Depression and the Dust Bowl, and now the Social Security Administration and Medicaid exist. I take pictures of lighthouses for desk calendars. So much for saving the world."

"Hey," Ty said, "your pictures could save that lighthouse. It's a piece of history. That light saved lives, and you can return the favor. People see that lighthouse and they start to care about it. Out of sight, out of mind, right? So isn't the reverse in sight, in mind? Maybe if somebody like you took pictures of these islands a hundred years ago, they wouldn't be in the shape they are now. And even when that lighthouse is gone, when all the islands are gone, we'll have your pictures. Better than nothing."

"Right. Better than nothing."

Faye smiled and looked at her pictures again. She couldn't believe her luck. A dozen gorgeous shots, any one of them could grace the cover of the calendar. A home run on her first at bat. That never happened.

Ty started the boat's engine up again. With a relaxed, practiced air, he steered them around the ruins of the pier and back into open water.

"Where to now?" Faye asked, slipping her camera back into her bag.

"Dinner. Oysters if you can handle it."

"I can handle oysters. You buying?" she teased. She'd never make a college kid buy her dinner.

"How about this? I'll give you the oysters in exchange for the clam."

Faye stared at him. "That is the grossest thing anyone has ever said to me. I'm almost impressed. No, I am impressed. Good job." She slapped him on the back.

"Thank you, baby. I'll be here all week."

Faye was too amused and too happy to be offended. Not that Ty could offend her if he tried. After four years in a bad marriage, one dirty pussy joke couldn't begin to ding her armor. Oh, but that smile of Ty's, that sweet, sexy smile could. It wriggled its way through the chinks in her chain mail.

Tonight she was going to make very bad decisions.

The rest of the evening passed in a blur. Faye and Ty both had a little to drink at dinner and then a lot to drink back at the Church Street house. So it wasn't that much of a rude awakening to find Ty still in her bed when she woke up around 3:00 a.m.

He lay on his stomach, facing away from her, looking so painfully young and terribly sweet. She forced down any guilt she might have felt. This hadn't been his first time, and it wouldn't be his last. Might not even be his last time tonight. She'd almost told him during their first round that it was the best sex she'd had since getting married, but she kept that comment to herself. After all, Hagen had set a low bar.

Faye slipped out of bed, put on her bathrobe and went to the bathroom. Ty stirred as she slid back in next to him.

"Just me," she whispered as Ty rolled over to face her.

"Did I fall asleep? Sorry. Your bed is bigger than mine."

"I don't mind. Just be careful sneaking out. I don't want to get in trouble with Miss Lizzie. She seems a little on the religious side."

"She makes Mother Teresa look like Miley Cyrus." Ty slid from bed and started gathering his clothes. She rolled over onto her side to watch him dress in the dark. "Luckily she sleeps so hard we could knock the headboard through the wall and she wouldn't wake up."

"That sounds like the voice of experience."

"Did you think I was a virgin?" he asked, crawling over the bed to her.

"No, but I was."

He laughed softly and kissed her. "Hope you had fun," he said.

"I did."

"You sure?" he asked. Faye blushed in the dark. She hadn't

been able to come during the sex. She'd tried, but it was going to take a while before she figured how to use her body for anything other than baby making again. But Ty didn't need to hear that.

"I did have fun," she said. "Don't take my lack of orgasms personally. I'm a little out of practice."

One more kiss and one more smile. "Practice makes perfect."

On his way out of her room she stopped him with a whispered question.

"Hey," she said. "What's the name of the island with the lighthouse again? Not Bride Island, the real name? Sea Island?"

"Seaport Island."

"Thanks. I need it for the caption."

"I'll take you out there again anytime you want."

"I might take you up on that. How much will you charge me for it?" she asked, smiling.

"One clam."

Ty crept into the hallway and was gone, leaving Faye laughing in bed. She didn't hear a single footstep creaking on the hardwood.

Faye tried to go back to sleep, but it eluded her. Her new life had officially begun with a bang and a whimper or two. Sliding out from under the covers, she walked naked to her camera bag sitting on the floor. She enjoyed the breezy tickle of the night air on her breasts as it wafted in under the blinds. It made her tingle in a pleasant way.

She hadn't had a chance to upload today's pictures yet and wanted to see the lighthouse again. She plugged her camera into her computer. Ah, there they were, her beautiful photos. The stork, the trees, the glimmering ivory lighthouse. Faye would get this photo printed out and she'd hang it in her room. It was possibly the best work she'd ever done. Maybe she'd finally found her subject. Man Ray had his nudes. Dorothea Lange had her migrant workers. Ansel Adams had his landscapes. Maybe Faye Barlow would have her lighthouses.

She typed "Seaport Island Lighthouse" into the spreadsheet she kept to label her photographs. Out of curiosity she entered that phrase into Google image search to see who else had been taking pictures of the lighthouse. She found a few amateur pictures of the island, most of them obvious iPhone pictures posted on Pinterest. As she scrolled through the results she found a few historical pictures. One of the iron skeleton of the lighthouse as it was being built in 1884. Another when it was completed.

Faye was about to shut her computer down when a tiny thumbprint photograph caught her eye. It was a faded and sepia-toned picture of one of the lighthouse's keepers who'd been stationed there after World War I, according to the caption.

Faye narrowed her eyes at the photograph. Her heart raced. She clicked on the link and enlarged the picture until the face of the lighthouse keeper filled up the fifteen-inch screen.

"No way..." she breathed, putting the laptop onto the sewing table and leaning in closer, staring at the photograph until her eyes watered. And she stared at it even longer until the watering turned to tears.

Faye reached out to touch the photograph on her screen.

She knew the face in the photograph, knew it well.

It was the face of the only man she'd ever loved.

Will's face.

4

When the Beaufort County Library opened the next morning, Faye was the first one through the double doors. Unfortunately, the librarian at the reference desk was fairly new to the area, a transplant from Tennessee, and she'd never heard of Bride Island and/or Seaport Island and had no idea there was a lighthouse other than the Hunting Island Light. She suggested Faye walk down to the local tourist center with a smile and a "God bless."

Thankfully everything that wasn't an island was within walking distance in Beaufort. The tourist center was housed in a clementine-colored brick storefront house on Bay Street. Between last night and this morning, the wholly uncanny feeling of the lighthouse keeper's photograph had faded from her consciousness the way a nightmare fades, mostly gone but leaving a strange, smoky pall over the day.

And yet…it was strange. Too strange to ignore, although too strange to take seriously, as well. But finding out the man's name wouldn't hurt, would it?

In the front window sat six watercolor paintings on easels.

All of them were paintings of Lowcountry—the beach, the Hunting Island lighthouse, the Penn School...

And there it was, set off behind the others, a single painting of a solid white lighthouse and the pier that no longer existed. At the end of the pier stood a woman in a light gray trench coat. The woman faced the ocean and seemed to be holding something in her hand, something Faye couldn't see. And behind the woman on the pier?

A large white bird perched on a pillar.

Faye froze, unable to walk away from the painting, unable to look away. The uncanny feeling returned times a hundred. First the photograph and now this...

What the hell was going on?

Faye tore herself from the painting and entered the tourist center's front office. She found a teenage boy with his nose buried in his phone manning the receptionist's desk. Either covering for his mother, she surmised, or doing community service for any of the usual teenage misdemeanors that deserved a punishment more than grounding but less than prison.

"Do you know anything about that painting of the lighthouse in the window?" she asked.

"Which one?"

"The one with the lady in the painting."

"Lady painting. Um...hold on," he said, sounding tired, hungover, stoned maybe. He wasn't moving very fast, either, as he took a binder off a shelf and flipped through the pages. She'd been amused by the terrapin-crossing warning signs she'd seen around Beaufort with the outline of the turtle in the middle. If she had such a sign she'd hang it over this boy's head. Then she would clobber him with it.

"Okay, here it is," the boy said between yawns. "Watercolor. Sixteen by twenty inches. *The Lady of the Light*. Fifty bucks."

"That's it? That's all it says about the painting?"

"Um…no. It says if you buy it, the artist accepts personal checks made out to the Historical Society."

"I wasn't planning on buying it. I want to know who the woman in the painting is."

"I told you—the Lady of the Light."

"Who's that?"

"Some lady."

"Okay," Faye said, counting to ten before she murdered this boy. "What about the artist? From the angle of the painting, it looks like he or she painted it from the beach, which meant they were out there. You're not supposed to be out there, since it's a private island. You know anything about any of that?"

"Um…"

"I'll take that as a no."

"You can ask Father Pat about it, I guess."

"Father Pat?"

"He's a priest."

"Why would I ask a priest about the painting?"

"Because he painted it."

"He's a priest and a painter?"

The boy shrugged. "What else are you going to do if you're a priest? Not like you can join Tinder. Maybe you can. I'm not Catholic."

"Is his number in the phone book?"

"What's the phone book?"

Now he was just messing with her. She hoped.

"His number's in here. Hold on." The boy waved her off

and flipped through the binder again. Finally, he found the phone number and wrote it down for her.

"Thank you," she said.

"You should buy the painting. Father Pat would really like that."

"I just got divorced. Took one week. Do you know how much money I had to give up to get my divorce finalized in one week?"

"You can have it for twenty-five dollars. It says so in the book."

"Fine. Give it to me."

Faye wrote out her personal check to the Historical Society. At least it was a tax write-off. The boy offered to wrap up the painting for her in some newspaper—she was shocked he knew what a newspaper was—but she declined and carried it back to the Church Street house. Faye wondered if sweat could damage a watercolor before recalling how much she had paid for it. As she opened the gate, Ty opened the front door. He stopped, looked at her and at the painting.

"Don't ask," she said.

He held up his hands in mock surrender. "I'm not asking a thing," he said before putting on his helmet and scootering away.

Faye set the painting on her desk, propping it against the wall. Father Patrick Cahill might be an amateur, but he was a talented one. His work had a Degas flavor to it, blurry, shaky, giving the impression of the lighthouse and the outline of the woman without giving way the details. She wondered if he painted en plein air or if this had been a work of pure imagination. He could have seen the lighthouse from a boat like she had and then painted it at a different angle later. But what about the woman? What about the white bird on the pier? Either the universe was trying to tell her something, or...

She was losing her mind. Faye thought she could put money on the second option.

First, so as not to be intrusive, Faye attempted to send Patrick Cahill a text message. She composed it carefully, saying she had bought the painting of the lighthouse and the lady and admired it greatly, and if it wasn't too much of a bother, she'd like to ask him a few questions about it. She signed her name and sent the message. She received an immediate error message.

It was a landline.

Fabulous. Father Cahill had a landline. How quaint. Now Faye understood why Hagen was so annoyed with her wanting to live in the past. She took a deep breath and dialed the number next. She hated cold-calling the man. Priests didn't make her nervous, but she'd talked to very few of them in her time. Even when on assignment photographing the interiors of churches, she'd spent more time with the secretaries and deacons than the priests, who had more pressing matters to attend to. Father Cahill didn't answer, but he did have an answering machine. Not voice mail. Answering machine. Would she need a time machine just to find the man?

She relayed her message to his answering machine and thanked him profusely for his time, which he actually hadn't given to her yet. Still, this was the South, and she knew it was best to play the honey card instead of the vinegar card if she wanted a man to do her bidding.

After gathering her gear, she set out again to work. She had never accomplished anything by sitting and waiting for the phone to ring, so she drove out to Saint Helena Island. She preferred shooting her outdoor photography in the early-morning and late-evening hours, but she didn't want to waste an entire day brooding and overthinking things. She'd done enough of that in her life.

First stop, the Penn School. According to its historical marker, Northerners during the Civil War had come to the region to start a school for the people newly freed from slavery. Faye could imagine how well that went over with the local white population. But the school, with its cream-colored exterior and red tile roof, was lovely even in the vertical noon sunlight. Faye made a circuit of the school, shooting it at every angle, even climbing a tree to get a shot of it through the branches sagging with Spanish moss. A good picture, but not good enough. She would have to suck it up and come back tomorrow morning around dawn to get the shot the way she envisioned it.

Next Faye drove down to the Chapel of Ease, or what was left of it. Four walls of tabby plaster, no roof and that was it. She took a few shots of the chapel but focused most of her pictures on the adjacent cemetery. A lovely, peaceful place until a bus arrived and belched tourists out onto the hallowed ground. Faye waited until they loaded up again and had driven off before taking the picture the way she wanted, with the chapel in the background and the cemetery in focus front and center.

The chapel's historical marker said the place had burned in the 1860s—a forest fire—and no one had bothered to rebuild it. Now it was a ruin, a beautiful relic, perhaps more loved in its wreckage and decay than it had been while intact. Were it still an active church, Faye would have driven past it like she'd driven past a dozen other churches on this stretch of road. Perhaps Ty was onto something with his sangfroid about the imminent destruction of the Sea Islands. Those people taking pictures of the Chapel of Ease wouldn't have set foot inside it during a Sunday service. Maybe it was simply human nature to only love a thing after losing it. Maybe they should all lose more things so they could appreciate what they had. Faye could count her possessions now on her two hands—car, camera, laptop, suitcase of clothes and shoes, phone, her beloved grandmother's necklace and an old ring she couldn't wear because it was much too big for her hands. Yet she wouldn't get rid of it. Not to her dying day.

The shots of the cemetery turned out better than she'd anticipated. If they didn't end up in the calendar, she could sell them to a stock-photo website. When she packed up her gear in the car, she had a missed call. The voice mail message said it was Pat Cahill calling and he was more than happy to hear someone had finally gotten suckered into buying one of his masterpieces. If she wanted to see him today, he'd be painting the marshlands on Federal Street, and she surely couldn't miss him. He'd be the old man on the front lawn covered in paint.

On the way to Federal Street, Faye's phone rang again. She didn't want to answer, not because she was driving, but because this time she knew who was calling.

"Hello," she said, keeping her voice even, flat, unemotional. It was easy for her to do, too easy.

"That's all I get? Hello?"

"Hello *there*? That better?" she said.

"You know I'm not the bad guy, remember? You can at least fake being polite to me."

"Hello there, Hagen. How are you?"

"God, you are really something."

Faye heard his aggravated exhalation on the other end of the line.

"What do you want?" she asked. "I'm driving and can't really talk."

"I don't want anything. I'm calling to see how you're doing. Call it a bad habit."

"I'm fine. Just working. How are you?"

"Working. Look, I found some stuff of yours in the guest room closet. Do you want it?"

Faye should have known he wasn't calling just out of the goodness of his heart.

"What is it?"

"I don't know. Do you really want me digging through your stuff?"

Faye sighed. Hagen had a gift for making things more difficult than they needed to be.

"How am I supposed to tell you if I want it or not if you won't tell me what it is?"

"You could come here and look at it."

"You can look in the box."

"I don't want to."

"Hagen, I didn't keep pet snakes. You can look in the damn box."

"I think it's Will's stuff."

Faye fell silent. She saw a gas station on the right, pulled in and shut off the car. It took her ten full seconds before she could speak again.

"It's not Will's stuff," she said finally. "I have a few things, and his family has the rest."

"And what about, you know... Will?"

Faye rubbed at her forehead. "I would not leave Will's ashes in a cardboard box in a guest room closet. I scattered them in the ocean two years ago."

"Without me?"

"I was in Newport visiting family. It seemed like the right time and the right place."

"Without me, you mean. He was my best friend," Hagen said.

"He was my husband."

"Yeah, so was I." Hagen nearly shouted the words, and each one landed on her like a heavyweight champ's fist. A right, a right, a left and then a brutal jab straight to the solar plexus.

"I'm sorry," she whispered. "I had to do it alone."

"You were alone?"

"Yes," Faye said. "I mean, except for a bird. There was a big white bird there, too. Maybe he knew Will." She laughed at herself, and fresh hot tears fell from her burning eyes.

"You don't sound good, Faye. Where are you?"

She wished he wouldn't talk to her so gently. It made it harder to stay angry, and she needed her anger. It gave her energy.

"I don't have to tell you that."

"Jesus, do you think I'm going to stalk you or something? If I was obsessed with you I could have dragged the divorce out a couple years. It could have been ugly. I didn't, though, and I don't remember you saying thank you for that."

"I'm supposed to thank you for not torturing me with a protracted divorce? Okay. Thank you, Hagen. Thank you very much."

The pause between her last words and his next words was so long she thought he'd hung up on her. No such luck.

"I was never going to be Will," Hagen said at last. "And it wasn't fair of you to expect me to be him."

"I never expected you to be Will, and I didn't want you to be Will."

"Because no one could be Will, right? Except Will, because Will was perfect."

"Will wasn't perfect," Faye said slowly, as if speaking to a child. "No one is perfect. Especially not a man who left dirty dishes under the bed and never cleaned a toilet in his life. But this is what Will was—Will was the man who loved me, all of me, even though I yelled at him and called him a thoughtless child when he almost burned the house down trying to cure a baseball mitt in the oven. He cleaned the oven, he bought me flowers and he told me he was sorry. So no, Will was not perfect. Will was better than perfect. He was too good for this world. The world didn't deserve him and neither did I."

In the pit of the night when Faye was alone with her thoughts and her loneliness, she would tell herself that Will was too good for her. It was her only explanation for why he was taken from her. The only explanation that ever made sense.

"Hagen, I know—I do—that you thought by marrying me you were honoring Will, doing what he would have wanted you to do, doing what he would have done in your place. I thought so, too. But it was a mistake."

"I kept you from killing yourself for nearly four years and you call that a mistake?"

Faye shrugged, shook her head and remembered the night Hagen had taken the pill bottle out of her hand. By the next day every gun, knife and pill in the house had been locked in a safe.

She didn't have the heart to tell him half the reason she'd had that pill bottle in her hand was because she'd married him.

"Hagen, I really have to go."

"Can I ask you one thing now that's it's all over? One question, one answer. I think you owe me that after four years of marriage and carrying my child and eating my food and sleeping in my bed and living in my house and taking my cock without complaint all that time."

Faye sighed. She'd been pregnant for a mere six weeks three years ago and Hagen still talked about that lost pregnancy like she'd given birth to a living child who'd died in his arms. He'd lost children. Faye had lost herself. They couldn't even grieve together.

"Faye?"

"Ask," she said. "But don't get pissed at me if you don't like the answer."

"Did you ever love me?"

"I tried." Faye closed her eyes, and twin tears rolled down her cheeks, scalding hot on her cold skin. "I swear I did try."

"So no?"

"No," Faye said.

This time when the silence came she knew Hagen had hung up.

Faye hated this part, hated when it hit her full body like she'd been thrown against a wall and nothing could stop her from feeling everything she didn't want to feel. Her chest ached and her face, too. Her throat tightened like a strong man's hand was clutched around it, squeezing. Her stomach roiled like boiling water. From her feet to her guts to her heart to her eyes, she ached with pure unadulterated panic. She hadn't had a panic attack since before Will died. But she remembered this feeling, this vise on her chest, this unbearable urge to run away, to scream, to fly and to fight. She'd tumbled headfirst into the pit, and nothing could get her out of it—not a rope or a pickax or her own bare hands clawing at the dirt walls.

She lowered her head to the steering wheel and squeezed the leather as hard as she could. In her twenties her panic attacks had been triggered by her student loan debt combined with her erratic income from freelancing. One bill could send her spiraling into the cold sweats, nausea and a sense of being choked to death by an invisible hand. Pills helped a little, but nothing helped more than Will putting her on his lap and holding her as he rubbed her back.

"Breathe, babe. In and out," he'd say, his voice strong and calm as she gasped and swallowed air. "It's not the end of the world. It only feels that way. We'll just be poor," he would say to make her smile. "We'll live in a cabin in the middle of nowhere with no electricity or running water. We'll smell horrible. We'll grow our own food. We'll have cows and chickens and no TVs. We'll have so much free time, babe. I don't even know what we'll do with all that free time... Wait. I got it. Blow jobs three times a day."

And Faye would laugh through her tears, which only Will could make her do.

"What about baseball?" she'd asked him.

"Just a game, babe. It's just a game. You and me, we're the real thing. Right?"

"Right." She'd put her head back on his big broad chest and ride out the wave of her panic in his arms.

"Breathe, sweetheart," Will would say, rocking her like a child. "I'm here, and I love you."

But he wasn't here anymore.

And he didn't love her anymore.

If the dead could love, they had a terrible way of showing it.

But breathe she did—in and out—and sure enough, when she raised her head she saw people walking into the gas station, a little boy racing to beat his sister to the door so he could be the one to hold it open for their mother. A robin pecked at a rotting pretzel on the asphalt. A shiny blue Corvette with Georgia plates pulled in for a fill-up. Life. It was still happening. The world hadn't ended. Not even her little corner of it.

Once she was back in control of her emotions, Faye started her Prius. As always she was taken aback by how quietly the car ran. She really never knew if it was running until it moved. Same with her—she didn't know she was alive unless she was moving—so she kept moving.

The phone rang again. Hagen calling back, either to keep fighting or to apologize. She ignored the call, and she also ignored the urge to toss the phone out of the car window into Port Royal Sound.

Faye found Federal Street easily, thanks to her tourist's map. Father Pat Cahill had said he'd be painting the marshlands, but that didn't narrow things down much. The entire place was surrounded by marshlands. She drove to the very end of the road; if she'd kept driving she'd drive straight into the water. Although tempting—today especially—Faye imagined with her luck the car would land on a dense patch of swamp, and she'd have a few hours to wait before sinking enough to even get her feet wet. Although she couldn't think of many good reasons to go on living, she also couldn't think of any good reasons for dying. So she went on as most people did for want of a viable alternative.

Two beautiful old white houses stood proud and dignified on either side of Federal Street, but only one of them had a man sitting on the lawn in front of an easel. The house he painted was a grand antebellum mansion, three stories, white, red roof, green shutters and a porch one could get lost on without a map and a compass. Before leaving the car, Faye checked her face in the mirror looking for any telltale signs of her recent breakdown. The makeup was an easy fix, but she couldn't do a thing about the redness in her eyes except hope Father Cahill didn't notice it. She grabbed her camera bag from the backseat. Might as well get some work done while she was here.

She strode across the lawn toward him, and he turned her way and gave her a broad smile.

"Are you my new patron?" he called out. "If so, I thank you and owe you an apology."

Faye smiled back. "No apologies necessary. The kid let me have it for twenty-five bucks."

"Twenty-five? Highway robbery." He rubbed his palms on his paint-smeared khaki slacks, and then held out his hand to her. She was struck by how much he looked like Gregory Peck in the late actor's last years. Minus the mustache but still with the glasses. His black T-shirt was as paint riddled as his pants. Did he wipe his paintbrushes on his clothes?

"Thanks for meeting with me, Father Cahill." He had a nice handshake, firm and friendly.

"Pat, please. And I'm retired, so it's not like I have a full dance card. Pull up the stool and tell me about yourself." He didn't say *card*, he'd said *cahd*. She knew she was dealing with an old Boston boy. If Kennedy had lived, this was probably how he would have sounded in his seventies.

He passed her his wooden stool and he sat on the stone bench where he'd set up his paints and brushes.

"Not much to tell. I'm in town for a couple months taking pictures for a fund-raising calendar."

"I know that calendar well. They preservation society ladies are nice enough to buy my paintings every now and then. Their mission in life is to take pity on old relics."

Faye laughed. "You're not an old relic."

"What makes you think I was talking about me?" He winked at her to show he was kidding. "How'd you swing this gig? You're not a local. Sound like a damn Yankee to me."

"Friend got me the job. But you're not a local, either," Faye said.

"What gave it away?" he asked.

She smiled. "I'm from New Hampshire. You're not my first Masshole."

Pat laughed loudly, a good rich laugh.

"Guilty. I was a pastor here in the midsixties. My first church. Fell in love with the islands back then. Always planned to come back, and here I am."

"Midsixties? You must have been a baby."

"I was. Big twenty-seven-year-old baby. God help that dumb do-gooder kid. I was not ready for the South during desegregation. Let me tell you this—anyone nostalgic for the past never lived there."

"Says the man who is painting a two-hundred-year-old plantation house. Thought you were painting the marshes."

"Marshlands. That's the name of the house. The owner wasn't a planter. He was a doctor. The doctor who discovered a treatment for yellow fever. You discover something that can save lives during an epidemic and you get a free pass to own a nice house."

"Fair enough," she said. "It is a gorgeous house." Faye pulled out her camera and examined it through the viewfinder.

"Light's not very good today," he said. "Too overcast. I doubt you'll get a decent shot. At least in painting I can pretend the sun's there."

"I'll come back tomorrow if the sun's out. I got some beautiful shots of the Bride Island lighthouse yesterday. A friend took me out on his boat."

"Yes. It's very nice." He didn't sound as enthusiastic as she'd expect from someone who had painted the lighthouse so lovingly. Very nice? That's all?

"What can you tell me about the lighthouse?"

"Not much. Only what Ms. Shelby told me. She said it was built to protect ships from the sandbar. Third-order Fresnel lens. Seven-second night mark. Solid white day mark. Decommissioned in, oh, '45, '46? It's been rotting there ever since. That's about it."

"Ms. Shelby? You know her?"

"I do. Met her at a party, and she and I had a nice talk. I asked if I could paint it, and she said I could go out there anytime I want as long I stayed out of the lighthouse. It's not structurally sound anymore. That whole corner of the island is very dangerous."

"What else is out there?"

"Ms. Shelby prefers to keep the land as pristine as possible. There's not much out there." He flicked a fly off his canvas. "Trees. A few houses, but those are on the south side of the island. A barn. Handful of horses and horse trails. A few ruins. A few graves. And then there's the lighthouse and what's left of the keeper's cottage, which isn't anything but the stone foundation."

"How did a lighthouse get on private property?"

"The government leased the land from the old owners. Four acres, which is a postage stamp on that island. That was back in the 1800s, when lighthouses were popping up along the coast. After they decommissioned the light in the forties, they left it up. Cheaper to let the elements have it than tear it down. Can I ask what your interest is in the lighthouse?"

Before Faye could answer, a small gray tour bus rattled up the driveway to the Marshlands and stopped. Pat gave a dramatic sigh as it unloaded a batch of tourists onto the lawn.

"Now, before we go into the house," the pretty young tour guide said, shouting over the murmur of elderly tourists, "let's walk over to the telescope and take a look at the sound."

"Every single damn day..." Pat sighed. "I should have found a different mansion to paint."

"Through the telescope," the tour guide went on, oblivious to Pat's annoyance, "you can see the sound side of Seaport Island, or what we locals call Bride Island. It's an unusual island rich with history. If you look up you'll see the top of a beautiful white lighthouse peeking through the tree line," the woman said in her sweet-as-pecan-pie accent. "Pretty as it may be, the lighthouse is closed to the public. The water is notoriously choppy at the north seaside of the island, and more than three dozen people have lost their lives in those waters in the past hundred years—"

"Including the Lady of the Light," Pat recited along with the tour guide, word for word, not missing a single beat. "Faith Morgan, the lighthouse keeper's beautiful teenaged daughter..."

"You've heard this all before?" Faye asked.

"It's enough to make a man toss a tour guide into the swamp. That's her in the painting, by the way."

"The tour guide?"

"No," he said. "Faith Morgan."

"The girl on the pier with the bird? That's her?"

Pat nodded as he capped a paint tube and dropped it into his gear bag.

"Why did you paint her?" Faye asked. "Why not the Bride of Bride Island? Didn't she drown, too?"

"The subject picks the artist, not the other way around."

"That's not very helpful."

Pat glanced at her before turning his attention back to his painting.

"I didn't realize you needed my help," he said.

Faye sensed she was asking Pat questions he didn't particularly want to answer.

"I'm sorry," she said. "I know I'm being nosy. I have a reason for asking, I promise."

"What's the reason?"

"It's a stupid reason."

"Tell me your stupid reason, Faye. You've piqued my curiosity."

"I just... When I saw the painting, I thought she was someone I knew. That's all."

He gave her a long searching look.

"Someone you knew. Who?" he asked.

"You'll laugh."

"I'd never laugh."

Faye sighed. She was pretty sure the man would laugh.

"Who did you think the woman in the painting was?" Pat asked, his voice awash with the tender concern that must have served him well in his decades as a priest.

"I thought, maybe... I thought she was me."

5

"Sounds crazy, right?" Faye asked. "You can laugh."

"I'm not laughing." He wasn't. He wasn't even smiling. Maybe she'd scared him. It kind of looked like she had. "Like I said, that's Faith Morgan in the painting. She was the old keeper's girl."

"I see. So if she was the lighthouse keeper's daughter," Faye said, "then who was the lighthouse keeper?"

"A former naval officer by the name of Carrick Morgan manned the light back then. Transferred from the Boston Light to Seaport in the fall of '20, and his girl, Faith, joined him that next June. I think they say she was seventeen or so."

Faye felt a mix of relief and embarrassment, all of which must have shown on her face. God, she felt so foolish. Well, she'd been a bigger fool before and survived.

"Never seen you before today," he continued. "Honest. And even if I had, I'm not that good a painter. There's a reason I paint landscapes and not portraits."

He smiled gently. "What on earth made you think she was you?"

"Someone I loved died," Faye said. "I went to a pier like the one in your painting to spread his ashes. It was cold, and I had on a gray coat. And I walked to the end of the pier holding the urn in my hands. The girl in the painting looks like she's holding something. And there was this white bird on the pier when I was there. It was just like your painting. All of it. Minus the lighthouse, I mean. God, that does sound crazy." Faye rubbed her forehead. "I'm sorry."

"Don't be sorry. Anyone would be a little spooked to see a scene from their own life on canvas."

"And that's only half of it," Faye said, laughing at herself.

"Well, let's go over to the dock and talk about it. I want to hear the other half."

Faye helped him gather his tools, and she slung her camera over her shoulder. They walked across the lawn in silence to the dock. Faye's wedges sounded loud and hollow on the faded wood boards as they walked to the end and looked out onto the water. They were silent for a long moment. Faye sensed Pat sizing her up.

"So talk to me, Miss Faye. What are you not telling me?" Pat asked as they stood side by side, elbows resting on the dock's wooden rail.

"Did you know that lighthouse keeper?" she asked.

"I knew him, yes. Long, long time ago."

"Can I show you something?" she asked.

"Go right ahead."

Faye took a printed piece of paper out of her bag and showed it to Pat. "Do you know who this man is?"

"He was much older when I knew him, but I'd know that face anywhere," Pat said. "That's Carrick Morgan."

"Is it? Are you sure?"

"Of course I'm sure."

Faye went silent a moment. His certainty had scared her. "Faye?"

"Sorry. Can you maybe tell me more about him?"

"Carrick?" He shrugged. "When I knew him he was retired and living off his navy pension."

"Interesting name. Irish?"

Pat nodded. "Son of Irish immigrants, named for the village they'd come from."

"How'd he get the job as lighthouse keeper? I thought the Irish had trouble getting good work."

"He'd been working at the Boston Light after the war. Carrick was brought down as an assistant keeper, took over as principle keeper when the previous family got transferred."

"You said his daughter moved in with him," Faye said. "What about his wife?"

Pat shook his head. "He said he was a widower."

"But he had a daughter?" Faye asked. Interesting Carrick Morgan "said" he was a widower. Did that mean he wasn't? Was his daughter illegitimate? That sort of thing didn't fly back in the 1920s like it did now. Faye could easily imagine a man in a government job trying to protect his daughter from the stain of scandal by lying about his past.

"Where did you find this picture?" Pat asked. He hadn't stopped staring at the picture since she'd handed it to him. "I've never seen it before."

"I took that picture," Faye said.

Pat's brow furrowed. "Not possible. Carrick was dead long before you were born. Died in '65."

"It is possible, Pat, because this isn't Carrick Morgan. This man's name is Will Fielding."

"Who?"

"My husband, Pat. My husband, who's been dead four years."

"My God..." Pat breathed. His shock was palpable. Faye felt it, too. "They're twins."

"Twins born a hundred years apart?"

Pat shook his head in obvious disbelief.

"Pat?"

"I'm sorry," Pat said. "It's just...strange. Very strange."

"Imagine how I feel," Faye said. "First I see a picture online last night of a man who looks like my dead husband. This morning I see a painting of a woman who looks like me the morning I scattered his ashes. And now I find out they were father and daughter? Oh, and that damn bird is back." Faye looked up at the overcast sky and shook her head. "I am going crazy."

"No, you are not, Miss Faye."

"You sound pretty sure of that," she said. "Wish I could be."

She crossed her arms over her chest and faced him.

"Why did you paint her on the pier like that? You wouldn't have been alive when she died."

Pat turned and leaned back against the railing of the dock, putting the Marshlands before him and the lighthouse behind him.

"Retirement age for a priest is seventy. Did you know that?" he asked. It wasn't what she expected him to say, but she trusted he had a reason.

"No. I'm not Catholic."

"I retired from the Church when I was sixty-four. I should have hung on for six more years, but I couldn't do it anymore."

"Why not?"

"I've painted all my life. It's my second religion. A few years ago my hands started shaking when I held anything heavier than five pounds. Then it was four pounds. Three pounds. A priest isn't supposed to drop the communion wine. I had to take early retirement."

"I wondered about your painting style. Kind of impressionistic, like Degas."

"Degas was almost blind at the end. And I can't hold a pen without it shaking like a leaf. I used to paint in a more realistic style. Impressionism was all that was left to me after the tremor started."

"Your work is lovely."

"It wasn't, in the beginning. It was just awful, embarrassing. Whatever technique I'd developed over the years was gone. I painted like a child. Imagine if someone took your camera from you."

"They can pry my camera out of my cold dead hands."

"That's what I always said about my brushes. But no one had to pry them out of my hands. They fell out."

"I'm so sorry," Faye said.

"It was hard to keep my faith after the tremor took the priesthood away from me, took painting away from me. My only two loves. So I went out to the lighthouse with a heavy heart. I had lied to Ms. Shelby, telling her I wanted to paint the lighthouse. But that wasn't the real plan."

Faye heard a note of shame in his voice, embarrassment maybe. She pictured herself curled up on the floor of the bathroom, the pill bottle in her hand while she worked up the courage to take off the lid. That was how Hagen had found her. The real plan, Pat had said. Yes, she knew exactly what the real plan had been.

"That would be quite a fall from the top of the lighthouse, wouldn't it?"

"And onto rocks," he said. "When the tide's out, it's nothing but rocks. A quick drop to a certain death."

"I've been there," Faye said.

He nodded. "I imagine a widow would know that place all too well."

"What changed your mind?" she asked.

"The lighthouse. I won't pretend a miracle happened. No angel stayed my hand. No voice from heaven. The lighthouse has always been a beacon of hope. That's why you see it so often in Christian art. 'A city set on a hill cannot be hidden. Nor do people light a lamp and put it under a basket, but on a stand, and it gives light to all...'"

"Very pretty."

"Matthew 5:15. I suppose it's a cliché to say I saw the light. But there was a moment, an instant where I thought I saw the lighthouse lamp burning again. Just the sunlight tricking my eyes, I know. But it... I don't know, it made me feel something I hadn't felt in years."

"Hope?"

He nodded. "Hope. Something told me to paint the lighthouse. And when I did paint it, I painted it well. Not like my old style, but not bad. And I painted it again. Eventually I wanted to paint it more than I wanted to throw myself off the top of it."

"And the lady in the painting? The Lady of the Light? Why did you paint her?"

"Carrick never got over losing Faith. Maybe I just wanted to bring her back to life. The lighthouse gave me my life back. I guess I wanted to return the favor."

"Pat," Faye said. "I need to get out to that lighthouse."

"Bad idea."

"Why?" she asked.

"That lighthouse is dangerous."

"You said it saved your life."

"It could have taken it, too. It's not safe out there. Some kids went out there a few years ago, got drunk on the beach and drowned when they went for a midnight swim. The lighthouse was there for a reason. There's the sandbar and one hell of a riptide, too. We already have one Lady of the Light. We don't need another."

"How did she get that nickname?"

"People swear they see her sometimes. But lighthouses are notorious for having ghost stories attached to them. Parents use her as a warning, a scare story to keep their kids from breaking into the lighthouse or swimming near that corner of the island. The real story is much sadder. Faith hadn't been at the lighthouse long. Just a few days. Nobody knows why she went out on the pier at night, but she did. A wave hit hard and high, and she fell into the water."

"How old was she?"

"I can't say for sure. A young woman."

"Where was she before? In school or something?"

"She was with other family members," Pat said.

"And why did she come down here?"

"A love affair gone wrong," Pat said. "She was a beauty, they say. But you wouldn't know anything about that, would you?"

"Stop it."

"I'd love to paint you. I'd have to get the right purple paint for your eyes. Elizabeth Taylor eyes."

"Got them from my grandmother. I swear, I think her proudest achievement in life was passing her eye color on to me. She wanted to be Elizabeth Taylor when she was a girl. Even did her hair like hers. Black bouffant even in her sixties."

"I might have had to go to confession after seeing *Father of the Bride* as a boy."

"You know, I can tell when someone is changing the subject. Why don't you want to talk about Faith Morgan?"

"It's..." He waved his hand dismissively. "Some things just don't make sense to me. Priests want things to make sense. She came down here to start a new life. Instead she died. And Carrick never recovered from losing her."

"Ah," Faye said, nodding. "Carrick and I have something in common then."

Pat crossed his arms over his chest. He would have to be seventy-six or seventy-seven if he was twenty-seven in 1965. He didn't look much over sixty to her. But now he did look older, just for a moment. Faye saw his hands tremble slightly. He clenched his fists, released them, and the tremor was gone.

"Poor girl," he said. "Had it been today she might have been fine. She had a dress on, a heavy dress, heavy shoes. And she couldn't swim."

"A lighthouse keeper's daughter who couldn't swim?"

"Women didn't do a lot of swimming back then. Carrick tried to save her and couldn't. Jumped in the water, swam after her... Waves got her. Haunted him the rest of his life."

"It wasn't his fault."

"Ah, but Carrick was a lighthouse keeper, a man whose job was keeping people safe. To lose her like that, on his watch...and then to find her body days later."

Faye held up her hand to stem the tide of his words. She didn't want to hear any more. She'd been spared seeing Will's body until they'd cleaned him up at the hospital. And that had been bad enough, the sickening indentation in the side of his forehead, the shaved patch of hair, the crude stitches, the blue-gray pallor of his cold skin, the sheet pulled up to his neck hiding his otherwise perfect corpse from her. But to find the body of your own child...bloated, battered by the current...

"It was the beginning of the end of the lighthouse when Faith died," Pat said. "Carrick couldn't keep the light anymore. They merged the Bride Island station with the Hunting Island station and automated the light in 1925, which was a tragedy of its own."

"How so?"

"Lighthouse keepers did more than just keep the lighthouse. They watched the coast, too, gave aid when necessary, rescued people in distress when called for. In the fall of '26, a fishing boat broke apart right off Bride Island's north shore during a storm and all fourteen souls aboard died. If the lighthouse had been manned at the time, those men might have lived. The world needed Carrick's light but losing Faith... That snuffed it right out."

Pat took off his glasses, wiping them with the only clean corner of his T-shirt.

"Carrick moved down to Savannah after leaving Charleston. He worked for a shipping company and then the Georgia Port Authority. By his own account it was a long and hard and very lonely life. He came back to Beaufort after he retired just like I did. He said it was the last place he was ever happy."

"Was he a good man?"

"Too good," he said. "Too good for this world anyway."

"Funny," Faye said, although it wasn't.

"What is?"

"Today I said exactly the same thing about Will."

Faye sat in the living room of Father Pat's little Duke Street cottage, a pretty fern-green one-story nothing-special sort of house. Nothing special on the outside, but the inside was an art gallery, a Pantone dream. He'd painted every room a different hue—sunflower gold for the kitchen, cornflower blue living room, lagoon-green bathroom. And every wall boasted watercolor paintings of the sea and the sun; every horizontal surface held books on paintings, on how to paint watercolors, on the history of painting. She expected something in the house to give a sign that it belonged to a priest, but there was nothing, not a cross in sight.

Pat got her settled on his sofa and gave her iced tea in a Pilsner glass.

"I'd never guess you were a priest," she said. "By your house or anything really."

"Ah, that's the point. Now show me your husband. You have me intrigued to the point of day drinking."

Faye opened her laptop and showed Pat both pictures side by side as he sipped at his beer and she her tea. She'd taken an old picture of Will and run it through Photoshop, aging the background, changing the colors. But she hadn't touched his face, hadn't changed the way he looked at all. Pat stared at them a long time before closing the lid of her laptop and passing it back to her.

"Okay," he said. "So I told you about Carrick and Faith. Now you tell me about Will and Faye."

"I'm a baseball widow. Ever heard of us?"

"I've heard of you. Women who say goodbye to their husbands in April and don't see them again until October?"

"I'm a real baseball widow. My husband was a professional baseball player."

"What team?"

"When we met Will was playing on a Triple-A team in Rhode Island. I was the local paper's photographer. One game I took a good picture of him making a double play. You should have seen it. This huge guy barreling toward second base, starting a hard slide, and Will tagging him, one arm in the air for balance and his glove just brushing the guy's back, inches from the bag." Faye mimed the move, the image burned into her brain. She'd been a baseball fan all her life and had never seen anything so athletic, so elegant as Will Fielding spinning like a bullfighter to get the out. "The picture ran in the paper with the caption, 'Olé!' I didn't think anything of it other than it was a good shot with lucky timing. But the very next game after the photo ran, Mr. Olé came up to me and thanked me. His teammates had given him the nickname 'The Matador' after that. He'd always wanted a good baseball nickname. Hank Aaron was 'Hammer' and Ruth was the 'Sultan of Swat.' Now he was Will 'The Matador' Fielding. He said I'd made his dream come true with that picture. I was supposed to say something to that like, 'No problem' or 'Just doing my job.' But here was this big, tall wall of pure American maleness. Handsome and brown-eyed and grinning at me, and I ended up saying something like, 'I will take pictures of anything and everything you want me to.' And only after the words came out did I realize it sounded like I'd just offered to take naked pics for him. I probably would have had he asked."

"That handsome?"

"Took my breath away," Faye said. "But he was a good guy and didn't ask for naked pics. Instead, he asked me about my work. When the game started he said he'd love to keep talking to me later. That night was our first date. Before Will I dated coffee-shop guys. You know, the skinny intellectuals with the earbuds and the Macs who drink expensive coffee and write thinkpieces for their incredibly boring blogs and magazines? Those guys. Never dated a guy who drank gas-station coffee before, who didn't own a Mac but did own a grill and a drill. We met in July, got engaged in September and got married the next spring. Sometimes you just know. And we just knew."

"I've known many a couple who just knew. A priest has to believe in love. It's part of our job."

"The day after Will asked me to marry him, he hit two home runs. He said I must be his good-luck charm, and who needed a rabbit's foot when he had me? He called me Bunny sometimes, and you better believe he was the one man on earth who could call me Bunny and live to tell the tale."

"I can tell you loved him," Pat said.

"God, I loved him." She blinked back her tears. "Will was one of the last good guys. The really good guys. Good inside and out. His dad worked at Jiffy Lube and his mother was a hospice nurse so…definitely not the most exalted of

origin stories. But it was meant to be. You don't grow up
with the name Will Fielding without being destined to be a
baseball player. And even when he was in the minors making
less than minimum wage and living in cramped buses and
roach motels, four players to a room, he felt like the luckiest
man on earth. I can hear him in my head right now. 'Babe,
think about it—who gets to do what I do? Play baseball
for a job? What's next? Pay me to eat candy and sleep with
you?' He'd say that all the time with this look on his face
like, 'Really? Me?' He never once thought he deserved it.
He was just happy to be there. And he made me so happy."

"I bet you made him happy, too."

"I tried. And you know what? I did. I did make him
happy. And it was my pleasure to do it. I hate sports puns,
but Will was out of my league. I was as happy to be his wife
as he was happy to be a ballplayer."

"You're the prettiest lady I've set eyes on in a long time.
You aren't out of any man's league."

"You're sweet to say that, but it's not what I meant. I
don't mean looks. I mean…before Will I was self-centered.
Not in any way that anyone else isn't self-centered. When
you're single, you don't have to think about anyone else, and
I didn't. I couldn't. I was broke, in student loan debt, worked
constantly. But then Will came along, and I watched him
spending his very few days off at children's hospitals visiting sick kids and helping out underprivileged Little League
teams. That was Will. You have any idea how grueling life
is in the minors? He never once complained. He said a ballplayer complaining about road trips and sore shoulders was
like a rich man complaining he had to hire an accountant
to count all his money. I've been a feminist my whole life,
independent. I went to an Ivy League school. I paid my own

bills. I knew even if we had kids I'd never quit my working to be a stay-at-home mom. And you know what?"

"Tell me," Pat said, looking her straight in the eyes.

"I'd give up the right to vote just to do one more load of Will's dirty laundry."

She laughed at herself—better to laugh than to cry again.

"I promise I won't tell Gloria Steinem on you," Pat said with a wink.

Faye laughed even harder at that.

"Will had these baseball T-shirts," she said, trying to compose herself. "So many baseball T-shirts. Every team you could think of. Two weeks after he died I found a Bronx Bombers shirt in a bag under the bed. Can you imagine? A kid who grew up on the Sox with a Yankees shirt? Goddamn it, Will."

Those stupid baseball T-shirts, they were all he wore when he wasn't naked or in his uniform. The single time she'd seen him in a suit was at their wedding. Those shirts... He had so many of them she'd wash them all in one load. Laundry was sorted into whites, darks, towels and baseball shirts. She'd given the shirts away after he died to relatives and close friends who needed something of his. She'd kept one for herself—the soft heather-gray one with the big red *B* on the front that Will had worn on their first date. That was the one she'd always slept in when he was on his road trips. She didn't sleep in it anymore. Crying oneself to sleep only worked in the movies.

Pat handed her a handkerchief and pressed it to her burning cheeks.

"Sorry about the 'goddamn it.' I shouldn't swear in front of a priest."

"You must not know any priests. You can say whatever the hell you want. Trust me—I've heard worse. Said worse, too."

"Thank you," she whispered, slowly bringing herself back under control. "Will really looked good in his T-shirts. Had the arms for them. Gotta say, there are a lot of perks to being married to an athlete. Having the sexiest husband at the beach was one of them, and I'm shallow enough to admit that." She laughed again, remembering…remembering… "Will had this great baseball player walk. It wasn't like a strut, more like an amble. This loose-in-the-hips amble. When he was leaving the house to go on a road trip, I'd always tell him, 'I hate to see you go, but I love to watch you walk away.' I didn't know the last time I watched him walk away would be, you know, the last time I watched him walk away. If I'd known, I would have stared at his ass longer."

Faye laughed again and cried again. Her body ached for Will. She could talk about his T-shirts but what she really missed was his body. The way he smelled after a game—sweat and leather. The way he picked her up and threw her into bed like a rag doll just because he could. The way he made love to her. He was twenty-three when they met and had just broken up with his high school sweetheart, the only girl he'd been with before her. But during sex he made her feel like she was the only woman in the world, and he was the lucky schmuck who got to have her. For a long time she had to think of Will to orgasm during sex with Hagen. That wasn't something she had told anyone. Widows might as well be nuns for the careful way people treated them. What would people think if they knew what she missed most about her late husband was the sex? The hard-core full-body, full-soul, all-in, nothing-held-back sort of sex you could have with someone who knew everything about you. Will filled her up and emptied her out and gave her what she needed. And what she needed was him, just him, but all of him.

"I should be ashamed of myself for how much I miss having sex with him. Kind of shallow, I guess."

"Taking pleasure in your own husband doesn't make you shallow. I know a lot of husbands who wish their wives saw them like that."

"Will was one of those guys born for heavy lifting and getting stuff off the top shelf. He made me feel small, and he made me feel safe, and it takes a special kind of man to make a woman feel both at the same time. One day I teased him that I heard 'Like a Rock' by Bob Seger automatically start playing when he walked into a room, and at the very next game, they played that as his walk-up song." Faye laughed. Will had always looked for a way to make her smile. Even now, even through the tears, here she was smiling because of him.

"He sounds like one in a million."

"He was. And we were so happy it doesn't even seem real now. As good as it was, it somehow managed to get even better. I found out I was pregnant the same week Will got called up to the majors. Which meant, of course, I got called up, too. I was officially a WAG."

"WAG? What on earth?"

"WAGs. Wives and Girlfriends of pro athletes," Faye said.

"I see," Pat said. "We don't get to have those in the priesthood. At least, we're not supposed to."

Faye grinned as she wiped her face. "Probably for the best," she said. "A couple days after Will went to Boston, I got invited to a WAG party at the house of one of the pitcher's wives. Nice women, but every last one of them warned me my life was about to change, and not for the better. So many women told me about the jobs they'd had to quit, the dreams they'd had to give up for their husbands' careers. And if I wanted to keep doing my little photography thing, they said, I should probably save it for the off-season, treat it like a hobby. I thought they'd be happy when I told them I was expecting. I just got this look like…"

Faye mimed the look of disapproval.

"I had committed the cardinal WAG sin," Faye continued. "I was going to give birth during the season."

"Shameful," Pat said. "How dare you? I shouldn't laugh, but…"

"You can laugh. Will did. He rolled his eyes so hard I thought they'd fall out of his head. He told me…" Faye paused, caught her breath. "He told me he would quit baseball before he missed the birth of our child. And he would never ever forgive me if I let his dreams get in the way of my own. He said the day I put down my camera, he would put down his bat and glove. He made me promise I would never give up my work for his. And if you were wondering why I said he was the best man who ever lived, that's the reason."

"He's giving Carrick a run for his money."

"There are no words for how happy Will was, how happy we both were. Then I went to shoot some pictures for a project I was working on, and Will went out to buy flowers to surprise me when I got back. On the way home, he sees two guys on the side of the road trying to change a flat. This was Will's area. Son of a mechanic. He helped more stranded drivers than AAA. But they weren't stranded drivers. They were a carjacking team. They went for the car, and Will tried to stop them. One of them hit him in the head with the tire iron. He died on the operating table from a rapid intracranial hemorrhage. They killed my beautiful husband for drug money and a 2005 Ford Focus."

Faye exhaled and leaned back on Pat's sofa, her hands on her face, trying to stifle the animal howl of grief welling up within her. A gentle hand touched her knee, and she grabbed Pat's hand and held it like her life depended on it. She breathed through it—*In and out, babe. The world's not ending*—and slowly found her voice again.

"He'd been in the majors all of one month. Batted .364. Best September of our lives. I'm always a wreck in September now. And I can't even watch baseball anymore."

Pat bowed his head and she wondered if he were praying for her. She'd take any help she could get.

"The police got the guys who killed him. Even got the car back. But they couldn't bring me my husband back. I had that car, though. That stupid car."

Pat clasped his hands between his knees and sighed. "If there's anything fifty years in the priesthood taught me, it's that I can't say a damn thing to make you feel better right now."

"At least you know that. 'Everything happens for a reason' sure doesn't cut it."

"Everything does happen for a reason. Sometimes it's a bad reason."

"Sounds like my second marriage," she said, sitting up again, wiping at her face and then giving up. Too many tears, not enough tissues in the world. "After the funeral, Will's best friend from college, Hagen, started hanging around our place all the time. It was nice. It helped, it really did. He said it was what Will would have done. And then a couple weeks later, he sat me down and told me he thought we should get married. It wasn't much of a proposal. More like an escape plan. Like this would solve all my problems. I thought he'd lost his mind. Then Hagen said the magic words again— 'It's what Will would have done.'"

"Was it?" Pat asked.

"If it had been Hagen who'd died, Hagen with a pregnant wife left behind, Will would have stepped in and been a father to that kid. So Hagen and I got married. Hagen had money, a big house. He told me I could have my own room, that he wouldn't expect me to act like his wife until I was ready for it. Sounds like the beginning of a beautiful romance, doesn't it? Hollywood thought so, too. A story ran in the *Boston Globe* about Will and me and Hagen, and the next day a producer called and said he'd already talked to a screenwriter about putting Will's Cinderella story on the big screen—nobody kid from Nowhere, Mass, drafted in the forty-first round, ends up playing for the Red Sox. And it would end with me giving birth to Will's baby. Triumph out of tragedy. Whatever. I talked to them because you go crazy when you're grieving like that. And I just wanted Will to be remembered. Then I lost the baby at sixteen weeks and they stopped calling. Not even Hollywood could give me a happy ending."

She didn't tell Pat about the years of trying to get pregnant that came after losing Will's baby. She could barely face her grief over losing Will. If she had to grieve for those lost years, she'd never make it out of this house in one piece. And Hagen? She couldn't talk about Hagen, how once she'd lost the baby, he'd turned into a ball of quiet anger, like it had been her fault she'd lost the last part of Will left in the world.

Faye took a shuddering breath and forced herself to drink her tea. Crying so hard had given her dry mouth, and her throat felt like it had been dragged down a gravel road.

"I promise I'm not vomiting this whole story onto you for the fun of it," Faye finally said, carefully lowering her glass to her knee. It left a wet ring on her white jeans, but she didn't care. "I'm just so...freaked out, I guess. And I don't even know why. So what? So Will and Carrick Morgan looked alike. What does it mean? Nothing. I know it means nothing. I've seen those internet clickbait stories where they show celebrities who look like people who've been dead for a hundred years. It happens. There are only so many faces in the world, I guess. But it feels like it means something. Do I sound crazy? You can tell me if I do. I can take it. Oh, and I think a stork is stalking me. Yeah, I sound crazy. I can hear it."

"My job entailed me turning wine into God's blood, so I don't think I can judge you too harshly. I'm an open-minded spiritual man by trade."

"I appreciate you listening to me. I can't talk to anyone about Will. Hagen and I are divorced, and we can't talk about anything anymore without it turning into a fight. Will's parents are doing better than I am. They have grandkids from Will's sister, and those kids are their whole life now. Every time I visit them, his mom has a breakdown and it takes weeks for her to get back on her feet again. I stopped talking to Will's family two years ago. Too hard on all of us."

"And your parents?"

"Dad died. Mom has dementia. I was an oops baby when they were both forty."

"Friends?"

Faye shook her head. "I had friends. They were great until the funeral. After that, they had their own lives, and nobody knows what to say to a twenty-six-year-old widow. Will's friends and teammates weren't thrilled with me for getting married again so soon after he died. The medical bills and funeral expenses wiped out the life insurance. There I was, almost broke with student-loan debt up to my eyeballs and pregnant. I ran out of shoulders to cry on a long time ago."

"You're Lady Job," Pat said with a sorrowful smile.

"Who?"

"Job, in the Bible. A very old Jewish story, very strange and mystical. You've heard the phrase 'the patience of Job'?"

"Oh, that guy. Yes, I've heard of him. I don't know if I've ever read the story."

"Odd little book, but some of the loveliest poetry in the Bible. A man named Job has a wife, children and wealth. And he's a good man. Satan goes to God and makes a sort of bet with him, saying that Job is only good because he's blessed, but if you take his blessings away, he won't be righteous anymore. God takes him up on that bet and wipes out Job's entire family, his wealth and his health. He's literally sitting in ashes using potsherds to scrape the sores off his body."

"Oh, my God, that's disgusting. Even I didn't have it that bad."

Pat laughed. "I told you it was a strange little book. But it does have a happy ending. Job keeps his faith in God, though he demands God explain himself."

"Does he?"

"God shows up and gives the 'who do you think you are?' speech to end all speeches. The short version is basically 'I am God. You're not, so stuff it.'"

"Very poetic."

Father Pat smiled but didn't laugh. He took a breath and met her eyes.

"'Where wast thou when I laid the foundations of the earth? Declare if thou hast understanding. Who hath laid the measures thereof, if thou knowest? Or who laid the cornerstone thereof, when the morning stars sang together, and all the sons of God shouted for joy? Or who shut up the sea with its doors, when it brake forth, as if it had issued out of the womb? Hast thou entered into the springs of the sea? Or hast thou walked in search of the depth? Have the gates of death been opened unto thee?'"

Pat stopped and sighed. "It goes on like that for a long time. God wanted to make sure Job got the point."

"That's beautiful," Faye breathed. "What does it all mean?"

"It means a lowly man may never understand the ways of God."

"And you find that comforting?" she asked.

"A little. If lowly little me could understand God, then he wouldn't be much of a God, right?"

"I guess," Faye said.

"I do find this comforting, though—even after God tells Job off, he restores him. New wife. Children. Even more children than he'd lost. Twice as much wealth. And a life so long he meets his great-grandchildren."

"If only," Faye said.

"Yes," Pat said. "If only."

Faye wiped her face with Pat's handkerchief again. She didn't know many men who still carried handkerchiefs. Will always had—a red bandanna in his back pocket just like his dad.

"When Will and I got married, we did all the usual wedding vows. Love, honor, cherish, until death do us part. But that wasn't good enough for Will. He added one more vow. He said…" She stopped to breathe even though it hurt to breathe, but she kept on doing it. Will would have wanted her to. "He said, 'Come heaven or hell or high water, I will love you and take care you of you as long as you live, Faye.' I asked him, 'Don't you mean as long as *you* live?' He said no. He wasn't interested in till death do us part. Even if he went first, he would find a way to take care of me. I treasure that vow. I hold it right here," she said, touching her chest over her heart. "But I'm still waiting for him to keep it."

Faye squeezed Pat's hands again. He had nice hands, a younger man's hands. A painter's hands even if they did tremble.

"You can't go back, you know," Faye said.

"Go back where?" Pat asked.

"Once someone loves you that much, loves you more than you deserve, you can't go back to being loved the normal way," she said. "You ever been loved like that?"

"Only by my creator."

"Pat, I have to tell you something else crazy," she whispered.

"Tell me something crazy."

"I think I'm supposed to go the lighthouse," she said. "I think... I don't know. I feel like someone wants me out there."

"What do you hope to find there?" Pat asked, and Faye could tell he really wanted her to think about it before answering. So she thought about it and admitted she didn't know the answer.

"I don't want to see any ghosts, and I know Will's not going to be there waiting for me. But it feels like I've had a nightmare, and if I got out there, I'll wake up and know it was all a dream. I just... Maybe it would help me. Like it helped you."

Pat took a steadying breath and nodded his head.

"All right. I'll get you there. But if Ms. Shelby's out there and catches you, you don't know me, right?"

"Right. Promise. Never met you."

"And you have to swear to me you'll be careful. That lighthouse is old, and the water there is choppy as hell. It's more dangerous out there than you can imagine. You swear you'll be safe?"

"I swear," she said.

"You swear you'll stay out of the water?" he asked.

"I swear," she said again. He gave her a long, searching look, then sighed like he knew he was wasting his time. Pat got a sheet of paper and scribbled a little map for her and walked her through the steps of how to find the road with the bridge, what turns to take and when to take them.

"Good enough?" he asked.

"Perfect," Faye said, folding up the map and shoving it into her back pocket. "Thank you. I should go. I haven't eaten much today, and I know I've taken up way too much of your time." Faye's head throbbed from hunger and crying so hard. She'd lost control of herself, something she rarely did. She didn't want to lose it again in front of this kind old man.

"You made my day, young lady. Beautiful woman in my house? The neighbors are loving this. They can't wait to find out what I've been up to with you in here."

"Keeping me from having a nervous breakdown."

"That's not a very sexy rumor. We'll have to do better than that."

"I'm sure you'll come up with something good. Feel free to ruin my reputation. I wasn't using it anyway."

"Count on it." He helped her to her feet.

Before letting her leave, Pat pulled a small red book off his shelf and pressed it into her hands.

"Take this," he said.

"What is it?"

"It's a prayer book, a very special one," Pat said.

"I'm not really religious."

"I'm not giving it to you because I want to convert you. But I think you should have it. Please."

"Are you going to pray for me?"

"For you. For Will. And for Hagen."

"For Hagen?"

"Ex-husbands are people, too," he said.

"If you say so," she said and smiled.

He kissed her goodbye on the cheek and held her hand.

"I hope you find what you're looking for, Faye," he said. "But if you don't find it…"

"I'll be okay."

"Just stay out of the water," Pat said again. "Please."

Faye promised him faithfully she would and then took her leave.

By the time Faye made it back to the Church Street house, she felt almost human again. She took a long shower, ate some homemade spaghetti with Miss Lizzie and another girl staying at the house that summer. Afterward she went up to her room to upload her pictures from the Marshlands.

As she suspected, most of the pictures were a bust. Maybe she could salvage a couple she'd taken off the dock for a stock photo site, but they wouldn't do for the calendar. It was what it was. She'd get back to work tomorrow.

Although it was barely seven o'clock, Faye was already sprawled in bed wearing nothing but her black silk robe. Her summer robe, a gift from Hagen. A thoughtful gift. Pretty and practical. She could say that much for Hagen; he gave good gifts. They'd skipped dating, being engaged, but at their wedding he'd given her a band and a four-carat diamond engagement ring. Both were in her makeup bag. If she ran out of money, she'd have them to pawn.

An old Catholic prayer book, on the other hand, might be the oddest gift anyone had ever given her. She'd read it maybe. Who knew? She might find the perfect prayer for her. A prayer for a widow who had remarried too soon and had lost her late husband's baby. Perhaps the generic "Prayer for Someone Suffering" would cover all that. Faye turned to the back where the index should be and found some handwriting in pen on a page.

The handwriting looked as old as the book, and the book, according to the title page, was printed in 1954. The ink was faded but the script neat and sturdy.

Lord, I give Thee thanks that Thou didst die upon the cross for my sins. Forgive me the blood on my hands. Forgive me the life I took and wash the blood from my hands and the stain of sin from my soul. Thou art infinite in mercy. Shower Thy mercy upon Thy son.

And the prayer was signed.

It was signed "Carrick Morgan."

Faye sat straight up in bed.

This was Carrick Morgan's prayer book? The lighthouse keeper?

Faye's hands shook as she gingerly laid the book open on her lap and traced his words with her fingertip. Carrick Morgan had a beautiful signature, an old-fashioned, elegant script. She should have guessed he was Catholic, being of Irish stock. The prie-dieu in her room... Had he carved that himself? And he prayed for forgiveness and for mercy because he took someone's life. He'd killed someone. Who? Father Pat had owned this book for years. Carrick Morgan himself must have given it to him. Pat would have known about the prayer for forgiveness, and yet he'd called Morgan the best man he'd ever known. It made no sense. None of it did. Staring at Carrick Morgan's words in the prayer book made it impossible for Faye to sit still in her room and wait for tomorrow. It felt like an alarm was blaring somewhere and she had to go to the lighthouse to find a way to turn it off. It was growing dark, too dark for pictures. But this wasn't about the photographs anymore.

Faye dug through her suitcase for a clean top and spied her little jewelry bag under her black tank top. When she opened it she found Will's old college championship ring that he'd given her right after they started dating. "Does this mean we're going steady now?" she'd said, teasing him. She'd worn the ring on a necklace until they'd gotten married and he'd slipped a wedding band on her finger—one that fit.

Though she no longer wore it, Faye treasured the ring. She wouldn't pawn it, not if she were starving. The ring was white gold with a blue stone in it, Will's name and a baseball insignia emblazoned on both sides. It comforted her to look at it, to hold it. She slipped it over her thumb and felt calmer in an instant. Here was the reason her marriage to Hagen had been so hard. It wasn't that she'd had to pretend to be in love with Hagen. It was that she'd had to pretend she wasn't in love with Will. She didn't have to pretend anymore.

"I love you, Will," she whispered, then kissed the ring for luck.

Faye pulled on her jeans and T-shirt, grabbed her camera bag and her car keys and headed out. Earlier that day Pat had asked her what she thought she'd find at the lighthouse. She hadn't known the answer then, but she knew it now.

She went to the lighthouse for the same reason anyone went to a lighthouse.

She went because she needed the light.

7

Faye had to Google directions to find her way to where Pat's map began. After one wrong turn on Hunting Island, she righted herself. She crossed the one-lane bridge, which was green with old paint and red with fresh rust. On the other side of the bridge she found a gate unlocked and standing wide-open. She usually wasn't the sort of person who believed in things like "signs," but usually she didn't see photographs of men who'd been dead since the sixties who looked just like her husband. The gate being open was either a sign the universe wanted her on the island tonight or, more likely, a sign someone had forgotten to close it. Either way, here she was.

As she crossed over onto the island, Faye's heart started a steady march through her chest with the feet of a thousand soldiers pounding the pavement. She could see it now—the cops would show up, arrest her for trespassing, and then she'd have to call Hagen to come and bail her out. She'd rather spend the night in jail than call him for help.

She drove slowly down the tree-lined path, the branches of

the oaks forming a tunnel. Low-hanging branches scratched her car roof, and she winced. There wasn't any money for a new paint job, so she better take care of the one she had. She wished she had some idea of where this road led—south beach or north beach or straight into a swamp? Pat's map didn't help much. The dense tree canopy threw off her usually strong sense of direction. Behind her she saw the last rays of the setting sun through a break in the treetops. The sun set in the west, which meant she needed to take a left to go north. She found a narrow road and turned onto it. Pat hadn't exaggerated when he'd said the island contained nothing but trees. Faye saw no houses, no ponds, no street signs, no flowers. Only a few dirt horse trails, and a gravel road here and there and the trees.

Finally Faye spied the top of the lighthouse dead ahead. The last of the day's sunlight gleamed off the bell-shaped black dome, and for a split second she thought she saw the light flash. But the lighthouse hadn't been operational in decades. The keeper was gone. No one was home. The light had been extinguished, never to burn again. No streetlamps or spotlights on Bride Island, either. Once the sun set, there would be no light on the island except what the moon and the stars deigned to offer. She had to hurry if she didn't want to be stuck on the island in the pitch dark.

The trees opened up to a clearing, and Faye parked on a patch of trampled-down scrub grass. She hopped out of the car, leaving her camera behind. This wasn't the time for work. She simply needed to see the lighthouse, to be in the moment, to listen to whatever the universe was trying to tell her.

Plus she had no idea what the tide was doing right now, and if she got her camera wet, she would be screwed—and not in the good way that involved alcohol and sexy college boys covered in black fish tattoos.

Faye picked her way down a rocky path toward the beach. The air was warm and smelled of salt and nothing else. An entire flock of little birds, sandpipers maybe, danced at the water's edge on their tiny little legs, leaving V-shaped tracks in the soft wet sand.

The sun was rapidly setting as Faye walked around the lighthouse, astonished by the sheer size of the monument. It hadn't looked nearly so wide from the water. The lighthouse was built like a cone that grew narrower as it neared the top. Three vertical windows were cut into the side and looked out onto the ocean. Faye stepped over a long line of square rocks that must have marked the foundation of what had once been the keeper's cottage. The lighthouse, on the other hand, composed of concrete and iron, had survived hurricanes.

Very likely it would survive her, too.

The door to the lighthouse looked like it belonged on a cathedral. It was tall and dark and made of thick planks of oak with iron hinges and an iron handle. She had to put her shoulder into it to force the door open enough that she could slip through the gap.

"Hello?" Faye called out, not expecting an answer and truly not wanting one. She merely hoped to spook any birds or bats who'd made the lighthouse their home. Better to roust them out while she could run for it than when she was already halfway up that staircase to the top. She heard nothing—not wings nor coos nor her own voice echoing back at her. Inside the lighthouse it was airless and stuffy, and sounds were muted but for the relentless roar and rumble of the ocean outside. Waves rushed the shore, retreated, only to rush back seconds later like a forlorn lover longing to leave and having second thoughts before reaching the door. The sun shone through the three windows and cast arched shadows onto the interior wall and the spiral staircase. Faye had to take a deep breath just looking at it. Dizzying, truly, and Faye didn't get dizzy when faced with heights. It looked like something from an Escher drawing. Although Escher wouldn't have painted his spiral staircase solid green. The color was fitting as the banister, plus every single slat and step was molded into the shape of a trailing leafy tendril of ivy.

Pat had said the only people who were nostalgic for the past had never lived there, and he did have a point. Yet she couldn't help but long for a bygone era when craftsmen took the time to make something both functional and beautiful, even knowing how few people would ever see their work. It was foolish to tell a grieving widow not to long for the past. She'd heard the saying that the past was a foreign country. True? Yes, but it was the foreign country where Will lived.

Faye wiped the sweat off her forehead. She should have brought a bottle of water with her. Faye started up the staircase, testing each one with her foot before trusting it with her full weight. If she fell and hurt herself, that was it for her. No one knew she was here. No one in the world. While foolish and dangerous, it was also exhilarating. Hagen had always insisted she keep her phone with her at all times, always charged no matter where she went. He insisted she tell him her schedule, when she'd leave, when she'd return. He'd been more a father to her than husband at times, and an overbearing father at that.

Not even sleeping with Ty had made her feel this free— being somewhere no could find her, and knowing that if something bad happened, she was on her own. Pat had warned her not to come out here, warned her it wasn't safe. She'd been playing it safe since Will had died, marrying Hagen for health insurance, getting pregnant because she'd known that was what Hagen wanted... But Hagen wouldn't want her doing this. This was something she and Will would have done together. Sneaking onto private property, giggling and whispering, Faye threatening to disavow all knowledge of Will and this mission if they were caught in the act. She'd gone on several of his team's road trips, and she and Will had had sex in three different minor-league ballpark locker rooms and one major-league dugout. Will had told the security guard that he'd left his contact-lens case in the dugout, which was easily the stupidest lie Will had ever come up with to get laid. And the security guard had known it, too. He'd looked at Will, then looked at Faye and then looked back at Will. He'd said, "She's cute, so I'll give you fifteen minutes. Make it good."

They'd made it good.

As she climbed up the spiraling staircase her body trembled with nervous excitement at doing something she knew she shouldn't. It was a delicious feeling, taking a risk again, getting out of her comfort zone and into the danger zone. It felt like her old life.

"I only wish you were waiting for me at the top of this lighthouse, Will," she whispered. "Not quite the mile-high club but close enough, right?"

She made it to the top at last. Her legs screamed at her and her lungs burned, but she made it. She found the door to the lantern room. She stepped inside and walked straight into a spiderweb. Screaming, she stepped back, batting at her hair and face, before laughing at her wild overreaction to something she should have anticipated. Of course there were spiders up here. Maybe even rats. Luckily it seemed the architect of the web had abandoned her handiwork long ago. Once more into the lantern room Faye ventured. She found it free of any other creatures or cobwebs. She also found it a dirty, disappointing mess. She couldn't even see through the muck-encrusted windows. The lens that had magnified the wick was long gone, no doubt residing in a museum somewhere or converted into a chandelier for some rich man's ceiling. Faye found the exterior door to the widow's walk, took a deep breath and walked outside into the open air.

"Wow," she breathed, unable to stay silent in the presence of such a magnificent vista. She could see all the way to Hunting Island. And the ocean... The ocean stretched out to the very edge of the horizon before dropping out of sight where the earth curved away from her. Close to the shore, the water was a greenish brown, like river water, but farther out it turned a bluish black where the continental shelf ended and the deep waters began. From this height, she could see the outline of the sandbar that had spelled disaster for so many ships before this lighthouse had been erected to guide them to safety. She wondered how ships avoided the sandbar now. In the distance, she heard the gentle tolling of a bell buoy. *Ah, that's how.* Less expensive than manning a lighthouse, but hardly as romantic.

Faye wandered the full perimeter of the widow's walk, taking in every inch of the view. So much beauty, she could hardly stand it. The trees of Bride Island looked like a soft green carpet, and the beaches at the edges of the island looked like delicate pie crust. From above she could see the roofs of several houses closer to the south beach. That must be where Ms. Shelby lived when she stayed here. If Faye had her own island, she'd never leave it, not for anything.

Closer in, Faye spied another area near the center of the island that had been cleared of trees. Had those trees been
taken for Ms. Shelby's bourbon barrels? Or was that the location of the ruins and the graves Pat had told her about? She
wouldn't want to plant trees or build houses over a cemetery, either, although she imagined if one dug deep enough
anywhere on earth, one would find the remains of someone
who wouldn't want a house erected on top of them. That was
one reason she'd chosen to have Will cremated. She didn't
want to give him a grave that in a few centuries would be
the foundation of someone's house or office complex. And
she couldn't imagine putting her husband into a hole in the
ground. Not her Will. She'd given his ashes to the water off
the pier where he'd asked her to marry him. And looking at
the sun setting on the ocean, at the long slant of light that
stretched like a reaching arm from the sound to the sea, she
knew she'd entrusted the ashes of her husband to the only
place worthy enough for them.

Already Faye regretted not bringing her camera with
her. She could have taken a whole series of sunset-on-the-
water pictures.

In reverential silence, Faye stood at the railing facing the
water and watched the last of the light fading and the sky
turning from gold to red to blue to black. Up here, watching
the sky change color as time passed, the thought of growing older and dying wasn't nearly so terrifying. She'd just
watched an evening turn to night, and if she stood up here
long enough she'd see the night turn into morning.

One...two...three... Red...blue...black... Time turned
colors as it passed. That was growing older—watching the
colors of one's life changing. And death? What was death but
falling asleep? Faye fell asleep every night. What did it mat-

ter to her if one morning she simply didn't wake up again? Had Will known? Did he have any idea that the blow to his head would be fatal? When he'd nodded off in the ambulance after muttering, "Somebody call my wife, please," did he know he would never wake up again? No. Surely not. If he had known, his last words would have been a declaration of love to her, and she knew that in the marrow of her bones. If she could take any comfort in Will's death, it was this—she hadn't needed him to tell her he loved her in his last words. She'd known. He'd told her that morning. He'd told her every day. That was why she knew if there were any ghosts in this world, Will wasn't one of them. The particular unfinished business she and Will had wasn't the sort of unfinished business one could finish without a body. No offense to his beautiful spirit.

"This is me, Will," she said to the empty air around her. "I'm just like this lighthouse. Still standing, still here. But I'm falling apart. The light's off, and I don't know how to turn it back on again."

She blinked back tears and took a long, shuddering breath.

"Your wife is turning weird. I'm talking to myself. I banged a college kid. I'm being stalked by a stork. I even talked to a priest about you—retired, but still. Oh, and did you know the lighthouse keeper of this very lighthouse looked just like you? So now I have a crush on a guy who's been dead for fifty years in addition to a guy who's been dead four years. I'm glad you're not here to see what a mess I am these days. If I go to see a medium next, you have my permission to kill me from beyond the grave."

She could hear the memory of Will's warm laugh in her mind, and his voice taunting her.

Can't hold the college kid against you. He was damn cute. You always did want me to get a tattoo.

"Don't laugh at me. This is all your fault."

How is it my fault you banged a college kid?

"Because you died for a car. Do you really think I cared if our car got stolen? I mean, maybe if it was a Corvette or something, but a Ford Focus? A beige Ford Focus? Come on. Couldn't you have at least died for a sports car?"

The flowers were in the car, Bunny.

"Oh, screw the flowers," she said.

That would hurt. They had thorns.

"You know what I mean. I can grow my own flowers if I want them. I can't grow another you. And I tried. My body is not made for having babies, apparently. Not even yours."

Don't feel bad. My body's not made for having babies, either.

"No, but your body was made for making them."

I'm sorry about the baby, too, sweetheart. You know that. But we would have had fun trying again, wouldn't we?

"God, yes." She closed her eyes and let herself remember images, moments, his hands in her hair, his lips on her stomach and going lower, lower… "Remember that thing you used to do to me? You know, when I'd wear a scarf in my hair and you'd pull it out and wrap it around my wrists, drag me into the bedroom and use the scarf for evil?"

I used it for good. If it ends with you having a screaming orgasm, then it was for good.

"You're a pervert."

I resemble that remark.

Faye sighed, then gave a little drunken laugh. Drunk on memories. Drunk on loneliness.

"You're not making this any easier," she said, still laughing because it was the one thing that kept her from crying.

"You know, it's been almost four years. I should be over you by now. I've been widowed four times as long as we were even together. One year wasn't enough."

I hate to tell you this, but...

"But what?" she asked, knowing that when Will said he "hated" to tell her something, it meant he was really *really* going to enjoy what he was going to tell her.

One thousand years wouldn't have been enough. One thousand years, and we would have just gotten started...

Faye smiled. "You sweet talker, you." This time she couldn't hear Will's smart-ass answer. Probably because if he'd been there for real and not just in her mind, he wouldn't have said a word. He would have kissed her and kissed her and kissed her. And eventually she'd be on her stomach in bed with his mouth on the back of her neck, and no words would be necessary for all that would inevitably follow. But her eyes were dry, and her throat was clear. How long had it been since she'd been able to smile while thinking of Will? Just smile? No tears, no panic, no pain? Coming to the lighthouse had been good for her, if for no reason other than it had given her this one little moment of peace.

Looking up at the sky, Faye searched out a shooting star, but they all seemed firmly fixed in place. That was fine. The lone wish she harbored in her heart was for one more night with Will, and it wouldn't have been polite to ask something of a star that a star couldn't give her. She did see something in the sky, though, something large with white wings. It landed on one of the old pier's remaining pillars.

"You again," Faye said to the stork. "Stalker."

Faye left her perch on the widow's walk—wasn't everywhere a widow walked a widow's walk?—and went back down the stairs. She made her way around the wide base of the lighthouse, looking up at it from below. On the side facing the water she saw a rectangular brass plaque screwed into the plaster. The moonlight illuminated the words, but the plaque was old and the typeface worn down. Faye ran her fingers over the indentations, reading the words with both eyes and fingertips.

"In Memory of Faith Morgan. Born May 30, 1904, died June 10, 1921. The Lord brought her to us, and the Lord took her home. May her spirit forever live in this light."

Who had placed the plaque on the lighthouse? Her father, Carrick? The people of the area? Seventeen years old and dead. Will hadn't lived much longer. He'd died at barely twenty-four. Faye placed her hand flat on the plaque. She mourned for anyone who died too soon, even this young woman she'd never met.

"Faith," Faye said, "if you see my husband wherever you are, tell him I miss him. And please remind him he promised to take care of me. I could use his help."

She sighed and let her hand fall away.

"And now I'm talking to dead girls," she said.

Faye pulled herself away from the plaque and strolled to the edge of the water, looking at the sand. Apart from a line of broken shells at the swash line, the beach was free of debris and litter. The tide was high and rising. It chased her as she walked down the beach so Faye took off her shoes and set them on a dune in a clump of sea oats, where the water couldn't reach them. She rolled her jeans up to her knees and waded into the ocean. Bathwater warm, the water wrapped around her legs and scooped the sand away from her feet. The ocean played at her feet, pausing every now and then to kiss her knee, her thigh.

"I am loved," she said aloud, and only after saying it did

she wonder where that had come from. But she realized she knew. The ocean, of course. She had scattered Will's ashes in the ocean. If any part of Will was in the water, then the whole ocean must retain some of his love for her.

No wonder she felt so calm and happy near the water. No wonder she felt like she belonged in this place, where a man who looked just like Will had lived and worked and cared for a daughter who had died here. Carrick Morgan's heart was in the ocean as much as Faye's was. The water was warm with love tonight. It loved her, and she loved it in return.

Faye brought her fingertips to her lips and kissed them. She bent and pressed them to the ocean's surface. As her hand touched the water, Will's championship ring slipped off her thumb and the tide snatched it away.

"Shit." She dropped to her knees, not caring that she hadn't brought a towel with her, not caring about anything but getting Will's ring back. She clawed at the water, chasing the ring's silvery glint into the sand. She panted in her panic. "Shit, shit, shit. Damn it, where are you?"

A wave struck her hard enough to knock her over. Another wave followed it, even higher, even harder, and struck her again, dragging her under with the force of a hundred hands. She fought to find her footing but couldn't get her legs under her. Was this the riptide Pat had warned her about? A sneaker wave? She scratched her way to the surface and caught one breath. In that breath she saw something that made no sense at all, something that convinced her that if she wasn't dead already, she was dying fast. She saw a beam of white light, bright and strong and steady, shining out from the top of the lighthouse. Before she could make any sense of it, a current jerked her backward and dragged her under again. A force stronger than wind or gravity was sucking her out to sea.

"Faye!"

Her name echoed across the water. Someone was screaming for her.

"Faye! Where are you?" the voice yelled at her again.

Someone was out there. Someone had seen her. Someone could save her if she didn't give up. But if she gave up...if she gave up, she could see Will again, couldn't she? Maybe? Or at least if she gave up, she wouldn't miss him anymore.

But she wouldn't give up.

Faye's mouth broke the surface. She managed a single scream before the water claimed her again. She continued fighting, but only occasionally surfacing for air as the water dragged her back and down, back and down.

Until, finally, it was too much.

She let go.

She wasn't afraid. The panic had dissipated entirely. She assumed that if one was awake when facing death, one would know the fear of it. But there was no fear. There was nothing, not even the burning in her lungs as she used up the last of her oxygen.

Far away she heard a voice, strong and steady. "In and out, love. Breathe for me. I'm here. The world's not ending."

And she believed the voice.

Because someone was here. She could feel his hands.

Then the world ended.

8

So this was death.

Death wasn't that bad.

It wasn't what Faye had expected. First of all, she was wet. She knew babies were born wet and covered in blood, but she never imagined death would feel like being dropped into a carnival dunking booth. Also, death felt very alive to her. Alive and corporeal. She wiggled her fingers, her toes. She filled her lungs with cool night air and exhaled. Clearly she did have a body in this afterlife, whatever it was, even if it didn't quite fit her the way she remembered her body fitting.

Maybe she wasn't dead after all.

When she at last dared to open her eyes she saw that strange white light again. In all the stories about dying she'd heard or read, there was a white light, but it was outside a window. She hadn't heard about the window in the near-death experiences stories. A tunnel, yes, but no windows. And there was a bed, definitely, and she lay on it. The bed sat by a wall across from the window. Through the window—open and without a screen—Faye could see the light flashing from the top of the lighthouse. It blinked out, then flashed on, blinked out, flashed on. She counted the seconds between darkness and light.

Darkness.

One. Two. Three. Four. Five. Six. Seven.

Light.

So Faye was not dead. At least she was fairly sure she wasn't. Was she dreaming? If so, she would wake up eventually. But if this was a dream, it seemed an unusually vivid one. Still it was the best explanation she had for why she could see and hear and smell and touch and feel. She could feel her heart running wild in her chest. She could feel the clinging of her wet hair to her cool skin. At some point while walking on the Bride Island beach she must have lain down to rest and fallen asleep. She'd dreamed she drowned in the ocean, and now she was dreaming she'd woken up in someone's house next to the lighthouse. Lucid dreaming? She tried to will herself to levitate off the bed. If she was dreaming she could fly. She'd done that a time or two in dreams past. But she remained on the bed, feeling alive and awake and earthbound. Faye turned her attention back to the light. Again it flashed and winked out of existence. Seven seconds later it flashed back into life. She kept staring at it, hoping it would reveal itself to be a helicopter searching for her or the reflection from the spotlight off a coast guard cutter. But she didn't hear the blades of a helicopter beating the air or the sound of a ship passing close by. She heard the ocean only and her own breathing.

In the darkness she heard a small sound. A flick and a sizzle, the distinct sound of a match being struck and flaring into life. A glowing flame no bigger than a moth fluttered into existence, and she watched as it moved to a wick and became a brighter light. A glass shade was brought down over the flame, the wick adjusted with a small knob.

"A hurricane lamp," she said, and her voice sounded off to her. Not off-key, merely off. It was her voice, only throatier, as if she'd been ill or screaming for hours at a concert. "I haven't seen one of those in years. My great-grandmother had one in her house in Portsmouth..."

The light illuminated a man's torso. His shirt was open, and she saw a broad chest and a hard, bare stomach dusted with a line of dark hair that disappeared into a loose-fitting pair of brown trousers. Faye blinked, confused but not displeased by the path this dream was taking. She followed the progress of the light as it floated across the room to where she lay on the bed. It wasn't her bed at the Church Street house or the bed she'd slept in with Hagen during their marriage. This was an old-fashioned cannonball bed, a full size if that, covered in a crazy patchwork quilt of every pattern and color known to man.

"Where am I?"

"Did you hit your head when you fell off the dock? You're home, love."

Faye recognized the voice. Of course she did. She would have known that voice across the sea or in a storm, in heaven or in hell or wherever she was... She knew that voice.

At once she sat up in bed and reached out, gripping and grabbing and grasping at the source of the voice. Yes, she was dreaming, of course she was, but she didn't care. If she could have Will alive again in her dreams, she would sleep forever. Waking be damned.

The bed shifted as he sat at her side, and Faye threw her arms around him. She couldn't get enough of him.

"Tighter," she said as his arms encircled her and pulled her hard against him.

"You're all right, lass. You're all right. You were on the dock and a nasty, big wave got you. But I got you back. I got you back, sweet girl. You're safe now. You're fine."

"I'm not," she said, gasping and wheezing in her shock and relief. "I thought you were dead. You were dead for so long."

"Bad dream. That's all." He cupped the back of her head, rocked her against him like a child. "I'm here and so are you. But you have to stay off the end of the pier. You know the water gets choppy there."

"I'll stop," she promised, not knowing what she was promising but willing to promise him the sun and the moon and every beat of her heart as long as he didn't let her go. His lips brushed her forehead, and his chin stubble scratched her cheek. It was Will, and he was alive and real. She would have known that voice and those arms and that stubble and that kiss anywhere in any time and for all time.

"I had to get you out of your wet clothes. I'm sorry," he said, as if her own husband weren't allowed to see her naked. The shirt she wore was white and heavy cotton, too large for her by far. One of his shirts? But she never remembered Will wearing a shirt this style.

"You were gone, and I missed you so much," she said, crying against his strong shoulder, her chest heaving with the force of her sobs. "You don't know how much I missed you."

"Hush now," he said, patting her back. "You'll make yourself sick crying like this—and all over a dream. Getting knocked off the pier isn't much fun. I thought I'd lost you when that wave hit. You're the one who was nearly fish food tonight, not me."

She clung to his body, absorbed his heat, inhaled his scent, salt water and sweat. His hair was wet and lay in messy rust-colored waves over his forehead. She rubbed his chest and neck, needing to feel the solidity of him, the realness, the flesh and bone of him. His heart beat under her palms, steady and hard, even as her nervous hands fluttered like butter-flies. Faye looked up and into Will's light brown eyes. They gleamed like copper in the lamplight. He had a few wrinkles around his eyes that she'd never noticed before. He looked older in this dream. Thirty-two? Thirty-five at most? She smiled wider. The stupid man was even more handsome with crow's-feet than he was without them. How unfair.

"You grew a beard," she said, laughing and crying and smiling and gasping all at once. She touched his face, ca-ressed his cheeks. "Is it the play-offs already?"

"You did hit your head, didn't you?" He ran his hand over her hair gently. "Did you lose time? I've had the beard ever since you got here."

"Yes, I lost time. So much time. Years," she said, play-ing along, afraid if she contradicted him the dream would evaporate. And she had lost time; it was true. Four years of her life that she should have spent with him. She brought his mouth to hers and kissed him.

The kiss seemed to startle him—he grabbed her by the upper arms and held her away.

"What?" she asked, panting.

"You kissed me," he said.

"Is that bad?"

His eyes were wide with shock. "Yes, and you know it."

"But I don't know it," Faye said. "Why can't I kiss you?"

"More reasons than I can count."

"What reasons?" Could this dream be any stranger? Why

would she dream of her husband and then dream he wouldn't kiss her?

"I..." He looked at her in the bed, at the V in the shirt and her bare legs against his thigh. "I knew them a minute ago."

"Kiss me, and maybe you'll think of them," Faye said.

"Good idea," he said and kissed her.

The kiss was undeniably Will's. Playful when he nipped her bottom lip with his teeth. Passionate when he waited for her smile to press his tongue into her mouth. Intense when he gave her no mercy as he kissed her and kissed her until her whole body ached and tingled and she could hardly breathe and didn't want to. But who needed to breathe when she had Will? Who needed anything at all?

"I swear I thought I'd lost you tonight," he rasped into her ear. His arms encircled her, and she'd never felt so safe. Lost her? She'd never been so found. "You took the heart right out of me. Don't scare me like that again."

"Never," she said. She had no idea what she was saying, because she would say anything to keep him kissing her.

He kissed her from her mouth to her ear and up and down her neck. He kissed her like he'd been waiting years for this kiss and had planned it in advance so that when the time came, it would be perfect. And it was perfect.

But it wasn't enough. Faye reached between their bodies, seeking out the top button of his pants. He inhaled sharply and pulled back.

"Whoa, there, love." He captured her hands again. "That is more than kissing there. And you've had a hard night."

"I want a hard you," she said.

He held her by the upper arms and looked at her face, studied it as if seeking an injury or recognition.

"What has gotten into you?" he asked, laughing nervously

at her ardor. Was this a game? Was he playing hard to get? Did people in dreams do that?

"I thought you were dead," she said. "And you aren't."

"You're the one who fell off the dock tonight."

She touched his face again, caressing his cheeks and delighting in the softness of his beard and the little lines around his eyes. He was breathing hard and shallowly, like he always did when aroused. But he looked scared, too, nervous. Why would her Will be nervous to make love to her?

He pushed a lock of wet hair off her face. What could she say to convince him?

"I love you," she said.

"You do?"

Faye nodded. "All this time I loved you." It was true. She'd never fallen out of love with him. The dead can't love the living but the living can love the dead, and that was the greatest tragedy of her life.

"You love me?" He narrowed his eyes at her. "You're sure?"

"I've never been more sure of anything in my life."

He looked away to the corner of the room, his brow furrowed, his hands clenched into fists as if he was trying to hold himself back from touching her again.

"Don't you love me, too?" Faye asked.

He pressed his lips to her forehead and his body vibrated with the shuddering breath he took.

"Will..." she said, pleading. She would wake any minute, any second. They had no time to lose.

"Will I what?" he asked.

The question puzzled her.

"Faith? What's the matter?" he asked. Faye narrowed her eyes at him, slid back on the bed a few inches to put some distance between her and him. He looked at her, confused, and she saw he had a scar on his rib cage, reddish pink and about six inches long. Will had no such scars. No scars and no beard and no crow's-feet.

For all that he looked like Will... Faye had the sudden sinking sensation that he wasn't Will at all.

She remembered something. Another name. A familiar face but another name.

"Carrick," she said.

"Aye, lass?"

Faye clamped a hand over her mouth, silencing a scream.

"Love?" he said. "What is it? Say something. You look half-sick."

"I..." Faye didn't know what to say. Her body shook as if she were freezing, and yet a sheen of sweat covered her from head to toe. The urge to vomit was nearly overwhelming but her mouth was dry and her stomach empty.

Carrick.

Carrick Morgan.

This man wasn't her Will. And this wasn't 2015. And this wasn't happening.

But it was happening.

Faye started at the earsplitting sound of an old-fashioned windup alarm clock ringing madly in another room.

She gasped. Her heart was caught halfway between her throat and her mouth.

"It's just the alarm," he said as if she should know. "You know, for the clockwork."

"The what?"

He stood up and pulled the covers over her legs.

"I'll be right back—promise," he said. "Just rest. You had a rough night."

When he reached the door she said his name again, practicing it.

"Carrick."

"Yes?" He turned in the doorway to face her.

"When someone hits their head you're supposed to ask them to name the year and the president and that sort of thing."

"Are you?" he asked, skeptical.

"Yes. But I don't know my name or the year or the president. Tell me."

He came back to the bed and sat down in front of her.

"I can't blame you for not knowing your name. I keep forgetting it myself. But you're Faith Morgan now. It's '21. And you're better off not knowing who the president is. I wish I didn't know."

Faye racked her aching brain. She'd majored in American studies in college. She should know. Better off not knowing? A bad president, then. And 1920s?

"Warren Harding," she said.

Carrick smiled. "That's it."

"And I'm Faith Morgan. And it's 1921."

"See? You're all right. Now stay here and rest. I'll be back in a flash."

She sensed he wanted to kiss her again but held back. From the doorway he gave her one last look before walking away into the darkness of the hallway beyond.

He'd left the hurricane lamp on the bedside table and Faye saw a pile of wet clothes on the floor. She left the bed and knelt on the floor. These weren't her clothes. She'd been wearing a black tank top and jeans. In her hands she held a long skirt made of heavy cotton and a fussy white blouse with a collar that would cover her all the way to her throat.

The room might have been lovely had it been a room in a bed-and-breakfast in Charleston, but in her present circumstances it horrified her. No television. No radio. No electric lamps. No cords. No outlets. She opened the side table drawer and found it packed with delicate lace handkerchiefs, a small Bible, and some matches. She took one handkerchief from the drawer and studied it. The edges were embroidered with pink-and-yellow flowers, and in one corner she saw someone had starting sewing a monogram into the fabric.

An *F* and then part of an *M*.

Faith Morgan.

This was Faith Morgan's handkerchief.

And this was Faith Morgan's bedroom.

And that man, the man who'd kissed her, was Faith Morgan's father, Carrick Morgan.

And Carrick Morgan had kissed her.

No…

Faye shook so hard she couldn't stand. She sat on the bed again because if she didn't, she would faint. Yet she also wanted to faint, to slip into oblivion again in the hopes when she woke up this nightmare would be over.

"I hit my head," she whispered to herself. "I went to the lighthouse, and the wave hit me, and there must have been a rock. There must have been a rock under the water. The water dragged me under, and I hit my head. And now I'm in a coma or hallucinating or delusional. This isn't real. None of it is real. It's not 1921. That's not possible. Head injuries are possible, and going back in time isn't possible. This is a fantasy. This is a dream. This is a hallucination."

On the bed Faye rocked back and forth, back and forth, trying to soothe herself. She put her hands into her hair and touched her scalp all over, looking for a wound, a bump, proof of an injury that would explain why she was seeing what she was seeing. She didn't feel anything, but that meant nothing. A bump might not have come up yet. She could have intracranial bleeding. Her brain could be swelling right now, and any minute she'd slip into unconsciousness and die.

"Am I dying, Will?" she asked. "Can you hear me, baby? Are you there? Am I going to die?"

Hot tears flooded her eyes and rolled down her cheeks. It struck her then and struck her hard, the sudden certainty that she did not, absolutely did not, want to die.

"I don't want to die," she said. Even as she said it, she realized it was possibly the first time in four years she could say that with 100 percent honesty. Maybe she was experiencing a severe head injury. Surely that was the only explanation. Death stared her in the face. Death called her name. Death held out his hand to her. Over the past four years she'd been tempted to take Death by his outstretched hand, but there on that crazy quilt in that lamp-lit room with the lighthouse blinking behind her, Faye knew she did not want to die.

She heard footsteps in the house. Impossible not to when it was so eerily quiet. No air conditioner kicked on and off. No fluorescent lights buzzed. No traffic rumbled in the distance. Faye closed her eyes tight, pressed the heels of her hands to her forehead and rocked back and forth again. It was in that position the man found her. She heard him enter the room, and felt him sink onto the bed beside her and gather her into his bare arms and against his bare chest. His body was hot from exertion.

"Breathe, sweet girl. In and out," he said, his voice strong and calm as she gasped and swallowed air. "In and out..."

"Am I dying?" she asked.

"No, ma'am. Not on my watch."

Faye wept openly then, shaking and shivering in his arms. She wept because he had Will's face and because he spoke Will's words. But he wasn't Will. And if he wasn't Will, why did she want to love him?

Slowly, breath by breath, Faye's shaking subsided. Fear still held her by the heart, and its iron fingers would not let go, but she could breathe again. A small victory.

"I must have hit my head," she whispered against the man's chest. Carrick's chest. "Something's not right."

"I can call over to Hunting for help. We'll go into town, take you to the doctor."

She shook her head. "No. No doctors."

If it was 1921, then a doctor would do more harm than good. Who knew what dangerous drug he'd prescribe, what unnecessary surgery he'd perform and in what sort of unsanitary conditions? And if she had no visible injuries and was still hallucinating, she could easily end up in an insane asylum.

"If you're hurt…"

"No doctors," she said again. "I won't go."

"All right, then. I can't make you."

"Why can't you make me?" Faye asked. "Aren't I your daughter?"

He laughed softly, a sort of ironic-sounding chuckle.

"That's what we tell them," he said. "Come on now. Look at me, love."

She slowly lifted her head and met his eyes. Once more she started, stunned nearly senseless by his resemblance to Will. How could it not be him?

"Hold still," he said, and he raised his hands to her head and gently rubbed his fingertips through her hair, over her scalp. His brow furrowed. "I don't feel a bump or a knot. The skin's not broken. Does it hurt anywhere?"

"No. How long was I under water?"

"Too long."

"Maybe I'm... Maybe I have oxygen deprivation?"

"Oxygen deprivation?" He smiled as he said it, as if she'd suddenly broken into a foreign language. "I suppose that could be why you're so out of sorts."

"I kissed you."

"We'll blame the oxygen deprivation," he said, letting his hands drop from her hair.

"You kissed me back."

He exhaled heavily.

"Don't know what to blame for that. Wish I did."

She laughed despite herself. It sounded just like something Will would have said.

"I'm not... I'm not your daughter."

He raised a finger to his lips, shushing her.

"Our little secret."

9

What was the secret? She wasn't his daughter. But if she wasn't his daughter, who the hell was she?

"I should sleep," Faye said, suddenly needing to be alone. She had to think, to figure things out, and she couldn't do that with Carrick here. He'd ask her questions she wouldn't be able to answer. If she told him the truth, that she was either hallucinating or had somehow traveled ninety-four years back in time, she would end up in a padded cell. There were no high quality mental hospitals in 1921. It was the cuckoo's nest—water cures that were water torture, brain surgeries and straitjackets.

"That sounds like a fine idea. You want me to stay?"

"No." Faye shook her head. "You can go. I'll go to sleep right now."

"I'll check on you in an hour or two. I won't wake you unless I think I oughta."

He kissed her forehead again, and Faye closed her eyes as his lips met her skin. For one second she allowed herself to pretend it was Will, her beautiful Will, and he'd come to her in a dream and now he'd leave again, but not without kissing her goodbye first. Will would never leave her without kissing her goodbye. The only time he ever had was the day he died.

"Sleep well, sweet girl," he whispered. He stood up as she lay back in the bed. "You'll feel better in the morning."

He gave her one last look, almost longing, and left her alone in the room. She listened in the dark, heard his footsteps travel down the hall, the house creaking with his every step. She heard his sure feet on a staircase, heard a door open and close, making a grunt as it rubbed against the frame. Faye closed her eyes and whispered words to herself in the dark.

"My name is Victoria Faye Barlow. I've always gone by Faye because Vicky is my mom. I was born June 5, 1985 in Portsmouth, New Hampshire. I went to Columbia and graduated with a bachelor's in American studies because I couldn't figure out what else to major in. I was twenty-five when I met William Jacob Fielding who was twenty-three and played shortstop in Rhode Island for the PawSox. We were married on a pier in Newport, Rhode Island. We were happy together, happier than anyone has a right to be. He died the next year during a carjacking. I would have died of the grief, but I was pregnant and had Will's baby to take care of. I am not crazy. I did not make any of that up. And when I open my eyes it'll be June of 2015, and I'll be at the Church Street house and I'll go to Ty's room and tell him about the crazy dream I just had, and he will laugh at me and I will feel better. Just as soon as I open my eyes..."

Gradually...slowly...millimeter by millimeter, Faye opened her eyes.

She saw a white light flash outside the window, saw a

crazy quilt lying over her body, heard the ocean rushing and retreating on the shore.

"Shit," she said.

She tried it again, her incantation. But no matter how many times she told herself who she was, when she opened her eyes she was in a cottage by a lighthouse manned by a keeper named Carrick Morgan.

A keeper named Carrick Morgan who looked just like her dead husband.

It wasn't a dream and it wasn't a hallucination.

It was real.

Faye rolled onto her side and pulled her knees in tight. She had to plan. She had to think. She had to…she had to leave. She definitely had to leave. There was no way she could stay here. But where could she go? It was 1921, and her grandparents weren't even alive yet. Her mother's father wouldn't be born for three more years. Her mother wouldn't be born for thirty more years. Could she go to her great-grandparents? Could she even find them? Her maternal great-grandparents had lived somewhere in Massachusetts and would be newlyweds. What would they do if she showed up at their door and told them she was their great-granddaughter from the future and that they would both be dead before she was born? Maybe she could go to New York or Washington, DC, and start a new life. She could be a working girl. She knew how to type, although she'd never used a manual typewriter in her life. She didn't know shorthand or how to take dictation. And she'd need money to get there. Was there any money stashed in this house? Did anyone in South Carolina have money in 1921? Maybe she could be a fortune-teller. She'd warn everyone of the stock-market crash looming and the threat of Nazi Germany on the horizon. Could she change the outcome of world events? Or would she simply get tossed into an asylum?

Faye heard the door rattle, followed by a soft knock.

"I'm fine," she called out.

"I'm coming in," Carrick said. Faye sat up straight and pulled the covers up to her neck.

Carrick cracked the door open and looked inside at her with Will's eyes in Will's face. She thought she even saw a little of Will's old love in his expression, but she pretended not to see it.

"I brought you some milk."

He handed her a blue-and-white tin cup, warm to the touch.

"Thank you."

"Do you need anything before I go back up?"

"Up?"

"Up." He pointed up.

"Right. Up." Up the lighthouse steps to do whatever it was lighthouse keepers did.

"How's your head?" He gently caressed the side of her face.

It took everything Faye had in her to not recoil violently from the touch of his hand. Why was he so gentle? Why was he so like Will? She enjoyed his touch despite a voice inside her screaming in protest.

"It doesn't really hurt," she said.

"Good." He nodded. "You can't sleep?"

"Rough night."

"That it is," he said.

"You saved me, didn't you?"

"Saved you? Nah. I saw you fall off the dock and pulled you out of the water. That's all."

"That's kind of the definition of saving someone."

"What was I going to do? Let you drown?"

"I guess you could have?"

"I'd be the world's worst wickie if I let someone drown out of my own damned house. Sorry."

"Sorry? For what?"

"I'm not used to a lady in the house. Well, a lady who can hear my foul mouth."

"I don't mind your foul mouth," Faye said.

"That's good. I'm out of practice. Give me another week and I might remember how to talk to a girl again."

"Another week," she said. "I haven't been here long." She could tell that from his tone and his words.

"No, but you'll settle in if you give it a chance. I know it's been hard for you these past few days. I know this isn't what you hoped."

"I'll be fine," she said. It seemed to be what he wanted to hear.

"I hope so. I…" He paused, stuffed his hands in his pockets. He'd put on another shirt, and he looked the very picture of a rough workingman in the 1920s. "I need to know… you did just fall tonight, didn't you? A wave caught you and that was all?"

He gave her a searching look.

"What else would it be?"

"Don't hate me for asking this," he said. "I saw you on the pier and looked away. Second I looked back you were gone. You…didn't mean to fall off the pier, did you? You didn't jump, I mean?"

"What? No." She shook her head. "I thought I dropped something, and I went to grab it out of the water. A wave got me."

"I had to ask. I know you haven't been happy. I know being here is hard for you. But you might come to like it. I did."

"I'll try to like it," she said, her voice hardly more than a whisper. Smiling wasn't easy, but she forced herself to play along. "I'm going to try to sleep now."

"You should. I'll be up if you need me. I'm always here if you need me."

He didn't seem to know how to tell her good-night. She could tell he wanted to kiss her again, but she held back, not wanting to encourage further intimacy.

"Thank you for the milk."

"Sleep well, love," he said again. "Don't fall out of bed."

"Carrick," she said when he turned to leave.

"Aye?"

"What I said earlier… I didn't know what I was saying. I'm sorry."

He shrugged again, hands deep in his pockets. He looked so much like Will then that it made her angry at him. How dare he steal her husband's face and voice and eyes and shrug and smile? How dare he look like the man she loved and not be him?

"First day I stepped onto dry land when the war was over, all over, and for good, I kissed the first ten girls who would let me and proposed marriage to five of them. You've been in a war of your own. I won't take it personally if you need to kiss a few boys to celebrate winning even if one of those boys is me."

He smiled at her and turned away, and she watched him walk down the dark hall until all she could see was the faint outline of his body in what bits of moonlight had managed to sneak into the house. Then she was alone again, alone and afraid.

Faye sat on the edge of the bed and took a sip of the warm milk Carrick had brought her. As soon as she tasted it, she spat it right out into her hand. It tasted sweet, very sweet, and heavier, thicker than normal milk. Of course. Whole fat milk, that was what it was. And it was probably unpasteurized. She took another sip of it and found it better the second time. By the third sip she'd warmed up to the taste. By the fourth, she decided she might like unpasteurized whole milk. She'd never been much of a milk drinker but she could get used to this. Except…this house had no electricity, did it? So where had Carrick gotten fresh milk?

Oh, God, it came straight from a cow, didn't it? Faye spit the milk out again. Carrick must have gone out in the night and milked some poor sleepy dairy cow and brought it to her straight from the udder. Rationally Faye knew all milk came from cow udders, but when it came directly from the udder with no stops in between? Faye groaned. She poured the rest out her bedroom window and onto the ground.

If the milk situation weren't bad enough, Faye had a full bladder. They had indoor plumbing in the twenties, didn't they? After some fumbling in the darkness relieved only by the flash of the lighthouse beacon every seven seconds, she found the matches in the bedside-table drawer. She lit the wick of the hurricane lamp again and sneaked out of the room. The floor creaked under her feet and she winced at every sound. Every step sounded like a snapping twig in the overwhelming silence. Every breath sounded like a windstorm.

"Thank you, God," she sighed when she found a bathroom. She saw pipes on the wall and a cooper tub and a toilet. She could have kissed it. She did her business as quickly and quietly as she could. So far she'd succeeding in getting from the bedroom to the bathroom silently. The toilet had a pull cord to flush it, and Faye tugged on it. The sound of the flushing was like a small but concentrated tornado.

She waited to hear footsteps or Carrick's voice. Nothing. Good, he was probably in the lighthouse. She was safe to walk around for now, safe to run if she could. But where?

First she found a set of dark stairs and crept down them. They were slick on her bare feet, as if they'd been freshly washed and waxed. With her left hand, Faye clung to the banister as she descended and clung to the lamp just as hard with her right. Death could come from a failure of either hand—if she slipped on the steps, she could break her neck, or if she dropped the lamp, she could burn the house down. It had been a long time since she'd felt fear like this, like fire in her blood.

At the bottom of the steps, she stopped and caught her breath. She'd survived this far. She lifted her lamp and gazed around the room, which appeared to be the living room or sitting room or whatever they called it here. It held a light fixture like the one in the bedroom, but Faye saw no electric outlets down here, either. She did find a candle box on the coffee table and two big brass candlesticks. The table sat in front of a cane-back sofa covered in blue cushions embroidered with wildflowers the colors of the setting sun. The focal point of the room was a brick fireplace. On the mantel sat two more candlesticks, which framed a wooden mantel clock on the left side. On the right, a peach-colored ceramic jug held an elegant array of yellow jasmine and white daisies. An indigo armchair with lace doilies over the arms sat to the side of the sofa with a bookcase against the wall just behind it.

She had seen rooms like this before, in books, in old hotels, in houses turned into museums. There should be red velvet ropes around this room and a tour guide saying, "And here's where the family would sit in the evenings and read together. Families spent more time together back then but not necessarily out of love. In winter, this would be the warmest room in the house… Now let's move on into the kitchen, folks. And please don't touch any of the antiques."

Antiques? Maybe in Faye's time, but here the sofa looked new and the ceramic flower jug on the mantel had no cracks in it, no signs of age. Even the books on the shelves looked new. Strange, but new. They were all hardcovers, every last one. Nice ones, too. Some were clothbound, others leatherbound. She flipped through a few. The colors of the clothbound covers were bright and bold and the pages had no foxing or staining. She knew some of the titles, the classics— *Jane Eyre, Ivanhoe, A Tale of Two Cities, Emma*… But the other books? *The Rosary* by Florence Barclay? *The Devil's Garden* by W. B. Maxwell? *The Tree of Heaven* by May Sinclair? *Ten Days That Shook the World* by John Reed? These were not Will's books. Will read Lee Child novels and Stephen King, all seven Harry Potter books, the occasional sports memoir and anything by Michael Lewis. He did not read *Ivanhoe*. Nobody read *Ivanhoe*.

Faye moved her lamp and saw a round-top table by the end of the sofa. Someone had painted a pretty little night scene on it—the moon, the stars, the ocean underneath them. On the table was something wrapped in brown paper and string. Faye carefully removed the paper and found a book inside—*The Moon and Sixpence* by W. Somerset Maugham.

The cover was a dull tan and the title and author's name were printed in black script. She opened to the copyright page. Faye dropped the book like it had bitten her. Copyright 1919. First American edition. The book was brand-new. The spine never cracked. The pages bright and the ink fresh.

Inside it was an invoice, a bill to be paid to a bookstore in Charleston, South Carolina. The date of the invoice read June 10, 1921.

It had been June 10 in 2015 when she'd woken up this morning. She'd also been Faye Barlow this morning. Tonight she was Faith Morgan.

But according to the plaque on the lighthouse, Faith Morgan had died on June 10, 1921.

How was Faith Morgan even alive? Hadn't Pat said she'd drowned?

"She did drown…" Faye took a shuddering breath. Faith Morgan did die tonight—or she was supposed to have died tonight. In 2015 Faye must have died and somehow come back here in Faith's place. But how? And why? What had Faye changed by coming here? Had she damaged the future? Fixed it? Did the life of this one girl in South Carolina in 1921 matter to anyone but Carrick?

Tonight as she'd been drowning in the ocean, she'd heard a voice calling for her. But now she understood the voice was calling for *Faith*, not Faye. It was Carrick's voice. He had saved her life but it wasn't her he meant to save. It was Faith, who he said was his daughter but clearly was not. If she wasn't his daughter, his biological daughter, then was she his adopted daughter? A stepdaughter? No, those were real daughters, and no decent man would kiss his adopted daughter or stepdaughter the way Carrick had kissed her. A foster child? No. Faye was no child. Neither was Faith.

She'd been seventeen at her death according to the plaque on the lighthouse. Maybe Carrick had taken her in? Faye's mind whirred with possibilities. Either the man was a monster or she wasn't related to him in any way. She feared the former, wanted to believe the latter. If she could ask him—but no, she shouldn't. Too dangerous. She would seem insane to him, kissing him, not knowing the year. It was a miracle he hadn't called for the men in white coats already.

Faye leaned against the fireplace mantel. She rested her head on her forearm and cried until she felt dizzy. It was 1921? Why did it have to be 1921? Of all the random, awful, stupid years to wake up in. Why not 2010 and she could meet and marry Will all over again? Why not 2006? She could have gone to the same college Will had. Even if he'd still died, she would have had him in her life for five years instead of only one. They could have lived in a world of indoor plumbing and electricity and vaccines and the internet. Had Carrick been Will, she would have given up all that and more gladly. But Carrick wasn't Will and she had to accept that. She'd thrown herself at him tonight, and if she didn't keep her guard up she would do it again, because it would be so easy—too easy—to pretend he was Will.

She forced herself to wipe away her tears.

"I'm in *Freaky Friday*, aren't I?" she said to the empty room. Faye sighed, stood up straight. Either she was calming down or the shock was setting in. She had no idea how to react. Collapse into tears again? Scream? Run away? Surely this was the first time in history this had happened to anyone. Or maybe not? Maybe this happened all the time, and no one ever found out because no one would ever believe someone who said she was from the future. Faye wouldn't.

And if Faye wouldn't, a lighthouse keeper in 1921 certainly wouldn't.

Faye picked up her lamp again and wandered through the house.

In the kitchen she found another antique that wasn't an antique—a black-and-white enamel stove. Copper pots hung from the ceiling. Cast-iron pans hung on the wall. And by the door there was a one-year calendar on a piece of white linen. A calendar just like her grandmother had in her house, a gift from a local bank. It said 1921 at the top, and underneath it was a New England farm scene. Faye backed out of the kitchen and into the living room again, where she bumped into the coffee table. On it she found a Sears catalog beneath a large hardbound Bible. No, not a Sears catalog—a Sears, Roebuck & Co. catalog. She picked it up and opened a random page. A men's three-piece suit was for sale—$24.95. Not a bad deal. The *Good Housekeeping* magazine on the coffee table had a picture of a little girl in green carrying a hat box. The issue was dated May 1921 and the ink still smelled fresh on the pages.

Faye continued her explorations of the downstairs. Off the living room was another bedroom much smaller than the one upstairs. The bed was a twin, and the headboard and footboard were iron. It looked a little like a monk's cell with nothing but the bed and washbasin and the prie-dieu. The prie-dieu? Faye examined it and found it identical to the one in her room back at the Church Street house. Sitting on top of the prie-dieu was a little red prayer book also identical to the one in her room back in Beaufort. Wrapped around the prayer book was a set of rosary beads, solid silver. The medal above the cross read S. Brendanus, *Ora Pro Nobis*. Faye eased the book out of the wrapping of rosary beads. Sure enough, on the inside cover was written a name—Carrick Morgan. And a handwritten prayer for God's forgiveness. A prayer she'd read a few hours ago. A prayer she'd read ninety-four years in the future.

Faye shut the book in an instant, wrapped the beads around it and returned it to its place.

Then Faye opened the closet door and saw clothes hanging inside—sturdy canvas work pants, sturdy cotton shirts, a long heavy coat, an oilskin slicker. Not a baseball T-shirt in sight. Yet there on the wall of the closet hung a black-and-white photograph—a photograph of a sailor in uniform. Brass buttons, chevron on the sleeve, US on a badge on the high stiff collar. It was Will in the photograph. It was Will in a US Navy uniform. Except it wasn't, because Will had never served in the navy. The only uniform he'd ever worn was his baseball uniform.

Faye couldn't take her eyes from the photograph. It was Will. Her Will. Younger than the Will she'd seen tonight by a few years, this was the Will she knew, the Will who only wore a beard during the play-offs—even if he wasn't playing in them.

"Will…" she whispered, touching the face in the frame. She knew she shouldn't do it but she couldn't stop herself. Carefully, she eased the back of the frame off and read the words written on the back of the picture in pencil.

Senior Chief Petty Officer Carrick Morgan, 1918.

The year 1918 was when World War I had ended. Carrick Morgan had served in World War I. The wound on his side…a war wound? She put the framed photograph back on the wall and closed the closet door. But only for a second before she opened it again. What she was doing was wrong, horribly wrong, but she had to do it. She'd spied a box on the top shelf and had to know what was inside. She set the lamp on the prie-dieu and held the box into the halo of light. It was a small wooden box, hand carved, the kind one kept secrets inside. Maybe there was one about her in there. Not her, but Faith, whoever Faith was.

"Oh, my God…" Faye breathed when she opened the box. It was full of medals and letters congratulating Carrick on earning them. A Navy Cross. A Distinguished Service Medal. A Good Conduct Medal. Even a Medal of Honor.

"You're a Boy Scout, Carrick," she said, shifting through the various medals, the letters of commendation from superior officers full of words like *noble* and *courageous, dauntless* and *indefatigable.*

"Forget the Boy Scouts," Faye said. "You're Captain Freaking America."

Faye knew there were seemingly good people who hid dark sides behind their masks of innocence or decency. But it was impossible for her to believe a man who could earn such honors, yet was humble enough to hide them in a box at the top of his closet, was the sort of man who would do anything as sick as kissing his own daughter. And since she couldn't believe it, she didn't. She wasn't any closer to finding out who Faith Morgan was, but she knew who Faith Morgan wasn't. She was not, in any way, shape or form, Carrick Morgan's daughter.

So who the hell was she?

Faye quickly packed up the medals and put them away before Carrick found her.

She left the little bedroom and pressed her hand to her forehead as a wave of panic and nausea rushed through her. It was happening again—the fear, the foreboding, the sense that she was losing all touch with reality. She had to get out of here, out of this house, out of this time and this world. How had she gotten here? The water had brought her. Maybe if the water had brought her, the water could take her back again. Fleeing the house, Faye ran to the ocean's edge and waded into the water up to her thighs. Nothing happened. She waited for a wave to hit her, but no wave came. The water behaved, merely licking and lapping at her legs. She waded deeper. She put her hands in the water; she put her arms in the water. She even knelt in the water, soaking herself through her shirt to the skin again. Nothing happened. The water was calm—no riptides, no hidden currents. And no denying it—Faye was trapped in 1921. The water had brought her here. The water seemingly had no intention of taking her back.

After a while, Faye grew cold. The cold helped in a way, calming her like a compress on a fevered forehead. She trudged out of the ocean and sat on the beach, almost bright as morning in the moonlight, her arms around her legs, shivering. She forced herself to breathe the way both Will and Carrick had made her. In and out, in and out. Whatever was happening, it wasn't the end of the world. Faye opened her eyes and looked around.

The water's edge was farther out than she remembered. At least forty feet farther out. And where before there'd been nothing but pilings, now she saw the long wooden pier. And where before there'd been only a line of rocks worn away by the elements, now there stood a two-story white house with dark trim on the windowsills and eaves. Green trim, maybe? Black? Hard to tell at night. The house was a perfectly symmetrical rectangle with a wide wooden front door in the center of the house and two casement windows on each side. Two brick chimneys jutted up on either side of the steeply pitched roof, and a painted porch ran the full length of the front. And where before the lighthouse had been dark and abandoned, now there was light. A bright beacon shining out from the top of the lighthouse and blinking on and off every seven seconds.

Father Pat had been right.

She should have stayed out of the water.

10

When Faye woke up, it was still 1921.

She knew this from the bed she lay in and by the clothes she wore and the smell of the salt water on her skin. Faye had opened her eyes as sunlight flooded the room. It seemed like she'd fallen asleep only a few minutes before and now it was already morning. Her first sensation upon waking was terror, which, in a way, was an improvement over her usual waking sensation of emptiness and despair. Sleep had long been a reprieve from the prison of her grief, and she woke up every morning back behind the iron bars of her loneliness. For four years she'd woken up disappointed to find herself still alive. That morning, however, was different. That morning she'd woken up scared she was going to die.

Stay calm, Faye told herself. Unless she was having the most vivid hallucination in the history of the world, she was actually in 1921. Whatever the reason she was here, she would need to drink water, eat food and cause as little trouble as possible until she figured out what the hell was happening. It wasn't much of a plan, but it was all she had.

Also, she should play dumb. If she had to blame a nonexistent head injury for anything strange she said or did, she would milk that nonexistent head injury for all it was worth.

Before Faye could get her bearings, a girl entered the bedroom. The girl glanced at her and flashed her a tight but polite smile before bending to gather clothes off the floor, which she then tossed in a large tin bucket. Not a bucket, a washtub. Faye had seen those in movies and photographs from the Great Depression. Or maybe she'd seen one on *Little House on the Prairie.*

"Good morning?" Faye said. The girl said nothing, just continued her circuit of the room—straightening and tidying and picking up clothes. She was a pretty girl, young and dark-skinned. She wore a bright yellow scarf on her head, tied in a bow at the nape of her neck. The scarf matched her yellow cotton blouse and red checkered skirt. Faye guessed her age as fifteen or sixteen. She had a teenager's spindly frame and thin wrists, but that didn't seem right. Why would a girl so young be cleaning her room?

From behind a chair, the girl picked up a coat Faye recognized. A gray coat, still damp from the ocean water. It was June, summer, South Carolina. Why had Faith Morgan been wearing a coat last night?

The girl seemed unnerved by Faye's staring.

"I fell off the pier and hit my head," Faye said. "Sorry if I seem out of it."

The girl only shrugged and said nothing. She merely stood and walked out, shutting the door behind her without saying a single word.

Who was she? Faye climbed out of bed and peeked into the hallway. The girl walked purposefully, knowingly. She had to be a servant of some kind. A housekeeper? She seemed far too young to be anyone's housekeeper. Then again, it was 1921. Were there any child-labor laws on the books yet?

The girl hadn't just tidied and picked up the laundry. She'd laid out clean clothes for Faye. It was then Faye saw the brass hand mirror on the dresser. Her hands shook as she lifted it and gazed into it.

It was her, Faye, and yet not her. They had similar faces, but not quite the same. First, the girl in the mirror was nowhere near thirty. Her nose was a little straighter and her hair a tad browner and much longer. The eyes were the same, though. Same violet color. Same loneliness.

Faye saw that she hadn't come out of her adventure last night entirely unscathed. Under her right eye she sported a yellow-green bruise, the exact shade of broccoli-cheddar soup. It looked disgusting, to say the least. Faith—or whoever she was—must have hit the water very hard. Or maybe she'd hit the corner of the pier when she fell.

Faye put the mirror down and took the clothes to the bathroom to dress. She ran water into the sink and held some in her hands. She sniffed it, studied it. The water was lukewarm and mostly clear. Faye tried splashing some on her face. When nothing bad happened, she worked up the courage to brush her teeth with it. In the bathroom cabinet she found a rather delicate-looking toothbrush and the initials MAC engraved on the handle. It had a white handle—bone maybe?—and thick worn-down bristles on it, more like a hairbrush than a toothbrush. She guessed they were animal hairs of some sort, but she tried not to think about that part too much. The initials were neither Faith's nor Carrick's, but she couldn't imagine this little toothbrush in Carrick's large male hands, so she assumed it was for her use. While she found no toothpaste in the cabinet she did find baking soda, which worked well enough in a pinch. It tasted acrid and weird, but it did the job. Then Faye washed her body as best she could with a wet washcloth. She discovered more bruises by daylight. Twin bruises on her thighs and one blue bruise on her arm that looked like she'd been grabbed very hard and pulled. That one made sense. Of course Carrick had had to grab her and haul her out of the water.

Most days Faye wore makeup—concealer, mascara, whatever she needed to look human for Hagen. But that wasn't an option today. She found no cosmetics at all in the medicine cabinet, which meant the bruises would have to stay out in the open. In this heat, she'd probably sweat any makeup off within an hour of applying it anyway. There was a jar of cold cream in the cabinet, a few bottles of this and that— mineral oil and lavender. Headache powders and cough syrup and scissors. If she needed any further proof this was a different time, the active ingredient listed on the cough syrup bottle was morphine. She'd save that in case any of them required surgery. Apart from that, she found a hairbrush, a comb and Carrick's shaving supplies, which he clearly hadn't used for a while.

Faye started to dress. She found in the clothes the girl had laid out for her the least attractive pair of underwear she'd ever seen in her life. These weren't granny panties. These were *great*-granny panties. But the white-cotton garment did fit her well. All the clothes fit her—the bandeau bra, the ankle-length blue skirt, the ivory-colored blouse with the matching blue tie. When she was done she looked at herself in the mirror.

"Oh, my God, I am Anne of Green Gables." Clearly the flapper style of the Roaring Twenties had not yet reached coastal, rural South Carolina. She'd just have to make do.

As Faye hadn't had hair this long since elementary school, she wasn't sure what to do with it. She had no elastics to use to pull it back or plastic hair clips. For ten solid minutes Faye fussed with her hair, braiding and twisting it until it was in a semblance of a Gibson girl topknot.

Scared of encountering Carrick again, Faye crept quietly from the bathroom. She returned to her bedroom and made the bed as best she could, since it seemed like the sort of thing a woman in 1921 would be expected to do. After Will had died, his mother held her in her arms and said, "When you're going through hell, just keep going." Faye would keep going. What other choice did she have?

Reluctantly, Faye left the bedroom and went downstairs, trying to walk as purposefully as the girl with the yellow scarf in her hair had. Surely the girl had a name. Faye would need to find it out quickly. Her entire being was concentrated on one task—learn everything she could about Carrick Morgan, Faith Morgan and this house so she could blend in the best she could until another, better plan presented itself.

Morning sunlight flooded every room in the cottage and Faye studied the layout. The front door opened to a mudroom with rain boots in cubbies and oil slickers on pegs. Through the mudroom door was a hallway. To the left was the living room; to the right, Carrick's bedroom. At the back of the house were the kitchen and pantry. The stairs went straight up from the center of the hall, her bedroom on the right and the bathroom on the left. A small house, lovely in its simplicity. Had she been here by choice, she would have fallen in love with the place instantly. But she wasn't here by choice. She was a hostage taken by time.

Faye found the girl in the small celery-colored kitchen cooking something that smelled so good Faye's mouth literally watered. It smelled like heaven, like love, like home and family and Sunday mornings at her grandparents' house. It smelled like...

"Bacon," Faye said with a sigh of bliss. She hadn't eaten real bacon in years. Too fattening. Too high in cholesterol. Too everything. In the large cast-iron skillet, the girl was also frying eggs. Eggs and bacon cooked in lard. Maybe there was something to be said for living in the past after all.

"That smells really good," Faye said, smiling at the girl. The girl smiled back but still didn't speak. "Can I help?"

The girl's attention was on her skillet, and she didn't reply, nor did she look at Faye this time. That was when it occurred to her that perhaps something was going on with this girl. Was she disabled? Mute? Deaf? That seemed possible. Faye had had a friend in college who was deaf. She'd worn a lanyard around her neck with a laminated "I am deaf, please face me and speak clearly" sign on it and hearing aids in both ears. But this was the twenties. Hearing aids probably hadn't been invented yet, and even if they did exist, Faye doubted a black teenage girl in rural South Carolina would have access to one.

Could the girl read? Could she write? Faye wasn't sure how to ask about this quiet young woman without revealing that she didn't know the things Faith Morgan should know. The girl was obviously comfortable enough with Faye to waltz right into her room without knocking.

Unsure what to do with herself, Faye walked out the back door and into the sunrise. The light was low in the sky, and the shadows were long—early morning still. She could see that the paint on the house was a warm off-white and the trim a deep dark green. Facing the back door, the lighthouse butted up against the left corner. Carrick wouldn't have to take more than ten or twelve steps to go from the kitchen to the lighthouse. Faye walked around the right side of the house and stood on the front porch facing the ocean.

It was lovely, yes, beyond lovely. Nothing this lovely could be had without a price. In her time, the lighthouse stood but the house was long gone, destroyed by a tropical storm or a hurricane decades ago. It was exposed, weak and far too vulnerable to the elements. If a storm came, she knew to hide in the lighthouse and let the wind and the waves take the cottage. In her time, the beach was gone, too. Fifty feet of beach and the pier. Had anyone bothered to take photographs of this place? Probably not. Faye hadn't seen any during her online search for pictures of the island. Did Carrick have a camera? Would he let her use it if he did? She would ask him if she could work up the courage. Where was Carrick anyway? Asleep? Did he work all night and sleep all day? Not all day surely. If his lighthouse keeping ended at sunrise, that would be around six in the summer. If he slept eight hours, he would be up around two. What would she do then? Claim amnesia and tell him she couldn't remember what to do or how to do it? No, she couldn't do that. She'd have to fake it as best as she could.

Faye rested her hands on the porch railing and gazed out at the water, watching the waves advance and retreat, advance and retreat, hypnotizing her with the beauty. She hated the beauty, hated it like she hated how much Carrick Morgan looked like William Fielding. The beauty felt like a trap. What if she fell for it?

Faye heard the door open behind her but she didn't turn around. She knew the sound of male footsteps when she heard them.

"Nice morning," Carrick said, standing at her side. He stared out at the water, and she stared at him.

"What time is it?"

"Seven or thereabouts. You sleep well last night?"

"Not really."

"Ah, well, that's to be expected."

"Maybe I'll sleep better tonight. You...you're going to bed?"

"Haven't eaten yet."

Faye nodded. So Carrick slept after breakfast. That made sense. He'd treat breakfast like dinner and dinner like breakfast. She would sleep during the day, too, if she lived in a house without air-conditioning in the South in summer. Better to sleep through the heat of the day so she could be awake during the cool of the evening and night.

"Dolly said breakfast was almost ready."

"Dolly said?"

Carrick laughed. "You know what I mean. She told me breakfast was about ready."

"Dolly," Faye repeated, committing the name to memory. "She works very hard."

"Aye, she does."

"She's young."

"Too young, I think, but she wants the job," Carrick said with a sigh. "Better here than in town, what with her ears and all."

"What exactly is wrong with her ears? Do we know?" Faye asked. "I don't remember if you told me."

"Her father said Dolly had a brain fever when she was one or so. That's their best guess."

"A brain fever..." That could mean anything in this time—meningitis, a viral infection, staph or strep or anything that made a child very sick. Wasn't it scarlet fever that had caused Helen Keller to go blind and deaf as a toddler? God, Helen Keller was alive in 1921. She'd been a grainy photograph in her second-grade textbook and a girl on a stage when they'd been taken to an amateur theater production of *The Miracle Worker*. But she wasn't a fictional character. The woman was real and alive and Faye could probably meet her if she wanted to.

"Her papa says she almost died," Carrick went on. "They're just happy she lived and has all her wits."

"People are so fragile," Faye said. "Scary to think about."

"It is," he said. "I could have lost you last night. I keep seeing it, in my mind. I was up on the walk, and I saw you on the pier. I looked away one second—one second—and you were gone."

"You didn't lose me," she said.

He leaned over and rested his forearms on the railing, glanced at her out of the corner of his eye.

"I won't let anything happen to you," he said. "If you trust me, stay with me, let me protect you, we'll be all right. It's better than the other choice, isn't it? Better than before? You don't want to go back, do you?"

"Back where?"

"Back home." He nodded at the expanse of water that if crossed would take her north. Was that where she'd come from? Somewhere north? "Back to him."

To him?

A clue. Finally, a clue.

Faith had left a man and come here.

"Do you think I should go back to him?" Faye asked.

"I know what the law would say. I know what the Church would say."

"What do you say?" she asked.

"I say if I see Marshall again, I'll throw him off the widow's walk into the ocean. Any man who raises his fists to a girl deserves no better, especially when that girl's his wife. But that's me. He's your husband."

Husband. Marshall. A husband named Marshall.

Faye inhaled sharply. It clicked into place all at once. Faith wasn't Carrick's daughter. Faith, whoever she was, was someone's wife. And that someone, Marshall Something, had abused Faith, and she had run away and come here for safety. And to avoid scandal, Carrick had lied and told everyone she was his daughter, the child of a marriage to a woman he was estranged from who had died. She could have laughed in her relief, could have wept. Instead, she said nothing until Carrick made a note of her silence.

"I shouldn't have brought him up," he said.

"It's all right," she said. "I just... I gasped because I'm sore. From the fall last night, I mean."

"Let me take a look at you."

She turned to him, and he touched her chin, tilting her face into the light.

"He's a dead man next time I see him," Carrick said. "But I hope to God neither of us ever see him again."

"Do they look that bad?" she asked. How strange it was to wear someone else's bruises, someone else's suffering. Hagen had been a thoughtless husband sometimes, even callous, but never ever had he hit her.

"They look a sight better today than when you turned up here," he said before lowering his hand.

"I left my husband, and you took me in," Faye said aloud, needing to hear Carrick confirm it.

"No decent man on earth would turn away a girl crying,

'sanctuary' on his doorstep. I don't know why you chose me, but I promise you this—I'll take care of you for the rest of your life."

"Don't you mean the rest of *your* life?"

"I meant what I said. Even if the good Lord takes me home tomorrow, I'll keep a watch on you. And I will never let that whoreson of a bitch hurt you again." Carrick winced. "Sorry. Told you I'm out of practice. I should put a penny in a jar every time I forget myself. We'll be rich by Sunday."

She swallowed fresh tears and turned to him. She wasn't Faith but she got a good glimpse into Faith's heart when Carrick said those words.

"Maybe that's why I chose you. Because you'll never let that whoreson of a bitch hurt me again."

Carrick met her eyes. It seemed he wanted to say something to her, but he stopped himself. Last night he'd kissed her so passionately there was no doubt in her mind that Carrick harbored deep feelings for Faith. How brokenhearted would he be when he learned Faith was dead? Faye knew. Faye knew all too well.

"I know this isn't any girl's idea of heaven." Carrick put his hand on the small of her back, and Faye stiffened at the touch. He rested his fingers there lightly and only for a moment before dropping his hand to his side again as if remembering he shouldn't be doing that. "Wouldn't have been mine at twenty years old, either. Especially since I know you're used to a different kind of life."

Different kind of life. Twenty years old. She knew she'd come from a very different place than this island now and she knew her age.

"If my old life were heaven," Faye said carefully, "I wouldn't have come here, would I?"

Carrick gripped the rail of the porch and stared out at the ocean like the ship he'd been waiting for all his life was just over the horizon.

"I should have stopped the wedding," he said. "I should have stopped the wedding and thrown you over my shoulder and put you on a boat bound for China. There are only two reasons a girl cries on her wedding day—either she's happy to be getting married or she's making the worst mistake of her life."

"And I wasn't happy," Faye said, remembering her two weddings. She'd cried with happiness when she had married Will, cried in sorrow and sickness when she'd married Hagen.

"Saddest girl I'd ever seen. And the prettiest, too. But I shouldn't be saying things like that to a married woman. Where's the jar? I'll put a penny in it."

Before Faye could reply, Dolly stuck her head out the front door and waved them in.

"Breakfast," Carrick said. "Come on, before I run out of pennies."

The kitchen table was round and painted green to match the trim of the house. It seated four, and three places were set. That was good. She was happy to see Dolly ate with them and not somewhere else like a servant. The question of whether Dolly could read or write was answered by the presence of a chalk slate on the table. Carrick picked it up and wrote "Dig in." Dolly laughed and Faye was so shocked by the sudden burst of sound from the girl that she jumped, which caused both Dolly and Carrick to laugh even more. She waited until they sat before taking her seat across from Carrick. Dolly sat between them. Would it be awkward and rude to talk to Carrick when Dolly couldn't hear or understand what they said? Probably. Faye stayed quiet while eating, staring out the kitchen window at the pier and enjoying the food so much she almost forgot she would have sold her right arm to be back in her own time again.

Dolly's cooking was wonderful. Wonderful if Faye could forget she didn't belong here. She could pretend Carrick was Will, Dolly was their daughter, and that nothing bad had ever happened to her and nothing ever would. A nice dream, but just a dream. The man at the table wasn't her father. But he wasn't her Will, either.

She'd just taken a bite of her bacon—a bite that had her wondering if she wasn't in heaven after all—when she heard the sound of an engine. Carrick stood up at once and walked to the window.

"We have a visitor," he said.

"Who?" Faye asked.

"Looks like John Hartwell. Must have gotten himself a new boat."

"Oh," Faye said as if she knew the significance of the name. "Should I...do something?"

"Just be yourself," he said. "Well, not yourself. Pretend to be yourself."

"That's not a helpful suggestion."

"Just be nice," Carrick said. "He's important 'round these parts. Or at least he thinks he is, which is worse."

Faye smiled at Dolly, who was looking from her to Carrick. Faye picked up her chalk slate and wrote, "Someone is visiting" on it as neatly as she could. Dolly's pretty dark eyes widened and she peeked out the front window before making an exasperated sound and running back to the kitchen.

At the end of the pier a man squatted by a pillar, tying up his boat. It was a beautiful boat, polished mahogany with a

red racing stripe down the side. Carrick clasped her hand a
moment, squeezed it and then walked to the front door. Faye
followed him, scared to go and too scared to stay. The man
had made it halfway from the pier to the porch by the time
Faye and Carrick opened the front door. He wore a suit and
a hat, plus what looked like goggles. Driving glasses? Well,
it was 1921 after all. The windshield hadn't been perfected
yet. As he walked up to the porch, he took off his hat, took
off his glasses and flashed a bright white politician's cam-
paign smile at both of them.

"Howdy, folks," the man called out, giving them a wave.

"I should be scared of him, shouldn't I?" Faye said to
Carrick.

"Why do you say that?" Carrick asked.

Faye looked behind her and saw Dolly hurriedly taking her plate away from the table and hiding her dishes in
the sink under a linen towel. Dolly grabbed the broom and
started sweeping the floor immediately, shooting cautious
glances at Faye and Carrick.

"Oh," Faye said, "just a hunch."

11

The man, Hartwell, mounted the porch steps, his right hand extended to Carrick, his left holding his hat, a straw boater, and a fistful of daffodils. His hair was black with a severe center part and combed back with some sort of gel. Each side had a perfectly symmetrical wave in it. He was the very picture of a tenor in a barbershop quartet. He had bright blue eyes, full lips, a well-trimmed beard and a toothy grin.

"Mr. Hartwell. Long time," Carrick said, shaking his hand.

"Ah, well, you know how it is. Been away on business since the winter. Seems like I stayed away too long."

"How's that?" Carrick asked.

"Let's see, when I left, you'd just came on here as Jack Landry's assistant keeper. Imagine my surprise when I come home to find the Landrys have shipped out, the assistant keeper is now running the whole station and making all sorts of changes and a man I thought was a bachelor like myself has a grown daughter all of a sudden. I couldn't stay away."

"I know the Landrys were sad to leave without saying

goodbye to their friends in town," Carrick said. "But with a malaria outbreak in the Keys, they had to shuffle a whole lot of us around fast."

"Well," Hartwell said with a shrug, "that explains the Landrys. Now, what about this girl of yours?"

"This girl of mine is right here. Faith, meet Mr. Hartwell. Mr. Hartwell, my girl, Faith."

"Hello, Miss Morgan. These, my dear, are for you. And I must say it is a pleasure and a half to meet you," Hartwell said, bowing his head, his hand over his heart. Good Lord, this man was ridiculous.

He flashed her that same ingratiating politician's grin he'd given Carrick. Faye found it unpleasant, although she smiled in return as she accepted the flowers.

"Thank you," Faye said, and she wondered if she was supposed to curtsy or not. Did people still curtsy in the 1920s? She tried a little bob, and it didn't seem to bother either Hartwell or Carrick. "Very nice to meet you, sir."

"Chief, you have a lovely gal here. Although…it looks like she's had a rough time of it. You all right there, Miss Morgan? You go a couple rounds with a grizzly bear?"

Faye raised her hand to her face. Since she had no memory of receiving the bruise, she had forgotten it was there. "I fell on the pier. It's slippery out there."

"You poor angel," Hartwell said, shaking his head. "I always did think it was a shame you ladies had to wear such silly shoes. You be careful now. We don't want anything bad happening to pretty ladies."

"Just pretty ladies?" Faye asked before she could stop herself.

"All ladies are pretty ladies. Aren't they, Chief?"

"Of course they are," Carrick said.

"Good man. The chief knows what's good for him." Hartwell gave her a wink that she was sure he meant to be charming. She did not find it so.

"Faith, Mr. Hartwell's father built this house we live in," Carrick said.

"Don't tell stories now," Mr. Hartwell said, still sizing up Faye's black eye. "My father was too busy to build anything but his reputation. But his was the company the government picked to build this house. Before Daddy came along, this place wasn't fit to be called a house. But you know the government. When it comes to their own houses, they won't spend a nickel when they can spend a dime, but when it's a lighthouse keeper and his kin doing real work out here, they won't spend a dime when they can spend a penny. They hired Daddy's company to do the building, and Daddy himself made sure y'all got a real nice place out here, even if he had to kick in a little of his own money to do it. I sure hope y'all like the place. We townsfolk have nothing but affection for our keepers and their families stuck out here on the islands."

"The house is very nice," Faye said to his self-serving speech. "Thank you. And thank you for the flowers."

"I'll pass your thanks on to Daddy. He'll be happy to hear y'all like the house. So is it just you two, then? We always hope for a big family to man the light. It gets lonely out here, I imagine."

"We stay busy," Carrick said. "The light, the house, no time to get lonely."

"I'm sure that's true," Mr. Hartwell said. "Now, I would love to see what y'all have done to the place while I was gone."

"We were having breakfast," Faye said.

"But it's no trouble," Carrick said, giving her a warning look. "If you don't mind the dishes."

"I don't mind the dishes at all. Shall we?" At that, Hartwell opened the door and walked right into the house like he owned it.

Carrick gave a little sigh. Faye knew exactly how he felt. He held the door open for her, then followed her into the house. It was a play, she realized. All she had to do was pretend she was an actress in a play. She didn't know her lines. She didn't know the script. But she knew her part was to look obedient, be quiet and not piss off someone who clearly had some power in this part of the country.

"I see you added a light in here," Mr. Hartwell said, standing by the fireplace and looking up at the hanging brass-and-white-glass light fixture in the center of the ceiling. His hands were in his pockets as he rocked back and forth on his shiny shoes.

"First thing I did to the house," Carrick said. "They dismantled a railroad station and sold me their lights and the wiring at a good price. Now that the lighthouse has been converted to run on acetylene, it wasn't anything to convert the house to run on it, too."

"Light makes a house a home," Hartwell said, running his fingers along the fireplace mantel as if inspecting it for dust. "You've got to modernize or you might as well be living in the past. You can't stay still. That's what I told Daddy when he said y'all made changes to his house. I said, 'Daddy— you've had indoor plumbing and gas lights for ten years in this house. Don't you think a war hero and his daughter deserve those same creature comforts?'"

"Not everyone who goes to war is a hero," Carrick said,

looking both humble and awkward. "But I wanted Faith here to have all the comforts of home. Any father would."

"You're too modest, Carrick. Is that an Irish trait? If so, I never heard of it. But anyway, Daddy conceded I had a point, and if you know Daddy, you know I had a good point."

"I didn't know your father objected to improvements," Carrick said.

"Oh, he thinks anything he touches is perfect," Hartwell said, shaking his head. "Myself included."

"The house is perfect," Faye said. "And with more light, we can see how perfect it is. You can't admire a Rembrandt in the dark, can you?"

Hartwell looked at Faye and narrowed his eyes. Then he laughed a big laugh.

"You're exactly right, Miss Morgan. That's what I'll tell Daddy if he brings it up again. You can't admire a Rembrandt in the dark. He'll like that."

"Good," Faye said. "We want to keep Daddy happy."

"Yes, Miss Morgan. Yes, we do." He turned and gazed around the rest of the living room. "It all looks mighty fine to me. Cozy. You're a good little housekeeper, Miss Morgan."

"Faith hasn't been here much more than a week," Carrick said. "Miss Dolly is our housekeeper."

"I'm sure you'll be running the whole show in no time at all, Miss Morgan," Hartwell said. "I see a big passel of books over there. Who's the reader in the house?"

"We all read when we get the chance, which isn't often," Carrick said. "But most of those were donations. Half of them came with the house, and the other half came in a crate after I moved in."

"Donations?" Hartwell moved to examine the titles.

"Well, that explains a few things. Some of these books over here might not be fit reading for a young lady. Or anybody." Hartwell held up a copy of *Uncle Tom's Cabin* and opened it to the middle. The book was upside down. He picked up a couple more and opened them, but seemingly found nothing worth his attention.

"Should we take a look upstairs?" Hartwell asked. "I imagine it looks a whole lot different without four Landry rascals running around."

"Upstairs is Faith's room," Carrick said.

"Is it? Wouldn't the lighthouse keeper want to stay in the room where he could best see the light at night?" Hartwell asked, fanning himself with his boater.

"The lighthouse keeper is awake all night, Mr. Hartwell," Faye said, although she'd planned on keeping her mouth shut. "He sleeps during the day."

"Is that so?" Hartwell said. "I stand corrected."

"A young lady needs a bigger room for her clothes and things," Carrick said. "And her privacy. Nothing to see really."

"Of course. Nothing to see," Hartwell agreed. Faye sensed he did want to see something upstairs. Was Hartwell acting funny on purpose? Or were all rich Southern white men in 1921 this high-handed, dandified and obnoxious? Whatever he was, he was driving her crazy. She needed to keep her mouth shut or she was going to say something to get herself into big trouble.

"Would you like to see the garden?" Carrick asked. "Now, that is something worth seeing."

Hartwell glanced at the stairs before pasting on a smile again.

"Lead the way," he said.

Faye followed Carrick and Hartwell to the back door. Dolly was currently squatting in the corner of the kitchen with a dustpan and a brush, giving all her attention to sweeping along the side and back of the stove and doing her level best to avoid eye contact with any of them. If Dolly had reason to mistrust Hartwell, Faye wouldn't trust him, either. Teenage girls could be uncannily good judges of male character.

"Hello there, girl," Hartwell said to Dolly. Dolly didn't look up or answer. "Y'all have a mouse in your house."

"She's deaf, Mr. Hartwell," Faye said.

"Deaf? Can she talk?"

"She's been deaf all her life," Carrick said. "She doesn't speak. She writes."

"Writes? Her? Well, I guess she had to learn something to take orders from y'all. Must be nice not having to hear her chattering away all day," Hartwell said. "I need a deaf-mute working for me. The girl at my place wouldn't shut up if you gagged her with a gourd. Let me know if y'all want to get rid of your mouse. I'll take her off your hands."

If this man didn't shut up, Faye was about to gag him with a gourd. She hoped there was some in the garden. They might come in handy.

"The garden's right out back," Carrick said, pointedly ignoring the comment. His jaw was clenched, and Faye could sense it took effort to unclench it. "We'll pick you something to take home."

As Carrick and Hartwell walked out the back door, Faye lingered long enough to catch Dolly's eye. She smiled at Dolly. Dolly didn't smile back.

When Faye reached the men, she found Hartwell standing

in the center of the garden surveying the cultivated land like his own private kingdom. Faye, too, looked around, trying not to gawk. It was her first time seeing the garden, as well. It was massive, half an acre at least, with a dozen rows of corn, a dozen rows of tomatoes and at least two dozen rows of potatoes. On top of that she saw cucumber plants, onions, head after head of lettuce, red cabbage and cauliflower. Did they grow all their own food here? Most of it, it seemed. Thankfully there were also strawberry plants and blueberry bushes. She wouldn't have to live entirely on vegetables.

In a small fenced pasture to the side of the garden, Faye spotted not a cow but three brown goats. Oh, joy. As if unpasteurized wasn't bad enough, she was going to be drinking goat's milk here.

Faye wandered among the rows and twisted a few ripe cucumbers off their stems while Carrick and Hartwell talked.

"Where were you again before they sent you all the way down here to our little light, Chief?" Hartwell asked. Both Carrick and Hartwell had their hands in their pockets, but their postures couldn't have been more different. Carrick looked humble and worn-out. Hartwell looked like a squire on a Sunday stroll.

"Boston," Carrick said. "I was up at the Boston Light."

"Boston. That's right. Nice town. I was just up there a week ago. Very busy city. So many people you could get lost in a crowd and never be seen again," he said, and smiled in Faye's direction. "I must say I'm happy to be back home in a place where we all keep an eye on each other. You like our islands, Chief Morgan?"

"Love it here."

"Good to hear. Very good. We're very fond of our lighthouse families," Hartwell said. He gave Faye a little wink over his shoulder. She pretended not to see that. "So how's that monstrosity up there work, Chief? You got to pour in the kerosene and light a match every couple hours?"

"Gas," Carrick said. "Acetylene gas. The mechanism was built in the Netherlands. You should be proud, Mr. Hartwell. This is the only lighthouse with a gas lamp running in the Carolinas. If the experiment works, they might try it everywhere."

"Now, what do you mean if it works?" Hartwell asked. "Doesn't it work right now? Didn't it work last night?"

"It works," Carrick said, wincing slightly. "It's just…ah… gas is a little unstable. There were a few accidents."

"Accidents? Big? Little?"

"Well, one lighthouse exploded," Carrick said. "But that's not going to happen here. Hope not anyway. You want to go up and see the improvements?"

Hartwell took a step back. "You know what, Chief? I think I'll admire it from afar."

Carrick was trying to scare the shit out of Hartwell on purpose—Faye was certain of that. After all, Carrick had run gas into the keeper's cottage, so surely it wasn't too dangerous. Then again, powering a house in 1921 with any sort of gas sounded about as safe as powering a house with lightning. Who knew? Maybe if the house blew up and Faye died again, she'd end up back in 2015 where she belonged.

"It's a pretty fine setup y'all have out here," Hartwell said, nodding at the garden and the house. "Nice view, even if you do have to live out here in the middle of nowhere."

"We're grateful to have the work," Carrick said. "Lots of men don't this year."

"Doesn't look like y'all are going to starve. I see cabbage. I see corn and peas and melons and summer squash. This must have taken some doing."

"Our Dolly's got a green thumb."

"Good to have a girl around like that. She lives here, I suppose?"

"No. She has brothers and sisters and parents," Carrick said evenly. "They need her at home when she's not here."

"So you all are all alone out here, aren't you? Just the two of you most of the time?"

"Who else would we need?" Carrick asked.

"Daddy told me the Lighthouse Bureau offered to find you an assistant keeper and you told them no. You don't want the help?"

"The light is automated now, so it mostly runs itself. I'm just here to wind the flash and run the foghorn. If something happens, Faith can radio the Hunting Island station. They have a keeper and two assistants, and one of them could be here in under and hour by boat."

"What if there's a storm and they can't make it over here?"

"I'm teaching Faith how the light works. She can take over if something happens."

"Seems like a lot of hard work for such a young lady." Hartwell glanced at her, a cursory glance, quick and dismissive.

"Wives and widows and daughters have been running lights for fifty years or more, Mr. Hartwell," Carrick said. "The keeper's widow is running the Red Point lighthouse as we speak."

"But a girl as young and sweet as Miss Faith? She'd blow away in a stiff breeze."

"I'm twenty, not two," she said. If there was anything she hated, it was being infantilized by a man. "I can handle the light if and when I have to."

"Twenty? I was under the impression you were seventeen. I must have misheard that figure."

Faye winced internally. She'd done it. She'd flubbed a line.

"Faith is twenty now," Carrick said hastily. "She was seventeen when I got out of the navy. Maybe the years got mixed up in the telling."

"You must have married young to have a daughter of twenty. You're thirty-five, if I'm not mistaken."

"Faith was five years old when I married her mother," Carrick said. "My late wife had lost her husband when Faith was still just a baby."

"Oh, I see." Hartwell smiled and put his boater back on his head. "Any plans to remarry? You're a young man after all. About as young as me."

"No plans," Carrick said. "I'm content as I am."

"You must have loved your wife very much."

"Very much," Carrick said with real feeling. "But I can't see myself remarrying. Not until my girl is safe and settled."

"Now it all makes sense," Hartwell said, taking his hat off once more and placing it over his heart. "Let me offer my condolences on the loss of your wife and Miss Morgan's mother. I lost my own mother at fifteen, and a finer woman there never lived. I understand when a woman is irreplaceable."

"Thank you," Carrick said and said no more. Faye struggled to say silent. She wanted to ask a thousand questions, but she couldn't risk it, especially not in front of Hartwell.

She'd already screwed up by revealing Faith's real age. Of course Carrick had told people his daughter was seventeen if he was thirty-five. They must have created a whole story to explain why a girl had shown up one day at the lighthouse and moved in with the keeper.

"Twenty years old," Hartwell said, interrupting her thoughts. "I guess you'll be getting married soon enough. Then you'll leave your poor father behind to tend the light all by himself. Or are you planning on devoting the rest of your life to your daddy?"

"No reason I can't do both," Faye said. "Right? The man I marry can be the assistant keeper, and we'd all live in one house under the same roof."

"You paint a pretty picture," Hartwell said. "But surely some handsome man is going to come along and sweep you off your feet. Carry you away to Beaufort or Charleston. I love living in Charleston myself. Quite a town. I think you'd like to see it, wouldn't you? I'd be happy to show you around whenever you like."

"I'm sure I'll be awfully busy out here," Faye said.

"Surely your father could spare you for one evening. I'd bring my boat out to fetch you and take my new Talbot tourer into town. We'd ride into Charleston in high style."

"Faith is right. We are awfully busy out here."

"Miss Morgan, tell me how are you going to find this magic man to marry who will be your father's assistant keeper if you don't leave the island?"

"I don't have to leave the island to find a husband," she said.

"You don't? You think he's going to come to you?" Hartwell asked, his voice teasing. But she didn't feel teased—she felt threatened.

"He already has," Faye said. "I'm engaged."

12

If it weren't for the knot of terror lingering in the pit of Faye's stomach, she might have laughed at the twin expressions of astonishment on Carrick's and Hartwell's faces. Carrick recovered first.

"You hadn't mentioned that to me," he said.

"I was waiting for the right time." Faye tried to sound girlish and apologetic, but she wasn't sure if she succeeded. She would never make it in a career on the stage. "I knew you wouldn't want me marrying a sailor. You told me so many times how hard the life is."

"When is the blessed occasion?" Hartwell asked in a too-friendly tone.

"We haven't decided yet. I met him in Boston but he had to ship out again. I don't know when he'll be back."

"And that's why I said I didn't want you marrying a sea-man." Carrick fell into the role of the concerned father as if he'd been born to play it.

"What's your gentleman's name?" Hartwell asked. "I'll keep my ears open for any news of his return to you."

Faye spoke the first name that came to mind.

"Pat Cahill," she said. "Patrick Cahill."

"A sailor, and of good Irish stock like your father. You must really love your father," Hartwell said, grinning that plastered-on smile again that made Faye think about shoving corncobs into dimly lit places.

"I know the life," she said. "That's all."

"My felicitations to the happy couple." Hartwell swept his hat down and gave her a bow. "Now, Chief, perhaps you'll walk me to my boat. It's a testy little critter. Then I'll be on my way and let you get back to work."

"To bed," Faye said. "He sleeps during the day and works all night."

"Sleeping all day and working all night doesn't sound like much of a life to me. If I'm going to be up all night, it sure as sin ain't going to be for work," Hartwell said, his smile widening. He wore his grin the way other men wore a gun.

"It suits me fine," Carrick said.

"Better you than me." Hartwell slapped Carrick on the back and the two of them set off.

Once they disappeared from view, Faye returned to the kitchen to finish her breakfast. The eggs had gone runny and the bacon cold, but it still tasted better than anything she'd let herself eat in a long time. Lard and sugar and butter and eggs—the four food groups of traditional Southern cooking.

Dolly had finished eating, washed her own dishes and put them away. Faye didn't see her anywhere, so she assumed she'd gone upstairs to work or hide. Faye didn't blame her for that. She'd hide from Hartwell next time he came to visit, too.

Faye put her dishes in the sink and stared blankly at them. She didn't see any dish soap anywhere. She felt guilty for taking her automatic dishwasher for granted all these years. When she got home, she'd get on her knees in the kitchen of the Church Street house and kiss Miss Lizzie's dishwasher.

If she ever got home.

Outside the house, Faye heard the sound of male voices calling back and forth to each other. She heard an engine start and the sound of a boat on the water zipping away.

Good riddance.

Carrick came back in the house through the back door. She glanced at him over her shoulder as she ran water over her plate.

"How hard did you hit your head last night?" Carrick demanded, coming to stand by the sink.

"I didn't hit my head last night," she said. "Or if I did hit it, I don't remember doing it. Which could be the case if I hit my head."

"You told Hartwell you were engaged?"

"I don't want him out here sniffing around Dolly or me. Did you hear what he said about her?"

"I heard. Arrogant shit," he said, shaking his head. "Sorry."

"You can swear in front of me. I am engaged to a sailor. I've heard salty talk before."

"I wish you'd told me before you told Hartwell that was your story. I looked like an ass out there with my mouth hanging open."

"It just came to me when he asked me to go to Charleston with him. I'd rather go swimming with sharks than out with him."

"He's not that bad," Carrick said, and she gave him the cockeyed stare she'd given Will when he claimed something "wasn't that bad" that was, in fact, "that bad." Like when he'd come home from a road trip with a "not that bad" bruise the side of a cantaloupe on his back courtesy of a ninety-two-miles-per-hour wild pitch.

"All right, he's that bad," Carrick conceded.

"He scares Dolly. Does she know him?"

"No idea. You better ask her what she knows about him, then."

"Me? Why me?"

Carrick gripped the ledge of the green tile of the kitchen counter and shrugged. "You know, it might be a female thing."

Faye rolled her eyes.

"I'll talk to her," she said. "After I do the dishes. You finish your breakfast."

Carrick nodded and went to the table.

"I'm sorry," she said, wiping her plate with a wet rag. "I didn't mean to let my real age slip out like that."

Carrick stabbed at his eggs with his fork.

"Not your fault. We got nothing but lies lying around here. Easy to trip over one."

"I tripped," she said. "I'll try not to trip again."

She dried her dishes and put them away as Carrick finished his breakfast. When he was done he tossed his plaid napkin on the table and leaned back in his chair.

"It was smart," he said.

"What was?"

"You telling Hartwell you were engaged to a sailor. Men can be out to sea for months, for years. And Hartwell seems like the gossiping sort. Once it gets around town you're engaged, we won't have to worry about suitors showing up. It was smart, even if you did catch me off guard."

"Thank you," she said. "I heard a story about the sister of

a lighthouse keeper who was engaged to a sailor. He shipped out and never came back. She waited for him all her life."

"Was that in a book you read?"

Faye started to say no but then thought better of it. Last year she and Hagen had gone to Savannah on a four-day vacation. He'd wanted to cheer them both up after a failed intrauterine insemination treatment. They'd played good tourists on that trip and had taken a carriage ride around town. The tour guide had pointed out a statue of a woman, the lighthouse keeper's sister, who'd greeted every single ship that came into port by waving a white towel at them in the hopes her beloved was on board and returning to her. By 2014 the woman was a local legend. In 1921, she was someone Faye could have tea with.

"Yes, I read it in a book a long time ago."

Carrick stood up and brought his dishes to the sink. Faye tried to take them from him, and he gave her yet another confused look.

"You're doing dishes now?" he asked.

"Of course, I—"

She nearly said, "I always do dishes" but that was Faye, not Faith.

"I only wanted to help," Faye said.

"You can help all you want. You just never have… I mean, I know you aren't used to housework."

Another hint. Another clue. Faye looked at her hands—Faith's hands. Smooth, no calluses, neatly trimmed nails. What sort of woman in 1921 wouldn't have done her own housework? A rich woman, that was who. The wife of a rich man. Faith's husband had money.

"There are lots of things I've never done before that I'm probably going to start doing."

"Yeah, I noticed that last night."

"Carrick, last night... I'm sorry. I was just overwhelmed," Faye said.

"You weren't the only one." He smiled, but the smile didn't last long. "About last night..." he began. "And the dishes. You aren't trying to earn your keep around here, are you?"

She found herself blushing, still humiliated by how she'd tried to seduce this man, this total stranger, simply because he looked like and sounded just like Will.

"Because I would never ask that of you," Carrick said. "You don't have to pay for room and board here with your body. You don't have to pay for it with anything at all. Not for me or Dolly. Dolly gets paid a good wage for her work, and she isn't complaining."

"She doesn't think I'm lazy?"

"Well, she does, but she thinks that about everybody, myself included."

"You're the lighthouse keeper."

"She sees me sleeping all day."

"Because you work all night.'

"That she doesn't see."

Faye laughed. She had been a pretty hard-nosed teenager herself. No one had met her impossible standards.

"I don't want to be lazy," Faye said. "I don't have much else to do. I'd rather help than sit around."

"I'm sure Dolly would appreciate a hand, and I appreciate what she appreciates."

"You're a good man."

"I wouldn't go that far."

"I threw myself at you last night, and you didn't take advantage of me."

"I'm not the sort of man to take someone else's wife to bed, even if that man doesn't deserve to kiss her baby toe."

"Right. Of course you're not," she said. "Now you should get to bed, right?" Faye needed to end this conversation before she said anything else wrong, anything else that might give her away.

"Going. Wake me if you need anything."

Once Faye was certain Carrick had gone to bed and shut the door behind him, she sprang into action. She couldn't make any more gaffes. First stop, the kitchen. Faye went through the pantry and the cabinets, wanting to memorize what they had and where it was stored. It wouldn't look good if Carrick asked her for a cracker or a cup of coffee and she couldn't find them.

In the cabinet by the stove she found familiar items— baking powder (Clabber Girl brand, which she'd had at home), along with condensed milk, molasses, brown sugar, white sugar, yeast, cornmeal, spices, salt and pepper and Jell-O. Even in 1921 there was room for Jell-O.

With the vegetable garden and all this dry food, at least she knew she wouldn't starve. She might drown, blow up in a gas explosion or contract malaria, but she wouldn't starve. And she wouldn't get scurvy, either, it seemed. Faye found several dozen jars of canned fruit preserves— cranberry, blackberry, cherry and orange marmalade. Plus, several cans of peaches, apples and cherries.

Under the sink she found bleach in an amber glass bottle and vinegar in a clear glass bottle. More baking soda, too. While the packaging wasn't what she was used to, everything in the kitchen was recognizable. She took comfort in the little girl with the umbrella on the Morton's salt canister. She never thought she'd welcome the sight of a familiar product logo. The kitchen reminded Faye of her grandmother's. And it was certainly well stocked with pots and pans and silverware. Nothing looked foreign to her, except maybe the millet, whatever that was. Surely they had a dictionary in the house. Asking Siri, "What is millet?" wasn't an option anymore. Faye almost missed Siri. Once in a dark and desperate moment she'd asked Siri to tell her a joke. She'd responded with "Two iPhones walk into a bar. They didn't get a good reception." That had been the night Hagen had pried the pill bottle out of her hand, the night she'd realized a telephone robot was her only friend in the world.

In the living room, Faye pulled the Sears, Roebuck & Co. catalog out from under the Bible, hopeful it would help her understand the world of 1921 America. She also wondered whatever happened to this Roebuck person. Had there been a dramatic falling-out, a breakup of sorts, between him and Mr. Sears? Were they the Beatles of their day—Sears was Paul McCartney and poor Roebuck John Lennon? On the cover in large letters it said, "Buy from the World's Largest Store."

"Oh, I get it," Faye said to herself. "It's the Amazon of 1921."

As she leafed through the book, she stopped at random pages studying the goods and their prices.

Blankets, cotton, white or tan—she could buy a pair for $2.75.

Men's silk socks in black or white—$1.48 a pair. Not bad considering the silk and cashmere socks she'd gotten Hagen for Christmas had cost more than a hundred dollars.

"Oh, my God…" Maybe 1921 wouldn't be so bad. If Faye had a spare $14.45, she could order a "Home Vibrator." The drawing showed a woman using the vibrator to massage her head. She'd always heard foreplay began with stimulating the brain, and this woman seemed to take that literally. The advertisement said it was for "Household Use." And she could hear Will in her head saying, "Household use? As opposed to what? Business use?" Too bad they didn't have electricity at the house, as the vibrator needed to be plugged into a wall socket. Then again, Faye was content to take her orgasms into her own hands if necessary. Or Carrick's.

"Not Carrick," she said to herself. Even if she wanted to sleep with him—she didn't—she shouldn't. Apparently she was married, and Carrick was Catholic with a decent streak as wide as the ocean. And she was in another woman's body in 1921. Was there any sort of birth control in the 1920s? The pull-out method, of course. She remembered the old joke—what do you call people who use the pull-out method? Parents.

Near the back of the catalog, she found houses for sale. Not real-estate listings, actual house kits that one could order and then assemble—brick and mortar not included. These weren't the generic-looking manufactured boxes of her day. No, these houses were nice. One model called the Castleton was a beautiful two-story home with a basement and a porch. Four rooms on the first floor, four rooms on the second. She wondered what the cost of shipping on a house was. You couldn't buy a house-assembly kit off Amazon.

"Get on that, Bezos," Faye said. "You're behind the times."

A two-story four-bedroom home, and all for the low price of $1,989.

That amount was about half the mortgage payment on Hagen's five-bedroom brick McMansion in their Columbia, South Carolina, gated community. She'd told him five bedrooms was a little excessive for two people. "But we'll have the kids," he'd said, as if children were inevitable and not, as they turned out to be, an unattainable fantasy.

Faye was almost scared to look at the cameras, but she made herself do it. There they were—on page 587. In 1921, Sears, Roebuck & Co. sold the Conley Junior film cameras in four sizes ranging in price from $9.85 to $17.25. The advertising copy promised they were "modern in every detail" and equipped with "Extra Rapid Rectilinear Lenses." The Conley Fixed Focus folding camera pledged "no focusing, no guessing at distances and snapshots always sharp." Film was for sale, of course, at forty-one cents per roll of six exposures. When Faye thought of the thousands of photographs stored on her iPhone…

She felt naked without a camera on her. She'd been a photographer since her junior year of high school. The editor of the school newspaper had been a sixteen-year-old smart-ass named Kev Conner who had been sexy in a junior-in-high-school sort of way. Being nerdy and gangly and not knowing how to flirt, Faye had joined the paper, since it had seemed like the best way to get closer to her crush. Quickly her loyalties had shifted from the guy to the job. She'd taken all the pictures for the newspaper that year, and most of the club and team photos for the yearbook. In front of a camera, she felt uncomfortable and trapped, but behind it…that was where she belonged. She'd felt powerful bossing the football players around, telling them how to stand for their team photo. And they'd done what she said. When she'd seen her name as the photo credit for the first time in the newspaper, Faye had found her calling.

It could be her calling again for the low price of $9.85 for the fixed-focus camera. She wanted to take pictures of the island and the lighthouse. The question was, did she have $9.85? Did Carrick? How much did he make a year? Did she have any money at all? Carrick had said she'd sacrificed a great deal to be with him. And apparently she didn't do housework, at least not until today. Once upon a time, Faith Morgan must have had money. Faye would have to find out if Faith still did.

Asking Carrick for a camera was out of the question. She'd pay for it herself or she would live without it.

Faye leaned back on the couch, her hands crossed over her stomach, which was aching now from a combination of fear and greasy food. Buy a camera? Why would she buy a camera? Was she planning on staying? What choice did she have? She was here either by accident or design, so she might as well face facts.

Faye slapped the catalog closed, placed it back on the coffee table under the Bible and headed upstairs. Last night it had been so dark in the house, Faye hadn't seen any rooms other than her bedroom and the bathroom. She'd assumed the door across from the bathroom was a linen closet or something, but when she leaned her ear against the door, she heard a low hum from inside, a sound like a wheel turning rapidly. Slowly so as not to startle Dolly, Faye opened the door and slipped inside.

"You have got to be kidding me." Faye laughed at the sight of the Singer sewing table. It looked identical to the one in her room at the Church Street house. Except this sewing table still had the machine on it and the treadle and someone using it like it had been intended to be used. Dolly sat at the machine, her foot pumping the treadle with an easy rhythm.

Faye glanced around the room, enraptured by its feminine beauty. A twin bed sat by the wall. The rectangular wooden footboard and headboard had been painted a pale yellow, and the quilt pattern was all yellow-and-white squares. Someone had sewn a pillow-size turtle and given it a green shell. The curtains were a lacy blue and the walls a soft buttercream color. The rug on the floor was blue and yellow, and someone had decorated the bed table with three perfectly formed conch shells, one large, one medium, one small. A mirror with a bamboo frame hung on the wall, reflecting a slender white vase set in the windowsill that held a single yellow daisy. If Faye had ever dreamed of what her and Will's baby's nursery would look like, it would be something like this. Only they'd have a yellow crib where the bed stood. She was in her dream house. What did you call a dream house when you dreamed it in a nightmare?

Dolly, sensing her presence, stopped her sewing and turned around.

Faye picked up Dolly's chalkboard and wrote, "This room is beautiful."

Dolly smiled at the words and wrote back, "Thank you."

Thank you? Faye erased the board and wrote a new question. "Did you decorate this room?"

To which Dolly replied, "Chief said I could."

The answer was wary, defensive. Did Dolly think Faye disapproved? And Chief? Was that what everyone called Carrick? She'd seen the writing on the back of his photograph last night—Senior Chief Petty Officer. Well, Chief it is, then.

"Did you sew the quilt?" Faye wrote. Dolly nodded in the affirmative.

"The curtains?" Faye wrote. Dolly nodded.

"Paint the walls?" Dolly nodded.

"Make the rug?" Dolly nodded.

This girl needed to own and operate her own interior design firm.

"Find the shells?" Faye asked.

Dolly gave her a strange look. "You did," she wrote on the chalkboard. Shit. Another gaffe.

"I forgot," Faye replied on the board. "You should decorate my room."

Dolly's grin was like a sunburst across her face.

"I will!" she wrote.

Faye laughed at the girl's eagerness for what amounted to doing extra work. Although she loved the look of beautiful homes, Faye never had the knack for interior decorating. Her apartment with Will had been functional and decorated mostly with his collection of baseball memorabilia and her favorite photographs in black square frames. Hagen had hired a professional for their house in Columbia, so Faye had been spared the task that Dolly seemed to relish so much. But really, what else was there for a teenage girl to do with her spare time in 1921? Not like she could play "World of Warcraft" or start a Pinterest account.

"Today?" Dolly wrote on her board.

"Maybe tomorrow," Faye wrote back. "We're busy today. What is that?"

Dolly unfolded the bundle of pink-and-white cloth. It was a dress, tiny and pretty with a white ruffle at the bottom.

"For you?" Faye wrote on the board, and Dolly laughed hard when she read it. She shook her head and the expression on her face seemed to say "Crazy lady."

"Baby sis," Dolly wrote on the board. "Church."

"Beautiful. I want one for me," Faye replied. A joke, but Dolly immediately pulled a tape measure out of her skirt pocket. Faye shook her head. "Not today," she mouthed.

Dolly sat down again. She wrote on her slate, "Do you need me, miss?"

Faye took the board back and wrote, "Call me Faith, not miss, please. Tell me what you don't like about that man who came today." She had to use both sides of the board. Perhaps they could order Dolly a conversation-size chalk-board from the Sears catalog.

Dolly shook her head as she read the question, not in refusal but in obvious disgust. She drew a picture on the board, a man with his leg sticking up and his foot in a giant boot. Faye narrowed her eyes at the drawing, parsing it out.

"Bootlegger," Faye said. She wrote back on the board, "How do you know that?"

Dolly looked at her with the most teenaged expression of "duh" and wrote two words in reply.

"Everybody knows."

Faye smiled. All right, that was Hartwell's game. Faye had forgotten Prohibition was in effect in this decade. Did people in 1921 call it Prohibition? Or did they refer to it as the Eighteenth Amendment or the Volstead Act? Was that why Mr. Hartwell seemed so disingenuous during his visit? Was he there scoping out the island for some reason? If Faye were going to be a booze smuggler, this wouldn't be a bad base of operations. The island was owned by a bourbon dis-tiller and from here one could take a boat all the way up the coast. And with no permanent residents on the island but her and Carrick, a bootlegger wouldn't have to worry too much about getting caught in the act. If bootlegging was Hartwell's only game, she'd let him play it as long as he left Dolly and her alone.

Dolly wiped the board clean again and wrote, "You need help?"

Their teenage housekeeper was eager to please, that was for sure.

Faye wrote, "Yes. I want to do chores. What should I do?"

Dolly went wide-eyed at the words. Apparently telling the boss's daughter what to do wasn't in Dolly's job description. Faye added an addendum to her question.

"He said I should help you more."

Carrick hadn't said that, but it seemed like a good explanation for Faith's sudden change in behavior.

Dolly wrote, "Chief wants you to help me?"

"Yes," Faye wrote. "What do you do around the house?"

Dolly heaved a sigh so loud it blew a spool of white thread across the table. Faye caught it just before it went over the side. With a shake of her head, Dolly pulled out a used envelope from a drawer and started writing along the back of it.

She wrote.

And she wrote.

And she wrote some more.

Faye took the envelope from Dolly and read the list of chores.

Clean house lamps
Weed garden
Fill lamps, trim wicks
Clean stove
Sweep & wash floors
Wash windows
Sew curtains
Make soap
Beat rugs
Bake pie
Milk Nanny

This house had a lot of damn lamps and that was a big garden out there. Make soap? What, was she supposed to be Granny on *The Beverly Hillbillies* now? Beat the rugs? What had the rugs done to deserve that?

Just reading these chores aged Faye a good ten years. So much for her pretty fingernails.

"This is a long damn list," Faye said out loud. Dolly looked at her in shock and confusion. Apparently Dolly could read lips a little bit and had seen Miss Faith say something entirely not very Faith-ful.

"You do all this?" Faye wrote.

Dolly nodded.

"What do you want me to do?" Faye asked.

"Can you milk Nanny?" Dolly wrote.

Nanny? Who was… Oh, yeah, Nanny. That had to be the goat Carrick had milked last night for her. Faye tried not to make a face.

"I'll try. I'm not great with goats."

Dolly was not sympathetic. She wrote two words. "Good luck."

Faye reread the list.

"I can bake a pie," Faye wrote. "And weed the garden."

Dolly smiled, looking both relieved and grateful. Better inept help than no help at all.

"Do you like working here?" Faye wrote.

Dolly nodded enthusiastically. Faye added *Why* to the beginning of her question.

Dolly wrote her answer on the board, and Faye read it. It told her all she needed to know about life on this island in 1921. And if a bus had pulled up outside with a sign on the side that said Destination 2015 with a travel time of ninety-four years, Faye would have boarded that bus then and there.

"Because it's so easy."

13

Maybe Faye wouldn't bake that pie after all.

In the cupboard over the sink, Faye had found a cookbook. She found the manual for the oven in the junk drawer under a notepad, a rubber band ball, a screwdriver, a set of jacks and some twine. And while she did have some experience baking an average dessert, that was in the twenty-first century with 2015 technology. The cookbook was not helpful. The ingredients for peach pie were simple enough—peaches, butter, flour, sugar. And the instructions were fairly straightforward—combine, stir, cream and so forth. The final sentence of the recipe, however, was a cryptic puzzle: "Bake in a moderately hot oven for forty-five minutes."

Moderately hot oven? That's it? No temperature listed? What did that even mean—moderately hot? How moderately hot were they talking here? George Clooney in *Ocean's Eleven* hot? Or Daniel Craig in *Skyfall* hot? Probably not Daniel Craig hot. That heat level would scorch any straight girl's peaches.

If the vague temperature directions weren't bad enough,

the recipe for the piecrust called for ice water. Ice? In June? In South Carolina? On an island? In 1921? Clearly this was a Northerner's cookbook.

Where the hell was she going to get ice water? Forget it. The crust would get tepid water from the tap, and it would just have to like it. Faye preheated the oven and started hauling bags of flour and sugar out of the pantry and setting them next to the cans of peaches on the kitchen counter.

She sighed.

"It's just a pie, Faye," she reminded herself. She had a degree from an Ivy League university, she'd taken photographs that had appeared in *Vanity Fair, Esquire, The Atlantic, Newsweek, TIME* and even *Garden & Gun.* Surely she could make a pie without falling apart.

Faye dug through the drawers and under the stove to find measuring cups, mixing bowls and the pie plate. When she stood up, Faye saw Dolly staring down thoughtfully at the assembled ingredients.

Faye sprinkled some flour on the counter, and in the white powder wrote, "Something wrong?"

"Crust?" Dolly wrote back in the flour pile.

Faye showed Dolly the recipe in the book. Dolly shook her head, then walked into the pantry. She returned with a box of saltine crackers.

Dolly wiped her hand through the flour, erasing the words. She wrote, "Watch me."

Faye watched her.

First Dolly took out several fistfuls of crackers and laid them on the counter. With a whack of the rolling pin loud enough to make Faye jump, Dolly smashed them. Faye saw a smile around Dolly's eyes as if she'd enjoyed making Faye jump. If Faye had to work a job this demanding at Dolly's age, she'd probably pull pranks on her employers, too.

Dolly rolled the pin over the crackers, breaking them into smaller and smaller bits. Instead of the measuring cups Faye had found, Dolly used a coffee mug and measured out two cups into the mixing bowl. The butter had already softened from sitting out, but Dolly melted it further in a small pan on the stove. From the junk drawer, Faye took the pad and with a little red stub of a pencil wrote down everything Dolly did. Dolly's nimble fingers would do any Cordon Bleu chef proud.

Wanting to help, Faye grabbed the jar of peaches and started to twist it open. Dolly waved her hand again, motioning Faye to follow her out to the garden. They walked past it and toward a small brick shed painted the same bright white as the lighthouse. A sign above the door read Oil House, and Faye could smell the faint scent of kerosene. But inside the shed she found nothing but a few empty old canisters and some old stained rags. Dolly lifted the cord to open a wooden trapdoor on the floor, lit a candle from a box on the inner wall and started down the steps.

Faye had no choice but to follow even though she was absolutely certain she was walking into the lair of the king of spiders and all his spider children. Was Dolly trying to scare her to death? Or kill her? It sounded as if Faith Morgan had never done chores in her life, so maybe this was some kind of baptism by fire. But no…it wasn't a spider's secret kingdom, although Faye did see a few of the creatures. Five of them. She counted. Five too many. Dolly didn't seem the least bit perturbed by their presence. And Faye had to admit it was kind of nice down there. It was a root cellar. Cool, damp air filled the room. Faye guessed its temperature at fifty degrees. If it weren't for the spiders, Faye might have been tempted to bring a chair and a lantern down here and do some reading.

Dolly pointed at the shelves. They were bleached planks, weathered, worn and full of nail holes. One had writing on it—SS something she couldn't read. These planks had been part of a ship once. A wrecked ship? Possibly. On the shelves were bags and bags of food. Faye found onions—red, yellow and white. And at least six buckets of potatoes. In the darkest corner of the cellar, Faye spied a black box the size of a piano bench or large ottoman. She lifted the lid and saw several blocks of ice inside.

"Oh, so that's why it's called an icebox," Faye said. "It's a box of ice." Now she knew where to get ice for ice water. Not that she'd want to ingest this ice. Who knew where it had come from? She wondered if the previous lighthouse keepers had saved and stored the ice from last winter. That ice could be six months old for all she knew. At least it was something she could use as a refrigerator or a freezer. She saw a large jug of milk in the box and some sides of meat wrapped in white paper.

Dolly pointed to a bag on the top shelf, and Faye pulled it down and found it full of peaches. They weren't as fresh as they could be, but they hadn't gone bad, either. Overripe bananas made for the best banana bread, and overripe peaches likely worked just fine when cooked in a pie.

Back in the kitchen, Dolly whipped up a bit of puff pastry to make the crosshatch shell. Faye stood behind Dolly and watched her roll out the pastry, cut it into strips and lay the pieces on top of the pie with an elegant precision even Martha Stewart would have applauded.

"You know more about running a house at sixteen than

I do at thirty," Faye said, glad Dolly couldn't hear her. "I don't know if you want to get married, but if you do, your husband will be a lucky man. You might not be lucky, but he will be."

Faye heard the sadness in her own voice, the bitterness. Married. This little girl married? But what other choice did a black deaf teenage girl in 1920s South Carolina have? Sure, there were black colleges, but did they cater to the deaf? Faye didn't know but she doubted it. This girl, so smart and talented and hardworking—did she have a snowball's chance in a South Carolina summer of doing anything with her life other than getting married, having babies or working as a housekeeper? Did Faye?

Since waking up in 1921, Faye had felt almost everything—fear and terror, confusion, anger, lust and loneliness. But for the first time she felt real regret. She almost wished she could send Dolly to 2015, and Faye would stay here in her place. No, it wasn't perfect in her time, but it had to be better than this?

Still…there was hope, wasn't there? Women had worked during World War I in unprecedented numbers. They'd had to. After that, many of them had fought to keep those jobs. And right now, out there somewhere, Dorothea Lange was learning her trade, a trade that would eventually lead to a job with the government taking pictures of the effects of the Great Depression and the dust bowl. If Dorothea Lange, a woman with a husband and children, could have a career as a photographer in this time, Faye could, too. Couldn't she? But before she could take on the world, she had to finish baking this damn pie.

Dolly gave Faye the pie, and Faye placed it in the moderately hot oven. When she instinctively went to set the oven timer, she found it had none. No egg timer, either. Had they not been invented yet? She'd have to check the clock on the mantel and peek at the pie every few minutes to make sure it didn't burn. The engineers of the world had figured out how to build lighthouses and steamboats and tanks and machine guns, but they hadn't invented a basic kitchen timer yet. As if Faye needed any further proof she lived in a world run by men.

The mantel clock said it was 11:40. With the pie taking forty-five minutes, she'd need to take it out at 12:25, if not sooner. Faye tested her prowess with the oven by making a pot of tea and then set out to weed the garden while it steeped. She'd had a flower garden at Hagen's house. The gardening itself had never been all that much fun for her, but Faye had loved taking pictures of the flowers as they'd budded, bloomed and died. Although she'd never had a vegetable garden, a weed was a weed, and she set to pulling them. Even with the ocean breeze wafting up from the beach, Faye still had to stop every few minutes, drink tea and towel herself off. She would have preferred a tall glass of ice water, but she didn't want to drink anything that wasn't boiled. The water for the house apparently came from a cistern and a rain barrel. Faye had no desire to acquire the Lowcountry version of Montezuma's revenge. Especially since the pie looked so good when she took it out of the oven. She wanted to survive to eat this damn thing.

After two hours of weeding, Faye was pretty sure she was going to die. Whoever had decreed that women had to wear full-length skirts and long sleeves while working outside was both insane and sadistic. Even wearing the large hat she'd found hanging on the back of the kitchen door, Faye felt the sun's heat like an ant under a magnifying glass. But if it killed her, so be it. If she died again, she'd either end up back in 2015 or in a morgue. She didn't care which—both had refrigeration.

When she went back into the house, she nearly knocked over Dolly, who was perched on a ladder in the center of the living room floor. She was cleaning the glass mantels on the light fixtures. The stuff on her cleaning rag wasn't just dirt. It looked like soot. Was that a side effect of gas lighting? Soot everywhere? No wonder Dolly put "clean house lamps" at the top of her chore list. Soot plus gas plus heat could equal a house fire. Was there anything in 1921 that wasn't specially designed to kill her? She should go outside in the next thunderstorm and throw metal lawn darts while eating some lead-based paint and huffing asbestos dust. How did anyone survive to adulthood? Many didn't, Faye knew, including Faith Morgan. Faith had drowned last night, hadn't she? And now Faye was here taking her place, living the life Faith would have lived. For what purpose, Faye couldn't begin to guess, but she would give anything to know.

Faye puzzled it over as she helped Dolly clean the downstairs lamps. Soon she was too tired to think of anything. Her arms ached. Her back ached. Her neck ached. Living in the past was literally a pain in the neck. Did naps exist in 1921? Even if they didn't, Faye would invent them.

When they finished the lamps, Faye called it a day before she fainted from the heat and the exertion. She stripped down to her slip and lay on top of the covers in her room. It was hot and stuffy in the house but she was too exhausted to care. The moment her head hit the pillow, she was out, and she dreamed of nothing, not even Will.

Eventually hunger pains woke Faye from the deepest, hardest, most dreamless sleep of her life. Hunger and the pressure in her bladder. She pulled her sore and tired body off the bed, groaning like an old man forced to rise from his rocking chair. When she fumbled for the light switch on the wall, she remembered the house had no light switches. Reaching up she pulled the cord for the gas lamp on the ceiling. A dim light no brighter than the tail of a single firefly sputtered into existence. Earlier today while cleaning the lamps with Dolly, she'd learned the secret of operating the lights—the right cord turned the lamp on, and the left cord turned it off. Simple enough. But as the lamps took several minutes to reach their full brightness, a candle or a kerosene lantern was the better option when light was needed immediately.

By the flickering light of the gas lamp, Faye found a match, a candle and a small silver candleholder. She slipped out of her room and into the hall, not bothering to put anything on over her white slip. Apart from her single small fire, the house was cloaked in inky darkness and eerie quiet. Would she ever grow accustomed to living in a house devoid of the usual sounds of modern life? The buzz of a refrigerator. The soft roar of air-conditioning. The whir of a ceiling fan. The hum of fluorescent lighting. Nothing made noise in this house but her feet, her breathing and the hardwood floors as she crept across their boards to the bathroom.

"Dolly?" Faye called out before realizing how incredibly pointless that was. Surely she'd gone home by now anyway. How long had Faye slept? It was dark out, but that could mean the sun had just set or the sun was close to rising again.

After leaving the bathroom, Faye took her candle and crept down the stairs.

"Carrick?" she called out and received no answer. She raised her candle to the mantel clock and read the time—

ten thirty. She'd slept for six straight hours, and Carrick was up at the lighthouse already. She made a mental note that if she ever got back to 2015, she'd write a book on the cure for insomnia she'd discovered in 1921—backbreaking manual labor.

Faye took advantage of the empty house to snoop some more. Luckily Faith had been living at the lighthouse for hardly more than a week, according to Carrick, so it made sense she'd still be settling in and learning the ropes. Faye had to wonder how Faith had gotten here and why she'd chosen to flee to Carrick after receiving what must have been a brutal beating by her husband, Marshall something. Faye admired the girl for running away. That was probably a rare feat in 1921, when even the law took the side of abusive husbands. The law, the Church and society, as Carrick had said. If Faith had trusted Carrick with her life, perhaps Faye could, too.

Unfortunately, Faye found no useful clues about Faith as she poked her nose in drawers and cabinets. The single item she found of interest was a telegram addressed to Carrick.

Chief Morgan
Received news that your daughter will join you at
Seaport Station
Pleased to have additional personnel at light
Records updated
Our thanks for your service

It was signed by Beck, Sixth District Superintendent, and dated three days ago. Carrick had taken quite a risk lying to his supervisors about her. He was a good man, which made it even harder to be there. Surely a good man deserved to know the truth, but Faye couldn't bring herself to tell him. What would she tell him even if she could?

Carrick, I know I look like Faith and sound like Faith, but I'm not her...

Carrick, do you believe in reincarnation?

Carrick, have you ever seen the TV show Quantum Leap?

No, none of those would work. She had no choice but to go on playing this role until God or fate or whoever was pulling the strings sent her back where she belonged. If that ever happened. She'd tried. She'd gone out to the water last night, waded in and waited for a wave to strike her and drag her under again. It seemed as if Faith had been doing the same thing last night. But not quite. She hadn't been wading in the water; she'd been standing on the end of the pier. It was worth a try anyway.

Faye went out the front door and down the path to the pier. The moon shone so brightly that she didn't need her candle. She blew it out and left it sitting on the seawall. Careful in her bare feet, Faye made her way down to the dock and stepped onto the wooden walkway, which extended fifty feet over the water. Overhead the lighthouse flashed its beam. At her feet the ocean swished and swirled around the pier. Faye's heart beat painfully hard as she walked to the end and stood with her toes overhanging the edge. As soon as she was there, she shivered as if someone were standing next to her.

"Faith," she said. "You were here, weren't you?"

Faye looked down at the water glinting in the moonlight. Above, the stars were so numerous, the sky looked like navy blue fabric covered in thousands of polka dots.

"Why were you here?" she asked. "What were you doing? Were you committing suicide? No, I don't believe that. Why would you run away from your piece-of-shit husband but then kill yourself once you were finally somewhere safe?"

Last night Faye had waded into the shallows and accidentally dropped Will's ring into the water, but what had Faith been doing out here? It seemed to matter, although Faye didn't know why. One more mystery she had to solve.

Faye turned her back on the ocean and returned to the house. In the kitchen she found that someone, Dolly no doubt, had left dinner waiting for her under a red-and-white-checkered dishcloth. Dinner tonight had been some kind of ham casserole and creamed something. Faye picked up the fork and took a bite. Creamed squash. Not bad. Better than she'd expected, certainly. She sat down and ate every bite of her dinner, and then hunted down the last quarter of the peach pie they'd made today.

Faye took one bite of the pie and decided that maybe, just maybe, she could get used to living in 1921. Even cool from hours of sitting under a dish towel, the first bite tasted warm in her mouth. The salty crust dissolved on her tongue, and the sweetness from the sugar and the peaches set her cheeks to aching. There were no artificial ingredients. No Splenda to replace the sugar, no low-fat margarine to replace the butter. Real sugar. Real peaches. Real butter. Real everything. It didn't taste like heaven, and it wasn't an orgasm in her mouth. It tasted like pie, pure, unadulterated perfect pie.

When she'd eaten her fill, Faye washed her dishes and put them away by candlelight. She found it almost...pleasant? Maybe that was the word. Something almost pleasant to Faye about the quiet, about the candlelight, about the solitude. Faye knew she should be scared out of her mind, and part of her still was. Yet another part of her drank up the beauty and the silence like a desert succulent in a rainstorm. Was this what the first astronauts who'd visited the moon felt? Equal parts terror and tranquillity?

Faye went back upstairs to dress. Her skirt and blouse were sweat-stained and dirty from the weeding she'd done that day. She was tempted to put on clean clothes but with Dolly doing the laundry—probably by hand—Faye didn't want to add to the wash pile more than necessary. And since Faye was helping with the chores now, she didn't want to add to her own work.

"Oh, God, the chores." Faye put her hand on her forehead and groaned.

She'd forgotten to milk the stupid goat.

Well, the goat surely wouldn't mind seeing her in her underwear.

Faye stepped out the back door and into the pitch-black night with nothing but her candle to light her path to the goat pen. When was the last time she'd experienced a world without electricity? Had she ever? A couple camping trips as a child? Then it had been a novelty, something to be enjoyed for a weekend before returning to civilization. Now it was her new reality.

She hardly needed the candle to find the goats. All she had to do was follow her nose. It smelled like a petting zoo, like warm animal bodies, sweat and oats and dung. The three goats drowsed lazily in their shed, seemingly content with their lot in life. They looked up at her with their weird eyes, their horizontal pupils dilating by the light of her candle.

"Hey there, goats," Faye said. "Don't mind me. I'm just here to grope one of you against your will. I'll be gentle, I promise."

The billy goat had terrifying curved horns on his head though otherwise he seemed fairly sleepy and innocuous.

The littlest one appeared to be a female, but Faye didn't plan on looking close enough to find out. Nanny eyed her curiously before bleating so loud Faye was certain Carrick could hear it all the way up in the lighthouse. Nanny had a rope around her neck, a sort of collar, and Faye winced as she reached for it. Thankfully Nanny seemed used to being handled and didn't put up any sort of fight as Faye led her through the wooden gate to a smaller holding pen. Faye assumed that was where the milking took place as a tin bucket hung off a hook there. She found a three-legged stool, secured Nanny to a post and put the bucket on the hay-strewn floor.

Faye sighed. "I have no idea what I'm doing."

Nanny bleated again. It didn't sound like a vote of confidence.

"Maybe I should get you drunk first," Faye said. "Maybe I should get myself drunk first."

"I might have some bourbon around here somewhere."

Faye started and turned around. Carrick stood in the doorway of the pen. It appeared he was trying very hard not to laugh at her.

"Where'd you come from?" she asked.

"Up. I was on the walk and saw you leave the house. Thought you might need some company."

"You said you have bourbon?"

"Don't tell," he said. "Want some?"

"Sure," she said. Carrick ran his hand along the inside of an unused feeding trough and pulled out a flask.

He handed it to her. Faye eyed it before unscrewing the cap and taking a sip. It hit her right between the eyes and she coughed.

"Good stuff," she said, handing him back the flask. "Where'd you get it? Hartwell?"

"Hartwell?"

"Dolly said he's a bootlegger. That's why she's scared of him."

"Makes sense. I found this in the house after the Landrys moved out." Carrick took a sip and then another before hiding the flask in the trough under some old hay. "But you didn't hear that from me."

"I didn't hear a thing," she said. Nanny butted Faye's leg with her head. "I am not drunk enough for this."

"Would you like some help?" Carrick said.

"Yes, please."

Carrick chuckled softly, shook his head.

"As I live and breathe, I never thought I'd be teaching a girl in her underthings how to milk a goat. Where's the bucket?"

"Here," Faye said, handing him the bucket. "And it's hot out. Why should I wear all my clothes when no one but you can see me and it's summer in South Carolina?"

"There's a good answer for that."

"What is it?"

"Put your clothes on and maybe I'll remember."

Faye rolled her eyes, laughed back and in her laughter realized she forgot for a split second he wasn't Will. Only Will had ever made her laugh so easily. Only Will had ever made her so comfortable with herself. Only Will knew how to tease her so that she felt better about herself, not worse. A rare gift, and it seemed Carrick had that gift, too.

"Ahem. The goat?"

"Right. Where's the bucket?"

"In your hands," she said.

"Right," he said. "Come on."

"Where are we going?"

"We have to wash the bucket."

"That's probably a good idea," Faye said. She followed him into the house and watched him pour bleach into the bucket and swish it around. It smelled like a swimming pool but she supposed that was better than contracting some sort of hard-core 1921 bacterial infection.

"Hands," Carrick said. She put her hands over the sink, and Carrick rinsed them with chlorinated water. At least in 1921 they knew about bacteria and sanitation. Better than trying to survive in 1821.

"Feels like I'm scrubbing in for surgery," Faye said.

"Surgery?"

"Oh, you know. Doctors have to scrub their hands and arms before performing surgery. So I hear," she said hastily.

"Ah, well, I'm cautious as a rule. My sister died of tainted milk. Killed her and her baby."

"I'm sorry," Faye said. "That's so awful."

"I hadn't seen her in years, but it still hurt to hear."

"You have any other family?"

He shook his head. "Not anymore. Nothing closer than a cousin or two out there somewhere. Mam died so young, and Dad, he never remarried."

"That's hard. I'm sorry. And you never got married?" She cringed inwardly. Surely Faith would know something like that. She shouldn't ask so many questions. But how would she survive here if she didn't?

"I'd planned on marrying Violet, but you know how it was. The flu took down more nurses than anybody in '18."

Flu. 1918. Faye racked her brain. That was the year of the Spanish flu pandemic, wasn't it? Of course a flu pandemic would target nurses. It sounded as if Carrick had lost as many people he loved as Faye had. Even more. Job, Father Pat had said. The man who lost everything. And yet, unlike Job, Carrick still seemed to have kept his head up.

"It's very hard to lose someone you love. I know how hard."

"I don't know if it was love, really," Carrick said. "But we got along well enough."

Carrick picked up a dish towel and wiped her hands with it. She let him do it even though she could have done it herself.

"Did you love him? Marshall?"

"I married him," she said. "Maybe I did at one point."

"You know it was your mother that wanted the match." Another clue.

"No," Faye said. "I didn't love him. But I loved someone else once, before him. And I lost him. And I lost myself when I lost him. And when you're lost like I was, lost at sea, it felt like…"

"Any port in a storm?" Carrick asked, smiling.

She nodded, tears in her eyes.

"Any port in a storm," she said.

"You'll be safe in this harbor," Carrick said, nodding around him. "Safe from him."

"He won't look for me here?" Faye asked.

"He might," Carrick said. "But it's me he'll find. It's me he'll find, and he'll wish he never looked."

Faye kissed him on the cheek. She hadn't meant to but she did it.

"Thank you," she said. "You make me almost happy I had to come here."

"Then I have a job to do."

"What's the job?"

"To take the *almost* out of that sentence."

She smiled at him. "You're not going to threaten to put a penny in a jar now, are you?"

Carrick shoved his hands into his pockets, then pulled them out.

"I'm out," he said.

Faye laughed. Carrick cocked his head, indicating she should follow him. They went back out to the little barn, Carrick holding the bucket in one hand and the kerosene lantern in the other.

In the barn, Carrick hung the lantern from the ceiling, put oats into a bucket and put Nanny onto some kind of feeding stand with a bar to hold her in place.

"It looks a guillotine," Faye said.

"You have quite an imagination," Carrick said, adjusting the wooden yoke over Nanny's neck.

"I'm sorry."

"Don't be. It's good to hear you getting your spirit back."

"I lost my spirit?"

"You've barely said ten words since you came here. Not until last night."

"I didn't mean to be rude," Faye said. "I was just…" What could she say? How could she explain herself?

"You don't have to apologize. I know shell shock when I see it."

"Shell shock," she repeated. It was what they'd once called post-traumatic stress disorder. Depression and anxiety, coupled with flashbacks, an intense startle reflex—something war veterans and abused women had in common. "That's a good way to describe it."

Carrick looked away. "Ah, well, Dad used to knock Mam

around so hard she'd forget her own name for days at a time. I still regret she died before I was big enough to kill him for her."

"Carrick..." Faye wanted nothing more than to reach for him, hold him. Carrick seemed to regret sharing so much. He looked at her, smiled.

"You ready to try this? Nanny's about to bust."

Faye exhaled heavily. "I'll try. But I feel sort of strange about this. I mean, Nanny and I, we barely know each other."

"She's a hussy," Carrick said. "She and Billy aren't even married."

"What a scandal," Faye said as she sat carefully on the little three-legged stool. "And now their baby is illegitimate."

"A stain on the family name."

"Carrick. What am I doing?" Faye asked.

"Hands on the teats."

"Both of them?"

"Both hands, both teats."

Faye cringed as she wrapped her fingers around the goat's udders. "This is so weird," she said, wincing. "Do I pull?"

"No pulling ever. Squeeze. Keep your first finger and your thumb right at the top. Don't move them. Squeeze down one finger at a time, but fast."

"That...makes no sense."

"Here. Give me your hand."

Faye reluctantly held out her hand to him. The more he touched her, the more she liked it. The more she liked it, the more she wanted him to touch her. Gently, he gripped her first and middle fingers in his right hand and squeezed.

"Like that," he said. "Feel it?"

"I think so."

"Try it. And hurry. She's going to run out of oats soon."

"What happens then?"

"Ever been kicked by a goat?"

"No."

"I don't recommend the experience."

Faye extracted her fingers from Carrick's hand and gripped Nanny's swollen teats again. She bit her lip, closed one eye and squeezed like Carrick had instructed. A tiny stream of white came out and sprayed the inside of the bucket.

"It worked!" Faye said, grinning up at Carrick.

"Good," he said, grinning proudly. "Do it again."

She did it again. It happened again. There was now approximately one tablespoon of milk in the bucket. Again she squeezed. More milk. And again. It was like squeezing a tube of toothpaste, sort of, and she almost said that aloud, except she wasn't sure if toothpaste existed yet.

"So I just keep doing this until she's empty?" Faye asked, still squeezing. She found a rhythm that seemed to work, and Nanny wasn't complaining yet.

"Until very little's coming out."

"I think we're there," Faye said. She squeezed and a few drops trickled into the bucket. "What now?"

"Well...you sort of have to rub them."

"Rub them?"

Carrick nodded, looking sheepish. "It helps keep them from getting sore."

"We wouldn't want sore nipples, would we, Nanny?" Faye said. "I've had them myself, and they're no day at the beach."

Carrick snorted a laugh.

"You're blushing," Faye said to him.

"Not used to ladies talking about their..."

"Nipples?" Faye asked as she gave Nanny the rubdown all ladies deserved.

"Those."

"Well," Faye said. "I was married."

"Are married," he said.

"Can we pretend I'm not?" She carefully picked up the bucket of milk and moved it far away from Nanny's feet.

"That's what we're trying to do," he said as he freed Nanny from the milking stand and put her back in her pen with her live-in lover and their bastard goat baby.

"You keep reminding me I'm married."

"No," Carrick said, shaking his head. "I keep reminding *me* you're married."

She looked at him, a long look, a look he tried to avoid by averting his eyes and watching Nanny make a bed of her straw.

"Tell me something," Faye said. "Tell me about the day you and I met."

"You were there."

"I know what I remember. But tell me what you remember."

The littlest goat wandered up to the gate and butted Carrick's palm with his head. Carrick scratched behind his ears, tugged his chin scruff.

"Hey there, Gruff," Carrick said. "Go back to sleep."

"Carrick, tell me," Faye said. "Please?"

He smiled to himself, a sad sort of smile.

"We were fools, me and Marsh," Carrick said. "He was the man who ran the ship, and I was the man who kept the ship running. We were close as brothers during the war. I trusted him with my life. I trusted him...with a lot. It didn't matter then we were from different worlds. Then the war ended."

"And it mattered."

"It mattered."

"He had money. Your family didn't."

"Not a red cent. I don't know why Marsh tried to stay friends. I didn't expect it of him. Maybe he just wanted to show off, stir up trouble. He asked me to visit him in his big place in Boston. I had a shift off from working the light and went to see him at the 'Old House,' and it was a house I expected to find. That was no house. That was a palace. I felt like a damn fool standing at the front door. Even the girl who opened the door wanted me to go around back till Marsh saw it was me. Then it was all right. He was happy enough to see me I could forget I didn't belong in his world. He brought me into his house, gave me a drink, the finest cigar I ever smoked."

"What day was it?" she asked. "Do you remember the date?"

"Never forget it. First day of summer in '19.

"I asked Marsh why he wanted to see me. 'To gloat, Morgan,' he said. 'I'm getting married.' Then he told me about you."

"What did he say?"

"It wouldn't be right to repeat all of it, but needless to say he was happy you'd said yes to his proposal. I gave him hell for marrying a girl half his age. Here he was, going on forty and marrying a girl of eighteen. He said anybody who ever said money can't buy happiness never had any of either. Your family needed the money, he said. He needed the young wife. And then he asked if I wanted to meet you.

I said I had to meet this girl who he'd wanted to give his heart to. Marsh said…"

"What did he say? Tell me."

"He said…" Carrick looked upward as if asking God for forgiveness. "He said you didn't do a damn thing for his heart, but it wasn't his heart he was going to give you. Sorry."

"Very classy," Faye said. "I married a prince among men."

"I thought it was just bragging. Marsh did that, and God knows sailors ain't known for sweet talk."

"That was the day we met?" Faye asked.

Carrick shrugged. "You were at the house. Do you remember? You and your mother. She took one look at me, and I thought she'd call the coppers. I should have worn my uniform."

"She was always a bit of a snob," Faye said, playing along.

"Ah, it was how she was raised. Except you weren't."

"I'm glad I wasn't a snob to you."

She stood at his side and reached into the pen. The little goat butted his head into her palm like he had with Carrick, and she scratched behind his floppy dark ears.

"No…you were anything but. Your mother didn't want me near you, and I'm sure Marsh wouldn't have taken me out to meet you personally, but to spite her, he did it. He dragged me out to the back garden, and there you were, on that swing in your white dress and your straw hat with the ribbon on it flying behind you, and I thought I'd walked into a picture postcard. You must not have heard us coming down the path because you kept swinging, high…higher. And Marsh said something to me about how he'd curb your hoyden's ways when you were his wife, and I said to him…

I said, 'Why? Why marry a girl with spirit and then snuff out her spirit?'"

"Because he wasn't marrying me for my spirit."

Carrick didn't seem to hear her. He looked off, out the open window at the night sky.

"You were so pretty. I've never seen a finer sight in my life, before or since. Not even land after a year at sea was a better sight than you in your dress with your white ribbons and that smile on your face and your eyes closed, dreaming whatever girls dream about. Marsh called your name, and you opened your eyes and saw us. And you remember what you did?"

"Of course," Faye said, bluffing.

"You jumped out of the swing and landed right in front of me. Then you stumbled, and I caught you."

"How could I ever forget?" Faye said.

"And you said, 'My hero.'" Carrick turned his head, met her eyes. "Of course, Marsh didn't appreciate that."

"I don't imagine he did."

"I still remember you giggling—that giggle filled the garden—after he sent you running into the house. I wasn't worried then. I saw you had a spirit not even he could break. But he tried, didn't he?"

Carrick touched her bruised eye with the gentlest of touches.

"He tried," Faye whispered.

"He couldn't do it."

"Because you took me in."

"It took more than spirit to run away from him than it took to let you in when you got here."

"I jumped," Faye said, covering his hand with hers. "You caught me. My hero."

Carrick kissed her. She'd known he would, and she'd known she wouldn't stop him when he did. They stood in the cone of light given off by the kerosene lantern as Carrick pressed his lips to hers and she pressed her body to his. They fit together, the two of them, as well as she and Will had. But Carrick wasn't Will and she wasn't Faith. She told herself that even as she parted her lips to let his tongue touch hers. She tasted something both familiar and unfamiliar. She'd never tasted it on a man's tongue before, but she knew what it was immediately. She pulled back and glared at him with narrowed eyes.

"What?" he asked.

"You've been smoking."

"So?"

"It's terrible for you."

"It is?"

"Yes. Absolutely awful for your health."

"It helps keep me up at night."

"I'll keep you up at night." She wrapped her arms around his neck and pressed her whole body into his. She traced a path down his back, following the line of his suspenders to the center of his back and down to his hips. His pants were loose—hence the suspenders, no doubt—and it was nothing to slip her hands under his T-shirt and caress the small of his back and the curve of his hip bone. They'd been two of her favorite spots on Will's body, and unsurprisingly she enjoyed them just as much on Carrick's. With her fingertips, she lightly scored the soft skin on his hard stomach, and Carrick inhaled sharply, his face scrunched up tight.

"Carrick."

"Stop," he said. Faye stepped back, held her hands up in surrender.

"We did it again," she said.

"We did," he said. He walked over to the railing, gripped it, hung his head down and breathed. "You make me forget things."

"Forget what? That I'm married? You can forget that if you want. I'm going to."

"Forget that I'm trying to keep you safe. And this isn't helping. If he finds out you're here and you've been with me..."

"But I haven't been with you. Not yet," Faye reminded him.

"Oh, good point," he said. "If we're going to pay for the crime, might as well commit it first." He reached for her then, pulled her to him. He pressed his hand into the small of her back, bringing her body even closer to his, chest to chest and hip to hip. Still, it wasn't enough for Faye. She craved more. She wrapped her arms around his neck, anchoring herself against him. Carrick groaned against her lips—a sound equal parts desire and frustration.

"Don't stop," she said.

"We have to." Yet he didn't stop. He kept kissing, kept grasping at her waist and her back and her neck with those huge hands of his. He wore only his work pants and a sweat-stained white T-shirt and she couldn't get enough of his arms around her—strong as iron still warm from the forge. She would know if there was Will in his heart by the way he made love to her. Will was forever ready with a smile, laid-back, a laughing soul, until he got her into bed or onto the floor or against the wall or wherever he could have her when he wanted her.

"Make love to me," she said into Carrick's ear. Carrick pushed her against the wooden wall of the barn. Not hard.

Not hard enough to hurt her, not a bit, but purposefully. And making love to her was the purpose.

Carrick pulled back as she gasped from the force of his passion.

"Stop me," he said, and he said it forcefully. He meant it. Only a word from her would stop him, and nothing else in the world.

She shook her head. They were both already shining with sweat in the little barn, sticky with it and glistening and smelling of the heat and the sweat and the warm bodies of animals.

Faye's back was against the bare wood, and Carrick had both his hands against the wall on either side of her head, boxing her in, though no parts of them touched.

"It's a sin to take another man's wife," he said with his eyes closed. "I'm not your husband."

"Does a man like that deserve a wife?"

"No."

"Then why care about betraying him?"

"Not him. Me."

That broke her heart. Here was a man of true faith, and he would flog himself for days to come for sleeping with a married woman. But the need to know him, to know him like she knew Will, was greater than her compassion. She reached for the top button of his work trousers, unbuttoned it and slid her hand inside.

"Good God" was all he said when she wrapped her fingers around him. The one word, a prayer, and then he shuddered like he'd been stabbed in the heart. His chin went up and she saw his throat like a tower and his strong Adam's apple move as he swallowed.

"Please," Faye said.

"A girl like you should never have to beg," he said.

"Then don't make me."

Carrick's mouth crashed down onto hers again, the kiss a hundred times hotter and hungrier than before. He slid his hands under her slip, cupped her bottom and pushed her against him so she could feel him against her legs when she sought him with her hand. His mouth massaged her neck and his hot breath warmed every part of her that wasn't already burning. This was more than the simple warmth of two bodies twined together. She licked a drop of fresh sweat off Carrick's shoulder, and the sound that came from his throat could have melted iron from the sheer burning heat of it.

"Carrick," she said, getting used to his name on her tongue. He started to push her underwear down her hips. As soon as they were at her thighs, he cupped her between her legs, seeking her heat as she'd sought his. His fingers slid inside, and she inhaled so hard she forgot to exhale until dizziness made her faint, and she breathed again out of sheer self-preservation.

She closed her eyes and pushed her hips into his hand. Will had this way of touching her with his fingers, of moving his hand inside her that made her lose her mind. No lover before had touched her like that, no lover since; yet here Carrick was, touching her exactly the way Will had, the way that made her wild, the way that made her remember she was a woman and forget she was a widow, and all at once. She cried out as she came in his arms, shuddering until he had to push her into the wall to keep her standing.

"Carrick, I…"

"Quiet," he said.

"But—"

"Shh…"

She slowly opened her eyes. He'd stopped touching her but she still stood framed between his arms. He looked alert, nervous. She didn't know why. Then she heard something, something she'd almost forgotten existed in this time and on this lonely island.

A car door shut.

An engine rattled to life.

Wheels and axles turned.

These were all unmistakable sounds.

"Stay here," Carrick said, his voice almost a whisper. He left her in the barn with the lantern and went out into the dark, unarmed.

"No..." Faye called out, her voice breaking into a sob. Anyone out there shouldn't be, and they could hurt him, kill him. She grabbed the lantern, raced for the door and found Carrick standing at the edge of the garden mere feet away from the dark oak forest.

"Are you all right?" She threw herself into his arms.

"All right," he said, patting her back. "Car's gone. It'll be halfway to the bridge by now."

"There's a road on the island?"

"You would know," he said. "You were on it."

Right. Of course. Someone had to have driven her here. It was either that or a boat that had brought her to the island.

"Sorry. I don't know what I'm saying. I was so scared."

"I'm not too pleased about it myself."

"You don't know who it was?"

"Could be someone from the Maddox family. They own the island. But they always stop by and tell us when they're coming so we can stay out of their way when they're hunting." He narrowed his eyes to peer at the edge of the forest. The trees were so dense Faye couldn't tell where one began and the other ended. It seemed to be all one tree with a thousand trunks and a billion branches and infinite roots.

"Who else would it be?" Faye asked.

Carrick looked at her, and she saw fear in his eyes.

"Your husband."

14

Husband? Faye didn't have a husband. No, Faye didn't. But Faith did.

"Marshall," she said.

"Come on," Carrick said, tugging her gently by the arm. "I'm taking you back to the house and putting you in bed, and I'm going to sit outside your door all night long."

"What about the lighthouse? Don't you have to man it or something?"

"I'll go up when it's time to turn the clockwork."

"Carrick. Stop."

He stopped on the back porch, looked at her by the lantern light.

"You can't protect me every second of every hour of every day," Faye said.

"Who says?"

"The car is gone. If it was my…Marshall, do you really think he'd leave without me?"

Carrick took a thoughtful pause. "No. If it was him, he would have tried to kill me so he could take you back. He wouldn't have driven away. Especially not if he knew what we were doing in there."

"You know, we didn't get to finish what we started back there."

"No, and we'll call that a blessing," he said, opening the back door for her. She went inside reluctantly. Carrick followed her to her bedroom and no farther. He stayed on the other side of the threshold, holding the lantern.

"Are you angry at me?" Faye asked when she saw his grim and stone-faced expression.

"Why in God's name would I be angry at you?"

"For what happened back in the barn."

"I'd be near as worthless as your husband if being inside a beautiful woman made me angry." Carrick's fists were clenched, and in the lantern light she saw the corded muscles flexing in his arms. Anger, yes. But not at her. At himself?

"I know you're trying to be true to your faith, and I'm not helping," she said.

"Nobody is to blame but me. I got carried away and carried you with me."

"I like it when you carry me."

"Faith. Love, please…" Carrick rested his forehead against the door frame, sighed and looked at her.

"I'm sorry," she said and truly meant it this time. "I know we shouldn't. I know it's wrong for a lot of reasons. It's just…"

"What, lass?"

"You remind me so much of someone I loved a long time…well, in a different time."

"He must have been a fool."

"Why do you say that?"

"Because you loved him, and any man you loved ought to be by your side right now."

Faye smiled sadly. "He died."

Carrick didn't look impressed by that.

"Nothing in the world more foolish than dying when a girl like you is in love with him."

Faye laughed softly and touched Carrick's face. He let her. She knew nothing more would happen tonight. It was safe to touch him. She stroked his beard. It was a well-groomed beard, not much more than thick stubble, and she could feel the contours of his face through it. The strong jaw, strong chin...just like Will's beautiful face.

"He didn't have a beard," Faye said. "Once, he did, but only for a couple weeks. I told him it was the dumbest thing I'd ever heard of, but he swore it brought him luck."

"It worked," Carrick said.

"Did it?"

"You loved him, right?"

"More than life," she said.

"Then it worked."

"Carrick..." Faye blinked back her tears. There was only one other man she'd ever known who'd said such sweet things to her, and he wouldn't be born for another sixty-six years.

"I'm trying to protect you," he said. "What happened in the barn... If I got you with child..."

"I couldn't stay here, could I?" Faye asked. Of course she couldn't. An unmarried woman pregnant in 1921? She'd have to go away, far away, to protect herself and Carrick. If not, the scandal would be enormous. She would be a pariah. And Carrick would never forgive himself for doing that to her.

"I should go up," he said. "I am going up. Right now." His gaze shifted and it seemed he wanted to say something more, but stopped himself. "Good night."

Faye had so much to say to him, so much to ask him, and yet all she could do was what Faith would do in her place, and that was say, "Good night."

Carrick gave her another look without speaking, then turned and walked away down the hall. Even his walk was like Will's walk, with that loose-in-the-hip rolling amble. Carrick might be a lighthouse keeper, but he walked like a baseball player. She almost called him back to her. Old habits died hard. Faye shut the door at last and crawled into bed. She curled up into a ball and whispered into the deep, dark quiet.

"Will, baby? He looks like you and he talks like you and he touches me like you. Is he you? Or am I just crazy?"

Of course there was no reply because Will was dead. Except this was 1921 and Will wasn't dead in 1921. Will wasn't dead in 1921 because Will hadn't even been born yet. Maybe that was why she couldn't hear his voice in her head the way she could sometimes back in 2015. Or maybe she didn't need to hear his voice in her head because she had Carrick's.

She rolled onto her back and stared out the window at the beam of the lighthouse. She counted the seconds—one, and the light went off. Two. Three. Four. Five. Six.

By seven she was asleep.

Faye dreamed, and in her dream she wore a black dress and a black veil over her face. Widow's weeds, but she wasn't a widow.

Though in the dream she wanted to be.

Faye crept through a long hall of an old house, a cavernous house, a house like a hotel with brass-and-crystal chandeliers hanging from the polished-mahogany ceiling. The floors were marble under her feet. The furniture fine and fancy. The bars on the windows were iron, like the heart of the man who owned the mansion, like the heart of the man who owned her. This was a house of wealth and privilege, and in the dream Faye had to escape it or she would die there.

And it wasn't the dying part she minded so much anymore, but she refused to die here. She would not die *here*.

She walked past a room and saw a man facing a window, and outside the window was a garden, and in the garden hung a swing. She couldn't see the man's face, but in the dream she didn't want to. In her dream she never wanted to see that man's face again.

Faye knew she had to walk past the room that held the man, and that if he caught her, he would kill her, and if he didn't, she could be free.

She took a step. *One.* The floor did not creak. She took another step. *Two.* And the floor did not creak. She took yet another step. *Three.* And the floor did not creak. By the fourth step she had passed the open doorway without the man seeing her. Now she had to make it to the street.

The urge to run was powerful, but in the dream Faye walked, counting her steps along with her breaths. Seven to the door. Seven to freedom.

One. Two. Three. Halfway there.

Every step hurt because her body was injured, outside and in. In her head echoed the furious voice of a furious man.

Did you honestly think I married you for love? Did you honestly think I would have married a stupid little girl like you for anything other than this? You have one purpose in this marriage, and it isn't spending my money.

And Faye felt hands on her thighs, wrenching them apart,

and a mouth on her neck, and then pain cutting her up the middle like the blade of a burning knife.

Four. Five. Six.

Seven. She'd made it. She opened the door slowly, cracking it and then opening it wide enough to slip out the servants' entrance. Behind a stone bench, she picked up a faded carpetbag one of the maids had left behind when she'd gotten married. In it were old clothes she'd pretended to donate to the Lady's Aid Society months ago. Even the widow's weeds she wore were borrowed, taken from her mother's closet after her funeral. Her mother wouldn't be needing them anymore, and it was good she wasn't alive to suffer her daughter's disappearance. She had a choice—she could disappear of her own volition or wait for her husband to make her disappear. So she would vanish into thin air. She didn't want anyone thinking she'd run away. A runaway could be found, but a girl who vanished, simply vanished, couldn't be followed. No woman would run away from home in broad daylight on a Thursday afternoon while everyone was in the house, including her husband in his office with the door wide-open, would she? But she would.

Once outside she walked straight to the street and turned a corner, then another. Old-fashioned cars drove past—Touring cars and Model Ts and even horse carts. In the dream Faye turned and waved her hand. A black four-door Oldsmobile with white doors pulled up alongside.

"Where to?" the driver said.

"The train station, please."

She got into the backseat of the cab, and the driver drove.

"You a widow?" the man said, looking back at her, eyeing her veil, which she'd pulled all the way down over her

face so that she viewed the entire world through a spiderweb of black silk.

"I am," she said, smiling behind the veil.

"Sorry for your loss, ma'am."

The smile widened.

"I'm not."

Faye awoke in a panic, pressed her palm to her sweating
forehead. Her other hand she pressed over her thundering
heart.

"Oh, God," Faye said, rolling into a ball. "Faith…"

She'd dreamed of Faith. Or maybe it was Faith's dream
she'd had. No wonder that girl had run from her husband.
He'd beaten her because she'd refused to have sex with him.
He'd not only beaten her but raped her. Faye pushed the
blanket off her and looked at her legs. Finger bruises almost
faded, but in the morning light she could still make them
out. Faith had fled a wealthy and dangerous man and had
drowned a week and a half later. And Marshall, whoever
he was, had gotten away with his crimes against his young
wife. The unfairness brought tears to Faye's eyes. Faith had
made it all the way here, made it to this sanctuary far, far
away from her monster of a husband. And Carrick could
have loved her, could have cared for her and given her a
new life with a new love. But she'd died a senseless, stupid
death before that new life could begin.

And someone out there had decided to bring Faye back
here to take Faith's place. For what purpose? Faye didn't
know, but she knew this much on her second morning when
she awoke in 1921—she would find out. For Faith's sake
and for hers.

When Faye's heart finally calmed, she sat up and looked
out the window. The sky over the ocean was gray and pink,

and the very first long yellow seams of dawn were starting to peek through the cracks in the clouds. Faye sat, mesmerized, as she watched the sun rise slowly over the horizon, changing the colors of the Atlantic Ocean from its nighttime black to a blazing red and morning blue. Faye wished more than anything she had her camera. She'd never seen such a sunrise. Was Carrick up in the lighthouse, watching the same sunrise? She saw the lighthouse flash once more before going dark again and staying dark this time. Carrick's workday was over. Hers was beginning.

Faye rose from bed and went to the dresser to find clothes for the day. She opened a drawer and saw the clothes Dolly had so neatly pressed, folded and put away were now in mad disarray. Faye opened the second drawer and found those clothes were also tossed about all over the place. By the light of morning Faye saw things she hadn't seen the night before in the near dark. The rug under the bed was wrinkled like it had been pushed a few inches away from the wall. She opened the drawer in the nightstand and found it, too, had been rifled through.

Faye ran and found Carrick leaving the lighthouse.

"Someone was in my room last night," she said.

Carrick's eyes went wide. He looked at her, pushed past her and went straight up the stairs to her room.

"They went through all the dresser drawers. And the bed's been moved." She pointed at the rug.

"Stand back," he said. "I'll check under the bed."

Faye pulled the nightstand away.

"Can I help—"

Carrick hefted the bed up by the base of the footboard and shifted it three feet over before Faye could say another word.

"You are seriously strong," she said.

He shrugged. "Not too many ninety-pound weaklings survive fourteen years in the navy."

Faye watched from the end of the bed as Carrick ran his hand along the wall, the floor and the floorboards. He knocked on the floor a few times, dull thuds like one would expect. Then he knocked again a few inches over and the sound was sharper, hollow.

"Here we go," he said. He pressed on the board here and there, and one end lifted an inch. Carrick pressed again and pulled the board all the way up.

"See anything?" she asked.

"I see room for stashing something. But nothing's down here."

"He must have gotten whatever it was. Money maybe?" she asked.

"Maybe. Not enough room to hide much else down here."

"Why would he go through my drawers if he wanted whatever was in that hidey-hole?"

He put the board back in place and stood up.

"Maybe he didn't find what he was looking for and went digging for anything he could find?" Carrick said, shaking his head.

"When Hartwell was here yesterday he seemed to want to come upstairs pretty badly. And did you see the way he was looking through the books?"

"You think Hartwell ransacked your room just to find a book?" Carrick asked. "Doesn't seem like much of a bookworm to me."

"Then what do you think he was looking for?"

"I don't know," he said. Then something seemed to occur to him, something that scared him. "If it was Hartwell... You don't have anything with your real name on it, do you?"

Was Faith not Faith's real name? Made sense. Who would go into hiding and keep their real name?

"Not that I know of." Maybe she did have something with Faith's real name on it. How would she know if she didn't know her own name? "Why?"

"Hartwell said he was in Boston a week ago."

"So?"

Carrick stared at her. Faye understood immediately. Carrick had been stationed at the Boston Light. Carrick had visited Marshall while he was living in Boston. That meant Faith also lived in Boston.

"Boston," she said. "You think…"

"I don't know what to think."

Carrick sighed, rubbed the back of his neck.

"Hartwell asked a lot of questions yesterday about us being alone out here," Faye said. "Then somebody tore through my drawers and under the bed while we were in the barn. If someone was after me, that someone could have taken me while you were up at the light and I was dead to the world with the door unlocked, right?" At least, that was what Faye wanted to believe.

"That's true," Carrick said. "And Hartwell didn't seem too happy to find out that the Landrys had been transferred eight hundred miles away while he was up north. Jack Landry had four little ones and a fifth on the way when they were sent down to the Keys."

"I'd start bootlegging, too, if I had five kids," Faye said. "Or stashing money or alcohol for a bootlegger."

"I'm sure you're right," Carrick said. "But I'd feel a lot better if we changed rooms. Just in case."

"Or I could stay up with you tonight, at the lighthouse."

Carrick glared at her, eyebrow arched. "I don't think that's a good idea."

"Why not?" she demanded.

"I recall, against my better judgment, mind you, what happened last night."

"What happened last night could happen again up there or down here. Every night we're alone together on an island, Carrick."

"Yes, but you sleep at night and I work at night. If you work at night while I'm working at night...we might not get much work done."

"Would you rather I stay down here at night alone?"

"No."

"So I can come up to the light tonight?"

"No."

"Carrick."

"Fine. You can come up tonight. Bring a blanket and a pillow, and you can sleep up there while I'm working if you get tired."

"Or I can help you."

"You want to help me man the light?"

"I want to do something," Faye said. Work had always given her happiness and purpose to her days. She needed that if she was going to survive this time. "Back in my old life I used to take pictures."

"Pictures?"

"I had a camera."

"I had no idea. You took photographs?"

"I did. I was pretty good. And I miss it. I need something to do other than housework. Even Dolly sews clothes in her free time and decorates. I'm sure she helps with the lighthouse, too."

"Dolly? Help at the lighthouse?" Carrick laughed. "She's so scared of heights, when I offered to show her the light you would have thought I'd asked her to kiss a snake."

"Okay, then… How about me? I could be assistant keeper. Hartwell said the lighthouse people wanted to send you one."

"I don't know about this."

"Didn't I hear you tell Hartwell that women help with lighthouses all up and down the coast?"

"Well, yes. I was only trying to shut him up about getting an assistant. Fewer people out here with you here the better."

"But I am here. So why can't I help?"

"Those are women. You're… You know."

"What?"

"A lady."

Faye pursed her lips and stared at him. "Last night I was milking a goat in my underwear and drinking bourbon from a dirty flask hidden in a feed trough. I am not a lady. I am a grown woman."

"You're a lady in my eyes. But I suppose you can be the lady of the lighthouse."

"The Lady of the Lighthouse?" Faye would have laughed, but she didn't want to explain why she was laughing to him. "It has a nice ring to it."

"All right, lady. You talked me into it." Carrick stuffed his hands into his pockets and nodded. "I'm not promising an official position or anything, but as soon as the sun sets you can come up to the watch room."

"Should I bring anything besides a blanket?"

"You should."

"What?"

"Well," Carrick said. "Considering what almost happened last night, a chastity belt."

"Trust me, this underwear I have on is bad enough."

Carrick sighed. "I meant for me."

He left her alone, and Faye rolled back onto the bed and stared at the ceiling. What the hell was she doing? She'd asked Carrick to show her how the lighthouse works. Why? Was she that bored already? No. Since waking up in this time, she'd been shocked, terrified, horrified, mesmerized, furious, fearful, attracted and aroused, but never once bored. That she'd seized on the idea of working with Carrick, being his assistant keeper, meant one of two very scary possibilities.

Either Faye knew she would never see 2015 again.

Or she was already falling in love with Carrick.

Or both.

15

Faye survived another day in 1921.

Barely.

She and Dolly tackled the rugs that day—taking them out of the house, throwing them over the clothesline and beating them with brooms. Halfway through the process Faye had the most horrifying epiphany of her life. This was why women in the old days didn't have day jobs. Because keeping house was literally a full-time job. No electric vacuums meant women had to remove the rugs from the floor to clean them manually. No air filtration systems kept the dust out. And the oil lamps spread soot everywhere they burned. She'd have given her right arm for her Swiffer.

By two in the afternoon, Faye was so sick from the dust and the heat she waded right into the ocean fully clothed and vomited. Dangerous or not, she was too hot and miserable to care. She even sank into the water and let it wash over her like a penitent sinner at her baptism. Dolly watched her from the beach in fascinated horror as Faye floated in the ocean fully clothed for a few minutes, then stood up, and waded back to the beach. She went into the house, stripped completely naked and went to sleep.

When she woke up, it was dark again. She must have slept for six or seven hours, at least. Faye dressed by the light of her little kerosene lantern. The overhead gas lamps were almost useless when she needed light for only a minute or two. They took nearly ten minutes to light up and another ten minutes to go off. Faye kind of liked living by the sun and the moon and the little oil lamp. Everything was prettier by lamplight, softer, more mysterious. Maybe that was why people romanticized the past so much. It simply had better lighting.

After Faye found her shoes, she walked out to the lighthouse just as the evening turned into night. The lighthouse door opened easily, much more easily than it had two nights ago. Two nights ago? It felt like years since that evening she'd driven from the Church Street house to Bride Island and ended up here, compelled by something and for reasons unknown. Time, before so concrete, had turned to sand and slipped through her fingers. The harder she tried to hold on to it, the more fell through her hands. Maybe she should just let it all go.

"Hello?" Faye called, and heard her voice echo off the stone walls.

"Ahoy down there!" came the echoing answer. "Come up if you dare."

"I dare," Faye shouted in reply and started quickly up the winding iron stairs. Halfway up the steps, Faye slowed her pace considerably when her screaming thighs reminded her she wasn't running a race.

"Okay, maybe I don't dare," she yelled up.

"Buck up, sailor," Carrick called back. "I used to climb more steps than that carrying a fifty-pound can of kerosene."

"Did you walk two miles to school every day and back?" she yelled.

"Four miles."

Faye shook her head, sighed. "Never trade hardship stories with a man born in 1886," she mumbled to herself as she started her climbing again.

Carrick opened the hatch to let her in, smiling at her as she gulped air and fanned herself.

"That's a lot of stairs," she said, panting still. "You must have amazing quads."

"Quads?"

"Leg muscles," she said.

"Ah, they get the job done." Carrick shut the door hatch behind her and locked it.

She'd been so eager to see Carrick again, she'd raced right up the lighthouse. Now with him, she had no idea what to say. She felt as awkward as a schoolgirl with a crush.

She looked around. "This the watch room?" she asked. In 2015 the windows of this room had been boarded up, but they were uncovered now and looked out onto the island and the sea. Various instruments hung on wall pegs—she saw binoculars, a spyglass, plus a large, beautifully carved barometer. And in the middle of the room sat a strange box made of brass, glass and steel.

"This is it." Carrick pointed at the glass box. "And this is the clockwork."

He took her by the hand and pulled her around the box. She peered in through the glass sides and saw large metal wheels and gears clicking and turning. On the side was a large handle, a crank of sorts.

"It's really a clockwork."

"It really is," Carrick said. "Like a giant watch. You have to wind it."

"What's it for?"

"It turns the light. I have to crank it every two and a half hours or it won't rotate and the light won't flash. But we're lucky here," he said. "I heard there's a few lights where the clockwork needs cranking every half hour."

"Can't they run the clockwork with an engine or something?"

"They could, but the Bureau is in no hurry to spend the money to make that happen. It's a miracle we have the sun valve here. They're all over Europe already."

"Sun valve?"

"It's up there," he said, pointing at a shape atop the clockwork box that Faye couldn't quite make out. "It uses sunlight to turn the beacon on and off. Sunlight warms a metal plate and the plate expands. That flips the switch off in the morning. At sunset it cools and contracts and flips the switch on. Acetylene gas powers it all night. All I have to do is replace the gas cylinders and crank the clockwork."

"That's amazing," Faye said. "All that without electricity."

"It's quite something," he said, a master of understatement. As he took a small oil can and rag to the crank's handle, she studied him, trying to see something in him that wasn't Will. He dressed differently, that was for sure. Carrick had on khaki-colored work pants, a white undershirt and suspenders. Will had never worn suspenders. If he had, she would have snapped them all the time, which would have landed her in all sorts of fun trouble. Carrick's hands were different, too. Little white scars on his fingers and the backs of his hands spoke of a lifetime performing manual labor. His eyes were a darker brown than Will's and his hair a shade redder. She clung to these differences, not wanting to love the man simply because he looked like Will. Maybe Faith had loved him with all her heart and Faye felt it like a sort of muscle memory. The heart was a muscle, wasn't it? Was that why hers beat so hard around Carrick?

She watched as Carrick took a watch out of his pocket and stood at the window. He clicked a button twice, then clicked it again.

"Perfect," he said. "Runs like clockwork."

"You were timing the light?"

He nodded. "Have to. A second's delay could mean life or death to a ship out there."

"How so?" she asked.

"Every lighthouse does double duty by day or by night. The paint job is the day mark. The light pattern is—"

"The night mark," Faye said, remembering what Ty had told her.

"That's right. Ships out there know that seven seconds between flashes means Seaport Station. Hunting Island Light has a different night mark. That's how you tell us apart in the dark. You see, a light's night mark is its heartbeat. You know a man by his heart. You know a lighthouse by its beacon."

Faye smiled at him. Impossible not to. "You have a bit of poet in you," she said.

"You spend a lot of time alone with your thoughts up here. They can turn fanciful."

"I know what you mean. I think I might have had a religious experience eating Dolly's pie last night."

"No shame in that. Dolly's pies can save a man's soul."

"Count me among the saints, then," Faye said.

"My first job was on the Boston Light, and all the wickies had to cook for each other. I saved no souls and might have damned a few stomachs."

"Wickies? Is that what they call you?"

"Before they converted this light to acetylene, they ran it on kerosene. And most lights are still run on kerosene. Gotta trim the wicks every few hours."

"Sounds like a lot of work."

"It was. Fill the well, trim the wicks, clean the soot off the glass..."

"Walk up those stairs again with a fifty-pound bucket of kerosene in your hand?"

"You get used to it," he said.

Faye walked around the room, eyeing the spyglass, the other instruments. Carrick had a book open on his desk, a large leather journal he'd apparently been writing weather reports in when she came up. She read what he wrote and smiled.

Temp at first light—78. Light wind. Clear skies. Every day here is more beautiful than the last. I am a lucky man.

"You really love it here, don't you?" Faye asked.

He shrugged. "Aye, it's a good job. You want to see the lantern room?"

"I'd love to. Can I?" Two nights ago in 2015, there'd been nothing in the lantern room but empty space where a light should be. But the lens wasn't gone in 1921.

"It's right up that ladder. I'll open the hatch and you can peek in. But don't look directly into the bull's-eye of the lens. It could hurt your eyes. That light's about fifty thousand candlepower."

Carrick opened the hatch, and Faye climbed the short ladder from the watch room to the lantern room.

"Oh..." she breathed when she stuck her head inside. It

was all she could say. The entire room was alive with light. The lens glowed like a giant white flower throbbing as it bloomed. And the prisms of the lens caught stray beams like butterflies in a net and released them across the glass in a flurry of a thousand wings and a thousand colors.

The sound was nothing she'd ever heard before. Faye closed her eyes and put her hands on the floor of the lantern room, feeling the sound as she heard it. Had anyone ever created a museum for lost sounds? She'd read somewhere that kids born in the year 2000 and after would never hear the sound of a telephone dial tone. It was an aural artifact. This sound should be in that museum, the whooshing hum of a living lighthouse run on gas and clockwork gears. She heard the gears turning and clicking in the box beneath her. The sound on her palms felt like a cat's belly as it purred or Will's chest when he snored, another artifact for the museum of lost and forgotten sounds. She was listening to the last heartbeats of a dying way of life.

"Like it?" Carrick called up. He stood at the base of the ladder, his hands on the backs of her calves to steady her.

"It's beautiful..." She had to shout for him to hear her but by his smile she knew he'd heard.

"I know. Come out to the catwalk. It's easier to talk out there."

Faye came down the ladder and followed Carrick out to the catwalk. Catwalk? She liked that term so much better than widow's walk.

"It's so pretty in there I can't stand it," she said. "All those prisms. It was like standing in a kaleidoscope."

"It's not too bad out here, either," he said, turning his gaze to the sea.

"No," she said. "Not bad at all."

They stood on the ocean-side edge of the watch room gallery. The lighthouse beacon flashed and shone over their heads, illuminating the water below them. White-maned breakers crashed on the sand and rolled back down into the water, where they gathered their strength to crash again and again. The breeze was salt scented and cool at the top of the lighthouse. It lifted her hair and tickled her legs.

"Did you always want to be a wickie?" she asked, hoping it wasn't a question Faith had ever asked him.

He shook his head. "Never really occurred to me. Went into the navy at eighteen. After the war, I needed a job. They were looking for a navy man for the Boston Light, and I qualified. Right age, I could read and write, haul heavy cans of oil, keep good records and stay up all night when it was my shift. I took the job because I needed it, not because it meant anything to me but a roof over my head and steady pay."

"It seems to suit you."

"I thought it would be just another job. But then I got out to the Boston Light and met Dan Chisholm—he was principal keeper there. He shook my hand and before he let it go he said to me, 'I know you're a military man, but the war's over and this is a civilian light. We keep people alive out there, and we don't ask what flag their ship flies. Everyone deserves light, Morgan. Whatever you do, keep the light burning.' Then he let my hand go. For an ex-navy man, that was quite something to hear, but I liked the sound of it—everyone deserves light. Lord knows in the war I got sick and tired of worrying about what flag the ships around me were flying."

Carrick shrugged and flashed her a sheepish smile. "I guess that sounds fanciful to you."

Faye swallowed a hard lump in her throat.

"No. It sounds…right," she said. "It sounds like something a good man would believe."

"Chisholm is a good man."

"I meant you."

He smiled again. "I try. All any man can do is try."

"Is this what you want to do for the rest of your life? Tend a light?"

"I thought about that. Truth is, I doubt I can count on this job for the rest of my life. If I live long enough, that is. They put the sun valve in here. Next will be the engine to turn the light. Maybe in ten years, twenty, all the lights will be run on electricity. Everybody thought horses would be around forever and, lo and behold, now we have automobiles. Won't be long before lighthouses go the way of the dodo."

"Progress always wins in the end," she said.

"You can't fight time. And you shouldn't even if you could. That is a losing battle."

Faye was losing her battle with time. Or winning it. She couldn't tell yet.

"Well…I have to say you might have the nicest office in the world." She waved her arm to indicate the island, the ocean and the wide night sky above. "And no mosquitoes up here."

"The sea breeze mostly keeps them away, and you don't get them much this high up," he said. "But you do have to watch out for birds. They think the light is something else and they fly toward it, and it kills them."

"Poor birds," she said. She knew just how they felt. She looked at Carrick, who looked so much like Will that it was impossible for her not to fly toward him, even knowing she might be flying toward a false light.

Standing at Carrick's side, she marveled at the view and the silence between them. It was a companionable silence, not the silence of strangers but of friends or lovers who knew each other intimately enough that words weren't necessary when the moment spoke for itself.

Faye yawned. "Sorry," she said. "Just woke up from my nap."

"You should go down, get back to bed."

"I'm fine. I'm waking up. I've never worked so hard in my life as I've worked in the past two days. And still, Dolly did five times the work I did. And she's what? Fifteen? Sixteen?"

"Seventeen. Just turned."

"Seventeen… So much work for a girl so young."

"Everybody works," Carrick said.

"Except ladies?"

He sighed. "Even ladies," he said. "So I've been told."

"Yes, even ladies. So tell me more about the lighthouse. If I'm going to be your assistant I suppose I should know everything there is to know about it."

Carrick stared at her a good long while, stared without saying anything. He did that a lot, and it worried Faye, made her think she'd done something wrong, something Faith wouldn't have done.

"You really want to stay here with me?" Carrick asked. "I mean, for good?"

"I keep asking myself that question," Faye said.

"Got an answer yet?"

"I don't know how long I'm going to be here. But I'm here now. And while I'm here, I want to learn everything I can."

It sounded good and it sounded true. And it was true in

a way—Faye still had no idea what her purpose was back in this time, but she knew she wouldn't figure it out hiding in her room. But the real truth was—and this she would not tell Carrick—that she simply wanted to be with him. With him and near him and around him and close to him. And if he spent his nights at the top of a lighthouse, then that was where she wanted to be, too.

"All right," Carrick said. "I'll teach you what I know. We'll start at the beginning—do you know how a lighthouse works?"

"Um… I know there's a big light up there." She pointed upward. "And it shines out there." She pointed at the ocean.

"It's a start."

Carrick dropped his arms to his sides, turned around and rested his lower back against the railing. Faye matched his pose and followed his finger where it pointed high up in the air.

"Working our way from top to bottom, that pole way up there is the—"

"Lightning rod?"

"Give the lady a prize."

"What did you say?" Faye stared at Carrick.

"Nothing. Just 'give the lady a prize.' You know, since you knew it was a lightning rod."

"Sorry. I just…" Will always said that to her. *Give the lady a prize.* It was what he said when she guessed something right, when she beat him at bar trivia, when she gave him a particularly good blow job that merited more than a simple "Thank you."

"It's grounded, right?" Faye asked to cover her confusion. "The lightning rod?"

"Of course it's grounded." Carrick's brow furrowed. "At

least I think it's grounded. I hope to God it's grounded. I'll
check on that tomorrow. Moving on down—that big ball
on top is the vent."

"Very big ball," Faye said, nodding her head in solemn
agreement.

"The bigger the lighthouse, the bigger the ball."

"I'm thoroughly impressed with your big ball," she said,
and from the corner of her eye she saw Carrick grin.

"You should be. Moving down farther is the roof. Nothing special there except it keeps the rain out. Then that
room up there is the lantern room, which you've seen. Every
morning and every evening that gets cleaned. I clean the
windows, I clean the lens, I clean off any dead birds that hit
the glass. Then I drape the lens and hang the curtains—"

"Hang curtains?"

"Around the lens," he said. "The sunlight can damage the
prisms. So I hang the curtains and clean the windows inside
and out. There are many fine things to being a wickie, but
washing windows on a skinny gallery in high winds or on
hundred-degree days is not one of those fine things. That's
why we do the window washing right after sunrise. The
light pops off and I start cleaning. Better do it then before
it gets hot out."

"That's smart," Faye said. "I can imagine the height and
the heat have caused a few accidents."

"More than one. But I have a rope and harness I strap
around myself when I clean the outside the windows. Moving down again, the light in there's a third-order Fresnel
lens. We salute the French for their ingenuity. They've saved
a million lives."

"*Vive la France,*" Faye said, and Carrick turned and gave
a jaunty salute in the vague direction of France.

"You know all about the clockwork and the sun valve," Carrick continued. "And the acetylene I'll show you tomorrow. The cylinders are stored in that building right there." He pointed down to a small brick shed at the base of the lighthouse. "I don't want you touching them unless you have to."

"Are they really that dangerous, or were you just trying to scare off Hartwell?"

"A little of both. They used to make the acetylene on-site at one station. Until there was a leak."

"What happened?"

"Goodbye, lighthouse. Goodbye, keeper."

"Oh, my God."

"Don't think about it," Carrick said. "That was back in '13, and we don't make the gas here. The tender brings the cylinders and we store them. It's safe—I promise."

Faye nodded. She didn't like the thought of living so close to something so explosive, but it wasn't like 2015 was without its dangers. She'd driven a two-ton death machine every day of her life since she was sixteen years old. Even in 2015, cars ran on gasoline and caught fire and blew up. Nothing and nowhere and no time in existence was without some sort of risk.

"The room below the lantern room is the one we were just in," Carrick said. "It's the watch room. I guess it's called the watch room because that's where the keeper keeps watch."

"I buy that."

"That's where the clockwork is, as you saw. It turns the rotors that the light sits on. And the counterweights drop all the way to the lighthouse floor."

"I didn't see any counterweights."

"Did you see that metal tube running all the way down the center of the staircase?"

"I did. I thought it was some kind of support beam."

"Young lady, this lighthouse is cast iron and brick. The stones are two feet by three feet and take ten men to lift. And inside the stone is copper rebar wrapping this lighthouse tight and holding it together like a corset. It doesn't need a support beam. That metal tube houses the counterweights as they slide down and turn the light. Then we turn the crank, like winding a grandfather clock to keep it running all night."

"I stand corrected. I never intended to disparage the might and solidity of this manly edifice." She matched Carrick's feigned Southern accent with one of her own.

"You are forgiven your lapse in common sense. I'm sure a young lady like yourself was simply overwhelmed by the sheer majesty of this monument."

Faye shook her head. Ridiculous man. "So how tall exactly is this majestic monument?"

"Well, that depends," he said. "Are we counting the height from the floor to the top of the lightning rod? Or are we counting from sea level up to the light?"

"From the base to the tip," she said, and Carrick cocked an eyebrow at her.

"About eighty-seven feet. Impressive, isn't it?"

"Impressive enough to give a lady the vapors. Hunting Island's light is bigger, though, isn't it?"

"It's taller, I suppose," Carrick said dismissively. "Mine's wider."

"Width matters, does it?"

"So I've been told. Mine is also younger and will likely last a lot longer."

"Are we still talking about the lighthouse?" Faye asked.

"I have no idea what we're talking about anymore," Carrick said, taking her face in his hands.

"Maybe we should stop talking, then," Faye said.

"Bad idea," Carrick said, but kissed her anyway.

Carrick kissed her, kissed her good and hard, kissed her until she couldn't breathe and kissed her until she didn't want to. She would have let him go on kissing her all night except he kissed her from her lips to her ear and then whispered a word.

"Faith…"

It hit her like a bucket of ice-cold water. She wasn't Faith. Faith was dead and Carrick didn't know it. It wasn't right to mislead him. Faye had a choice. She could either tell Carrick the truth or she could stop letting him kiss her.

"Stop," Faye said. Carrick stopped. Faye gave him a weak smile. "Sorry."

"Don't be," he said, panting.

"Kissing you is too easy," she said. Her head spun like a top. She felt faint and dizzy and happy all at once. "I keep forgetting who you are."

"I keep forgetting myself, too," he said.

"Go on," Faye said. "Tell me more about the lighthouse."

"Better call it a night before I do something I shouldn't. Again," he said. He stood up straight and put his back to the railing, to the ocean. He looked so beautiful in the starlight and the lamplight—strong and handsome and dependable.

"I want to stay," she said. "You know you get lonely up here, don't you?"

"Lonely? Me?" He shook his head. "Never. I have Ozzie."

"Ozzie?"

Carrick put two fingers in his mouth and whistled. Faye

heard the sound of metal rattling, and seemingly out of no-where, a small gray cat materialized at Carrick's feet.

"The Great and Terrible Ozzie," Carrick said, picking up the cat and carrying him into the watch room. "Principal rat catcher and lighthouse sentinel." He pulled a bit of food from a tin and fed it to Ozzie. The food looked and smelled like dried fish. "And a rascal. Caught him pissing off the gallery last night. Watered the plants ninety feet down."

"That's quite a skill," Faye said. "You would never do that, I'm sure."

"Course not. Well, maybe no more than once a night. Depends on how much coffee I had. But he doesn't drink coffee. No excuse."

"Don't listen to him, Ozzie." Faye stuck her hand out, and Ozzie pushed his head into her palm. She picked him up, and he let her hold him, purring loud enough she could hear it over the roar of the spinning lens. "You can piss off the lighthouse whenever you want. My Lord, you are loud."

"That purr could wake the dead," Carrick said. "I don't know if he eats the rats or just scares them away by purring at them, but I haven't seen hide nor hair of a rat or a mouse since the day Oz moved in."

"Did you name him after *The Wizard of Oz*?"

"Dolly did. She's a Dorothy, you know. Been Dolly all her life, though, her father says. One of the few words she says."

"I didn't know she could say anything. This is her cat?"

"She brought him here a few weeks before you came. They had one too many cats and kittens at their place, and her mother was threatening to throw them in a sack and toss that sack in the ocean. Dolly wouldn't stand for that, so she brought the three toms out here. Two ran off to God knows where, but Ozzie stuck around."

Ozzie kneaded her thigh through her skirt, and she tried to enjoy the affection and ignore the pinprick of his sharp little claws. Then he rolled up into a tight furry doughnut on her lap, purring so loudly she could feel the vibration down to her feet.

"Ozzie of Oz," she said, stroking the silver V between Ozzie's ears. *The Wizard of Oz.* That was exactly what this was, wasn't it?

"What are you smiling at?" Carrick asked.

"I feel like Dorothy in Oz. You know, since I came here," she said. "This place is so different from what I'm used to, like another world."

"Like Oz?"

Faye nodded.

Oz. Of course. Why hadn't she thought of it before? In *The Wizard of Oz*, the lady who played the mean teacher looked exactly like the Wicked Witch. The Tin Man, the Cowardly Lion and the Scarecrow all looked like men who worked on Uncle Henry and Auntie Em's farm. And here Carrick looked just like Will. And Dolly reminded her of someone, but she couldn't quite remember who. Like Dorothy, Faye had been swept away and carried off to another world. They'd both woken up in another land where everything was different and yet oddly the same. And Faye, like Dorothy, just wanted to go home.

Or did she?

"I keep thinking I'm going to wake up and it'll all be dream. Just like Dorothy did." Faye looked at Carrick and smiled. "And all this will be gone, and I'll be back where I came from."

Carrick narrowed his eyes at her.

"A dream?" he asked.

"You know," she said. "At the end of the—" She almost said "the movie," then remembered *The Wizard of Oz* wouldn't come out for years. "At the end of the book, when Dorothy wakes up from her dream about Oz."

"You must not have read the same book I did."

"What do you mean?"

"The Land of Oz isn't a dream," Carrick said. "Oz is real, and Dorothy goes back to it again and again in the other books."

"Oh, yes," Faye said, swallowing hard. She'd never read the book, although she'd seen the movie so many times she'd lost count. "That's right. Been years since I read it."

"If you ask me, I don't know why Dorothy ever wanted to go back to Kansas. I've been to Kansas," Carrick said. "Would you pick Kansas if you could have Oz?"

"Oz had wicked witches, you know. Kansas doesn't."

Carrick touched the bruise on her face, a touch as soft as a kiss.

"Everywhere's got wicked witches."

Faye wanted to press her face into Carrick's hand the way Ozzie had butted his head against hers.

"Tell me something," Faye said.

"Anything."

"What would you do right now if I wasn't married?"

"You are married."

"Pretend I'm not."

"I can't pretend. I don't have that good of an imagination."

"Can you imagine this, then? Imagine I didn't survive when I fell into the water. What would happen to you if I'd drowned that night?"

Carrick mulled that question over for a good long while. Faye held her breath and waited for the answer. She didn't know why she'd asked him, except something told her she needed to know.

"Have you ever seen an abandoned lighthouse?" Carrick asked. "Windows broken, paint faded and peeling and no light shining out from it?"

"Yes," Faye said.

"Aye, then, there's your answer."

16

On the third morning Faye woke up in 1921, she realized something.

She wanted to stay.

She wanted to stay so much that if a man in black showed up on Carrick's porch and offered her a key to a door to take her to 2015, she would politely decline, wish the man well, close the door and get back to work. The body she'd woken up in was her body. The face she saw in the mirror was her face. The life she inhabited was her life. Whether she had become Faith or Faith had become her, Faye didn't know and didn't care anymore. She fit this life like a hand in glove.

While Dolly cooked breakfast downstairs, Faye dressed, pinned up her hair and went to work in the garden. The garden that was her garden now. According to the almanac, which Dolly consulted on a daily basis, it was time to plant beets and carrots for an autumn harvest. Faye found the seed packets and went to work weeding and sowing. Faye had never been one to cook elaborate meals that required hours of preparation. And yet here she was, planting food in June she wouldn't eat until September. She caught herself smiling while she pushed seeds into the soil, even though the sun was hot and kneeling on the ground was uncomfortable. How long had it been since the salt in her eyes had come from sweat and not tears?

Faye sat back on her knees and admired her work. Three rows of carrots. Three rows of beets.

"Faith?"

Faye heard Carrick's voice calling to her.

"Is breakfast ready?" she called back.

"Stand up slowly, love, very slowly," he said, and Faye turned to him. He walked toward her, carrying an ax in his hand. An ax?

"What?"

"Stand up right now. Walk across the garden. Walk as fast as you can."

"I just planted it—"

"Now. Right now."

Faye heard a sound, a strange sort of shuffling, like footsteps dragging on the ground. Slowly she turned around.

Faye screamed.

An alligator lurked not ten feet behind her. At the sound of her scream, it opened its mouth, baring rows of white teeth, a dark cave filled with ivory stalactites. It charged toward her as she scrambled back on her hands, getting tangled in her skirt as she tried to stand.

She yelled Carrick's name. In a blur of movement, she saw him rush forward with his ax raised, but she didn't wait to see what happened next. She clambered to her feet and ran to the opposite side of the garden to the oil shed and hid behind the door. From behind the shed's door, she could hear grunting sounds, wet thuds and then...silence.

When she cracked the door open and peeked out, Carrick's silver ax head dripped with red.

"Hope you like alligator stew, love," he said, turning to her, wearing a look of false levity on his face.

"That... That's... Carrick, that's an alligator," she said, cowering in the oil house doorway.

"That *was* an alligator."

The alligator, or what was left of it, lay on its side, two fat legs dangling in the air.

"This island has alligators," she said.

"Yes, this island has alligators."

"You killed an alligator. With an ax."

Carrick nodded. "Didn't have time to load the shotgun."

"You killed an alligator with an ax because you didn't have time to load the shotgun."

"You're repeating me," he said.

"I was almost eaten by an alligator."

"I think he was after the goats."

"Carrick."

"Or you," Carrick said. "Can't lie, he might have been after you."

"I'm going to faint," she said.

"Don't faint. It's dead, I swear. You can come out of the shed now."

Faye didn't want to come out of the oil shed, but her rational brain reminded her she couldn't stay in there forever. Her rational brain also told her she should not be living on an island where an alligator could just sneak up on her.

"Come out," he said again. "You're safe. I got him."

Faye knew she might puke, so she waited a few more seconds until the nausea passed. Then she turned around and almost did throw up though nothing came out. It had happened so fast, so insanely fast she didn't know how to process it. She'd barely had time to be scared before Carrick had killed it. Adrenaline coursed through her veins. She wanted to run a hundred miles at a hundred miles an hour away from the creature. Instead, she crept from the doorway of the oil shed and walked over to Carrick, where he stood panting. Faye winced and turned away at the sight of the deep gashes in the alligator's body. She guessed its size at about ten feet long, more than large enough to kill a human being. Specifically, her.

"Not an endangered species," she said, looking at its long green-black body. Liberal guilt haunted her even in 1921.

"What was that?"

"Nothing. It's a big, big…thing."

"It's a big thing, yes. A big dead thing." Carrick nodded.

"You saved me from an alligator. No one has ever saved me from an alligator before. That's not a thing that happens to me. That's not a thing that happens to anyone."

"It happens on this island."

Faye sighed and leaned against his chest, his broad, strong chest that had the power to kill an alligator with a three-foot-long wooden ax. She giggled madly, giddy and dizzy, relieved to be alive.

"You are such a badass," she said, lightly pounding his chest with her fist.

"I'm a what?"

"Nothing. Just rambling. I'm fine—I promise."

"You regret coming here yet?" he asked, and she looked up at him sharply before remembering he meant coming here from Boston, not coming here from 2015.

She shook her head no and rested her forehead on his chest again. She smiled. A man had killed an alligator to save her. This would never have happened in her time, and yet it didn't make her regret coming here. She felt lucky. Lucky to be alive. Lucky to have Carrick. Lucky to know how lucky she was, which was the best sort of luck.

Carrick wrapped one arm around her shoulders and held her to him. Faye looked up at him, ready to kiss him senseless.

"Oh, my, am I interrupting something?"

Faye started nearly as hard as she had when she'd seen the alligator.

"Mr. Hartwell," Carrick said. "We've had an interesting morning."

"I see that." Hartwell strolled over the lawn to where they stood by the alligator's corpse. "Sorry to disturb y'all. Looked like you were having a tender moment."

"My, um…my father just killed an alligator that snuck up on me," Faye said. "Close call. I'm a little…" She waved her hands wildly to illustrate her agitation. "You know. Frantic."

"You are a lucky lady to have such a man to take care of you." Hartwell grinned temple to temple.

"I am, yes."

"What can we do for you, Mr. Hartwell?" Carrick asked. "Did you come for alligator stew? Alligator steaks? That's what's on the menu for the next week or so."

"I thank you for the hospitality, but I'll pass. That meat's a little tough for me. I was passing by. On my way to visit some friends over on Hunting, you know. Thought I'd say howdy."

"Howdy," Faye said.

"Howdy, indeed, Miss Faith. You feeling all right?" he asked.

"Fine," she said. "Apart from the alligator scare."

"That's good to hear. Real good," Hartwell said. "Since I seem to have caught you all at a bad time, I'll just be on my way."

Hartwell walked toward the kitchen door. At the door, he paused and turned around.

"Chief Morgan, I meant to ask… Y'all don't have a haunted lighthouse, do you?"

"Not that I know of. Why?"

"Oh, I hear it's common for lighthouses to have a ghost or two. You sure you don't have one?"

"Sure as I am of anything," Carrick said.

"Strange." Hartwell shook his head. "I was here a couple nights ago in my car, you know, just visiting the beach with some friends. We like to do that at night, do a little clam digging. Well, anyway," he continued, "I heard some kind of spooky, I don't know…*moaning* sounds coming from the house or the lighthouse or the barn. I must have imagined it. Or maybe it was just the wind…"

"Just the wind," Carrick said. "Been real windy."

"Probably so, probably so," Hartwell said, his hands in his pockets.

"Did you find any?" Faye asked.

"Excuse me, Miss Faith?"

"Clams," she said. "Did you find any clams while you were out here digging?"

"No, I sure didn't," Hartwell said. "But that's all right. I found something better than clams."

"Good for you," Carrick said.

"Very, very good," Hartwell said. "Y'all take care now. We sure do appreciate our lighthouse families out here." He winked and walked away. Soon as he was gone, Dolly came out of the house carrying a basket over her arm. She paused, looked at them, looked at the alligator, shook her head and walked on toward the chicken coop.

"Nobody goes clam digging in June," Carrick said.

"He knows about us," Faye said.

Carrick nodded. "He knows something. He knows you're not my daughter."

"Hope that's all he knows," Faye said. "Why did he ask how I was feeling? Was that a threat?"

"I don't know, but I swear if he tries anything with you..." Carrick said. He held up his bloody ax.

"You can't kill him like an alligator."

"True," Carrick said. "Next time I'll use the shotgun. On the alligator, I mean." The sound of Hartwell's motorboat intruded into their conversation. She almost preferred the alligator.

Carrick walked off, dragging the alligator by the tail behind him.

"Wait," Faye said. "Next time? What do you mean next time? Carrick? Are there more alligators around here?"

Carrick didn't answer, but she could swear she heard him laughing.

"I'm not eating that!" she yelled after him.

Then she went and got the ax from Carrick.

Just in case.

Three more days passed in a haze of hard work and happiness. No more alligators showed up to menace her. No Hartwells, either. Faye had survived almost a full week in 1921 and though her body was sore in ways it had never been before, her heart glided light in her chest like a sailboat in a strong, steady breeze. She had only one lingering complaint about her life here at the lighthouse, and that could be an easy fix if Faye could talk Dolly into helping her. Faye waited until Dolly was at work in her sewing room to go begging.

"I need clothes," Faye wrote on Dolly's slate. "Please."

Dolly sighed. "I made you three skirts two weeks back," she wrote back.

"Pants," Faye wrote on Dolly's slate. "I need pants."

Faye could handle Bride Island and she could handle 1921 and she could handle Hartwell, but she couldn't handle all of it in an ankle-length skirt and underskirt in South Carolina in June.

Dolly was not amused by the request.

"Pants? For a girl? No," Dolly wrote on her slate, shaking her head for emphasis.

"Yes," Faye wrote. "I hate doing chores in skirts." She underlined *hate* a few times for emphasis. Six times in fact.

"I do chores in skirts."

"You could save the world in skirts. I can't," Faye wrote, meaning every word. Faye had never considered homemaking an art before, but if it were, Dolly was Picasso, Rembrandt and Martha Stewart rolled into one. "I'll die of the heat. Help me."

Dolly shook her head again. "Chief won't like it."

Faye wrote on the board, "Chief says it's fine as long as I change when we have company."

That was a lie but a plausible one. Carrick seemed the sort who would merely roll his eyes at the sight of her weeding the garden and beating rugs out in trousers.

"Is this a Northern fashion?" Dolly asked, and Faye remembered that she was supposed to be from Boston or thereabouts.

"Yes," Faye lied. "The newest style."

"You been there?" Dolly asked.

Faye wrote, "New York."

Dolly looked mightily impressed.

"I want to go," Dolly wrote back. "More than anything."

Faye wrote, "It's a cool town" then quickly erased the word *cool* and replaced it with *wonderful*. She wasn't sure if *cool* meant *cool* yet or still only referred to temperature.

"If they're doing it in New York City, then I guess I can make you some."

"I promise," Faye wrote, "pants for women is the style of the future."

Faye pledged on her honor that Dolly would not get into any trouble with the Chief for sewing her two pairs of work pants. She also offered to do all Dolly's chores for a week as payment. Dolly wasn't persuaded.

"I do my own work," she wrote. "But you let me do your room any way I like."

That was all? Dolly wanted to redecorate Faye's room?

"Any way you like," Faye wrote back. "I'll help. You give the orders and I'll follow them."

The deal was done, and they shook hands on it. Dolly read Faye's promise, nodded her head and pulled her measuring tape out of her skirt pocket. When Dolly measured her waist, she gave Faye a look.

"What?" Faye wrote on the slate.

"You gained an inch. Eat less."

"Not my fault you're such a good cook," Faye wrote. Dolly only smiled and got back to work.

Five minutes later Dolly was tracing a pattern onto brown paper, and fifteen minutes after that Faye heard the sewing machine running, Dolly's foot working the treadle with gusto. Dolly warned Faye the only suitable material she had now was a sturdy oatmeal-colored linen she'd used to make her father some work shirts. It wasn't the most fashionable fabric in the world, but Faye didn't care about fashion. She just wanted to work without having heat stroke.

While Dolly sewed, Faye cleaned. Dolly warned her the lighthouse inspector could show up without any notice and so they should always be ready for an inspection. The house must be as shipshape as the light itself. Also, it was a rule that the lighthouse keeper's family must always show hospitality to any visitors who stopped by. If anyone, from a prince to a pauper, wanted to tour the light, well, they toured the light and had a picnic lunch after. So Faye dusted the furniture, polished the brass, took sheets and towels off the clothesline and folded them with geometric precision.

Thanks to all the cleaning, Faye now knew every inch of the house as if it were her own. If Carrick needed a pencil, Faye could tell him there were half a dozen black #2 Ticonderogas in the junk drawer. If Dolly wanted her to fetch the wooden clothespins, they were in a coffee can in the pantry. If Faye had a craving for chocolate some night, she knew where to find the cocoa and the milk, the saucepan and the mugs. She'd simply have to learn to live without marshmallows. For a free beach house, she'd made that sacrifice. Faye admired the tidiness of the little house. Everything had its place, and every place had its thing. The more hours that passed, the more time she spent working and the more nights she spent with Carrick up in the lighthouse, the more Faye would have her place here, too. She'd fit right in like a book on the shelf, like *The Wonderful Wizard of Oz*, third shelf down, two books to the right. Faye went straight to the back of the book. Carrick was right. Oz wasn't a dream at all in the book. Oz was real. As real as Bride Island.

And apparently the Emerald City was getting a paint

job. Faye slid the book back onto the shelf as Dolly walked through the living room and up the stairs with a paint can in her hand and a paint-stained tarp draped over her shoulder like a mink stole.

Faye followed her upstairs and found her not in her sewing room but in Faye's room.

"What are you doing?" Faye asked, mouthing the words carefully and eyeing the can and the tarp.

Dolly mimed the act of painting the wall, and there was a look of "obviously" in both her answer and her expression. Then she held up a pair of pants, waving them like a flag to prove she'd earned her redecorating spree. Faye took the linen pants from Dolly and turned them over in her hands. They looked like they'd fit. She ran down to the bathroom, stripped out of her skirt and slid them on. They were loose around the waist, but Dolly had fitted the trousers with a drawstring. Faye cinched the waist and rolled the bottom cuffs up. In her plain white cotton blouse and these pants, Faye looked like she belonged on the cover of an L.L. Bean catalog, the fun-in-the-sun summer edition. All she needed was a big floppy hat, and she'd look ready for a trip to the Hamptons.

In her new and fabulously comfortable pants, Faye returned to her bedroom. Dolly gave her an appraising stare while Faye turned a circle. Dolly nodded her approval.

"They fit good," Dolly wrote.

"Do I look good?" Faye replied.

"You look like a boy."

"Boys look good," Faye wrote. Dolly only rolled her eyes and went back to work.

Dolly had picked a pale green paint for the bedroom, the same color as the kitchen walls. Lead-based paint, of course.

Faye doubted one could find any other kind in 1921, but as long as she didn't eat the paint or lick the walls, she could probably avoid dying of lead poisoning.

Between the two of them and with a few minutes' worth of pushing and sweating, they managed to move the bed to the center of the room. The dresser wouldn't budge, however, as it was far too heavy for either of them and refused to slide no matter how hard they pushed. Faye pulled the drawers out and stacked them on the bed. Once the dresser was emptied of its load, it moved easily. Faye pushed, and the dresser shifted and wobbled, nearly toppling over. Faye looked down and saw why. One leg was shorter than the other by almost two inches. Someone had slipped a book under the dresser to even the legs out.

"Must not be a fan of Lucy Maud Montgomery," Faye said as she picked up the book, *Anne's House of Dreams*. Faye had read the whole series as a girl. When she opened the book, she gasped.

Dolly dropped her paintbrush on the floor, and if Faye had been holding a paintbrush she would have dropped it, too.

Someone had cut a rectangular hole in the center of the book's pages and stuffed money in it. Cash, and lots of it.

Faye looked at Dolly, who stared at the money in wide-eyed amazement. Faye riffled through the bundle of money and saw every bill was a Benjamin Franklin, and there were about one hundred Bens. That was about ten thousand dollars. Carrick had told her an assistant lighthouse keeper made about eight hundred dollars a year. Faye wasn't sure what that meant in 1921 money, but she knew if this cash constituted about twelve years' salary for a lighthouse keeper, it was a lot of money.

Dolly grabbed her slate and wrote quickly.

"I put that book there to steady the dresser," she said.

"When?" Faye wrote back.

"Right before you came."

"Hartwell," Faye wrote on Dolly's slate and Dolly nodded sagely.

So this was why Hartwell kept sneaking around the house. The Landrys had left money for him in this book, and Dolly had moved it before Hartwell could fetch it. She was stunned and relieved all at once. Hartwell didn't want to hurt them. He just wanted his damn money back. Even in 2015, ten thousand dollars was a lot of money. She'd want it back, too.

"Tell Chief," Dolly wrote. "He'll know what to do."

Faye slid the money back in the book and stuffed it in her dresser drawer. She hated to wake him up, but she knew this couldn't wait. For that much money, Hartwell was sure to come back, and he might not stop with just threats next time.

When she went to his room, Faye saw she needn't have worried about waking Carrick. She found him standing at the window of his bedroom wearing only his work trousers, a T-shirt and a worried expression on his face. She knew it was worry because she knew that look—the furrowed brow, the tight line of his lips, the hard set of his jaw. In his hands Carrick held his silver rosary beads. With his thumb he clicked through the beads, turning them over rapidly like a bicycle chain whirling in gear.

"What's wrong?" Faye went to stand next to him by the window. She tried to see what it was he saw, but apart from a cloudless sky she saw nothing.

Carrick slipped his rosary beads into the pocket of his pants.

"It's quiet out. Hear it?"

"I don't hear anything."

"Exactly. Listen again. Tell me what you don't hear."

Faye listened. She heard the water lapping the shore. She heard a rustle of wind in the trees. She smelled something like copper in the air. Nothing else. No sounds. No smells.

"Where are the birds?" she asked.

"Gone."

"What does that mean?"

"Nothing good."

"Hurricane?"

"Maybe. Maybe not. But bad weather is coming. Big, bad weather."

"How bad?"

"Bad enough to scare the birds away. The barometer's falling fast. It's going to be an ugly day. I want you and Dolly in the lighthouse with me."

"Won't her father be coming for her?"

"He knows better than to come out here in a storm. Pack up some blankets and food. We'll camp in the watch room tonight."

Faye's heartbeat hastened. She'd never been this close to the ocean during a tropical storm before. Hartwell and his dirty money could wait.

"I'll go get Dolly," Faye said.

"You do that—what on earth are you wearing?" Carrick had finally noticed her clothes. "Are those trousers?"

"I had Dolly sew them for me."

"They look like long underwear."

"Don't be mad. I told Dolly you wouldn't care if I wore them around the house when I was working."

"But pants?" He screwed up his face in a mixture of confusion and suspicion.

"Would you want to do your work in a long skirt?"

"Well...no."

"See? I promise I'll change into my very best dress the second someone comes to visit. While I'm scrubbing floors and weeding the garden, I want pants."

He took a step back and looked her up and down. With his index finger he made a little circle in the air, and Faye turned around with a heavy, put-upon sigh.

"What do you think?" she asked.

"They're different."

"Women will be wearing pants all the time everywhere eventually," she said. In a decade or two or three, but definitely eventually. "I'm sure of it."

"They're very..." Carrick paused. "Revealing."

"Revealing? These pants that cover me from waist to foot are revealing? You do remember the night you got me out of my wet clothes? All my wet clothes?"

"That's different. That was a rescue. This is... I can see your shape in them. Your hips, and that sort of thing."

"You already know what shape I am."

"True, but it's different seeing you like this. I think..."

"What?" she demanded sharply.

"I think I like them."

Faye laughed, and Carrick kissed her. A quick kiss from a scared man who knew a big, bad storm was coming, and if they didn't kiss now they might not ever get to kiss again. Faye returned the kiss with ardor, with hunger, forgetting, as she was wont to do, that she wasn't supposed to kiss this man any more than he was supposed to kiss her.

Faye heard a sound. A loud gasp followed by a tiny, stricken cry. She turned her head and saw Dolly in the doorway staring at her and Carrick in horror.

"Shit," Faye said.

"Faith!" Carrick said, aghast.

Dolly turned on her heel and ran out, horrified by what she'd thought she'd seen.

"I'll go get her," Faye said.

"What are you going to tell her?" Carrick grabbed a shirt out of his closet and pulled it on. He buttoned it up quickly and followed her out the door.

"I don't know. But let me handle it."

"Go. But hurry. This storm is kicking up fast."

"We'll be right back, I promise." She kissed him one more time because she just had to, then ran out the front door. Carrick hadn't been kidding. The sky darkened as she ran down the beach, and the wind blew hard enough to turn the water white. Thankfully Dolly had run down the beach instead of into the forest. Faye saw her ahead running pell-mell into the wind. Good thing Faye had her pants on. No way could she catch up with those long teenage legs otherwise. Faye reached out and grabbed Dolly's arm. Dolly gasped and spun around, struggling against her.

"Please," Faye mouthed, hoping Dolly could read that word on her lips. "Please..."

Dolly stopped trying to run away. She put her hands over her face and shook her head. A sound came from the back of her throat, a guttural moan of sorrow. *Poor girl.* What she must think of them...

Faye dropped to her knees, and Dolly looked at her, stunned. In the sand Faye wrote a single word with her finger.

Watch.

Dolly waved her hand, a dismissive "go ahead, see if I care" gesture.

Faye cut right to the chase. "Chief isn't my father or my stepfather."

Dolly's eyes widened as she read the words.

"I ran away from home," Faye wrote. She hoped that was close enough to the truth.

Dolly dropped down onto her knees in the sand.

"Why?"

"I'm hiding here."

"He's not your pa?"

"No."

"You his wife?"

"Another man's wife," Faye wrote. "An evil man."

Dolly shook her head, tears streaming from her eyes. "It's not right."

"I know." Faye scribbled as quickly as she could. The wind picked up, blowing her words away. "I'm sorry."

Dolly stuck her finger into the sand and wrote a question Faye didn't think she could answer yet.

"You love Chief?"

Faye stared at the question. Before she could answer it, a wave hit the beach so hard it slammed into them both washing all their words away.

Lightning cracked the sky wide-open. Thunder exploded like an atom bomb in the air. Even Dolly felt it and jumped. Grabbing Dolly by the arm, Faye pulled her toward the house. The ocean was roiling now, bubbling as wildly as a pan of water on high boil. Again and again waves slammed the shore, climbing higher every second. Running on hard wet sand was faster and easier than trying to wade through loose dry sand, so they skirted the waves as they raced back toward the house. Easier wasn't safer, however, and when the wind struck them again, Dolly was blown facedown into the sand. She came up howling and weeping, sand in her eyes, blood trickling out of her nose. In pain and unable to see or hear, she stumbled toward the water. Faye raced after her, pulling the terrified girl close and guiding her down the beach again. Sandy tears streamed out of Dolly's eyes. Faye looked up and saw Carrick running toward them. Before he could reach them, another wave struck, and the ocean dragged Dolly into the water with greedy arms.

"Dolly!" Faye screamed, forgetting the girl couldn't hear her. She ran into the water and tugged Dolly free from the grip of the current. Carrick arrived just in time to lift Dolly, sodden heavy skirts and all, out of the water. He set her down gently higher up on the dune before running back for Faye. He reached for her, and Faye reached for him. As their hands met, a current caught her by the legs and ripped her out of his grip, shoving her under the surface. She struggled against the waves, which tossed her like a chew toy in a dog's mouth. Even under the water, she heard Carrick calling for her, screaming for her, and she wanted him. She wanted him so much, but she just couldn't make her way to the surface.

No. She wouldn't give in. She'd just found Carrick, and she wasn't about to lose him. With all her strength, Faye clawed at the water, tore through it, digging an escape tunnel where none existed. Her heart felt like a drum in her chest, huge and pounding, ready to break out of her body. She surfaced with a roar of pain as air filled her scalding lungs. Broken and exhausted she limped out of the water, crawled on the beach and collapsed.

She heard the sound of birds calling.

Birds? Carrick said the storm had scared away all the birds.

And she heard music, too.

Music?

Faye forced her eyes open, lifted her head, and looked out onto the water. The calm, lazy water. She saw a boat. A yacht. On it a dozen twentysomethings lounged around in board shorts and bikinis, drank beers from cans and lay out on the roof in the sun. Faye looked down at her body. She had on jeans. Jeans and a black tank top.

Instinctively she looked to the lighthouse for comfort and it was there. Thank God it was there. But the house was gone. Her house. The seawall. The vegetable garden. The oil shed and the root cellar and the outbuildings and the beach. So much of the beach was gone.

And Carrick was gone. And Dolly was gone. And it was 2015 again, which meant Will was gone.

And she was here.

Goodbye, Oz.

Hello, Kansas.

17

Numb from shock, Faye dragged herself to her feet and wandered unsteadily down the beach toward the lighthouse. Her mouth was dry and tasted of salt water. Sand and sweat stiffened her clothes, chafing her skin as she walked. The lighthouse door hung open on its rusty hinges. The black-and-white tile on the floor was gone, replaced by bare cement.

"Hello?" she called up, and only a dusty echo answered.

She walked around the lighthouse, disoriented by her sudden reentry into this time. Her head swam and her eyes watered. A brown pelican swooped overhead, and Faye flinched, mistaking it at first for a vulture. In a daze, she wandered to her car. A fine layer of dust and sand covered the windshield, but the keys were still in the ignition, the doors unlocked.

The car started on the first try. "Thank you, Hagen," she muttered, grateful he'd given her the new car when she'd left. She'd been gone a week, and to have the car start up without any trouble was a relief. Wait. Six days? Was that how long she'd been gone? Her phone was dead and she'd left her charger in her luggage. She drove back to Beaufort slowly and fearfully, remembering how to drive as she drove. When she was off the island with the lighthouse miles behind her, she picked up speed as muscle memory kicked in. The more distance she put between herself and Bride Island, the more she remembered who she was and where she was and when.

"My name is Victoria Faye Barlow. I've always gone by Faye because Vicky is my mom. I was born June 5, 1985 in Portsmouth, New Hampshire..." she recited as she drove across the Sea Island Parkway bridge and merged onto Carteret Street. She pulled into the parking lot of the Church Street house and had a sudden panicked thought that her room had been given to someone else while Faye had been gone. Surely Miss Lizzie would have called the cops or something. And if not that, she would have chucked Faye's luggage out and given the room to someone who hadn't skipped out on her tab.

Feeling like a criminal, Faye slipped in the front door and peeked into the living room and TV room. No one there. She went back to the kitchen and saw Ty at the counter constructing a sandwich roughly the size of a human head.

"You," she said to him.

"Me?" He smiled and pointed at himself. "What about me?"

"I know you."

"Biblically," he said.

"What day is it?" she asked.

Laughing, Ty looked her up and down, whistled and shook his head.

"If you don't know, I'm not telling. Are you hungover?"

"Something like that."

"You look like shit, baby. No offense."

Faye rested her head on his shoulder a moment, before straightening up and crossing her arms over her chest, shivering.

"It's freezing in here," she said.

"You know how Miss Liz loves her AC."

"Where is she? Did she say anything about me being gone?"

He shrugged. "Not to me. Why?"

"You know how I asked you what day it is?"

"Yeah…?"

"Can you tell me what year it is, too? I know what year it is. I just want you to tell me."

"It's 2015. And you need this more than I do," he said, handing her his sandwich. "Go upstairs. Eat. Sleep. Take a shower. A long one, 'cause you smell like a sailor on shore leave."

"Thank you," she said meekly, obediently taking the plate from him and walking upstairs. When she reached the door to her room, she put the key in the lock and eased it open, worried someone else had moved in while she'd been gone.

But no, there was her luggage, her clothes, her camera equipment and laptop. Nothing had been moved, nothing touched. It was like she'd been gone a night and no longer.

"What the hell…" Nothing had changed. It was like no time had passed at all.

Dizzy and sunburned and exhausted to the bone, Faye sank into her desk chair and placed the sandwich in front of her. It was so tall she didn't know how to eat it. She extracted the top layer, which consisted of lettuce, bacon, tomato, onion, mayo, more lettuce, maybe Thousand Island dressing, all between two pieces of toasted wheat bread. She took a bite. Then another. Maybe Ty was onto something. She'd feel more like herself once she'd eaten, had a shower and slept. The shower was top priority, right after the sandwich. Faye leaned back in her chair and started to put her feet up on the desk. When she saw the Singer sewing emblem under the tabletop, she sat up again.

Hadn't Miss Lizzie said most of the furniture in her room came from the lighthouse?

"Dolly..." Faye ran her hand across the wooden surface, worn smooth by time and faded by wear. Dolly's sewing table. Tears burned Faye's eyes, and she could barely swallow. Dolly had been real, hadn't she? She couldn't have been a dream. Why would Faye's subconscious have invented a teenage Martha Stewart to be her friend and teach her how to make peach pie? No, surely Dolly was real. She needed Dolly to be real. Dolly had sewn her a pair of linen pants. No figment of her imagination had ever sewn her pants before.

Faye wept as she ate, and she didn't know why, other than she was homesick, so homesick, but she was already home and it was the wrong home.

When Faye finished eating, she took a shower. She stayed under the water for so long that when she emerged her feet and fingers were wrinkled as raisins. She dried her hair with the blow-dryer, and it felt like a luxury. Everything did. Air-conditioning and hot water in the shower that didn't have to be rationed because it wasn't rainwater stored in a cistern. The sandwich from the fridge. The blow-dryer. Face moisturizer. Towels fluffy and soft and smelling of Downy fabric softener.

Back in her room, she pulled the heather-gray Sox T-shirt out of her suitcase, the only one of Will's shirts she'd kept. She put it on and crawled into bed and waited for sleep. She knew then that whatever she'd been through, whatever had happened, it hadn't been a nightmare. Maybe a dream, but never a nightmare. How could it be a nightmare if she wanted to have it again?

Faye slept but did not dream. In the murky light of almost morning, during those last gray minutes between dark and dawn, Faye remembered the turtle. Two nights and ninety-four years ago, she'd been woken near dawn by a soft knock on her bedroom door.

"Carrick?"

"Open up, love. Someone here wants to meet you."

"What? Who?" she'd said, and opened the door to find Carrick standing with his hands cupped in front of him. He opened his hands, and on his palm sat the tiniest little green turtle she'd ever seen.

"Say hello," Carrick said.

Faye gasped and covered her mouth with her hands. She looked up at him.

"Is that a loggerhead turtle?"

"The beach is full of babies tonight. Want to see?"

"Do I want to see baby loggerhead turtles? Are you crazy?"

"I guess that's a yes."

"Oh, my God, yes yes yes. Grab the lamp before they're all gone. And give me that little guy."

Faye cradled the baby turtle in her hand as Carrick found the kerosene lamp and lit it. It felt so weird, the turtle did, wiggling and wriggling on her palm.

"I love him so much," she said, following Carrick out of the front door and down to the beach, the lamp slinging light back and forth as they walked. She could have started crying any second. She was frazzled from sheer happiness. A baby loggerhead turtle. She was holding in her shaking hands a baby loggerhead turtle. "Now I know how Kristen Bell felt with that sloth."

"Who?"

"Nobody. I'm going to name him George."

"You can't keep that turtle," Carrick said.

"Yes, but I can still name him."

"There they are..." Carrick pointed the lamp toward what looked like nothing but a dark blur against a light blur. Carefully, watching every step, they walked toward the blur. Faye saw the hole in the dune and the baby turtles creeping out of the hole and onto the beach.

"Keep an eye out for birds. They eat the babies," Carrick said. He turned the lamp down as their eyes adjusted to the darkness. Faye gently set little George onto the sand next to one of his or her siblings. Like a tiny windup toy, it wriggled across the sand, its flippers barely leaving any tracks as it followed Mother Nature's orders to get into the water right away.

"Amazing..." Faye smiled so wide it hurt. "I wish I had my camera."

"I thought you'd want to see them," Carrick said.

"You were right. They're so little and sweet. I just want to keep them all."

"For turtle stew?"

"No," she'd said forcefully. "And don't you even joke about that."

Carrick chuckled when she punched him in the biceps.

In silence they watched the babies until it seemed all the turtles had escaped the hole in the dune and disappeared into the ocean. Faye took the lamp and looked inside the abandoned nest. One last turtle was trapped at the bottom. She pulled him out and walked with him into the water ready to let him go. Something stopped her.

"Faith?" Carrick called out.

"Here," she said, turned around and walked back to him. "You put him in. Since you found the nest. You can let this one go."

"Come here, turtle stew," he said, and took the baby from her hand. "You wouldn't even be one spoonful. Better throw you back until you're worth eating."

He walked over to the water and waded in, letting the turtle go about ten feet from shore. Nothing happened. No waves. No magic. Carrick came back to her and picked up the lantern. The yellow light from the lamp turned the sand into gold dust all around them. And in that moment, that lovely little moment that meant nothing to anyone in the universe but the two of them, Faye had fallen in love with Carrick.

And now she'd lost him, too.

Faye rolled out of bed and took another shower to wake herself up and clear the cobwebs from her head. Also, she needed a reminder of the many benefits of living in modern times as opposed to say...1921.

Shower over, Faye dressed in a white sleeveless blouse and miniskirt, and she felt naked in them. In just a few days she'd grown so accustomed to ankle-length skirts and long-sleeved shirts that to show the world her bare arms and bare legs seemed positively wicked. Of course, in 1921 long sleeves and long skirts also kept her from severe sunburn. In a time before sunblock, modesty prevented skin cancer.

In the kitchen, Faye went about brewing her usual cup

of black tea for breakfast. She boiled water in a saucepan and found her tea bags. Ty came in and peeked in the pan.

"You cooking spaghetti for breakfast?"

"Just tea," she said.

"On the stove? Why not use the microwave?"

Faye looked up sharply.

"Right," she said. "Microwave. I forgot about microwaves."

"What do you mean you forgot about microwaves?" Ty stared intently at her.

"I mean… I forgot they existed."

"Are you still hungover?" he asked.

"Kind of feels like it."

"Did you drop acid?"

"No, Ty, I did not drop acid."

"You forgot microwaves exist. It was a fair question."

"I…" Faye sat down and rubbed her temples. "I sort of can't quite remember the past few days. Here. I remember things, but I don't know if they actually happened. But they had to have happened if I remember them, right?"

"Do you remember us having sex?" he asked.

Faye rolled her eyes. "Yes, of course."

"When was that? How many days ago?" Ty asked.

"A week ago, right?"

Ty nodded. "Okay. Come on. I'm driving you to the hospital. Where's your keys?"

"What? The hospital? Why?"

"Because yesterday you said you were so hungover you weren't sure what year it is. And this morning you forgot microwaves exist and now you think something that happened three nights ago happened a week ago."

"Three nights ago? No…that was…" Three nights ago

she'd been in the lighthouse with Carrick. He'd taught her how to use the logbook to record weather conditions.

"We went out on the boat," Ty said. "We went to dinner. We came back here to your room."

"Three nights ago." She knew the date and yet it seemed impossible that was only three nights ago. "Are you sure?"

"I'm sure I'm driving you to the hospital, and real damn quick."

"I can drive myself."

"You said you forgot microwaves exist."

"Right," Faye said, nodding. "Okay, yeah. You should probably drive."

It was a slow day in the ER, and an hour later Faye sat on the end of an examining table behind a white curtain as a doctor who looked five years her junior shone a light in her eyes and asked a series of increasingly personal questions. Finally, he lowered his light and put it in his white coat pocket.

"Let's talk," he said. He pulled up a wheeled tripod stool and sat down at the end of the table.

"Talk about what?"

"An MRI. You need one. Today."

"An MRI? Are you serious?"

"You said you weren't entirely sure what happened in the last three days, although your friend in the waiting room can apparently account for your whereabouts. If he knows what you were doing and you don't, something's wrong."

"I feel okay. I'm just...confused."

"Confusion and disorientation are both signs of a head injury," he said. "But there's being confused, and then there's amnesia."

She flinched at the A-word.

"I remember everything, just not..."

"The MRI is just to rule out traumatic brain injury re-lated to your near-drowning experience," he said. "I don't expect it to find anything."

"You don't."

He shook his head.

"Ms. Barlow." He smiled, and she didn't trust that smile. Whatever he said next she wasn't going to like. "Your first husband died four years ago and you recently divorced your second husband. Your father died last year and your mother has dementia, and you've suffered two miscarriages and sev-eral years of infertility treatments. Any one of these events could cause you to experience a temporary break with re-ality—a nervous breakdown, a fugue state, a major depres-sive episode... When you tell me you've been hallucinating another life, that tells me you either need a neurologist or a psychologist. I'm neither of those things, but I want to get you to the right person who can help you."

Faye swallowed a hard lump in her throat, and that lump was a pearl. The first grain of sand in the oyster had been Will's death, and after that every loss had added a layer to it.

The doctor glanced down at his notes again. "Your chart says you're on Ambien?"

"I took one Ambien my first night in Beaufort because I have trouble sleeping in new places. One. One Ambien is not going to trigger a six-day hallucination. I didn't even take it the day I disappeared."

"But you didn't disappear, and you weren't gone for six days."

"I remember six days. I remember..." Faye paused and held out her hands palms open. "Everything. I can tell you where the pencils are in that cottage. And what brand they are. And I can tell you what we ate for breakfast. I can tell you the books I read. I can tell you Carrick likes milk in his coffee and Dolly likes sugar. I can tell you that sometimes Carrick says 'aye' instead of 'yes' and Dolly can sew a pair of drawstring pants in thirty minutes. And there was a cat named Ozzie, a gray tabby, and he's got stripes on his head in the shape of an V. That's his favorite place to get scratched—right on his V. Is that normal? Hallucinating a lighthouse keeper, a sarcastic teenage seamstress and a tabby cat?"

"The brain is a mysterious organ. It can play some pretty impressive tricks on us. Let me ask you this." He pulled his stool a little closer. "What's more likely—that you traveled to 1921 and spent a week living in a house with a man who looks just like your late husband but isn't him and a teenage girl who reminds you of someone but you can't remember who, living the life of a girl who died? Or maybe you had a reaction to a sleeping pill with known hallucinogenic side effects, or received a head injury, or you had a temporary break with reality brought upon by a series of severe emotional traumas? What sounds more likely to you?"

Faye didn't answer. She didn't want to answer. He was so calm and kind and rational and right. He was right. She had taken an Ambien. She had nearly drowned. She had lost so much in the past few years. Any or all those things could have brought on some sort of break with reality.

"Ms. Barlow?"

Faye blinked and wiped tears off her face.

"Okay," she said. "Do the scan."

"Good choice. We're going to do blood work, just in case, as well. We can't be too careful when there's possible head trauma."

"Thank you," she whispered. She was glad he was taking this seriously, but she still felt like she'd betrayed Carrick and Dolly somehow, like she'd let someone convince her they weren't real when they were.

Weren't they?

They had to be. Why else would she miss them so much? The MRI turned up nothing, which was both a relief and a concern. Faye certainly didn't want to have a head injury, but she didn't want some kind of psychosis, either. And she certainly didn't want to think she had accidentally over-dosed. The ER doctor referred Faye to a psychologist, and she dutifully promised to call her first thing in the morning.

"You're lucky they didn't send you off to the funny farm," Ty said as he turned out of the hospital parking lot.

"I don't think you're allowed to call it 'the funny farm' anymore. It's offensive."

"You offended?"

"Only if they send me to the funny farm."

Ty snorted a laugh. "Here's my theory. I think you did exactly what I told you not to do. I think you went swim-ming off Bride Island, almost drowned like I said you would, washed up and got sunstroke out there. Fried your brain."

"I don't even have a sunburn, Ty. And I admit I went wading, but I don't remember stripping naked and going skinny-dipping."

"But you do remember spending six days on an island in 1921, so let's just say for the time being your memory is suspect."

"My memory is excellent. I remember everything that happened while I was gone. I don't know if what I remember was real, but that doesn't change the fact that I remember it."

"That makes no sense," Ty said. "We better go with my theory."

"I'm not saying your theory doesn't make sense. I even

get why I'd dream of a man who looks, talks and kisses just like my dead husband did. You don't need Freud to interpret that dream. But why would I dream about a deaf teenage girl who loved interior decorating and baking pie? I mean, that's really specific. I don't decorate. I'd never baked a peach pie in my life before I went there. Now I have. Now I can..." Faye glanced out the passenger-side window at a gas station in a strip mall. "Hey, can you take me to a grocery store?"

"Why? You hungry? We can go out to dinner if you want."

"I'll take you out to dinner as a thank-you for wasting your entire day with me at the hospital. Tomorrow. Now I need to cook something."

"It wasn't wasted. I met an insanely cute nurse. And I got her number." He held up his left hand, where a phone number had been written on the inside of his wrist. "Don't be jealous. I have a rule against dating crazy girls. A little *loco* is fun, but I draw the line if she's hallucinating other guys."

"I'm not jealous. I wouldn't want to date me, either. Plus, I think I'm in a relationship with a man who's been dead since the Johnson administration. Oh, and I'm married."

"You said you were divorced."

"I'm divorced in 2015. I'm married in 1921."

"Nice guy?"

"A monster who beat and raped his wife when she refused to have sex with him."

"And you want to go back?"

"Well, yeah. I'm cheating on him with a lighthouse keeper, or trying to. Is there a Facebook status for all that?"

"I'd file that under 'It's complicated.'"

"Are you taking me to the grocery store or not?"

"Depends on what you're gonna make me."

"Peach pie with a saltine cracker crust."

"Oh, hell yes, then. We're going right now."

The pie was simple enough—crushed crackers, butter and sugar for the crust, and peaches and more sugar for the filling. Faye didn't have a recipe. She had nothing to work from except her memory, but as she crushed the crackers and kneaded them with the softened butter, she knew she could do this. Although she'd never made a peach pie before in her life—in this life—she knew how. As she crushed the crackers and kneaded the dough, memories leaped out of her mind like dolphins breaching for air. She remembered Dolly's blue gingham apron and the yellow scarf she wore in her hair, not like a stereotypical housemaid's scarf but in a big bow over her right ear like a fifties-style pinup girl. She remembered the flour dusting Dolly's beautiful face, leaving a smattering of freckles on her smooth, dark skin. Dolly hummed as she worked sometimes, and Faye thought of that soothing tuneless sound as the sound track of the home—like an engine purring. Between the two of them, they'd managed to finish all the housework by two or three in the afternoon. They'd gone out collecting seashells one day and sat on the front porch the next reading and drowsing in the heat. Dolly read Sherlock Holmes short stories. Faye read *Villette* by Charlotte Brontë, a book she'd always meant to read but had never taken the time to. But in 1921 she'd taken the time, because she could. Because she had all the time in the world.

"'I believe that life is not all,'" Faye whispered to herself as she pressed the crust into the pie pan. "'Neither the beginning nor the end. I believe while I tremble. I trust while I weep…'"

She paused and looked up. She'd read *Villette* at the keeper's cottage. How would she remember lines from a book she'd never read?

Faye looked out the open kitchen window behind the sink. Crickets woke to sing, and flashing lightning bugs darted and danced under the Spanish moss hanging from the branches of the backyard's live oak trees. If she closed her eyes and listened, she could pretend she was back at the cottage again. Evening meant cooking dinner and waiting for Dolly's father to come fetch her. He'd pull up to the dock in his metal fishing boat that spewed diesel fumes they could smell all the way up at the house. Carrick would catch his rope and tie it to a pillar. Her father, a fisherman named Wallace, always brought them something from his catch—grouper or snapper or flounder—and Faye would give him something from their garden, corn or squash or onions. And without fail, every day he'd doff his hat and say, "Thanks to you and the chief for taking good care of our girl." And without fail, every evening Faye would reply, "We don't know what we'd do without her." Every evening, that was the ritual. It was so deeply embedded in her mind that when she'd passed a display of saltwater fish for sale at the grocery store, her nose had conjured the scent of diesel.

When the pie finished baking, Faye took it out of the oven and set it on the trivet to cool. It looked like Dolly's peach pie and smelled like Dolly's peach pie, but she wouldn't know for certain she'd made it correctly until she tasted it.

"Something sure smells good in here."

Faye looked over her shoulder and saw Miss Lizzie come into the kitchen, her broom and dustpan in hand. She cleaned the house almost as obsessively as Dolly had cleaned theirs.

"Peach pie," Faye said. "I hope you don't mind. I used one of your mixing bowls and your pie pan."

"I don't mind a bit as long as you wash them and give me a piece of your pie."

"Soon as it cools, it's all yours."

Miss Lizzie walked over to the oven and gave the pie on the trivet an appraising look.

"Looks good. You make it with the cracker crust? That's the way to do it."

"I think so, too. You've had it like that before?" Faye asked as she washed her hands.

"Many, many times," she said wistfully as she walked over to the broom closet and opened the door. "My grandmother always made it like that. Still my favorite."

Faye froze with her hands under the faucet. She picked up a towel, turned around and saw a faded blue-and-white-gingham apron hanging inside the broom closet on the back of the door.

"Didn't you tell me the furniture in my room was from the Bride Island lighthouse?" Faye asked.

"The desk is and the side table. Few other pieces around the house."

"How did you come to have them?"

"Passed down. They were my mother's first and she gave them to me."

"And your grandmother's before that?"

"They were. She worked out at the lighthouse, and they gave her some of the furniture when they automated the light. Same grandmother who taught me to bake pie, as a matter of fact."

"Dolly," Faye said, her blood chilling, her heart leaping.

"Dorothy," Miss Lizzie said. "Although I do think she was called Dolly as a girl." Miss Lizzie narrowed her eyes at Faye. "How do you know my grandmother's name?"

Faye walked over to her, shaking a little. There it was—Dolly's pretty nose right on the center of Miss Lizzie's face. Same eyes, too, wide with a little upturn at the corners—Diana Ross eyes.

"I'll tell you how I know in a second. But can I do something first?" Faye asked.

"Whatever you please," the older woman said.

"Can I hug you?"

18

Faye hugged Miss Lizzie like she'd hug Dolly right now if she could. Miss Lizzie suffered the hug gladly, patting Faye on the back the whole time.

"You're an odd one, Miss Faye, but you make pie like my grandma made it, so you must be a good one."

Tears sprung to Faye's eyes.

"Now, don't cry, girl," Miss Lizzie said.

"I miss… I miss my grandmother is all," Faye said, when what she wanted to say was *I miss your grandmother.*

"I miss mine, too. I miss her every day."

By the time Faye had finished crying and pulled herself together, the pie had cooled enough to eat. She and Miss Lizzie sat across from each other at the kitchen table, a piece of pie in front of each of them.

Faye lifted her fork and paused before she took the bite. If she'd screwed up the pie, then maybe it had all been a dream. Maybe she'd read about Carrick and Dolly while studying the lighthouse and it had all come together in some sort of brain stew in her sun-bleached brain while she'd lain passed out on the beach.

Faye took the bite, and it tasted like pie, like Dolly's pie, like a pie that could save your soul if it needed saving. And it tasted real and true, as real as the peaches on her tongue, as true as her time in 1921. Dolly and Carrick and the house—it hadn't been a dream. Faye had been there.

"I don't know how to make pie," Faye said to Miss Lizzie. The older woman took a bite and nodded her head.

"Tastes like pie to me," she said. "Just like my grandmother's pie."

"Maybe I found her recipe when I was researching the lighthouse."

"You said you found some papers about her?" Miss Lizzie asked.

"I found a few mentions of her," Faye said. She hated to lie, but she didn't want to burden this woman with the truth. "Dolly Rivers—she worked as a housekeeper at the cottage there. Kept the whole place running like clockwork."

"Those papers said that about her?"

Faye nodded.

"I believe it," Miss Lizzie said. "She was always a good housekeeper but you know, that just never was enough for her. In her forties after her kids were old enough, she got a job at a furniture store. It wasn't her dream job, of course. Until the day she died, she talked about how all she wanted was to go to New York and try her hand at being a real interior designer. It wasn't meant to be back in those days. She made the best of it, though. One lady who came into the furniture store all the time hired her to decorate her house. My grandmother did such a good job that before it was over, she'd done half the houses in town. Every lady within fifty miles of here wanted my grandmother's help. You know what my grandmother said to me about it?"

"No, what did she say?"

"She said, 'They let me in through the back door, but when I'm done I go out the front.' She made a lot of money doing those houses up, though she would have made more with her own business."

Faye grinned. Not even bigoted old white ladies could deny Dolly's talent. It would be like denying the wind while standing in a hurricane.

"Doesn't surprise me," Faye said. "The papers I read said she was the best cook around, and she decorated the whole place, made it a home. The keeper and his...his daughter loved her. They loved her very much."

"Oh, she loved them, too. Now, the first family she worked for in town, she didn't like them much. They treated her like she was stupid just because she couldn't hear. But the light keeper and his girl, she was close to them."

"I can't imagine anyone treating her like she was stupid. I mean, the stuff I read said she was smart and talented, very artistic."

"You sound like you know her," Miss Lizzie said.

"I feel like I do. Tell me more about her. She got married, I guess. And kids and grandkids..."

"Four children, ten grandchildren. And all thanks to her ears. About age twenty or thereabouts, her brother took her to Atlanta. They had a hospital there just for black folks. All black doctors and nurses, too. Now, they couldn't do anything for my grandmother's ears there, but one doctor decided he'd rather have her as his wife than as his patient. He didn't mind my grandmother couldn't hear. His nurses said he was the sort of man only a hard-of-hearing woman could love anyway." Miss Lizzie's face broke into a broad grin. "But that was Dr. Gerald Holt, my grandfather."

"A doctor. Good for Dolly." Faye wanted to find Dolly right this second and give her a high five.

"She was the talk of the town because of him. She wouldn't marry him unless he agreed to take her to New York on their honeymoon, and you better believe he took her there."

"Very smart man," Faye said. "I bet the wedding was incredible. I'm sure she made her own dress."

"She made a beautiful dress, but a month before the wedding her daddy died. But Chief Morgan, he stepped in and gave her away."

"Carrick gave her away? I mean, Chief Morgan did?"

"Oh, yes. They were like family, she said, she and the Chief were—that's what she always called him—Chief. And he'd lost a daughter and my grandmother lost her daddy... and they were close. Not in any way that wasn't right," Miss Lizzie said quickly. "They were the only two people there when his girl drowned in the storm. My grandmother watched it happen."

"A storm," Faye repeated. "His daughter drowned in a storm?" Is that what had happened? They'd watched her drown? Originally Faith had been killed a week earlier when she'd fallen off the pier into the water. Faye had changed the past, but only in the smallest of ways. The present, it seemed, was otherwise unchanged. Thank God for small favors.

"It wasn't quite a hurricane, but it was bad," Miss Lizzie said. "My grandmother never talked about what happened until the night before the Chief's funeral. Then she told us the whole story, about how it was her who'd almost died that day. She fell in the water and the keeper's girl dived in after her and fished her out. But before the keeper's girl could get out of the water, a wave hit, and she went under. Never came up. My poor grandmother had to drag the Chief out of the water before he drowned himself looking for her. They spent the night in the lighthouse. My grandmother said it was the worst night of her life. Every few minutes she had to stop him from running out and throwing himself in the ocean. She said she slept stretched out in front of the hatch to stop him. She said...she said she'd never seen anyone grieve like he grieved for that girl of his."

Faye leaned back in her chair, all appetite gone. Carrick... He'd mourned for her like she'd mourned for Will. He thought she was dead, and here she was, alive and well and eating pie. His grief was for nothing. She hadn't died, but how could she tell him that?

"I can't imagine watching someone drown, someone I loved," Faye said. "I don't want to imagine."

"My grandmother and the Chief carried that night with them all their lives. I recall my mother telling her she didn't want to go to Chief Morgan's funeral. He was a Catholic man, you see, and none of us had ever once stepped foot in a Catholic Church before, and this was a white church, very white. But my grandmother said, 'We are all going.' So we went."

Faye could scarcely breathe thinking of Dolly at Carrick's funeral, of her grief and Carrick's and all of it that could have been avoided somehow...should have been...

"I was fifteen or so then and liked my grandmother a whole lot more than I liked my mother. You know how girls are at that age. So I sat by her side through the funeral," Miss Lizzie continued. "You know, I had never seen my grandmother cry before. And she...she wept." Miss Lizzie said those two words with finality. "She wept so hard the priest tried to cheer her up afterward by asking her if she was Chief Morgan's girlfriend. I laughed at that—teenage girls find everything like that funny—but my grandmother did not. She never talked much outside the family. But that day she spoke, clear as a bell. She held that priest's hand and said, 'Father Cahill, the Chief was my friend.' And that was that."

"Father Cahill? Pat Cahill?"

"You know him? He lives around here now."

"I know him. And I think I need to go have a little talk with him."

Faye stood up and reached for her plate of half-eaten pie. Miss Lizzie put one finger on the edge of the plate.

"You can leave that right there," she said with a meaningful smile.

Faye grabbed her purse and her car keys and was heading out the door when her bag buzzed at her. When she pulled out her phone, she saw a text message from Hagen flashing on the screen.

Four simple words: I'm calling. Please answer.

Faye sighed. Sure enough, the phone buzzed in her hand. She sat on the bottom step in the foyer. Something told her she'd want to sit down for this call.

"Okay, I'm answering," she said to him.

"Thank you," Hagen replied. "I swear this won't be a fight unless you want it to be."

He sounded sincere. Sincere and panicked.

"I don't want it to be," she said. "What's up?"

"I got an email confirmation about an MRI for you from our insurance company? What the hell, Faye? Are you all right?"

Damn it. The insurance was still in Hagen's name, his

email address, his phone number. She'd forgotten to tell them to change it.

"I'm fine. I don't have anything wrong with me. They were just checking."

"Doctors don't do emergency MRIs for fun. Were you in an accident? Are you hurt?"

"Not hurt. I may have accidentally mixed up my Ambien with Tylenol. I blacked out. Nothing else." Ty's theory had been reasonable, a very male "stupid girl" theory that Hagen was likely to believe as it put the blame squarely on her.

"Jesus, Faye, you could have killed yourself. Are you keeping all your pills in one bottle? Were you drunk?"

"You know, our whole 'let's not fight' plan is not going to fly if you start accusing me of getting drunk and mixing booze and pills. Does that sound like something I'd do?"

"I'm not accusing. I'm scared. I've pried pill bottles out of your hand before."

"That was years ago."

"Now you're overdosing and blacking out," Hagen continued. The man could go on like this for hours if she didn't stop him. "I'm allowed to worry about the woman I was married to for almost four years. Even if that woman does hate me."

"I don't hate you. I never hated you."

"You hated being married to me."

"Not all the time."

The last thing she expected was to hear Hagen laugh, but he did. A real laugh, not ironic, not sarcastic. Just amused.

"Hagen?"

"We did suck at being married to each other, didn't we?" he asked.

Faye smiled. "We absolutely did. We sucked hard," she said, amazed Hagen had admitted it. Finally.

Hagen sighed so hard the phone rattled in her ear.

"Maybe you should come back for a few days," Hagen finally said. "Just until you're sure you won't have another blackout. You know the house is big enough you wouldn't have to see me if you didn't want to."

"You know that's not a good idea."

"Fine, go stay with your mom and aunt, then. Stay with somebody who will keep an eye on you."

"Aunt Kate can barely keep an eye on Mom. And I have friends here. One took me to the ER today and waited until I was done to drive me home. He'll take me there again if I have to go back."

"He? Are you dating somebody again already?"

"My personal life isn't your concern."

"So you are?"

"I'm hanging up now..." She sang the words, trilling them to him, something he always hated.

"Faye, please. Keep in touch with me, okay? I worry about you."

"You don't have to worry. I'm okay. Really."

"Because of this new guy?"

"He's part of it, yes." Faye didn't want to hurt Hagen needlessly but the sooner he moved on, the better for everybody involved, especially him.

"Who is this guy?"

"He's a lighthouse keeper."

"A what? I didn't think they existed anymore."

"They don't."

Faye told Hagen goodbye before he could get in another word. She hung up, got in her car and threw the phone in the glove compartment. She drove straight to Pat's house. When he didn't answer her knock on the door, she followed a hunch and drove over to the Marshlands. Faye spotted his white hair and his Gregory Peck profile parked in his usual painting spot in front of the house by the stone bench.

"Miss Faye, what brings you out here?" he called across the lawn. "Come to take pictures of the sound? Nice evening for it." He pointed his paintbrush at the sky. Red-and-gold clouds crowded together over the water, creating a ruby-and-citrine sunset. "Red sky at night, sailor and painter's delight."

Faye sat on the stone bench next to his chair and looked him in the eyes. At first he didn't seem to want to return her gaze, but eventually he gave in and looked at her.

"I need to know everything you know about Carrick and Faith Morgan," Faye said. "Everything. And I know you didn't tell me everything, so don't pretend you did."

"I don't know what you mean," he said.

"You know. You performed Carrick's funeral mass. I'm guessing you heard his confessions, too?"

"Faye, I'm a priest."

"You're a retired priest."

"Once a priest, always a priest. I won't betray a parishioner who put his trust in me. There are rules."

"I don't care about the rules. I have to know about them. I have to know what you know about Faith Morgan."

"Faith Morgan—why do you have to know about her? She died in a storm almost a century ago."

"In a storm? Are you sure? Because last time we talked, she fell off a pier and drowned."

Pat's eyes narrowed. He looked up to the sky. "Was it a storm? It was. I know it was. But a pier...that sounds right, too." He turned and met her eyes. She saw fear in his. He stood up and put his hands to his head, lowered them and faced her.

"The pier," he said. "I remember the pier. Faye, what's happening?"

"I don't know. But I think you do."

"You went into the water, didn't you?" he asked.

Faye slowly nodded. "Pat, I'm going to tell you about a miracle. You're a priest, so I assume you believe in them."

"I want to believe in them."

"Then believe in this," Faye said, taking his paintbrush from his hand and placing it on his easel. She took both of his hands into both of hers. Hers were steady. His weren't, but she knew they weren't shaking because of his tremor. In his eyes, she saw fear. Maybe he didn't want to believe in miracles. Maybe he was afraid to.

"What's the miracle?" he asked.

"I am Faith Morgan."

19

Faye told Pat the truth, all of it, and he listened without speaking until she reached the end of her tale.

She thought it had started raining until she realized the two drops of water on her wrist hadn't come from the clouds above but from the eyes of the priest whose shaking hands she held.

"You believe me," she said. It wasn't a question. A man wouldn't weep when told a lie, but he might when told a truth he didn't want to hear.

Slowly, he nodded his head. He pulled his hands from her grasp and stood. She followed him over to the dock that looked out on the marshy sound.

"'I grow old/I grow old/I shall wear the bottoms of my trousers rolled,'" he said.

"T. S. Eliot. 'The Love Song of J. Alfred Prufrock,'" Faye said. "I read that just last week at the cottage. Carrick has a first American edition on his bookshelves."

"Eliot died in '65. Same year Carrick did," Pat said, kicking a pebble off the dock and into the water, where it made hardly a ripple. "As for me, I could have died when I went out to the lighthouse."

"You said you decided against killing yourself."

"I did. It was a foolish whim, and when it passed I wanted to ask God's forgiveness. Despair is a sin, but I'd say it's the sin God forgives most often and most easily. So I rolled up my trousers, waded in the water and took my rosary out of my pocket. That rosary was special to me. Carrick gave it to me before he died."

"Silver beads? Medal that says 'S. Brendanus'?"

"Saint Brendan, yes. Patron of sailors. I was holding the rosary, praying my way through the first decade, when my hands got a tremor. Dropped it right in the water. I dived for it. A wave hit and threw me under. I really didn't think I'd come up again. What a nasty trick that would be for the ocean to kill me not ten minutes after I'd decided not to kill myself. But somehow I made it to the surface again. God knows I was fighting for my life. When I came up everything looked different. The sky was dark and getting darker, but the lighthouse, it was shining. I saw the light flash and I thought I had died. But then I saw the house that hadn't been there before and the long wooden pier in the water. I saw a woman standing at the very edge of the pier, like she'd found where the sidewalk ends."

"Did you see her face?"

"No."

"What did she throw in the water?" Faye asked.

"Herself," he said.

"Are you sure?" Faye asked.

"I'm sure. The water was choppy, but not choppy enough to pull a girl down off a pier. She jumped, Faye. I saw her jump into the water."

"Why would she jump? She was finally free from her husband."

"I don't know. And don't think I haven't wondered about that every single day of my life."

"What happened next, Pat?"

He shook his head. "I tried to save her. It was the damnedest thing. I took off swimming after her like I was twenty-five again. I knew how it felt to swim these waters when I was young and strong. I did it often enough when I was pastor here in the sixties. But before I could reach her, another wave hit me and I went under. When I came up again, the dock was gone, and the cottage, and the lighthouse was dark. I felt like an old man again. Sometimes I wish… I wish I could have stayed."

"Did you know what had happened? Did you understand it?" Faye's relief that she wasn't the only one who'd been there, who'd been part of this mystery was knee weakening. She could have cried.

"I thought I'd passed out," he said. "I thought it was all a dream. But telling myself that didn't sit right with me. I'm not prone to denial. I went to the hospital and got tests run. They all came back clear. I wanted to believe it wasn't real even though I knew better. On my better days I'm a man of faith. It's easy to say you believe in miracles and signs and wonders, and that there are more things in heaven and earth than are dreamed of in all our philosophies, but when something happens you can't explain except by calling it a miracle, you can't imagine how hard that is on your faith. Faith is believing without knowing, without seeing. But when you see…" He stopped and looked up at the sky as if seeking the face of God. She hoped Pat saw it. All she saw were clouds, but such beautiful clouds that if one believed in God, one might imagine Him or Her as a painter.

"I thought I was crazy, too, for a little while," Faye said. "When I woke up and there was Will in my bedroom, I kissed him. I thought it was the best dream I'd ever had in my life. And then when I realized I was somehow Faith Morgan, that I was Carrick's daughter, I thought I was in a waking nightmare."

"Faith was not his daughter," Pat said, his voice firm and final. "And Carrick Morgan would never lay a hand on a woman unless she wanted his hands on her. He was a good man."

Faye didn't tell him how much it hurt to hear Carrick spoken about in the past tense. Carrick *is* a good man. Carrick *is*, not *was*.

"He told you about Faith?" Faye asked.

"He did. And I can tell you a little of what I know because he told me over dinner one night, not under the seal of the confessional."

"Please tell me anything you can about her." Faye said *her* when what she meant was *me*. *Tell me about me*, she wanted to say to him.

"Faith's real name was Millie Anne Scarborough."

"Millie Anne Scarborough," Faye repeated, testing the name in her mouth and finding it foreign.

"Millie's parents were old money, but when her father died when she was sixteen, her mother discovered there was none of that old money left. No money, but plenty of debt and three daughters who needed husbands. The only way to get out of that debt was to marry the girls off to wealthy men. Luckily they found takers for all three girls. One senator's son, one bank president and one former navy officer who'd inherited a fortune from his industrialist father."

"Marshall."

"Lieutenant Marshall J. Carlyle of the Carlyle Steel fortune. He was forty years old when he married Faith, and she'd just turned eighteen. Marshall and Chief Carrick Morgan had been buddies in the war, served on the same ship. They kept each other sane, Carrick said. Kept each other alive. They were very close. Then the war was over and they returned to their civilian lives. Carrick took a job at the Boston Light. Marshall Carlyle finally decided to get married and have children. He wanted a young girl, and he wanted a pretty girl, and he had enough money he could snap his fingers and get both. Millie fit the bill. Carrick said Marshall caused a minor scandal by inviting him to the wedding. Rich, old-money socialites didn't usually invite poor-as-dirt Irish Catholic sailors to their weddings, especially not the society wedding of the year. Carrick went, though he didn't want to. Had a soft spot for Miss Scarborough himself."

"He loved her a little bit," Faye said. "He said something about wanting to stop the wedding. He saw her crying before the ceremony."

"No stopping that wedding. Not with a fortune spent and another fortune to be gained or lost. She married him— God help that poor girl. Her husband ruled the house with an iron fist."

"She ran away from him. I know that. How did she get to the island?"

"Train from Boston to New York. Hid in the big city a couple days, then hired a driver to take her to South Carolina. Marshall and Carrick had stayed in touch, so I assume that's how she knew where to find him. She didn't tell him she was coming, though. I don't think she told a soul. Just walked out of her house and disappeared. Turned up on Carrick's doorstep one night. She told him her husband had tried to kill her. So Carrick took her in, told everyone she was his daughter who'd come to stay with him now that she was out of school. A believable enough story then. People still think she was his daughter to this day. No need to correct them and cause a scandal. Might as well let sleeping dogs lie."

"How did she come to be 'Faith'?"

"Old nickname her grandmother had given her. She and her two sisters all had nicknames as little girls—Faith, Hope and Love. Millie was Faith."

"Is that why you painted her? Because you knew you saw her the night she died?" Faye asked.

"She didn't die that night. She died later in the storm. So strange," he said, raising his hand to his forehead. "I remember both."

"I had a dream about her. I dreamed I was running away from my husband. I wore a black dress and a black veil. Widow's weeds. It was Faith's dream. Or maybe one of her memories she let me see." Faye leaned her head back, looked at the darkening sky. "Why is this happening, Pat? What does it mean? Is it reincarnation? Was Will really Carrick in a past life? Was I Faith?"

"Catholics don't believe in reincarnation."

"Then what do you think it is?"

"You lost Will in a tragic accident. Carrick lost Faith in a tragic accident. Reconciliation, maybe? Restoration? Hell, it could be reincarnation. All I know is that I don't know."

"You're a priest. You're supposed to know these things."

"There's nothing in the Bible about time travel, my dear.

Seeing visions, yes, but not...not anything like this. We are in deep water here."

"It's not much of a restoration with me in this time and Carrick back in 1921. I can't stand the thought of him thinking I'm dead. He's there right now, broken the way I was when Will died."

"But he's not, Faye. Carrick's dead. Has been since 1965. I can take you to the cemetery right now and show you his grave. It's right next to..."

Pat choked on whatever he was about to say next. He simply stopped speaking and could not go on.

"Mine," Faye said. "Right? His grave his next to mine."

"Next to Faith Morgan's."

"The Faith Morgan who died in the storm?"

Pat nodded. "She's buried here in Beaufort. Anything with her real name on it was buried with her. Even after she died, Carrick wanted to protect her from her husband."

Faye's heart tossed and twisted like wind chimes in a storm. Her own grave was here in Beaufort. Strangely, it didn't bother her, the thought of seeing her own grave. But Carrick's? She couldn't bear to see Carrick's. She hadn't even allowed Will to be buried in the ground under a headstone, fearing that if she buried him in the earth and put up a monument to him, she would never leave his tomb. If she saw Carrick's grave...

"Pat... I refuse to believe I went back in time ninety-four years by accident. Of all the people to go back, it was me—the widow of a man who looks just like Carrick. The one woman on earth who would want to be there and stay there. Me. And I was the one who went. I won't know why unless I go back."

"Go back?" Pat faced her, stared at her, eyes wide and stunned. "You can't possibly mean that."

"I can mean that. I was happy there. Do you know what it means to be able to say I was happy anywhere?"

"You were there six days. Six. That's a vacation, Faye. You know what they say—nice place to visit, but I wouldn't want to live there. You don't want to live in 1921. Penicillin hadn't even been invented yet."

"I won't get sick."

"You can't know that. Do you know what the infant mortality rate was back then?"

"What does that matter to a woman who can't have babies?" Faye shook her head, wanted to laugh and cry, but did neither. "Pat—I was almost eaten by an alligator. Carrick killed it with an ax and Dolly turned it into stew for dinner. Trust me. I know that 1921 isn't safe. I also know my husband was killed in 2011 when he tried to change a tire for some meth heads. Life is dangerous and it kills us eventually. Right?"

"You can't live in the past."

Faye stood up and walked away from Pat a few steps before turning around and facing him.

"You sound just like my ex-husband. That's such a condescending, male thing to say. It sounds rational. It sounds like something smart to say, but it's meaningless. We are all the sum of every single day we've lived. We are our pasts. Not only can I live in the past, I did live in the past, and it was the first time I was living in a long time. And if the past wants me to live in it, why shouldn't I? At least the past and I have met. The future's a total stranger."

Pat walked over to her, put his hands on her shoulders.

"You know Carrick isn't Will and Will isn't Carrick. Will's no more alive in 1921 than he is in 2015."

Faye didn't meet his eyes, couldn't meet them.

"Yes," she whispered. "But he's not dead, either."

"Faye, look at me."

She sighed and met his eyes.

"Carrick doesn't know who you are," he said. "He thinks he's in love with his war buddy's young wife. You deserve better than being loved for something you aren't. You should be loved for you, as Faye. And Carrick—he's not Will. And he deserves better than that, too. He deserves to be loved for who he is, not who he reminds you of. I don't have to tell you that, do I?"

"I would have told him, but I thought...I thought he'd send me to a mental hospital. Wouldn't you?"

"Maybe I would have in his shoes. But I'm not Carrick. The man I knew would have heard you out, and he would have bent his own soul backward to believe in you."

"If I tell him the truth, he might not love me anymore."

"If you don't tell him the truth, it's not you he loves."

Pat's words hurt because they were true. She nodded. "I'll try."

"That's all I ask. Carrick was a dear friend to me during a hard time of my life. He told me his secrets and I told him mine, and we both respected each other more after. That doesn't happen often. I almost envy you. I'd like to shake his hand again, tell him how much his friendship meant to me."

"I'll do that for you. It would be my pleasure."

"You're really going to do this?"

"Dolly had to spend a night in the lighthouse with Carrick to keep him from throwing himself into the ocean. A seventeen-year-old girl—a girl I love and adore—had to sleep in front of a doorway to stop a suicide. If I can save her from that, if I can save Carrick from that... How can I not go back?"

"Is that the real reason? Or is that how you're justifying what could very well be a suicide attempt of your own?"

Faye crossed her hands on her chest over her heart.

"I love him, Pat."

"Carrick?"

She nodded.

"He's not Will," Pat said. "You know he's not Will."

"I don't know what I know anymore. But I think...I think I know this... Carrick told me about the night mark. You know what that is?"

"It's the name for the lighthouse's particular light pattern."

"That's right. Carrick said the night mark is the heart of a lighthouse. And Carrick and Will have the same night mark, Pat. They shine the same light."

"Oh, Faye, love." Pat looked at her and shook his head in pity and affection.

"I've been in the dark too long. I can't go back to living without that light. I can't. I just can't..." She swiped tears off her face until she gave up and let them fall.

"You go, then," he said. "And you walk in the light, any light you can find."

"You can come, too," she said, smiling at him through her tears. "You said you've already been there. Come back with me."

"Oh, no. I'm too old for that nonsense."

"You said you felt like a young man again in 1921. Why not come be a young man again? Take a second chance at your life. You lived one entire life as a priest who painted on the side. Now you could do it again and this time devote your life to painting."

"Nice fantasy," he said.

"You could get married."

Pat laughed. "Never been a top priority for me."

"What about helping people? You said you came here the first time because you wanted to help people. Imagine how much you could help them if you knew the future."

He shook his head, laughed. "Knowing the future and changing the future are two different things. I know the future already—my tremor will get worse. I have maybe two years of painting left. I will slowly succumb to heart disease like normal people do, and I'll die in a nursing home just like my father did. No way I can change the future. Knowledge isn't always power."

"You don't want to go back and try to assassinate Hitler?" she said. It seemed like the sort of thing a young and passionate do-gooder priest would want to do.

"Hitler's own men couldn't kill him, and many of them tried. I don't speak a word of German, but I've always wanted to get hanged or shot by a firing squad, so I might as well give it a go, right?"

"We could try to warn people what was coming."

"If a girl walked up to us right now and said unless we assassinate the prime minister of Britain, World War III will break out in ten years, would you believe her?"

"No," Faye said.

"How's this? I'll go back and try to kill Hitler. You go back and warn people of the Great Depression and the Third Reich. I'll end up in a hangman's noose and you'll end up in an asylum. And there'll be no one to get you out this time. One person can't change the world."

"We could change a tiny corner of it. Isn't that enough reason to go back? To save even one life?"

"Whose life are you saving by going back? Carrick Morgan and Dolly Rivers Holt both lived into old age."

Faye leaned forward and kissed Pat on the cheek. She had a feeling she would never see him again.

"Mine," she said.

She squeezed his hand one last time and started toward her car. Pat called out after her.

"Be safe, Faye. Please. I'd like to think I'll meet you again."

"You think you'll come back?"

"No, but I think if you live long enough, I'll see you in 1965. I'll be the baby-face priest who's scared shitless of his own congregation."

"And I'll be an old lady. You won't even recognize me."

"I'd know those Elizabeth Taylor eyes anywhere."

Faye smiled and blew him a kiss. She got back into her car and drove back to the Church Street house. She sat at her desk, at Dolly's sewing table. She had paper, she had a pen, but she had no one to write to. Her father was dead, and her mother hardly knew her anymore. If she did die tonight or disappear or whatever happened when she left this time, who would miss her? She'd drifted away from her friends after Will's death, and she'd remarried Hagen so suddenly...

"Dear Hagen," she wrote on her stationery.

What was there to say to him that she hadn't already said?

"You were wrong. I can live in the past."

She signed it, and as she did she knew no one would ever read this. No one had noticed when she'd left the first time. No one would notice this time. Did it bother her that time and the universe would cover up her disappearance like dirt over an unmarked grave? No. It didn't bother her. Maybe it should have, but she already felt like a ghost in 2015. She might as well haunt the past as the present.

Faye stood up and took a quick breath. *Time to go.* She only needed one more thing. The first time she'd dropped Will's ring into the water by accident and the water had carried it away, drawing her in like a fish on a hook. Pat had dropped Carrick's rosary and the same thing had happened to him. She needed an object, something from Will or Carrick, something to act as a key or an offering or a sacrifice. Faye dug through her luggage and found a small velvet box. She opened it and there they were—her wedding band and Will's. She'd worn hers up until the minute before her courthouse wedding to Hagen. Will had worn his from the moment they said, "I do" until the moment they'd slipped it off his finger before his cremation. She couldn't bring herself to sacrifice Will's band, so she took her own wedding band and hoped it would be enough.

When she made it back to Bride Island, she parked in the bare patch between the trees behind the lighthouse again. She walked to the beach again. She took off her shoes again. She waded into the water again.

Faye looked up at the lighthouse, at the white tower so silent and so somber, at the lantern room dark and growing darker as the sun disappeared. From her pocket, Faye took out her wedding band. She slipped it onto her ring finger.

"Will, honey, tell me if I'm doing the wrong thing. Tell me if I'm crazy."

You called me honey. That's cute. Is this a Southern thing you picked up down here?

"God, I miss you."

That's not a good reason to go tossing yourself into the ocean, Bunny.

"I miss me. How's that for a reason?"

You miss you? You're standing right there. I can see you. Your tits look great in that shirt, by the way.

She sighed and the sigh became a laugh.

"You know this isn't me. You know I haven't been me since you died. But back there, back with Carrick and Dolly, I feel like me again."

You love them?

"Like family."

Family is worth taking big risks for. And it's hard to be without family in this world. We aren't made for it, are we?

"Very hard. And I don't feel alone with them. I feel like I belong."

He takes care of you, right?

"He killed an alligator with an ax to protect me."

Well, I killed that spider in our bathroom that day. You remember that? Thing was as big as a baseball. Fucking tarantula.

"My hero."

I should have used an ax. That would have been way more badass than swatting it with Sports Illustrated.

"You're only saying that because you got spider guts all over the swimsuit edition."

Yeah, and we probably wouldn't have gotten our security deposit back if I'd stuck an ax in the wall.

"Will?"

Yes, babe?

"I want to love him like I loved you. Is that okay?"

Babe...

"Please, just tell me how you feel about that—yes or no?"

Faye, it's okay. I swear. I want you to love him as much as I want him to love you.

"You do? Why?"

Because I'm the goddamned greatest dead husband who ever lived.

She burst into laughter. "You are that. No argument from me."

Faye took a breath.

"Will, love? Is this you?" she whispered. "Are you doing this? Are you pulling these strings for me?"

Didn't I promise to take care of you until the day you died?

"Yes, you did, Will. And you're doing a very good job of it."

And with that, she tossed her wedding band into the water.

She waited.

The lighthouse beacon flashed once and went dark.

Faye counted.

One.

The water started running high. It lapped at her legs, at her waist…

Two. Three. Four. Five.

Faye heard the water rushing toward her, rumbling like an iron train on iron tracks.

"See you on the other side, my love."

Six.

A wave hit her with the force of that runaway train.

Seven.

Light.

20

Faye broke the surface with a cry, and a force even stronger than the ocean ripped her from the water and carried her to dry land. She couldn't see who it was for the salt and blowing sand in her eyes. She struck out with her arms, seeking warm bodies, and caught hold of the first one she found.

"What year is it?" she yelled. She had to scream over the screaming of the wind.

"What?" The word sounded like it had been ripped from his mouth and tossed away.

"What year?" she yelled louder.

She swiped at her face and blinked her way back to sight.

"It's the year you learn how to swim, love." Carrick knelt at her side, smiling like he'd won the grand prize in the carnival of life. He grabbed her by the shoulders, pulling her roughly against him. She clung to his arm, never wanting to let go of him again.

Dolly, still soaking wet, threw herself on the ground and wrapped her arms around Faye's stomach. Faye grabbed her, held her. Thank God or whoever was running this show, she was home.

"How long was I under?" Faye asked.

"Too fucking long," Carrick said. "I thought I'd lost you for sure this time."

"You swear like a sailor, Chief Morgan."

"I am a sailor. Now get into the goddamn lighthouse."

"Aye, Chief."

Carrick glanced at the ocean stampeding the beach like a herd of wild horses.

"Get Dolly," he said. "Hold her hand and you hold mine. Stay low to the ground. Ready?"

Faye took Dolly's hand, and they scrambled to their feet.

"Ready."

"Don't let me go," he said. "Now run."

He took off, her wrist tight in his hand and Dolly's hand tight in Faye's. The wind surged, turning the air into a sandstorm. Halfway down the beach the rain started, slamming into them like a thousand tiny bullets. She remembered riding a roller coaster in the rain once and having to cover her face from the pain of hitting the water so much faster than the water hit her. Now the water hit back. Dolly slipped and took Faye down with her. Carrick turned and grabbed them both by the hands.

Tripping and sliding, the three of them ran into the wind and through the whirling sand. Faye imagined they must have looked like a mad family on the maddest beach outing, a parody of a picture postcard.

Faye knew she should be terrified. One broken flying branch, one storm surge, one more fall and that could be the end of any one of them. But she couldn't be afraid, not when she was so relieved to be back. Elated. As soon as she could, she would kiss Carrick and keep kissing him until neither of them knew nor cared what year it was.

The wind blew hard north, picked up speed as it whipped around the stone seawall and slammed against the lighthouse. Carrick could barely get the door to crack open against the wind. Faye had to slide in through the gap and push it open with her back against the wood. Carrick pushed Dolly through and followed her in, right as a gust of wind caught the door like a sail and pulled it loose from the hinges. Carrick jammed the door into the frame the best he could, but there was nothing for it. The next gust blew the door in and onto the floor. Wind gushed into the tower, cold and wet and angry, and ran circles around the three of them. The lighthouse whistled and howled like a whole orchestra of off-key oboes.

"Watch room," Carrick screamed over the wind. "We can shut the hatch."

Faye took Dolly's hand again and coaxed her toward the spiral staircase. Carrick hadn't been kidding about Dolly's fear of heights. Dolly took two steps, shook her head and dug in her heels.

"Come on, sweetheart," Faye said, taking Dolly's face in her hands. "Please," she mouthed over and over, but there was no budging Dolly. She pulled back from Faye and tried to make a break for the open doorway. Carrick caught her around the waist and hoisted her up in his arms.

"I got her," he said as Dolly struggled, then went still, not out of surrender but in fear-filled paralysis.

"That's one hundred and ten steps?" Faye asked. "That's impossible."

"Follow me close. Whatever you do, don't let me drop her."

Faye followed but she knew they'd never make it. Dolly wasn't a child of six but a young woman of seventeen. While slender, she was tall and had to weigh at least a hundred pounds, especially in her wet clothes. Dolly let out a low moan of true terror. Faye took her hand. It was ice-cold. Faye locked eyes with her, smiled and squeezed her hand over and over as Carrick began the long, arduous journey up the lighthouse stairs.

Three sounds competed with one another for dominance in that tower as they wended their slow, torturous way up the lighthouse's spiral staircase—the wind, Dolly's moans and whimpers and Carrick's labored breathing. Faye could barely breathe herself as she kept pace behind them, one hand on Carrick's lower back for support and her other hand in Dolly's iron grasp. Although Dolly couldn't hear her, Faye whispered to her the entire way up, promising her they would be fine, it was okay, they were safe and they would be safe all night, they were almost there, getting closer, so close... She spoke as much for Carrick's benefit as Dolly's. She hoped to distract him, give him comfort, give him something. She wouldn't be able to walk up these steps carrying a gallon of milk in her hands, and here he was, climbing them at a steady rate with the equivalent of twelve of them.

Two-thirds of the way up, Carrick stumbled. He leaned against the wall, straining to catch his breath.

"Put her over your shoulders," Faye said. "Fireman carry."

"She's a girl," he said between hard breaths, "not a bag of oats."

"You can carry her easier."

"I can't put her down. She might bolt."

He spoke slowly, gulping air between words. Faye wished she could help him, but she could do nothing but stay close.

Dolly had stopped whimpering, but the fear was unmistakable in her eyes, which were as round as silver dollars and bright with tears. She'd dug her fingernails so tightly into the back of Carrick's shirt she'd torn the fabric and cut the skin.

Faye looked up. "Maybe thirty steps to go," she said.

Carrick started up again, and Faye stayed one step behind him. His shirt was drenched through with sweat. He must have done this in the other timeline when Faith had drowned and died in the storm, and Dolly had had to drag him to the lighthouse. He would've had to carry Dolly up the steps—a double weight, for he'd borne the weight of the living girl in his arms and the weight of the drowned girl on his heart.

One painfully slow step at a time, Carrick ascended the stairs. He had to stop for breath after each step, and soon he wasn't breathing but wheezing. Finally, after what seemed like an hour, they reached the watch room. Carrick set Dolly on her feet inside the door, and Faye pulled her in and dragged her to the opposite wall. She grabbed a blanket out of Carrick's supply trunk, laid it on the floor and drew Dolly down to it. Dolly pulled herself into the fetal position, facing the wall, hiding from doors and windows. Carrick let out a groan and bent double, still standing but resting his full weight back against the wall.

"Carrick?"

His face was red, and he was gasping like he'd just run a marathon or ten.

"I'm…" He gulped a breath and collapsed onto the floor.

"Carrick!" Faye ran to Carrick and dropped to his side. His heart beat so hard she could see it punching against the inner wall of his chest like a fist. He was breathing in short, shallow breaths that scared her. She could see the outline of the jagged scar on his rib cage through his shirt, which had gone transparent with sweat.

"Don't die," she begged, hating how white he'd turned, how cold. "Don't you dare die after all I gave up to be here with you. Central air and the internet and Oreos and antibiotics and vaccines and Netflix. Don't you dare..." Tears choked her throat. Did she do this by coming back? Maybe in the original timeline Carrick and Dolly had made it to the lighthouse after the wind had died down, and so the door hadn't blown off its hinges, and they waited the storm out at the foot of the steps. Had she traded her life for his by coming back? She'd never forgive herself. Better to have never come back at all.

"Sweet girl." Carrick breathed the words through chalky lips.

"Oh, God, are you all right?"

"I need—"

"Anything. Tell me." She would run to the house for food. She'd run to the cistern for water. She'd run a billion stairs into the heavens and grab God by the throat if Carrick asked her to do it.

He rolled over, stuck his head out of the door hatch, and she heard the unmistakable thick liquid sound of heavy vomiting.

Faye winced. Poor Carrick.

"Need me to hold your hair?" she asked, although she knew he couldn't hear her over the sound of his own retching.

She looked around, found his water canteen on his desk and brought it to the door.

He crawled back into the watch room, closed the hatch, and sat back against the curved stone wall.

"Feel better?" she asked.

He slowly nodded. "I think I vomited on Ozzie down there."

"Ozzie threw up a hairball in my wicker flower basket. Turnabout is fair play."

"How's our girl?" Carrick asked, still breathing too hard for her liking.

"Curled up in a ball and keening. So about as well as you."

She unscrewed the cap from the canteen and brought it to his lips. He drank deeply but carefully. When he nodded again, she put the cap back on. Carrick grinned.

"What?" she demanded.

"I would marry you if you weren't already married," Carrick said. "Do you want to marry me?"

"You nearly killed yourself carrying a teenage girl up one hundred and ten stairs. That was still the most romantic thing I've ever seen. If you weren't half-dead and if Dolly weren't up here with us, I'd do things to you to make a sailor blush."

"If I knew that's what put you in the mood, I'd carry a different girl up those stairs every day of my life. No, I wouldn't. That was the hardest fucking thing I've ever had to do."

"Watch your language."

"It's not true anyway. Standing there in the water waiting for you to come up again—that was the hardest thing I've ever done."

"Carrick, I'm sorry. I didn't—"

"I stood there watching the water like my whole life was there in front of me, and if you came up, I'd live, and if you didn't, I wouldn't."

"You would have lived."

"Aye, but I wouldn't have wanted to, and that's worse than death, isn't it?"

"Yes," Faye said. "That is worse than death. I've been there."

"When you went under, it killed me to think you might die never knowing that I've loved you from the moment I saw you, since the moment you flew off that swing and into my arms, since the moment you said—"

"My hero."

"God'll just have to forgive me for declaring my love to a married woman. I won't act on it. I won't. But I had to tell you. And if the day ever comes when that husband of yours takes a long walk off a short pier, I'll marry you by sundown."

Faye bowed her head and sighed, Pat's words ringing in her ears.

If you don't tell him the truth, it's not you he loves.

"What if we don't have to wait, Carrick?"

"Wait for what?"

"For Marshall to take a long walk off a short pier. What if I wasn't married?"

"I know you are. I was there."

"What if I said that wasn't me?"

Carrick looked at her long and hard. Then he sighed, pulled her to him. "I know it wasn't you," he said.

"You know?" She leaned away and looked at him.

"I know it was your mother making you marry him. But that doesn't change that in the eyes of the law and in the eyes of God you are married. I'd risk my soul for a night with you, but I won't let you risk yours. I'm not worth it."

She'd tried telling him and just couldn't do it. Not with the way he was looking at her, looking at her like a man in love. A man in love with a dead woman. Faye knew that look all too well.

"You're worth it."

Faye took his face in her hands and kissed him lightly on the lips. Right now he looked like Carrick, just Carrick, and not like Will at all. But she loved his face nonetheless.

She settled against him, clung to him. Faye's love for Will wasn't gone, but in Carrick's arms the ache of it dissipated like the waves on a pond after someone threw a stone into the water. The stone had sunk to the bottom and would remain there always, yet once more the water was calm, at peace. And so was Faye.

Faye saw Dolly raise her head. She saw Faye and Carrick clinging to each other and rolled her eyes. When Faye waved her over, Dolly came up on her hands and knees and crawled across the floor to join them in their pile of arms and legs and wet clothes and relief. Carrick held Faye. Faye held Dolly. Soon enough Ozzie bounded up the stairs and Dolly held him, too, as he purred loud enough to give the wind outside a run for its money.

The whole family was alive and well. Let the wind blow the world away tonight. This lighthouse was her ark and she had all she needed in here. Tomorrow they'd find dry land. Tonight they'd be one another's sanctuary.

Faye let Dolly sleep and Carrick rest while she took care of the beacon. She cranked the clockwork to keep the lens rotating all night, and even went up to the lantern room to make sure the windows were clear of debris. Faye monitored the anemometer readings and recorded them in Carrick's station log like he had taught her. When the winds died down to ten miles per hour, Carrick sent her and Dolly back downstairs to the house so they could get some real sleep in real beds. He would stay until the sun came up to clean the windows and the lens. It would certainly need it after this storm. Faye worried Dolly would have to be carried downstairs again, but no, Dolly devised her own solution for getting down the steps. She sat on them, and while clinging to the banister, she bump-bump-bumped on her bottom all the way down, Ozzie following Dolly and Faye following Ozzie.

When they emerged from the lighthouse, it was to an island that looked like it had survived a drinking binge. By the first gray and pale pink rays of dawn light, Faye spied tree branches littering the beach like broken glass on a bar floor. Sand had been swept all the way up to the back steps like spilled liquor. One green shutter hung sideways, giving the window the look of a bruised and swollen eye. Kelp hung off the corner of the roof like a discarded bra tossed aside in a drunken fling.

Yet for all the damage the storm bender had done, it was a lovely morning to be alive. The rain was nothing but the gentlest drizzle now, and the air smelled so fresh Faye felt clean just by standing in it and breathing it in. June 21 was less than a week away according to the kitchen calendar. Almost officially summer. Oh, it would get hot here this summer. Hotter. But cooler again in autumn. Would it snow on the beach in winter? She couldn't wait to find out. And she would find out, because she would be here. Because that house with the shutter askew and the seaweed hanging off the roof was her home. A little bruised, a little battered, but home.

Dolly headed straight to her bedroom, collapsed onto the bed and fell asleep in seconds. Faye stood in the doorway smiling at the sleeping girl. It was there that Carrick found her, and she leaned against his chest.

"How is she?"

"Exhausted," Faye said. "But alive and well, thanks to you."

Carrick put his arm around her and rubbed her back.

"I want a daughter," Faye said. "Just like her."

"Well, you can't have her. She belongs to someone already."

"I'll fight them for her," Faye said. Now that she'd returned, she knew she'd come back as much for Dolly as she had for Carrick, as much for Carrick as she'd come back for herself.

"She's a little wild for me. Look what she did." Carrick turned and showed her the back of his neck and the bloody fingernail scratches deep in his skin.

"Oh, no, you poor thing." Faye tried to sound sympathetic but ended up laughing at him instead. "Let's go in the bathroom. I'll clean those cuts up."

She put a chair by the bathroom sink and tried not to stare as Carrick shucked out of his shirt and undershirt. In her abject terror, Dolly had left sixteen scratches in Carrick's neck, shoulders and back. Faye counted them all. She also counted the tattoos on his back. Seven of them—all birds.

"This isn't fair," Faye said as she ran cool water onto a clean strip of linen cloth and pressed it against the dried blood on Carrick's shoulder. She washed off the blood, put iodine on the cuts. "I'm the one who should be leaving fingernail scratches on your back."

"Jesus, Mary and Joseph," he groaned, rubbing his forehead. "You'll be the death of me, woman, if you say things like that."

"I'm sorry," she said. "Ignore me. Tell me about the tattoos. What are the birds?"

"Swallows," he said. He had an entire flight of swallows on his skin, fluttering from shoulder to shoulder and shoulder to hip. Seven of them total. They made a C-shaped curve from his upper back to his lower back, red and black and yellow birds.

"They must have hurt," she said. She couldn't imagine how much getting tattooed with a World War I–era tattoo gun hurt. A whole damn lot, probably. Standing in front of him, she gently pushed his head down so she could put iodine on the cut along his hairline.

"Nobody but a fool joins the navy hoping to avoid pain." Carrick rested his forehead against her stomach. Will would do that, too, when she rubbed his shoulders after a long road trip. But the thought came and went, fluttering away like a swallow returning home. She didn't miss Will right now. She didn't miss missing him, either. She remembered him, but without the pain of loss. The wound had healed and left a scar, but the scar didn't hurt.

"I wouldn't think so. Does it mean anything you have seven of them?"

"You get one for every five thousand miles you sail. I was in the navy a good long time." Carrick pushed up the edge of her shirt to bare a couple inches of her stomach. He pressed a soft kiss against her side.

"That's my rib you're kissing, Chief Morgan," she told him as she dotted the iodine on the cut.

"No, ma'am, that's Adam's rib. He said I could kiss it."

"I loved that movie," Faye said.

"A what?" Carrick asked, confused.

Oops. *Adam's Rib* wouldn't be out for another almost thirty years.

"Nothing. Tell me more about your swallows. You traveled thirty-five thousand nautical miles?"

"Thereabouts." He lifted her shirt a little higher, kissed her again. Faye shivered with pleasure.

"That's the entire world, Carrick."

He shook his head. As he did, he blew warm air across her bare stomach.

"What are you doing?" she asked, shivering with pleasure.

"I was thinking about taking you to bed before I remembered I'm not supposed to do that. What are *you* doing?"

"I think I was arguing with you about how big the earth is while cleaning up your cuts."

"The earth is about twenty-two thousand nautical miles," he said. "I was nearing my second circuit when the war ended. Not that I minded not getting that eighth swallow. Three years on the *Kentucky* was long enough for me. Are you done yet?" He held her by the hips while Faye screwed the lid back onto the iodine bottle and pretended not to notice his roving hands. Now this felt like a marriage. How many times had she been attempting to do boring and important tasks like putting away dishes or paying bills while Will would kiss her neck or rub her ass or whatever it took to get her to give up her work and go to bed with him? Which was what she wanted to do all along but it was always much more fun making him wait for it.

"What's the *Kentucky*? Your ship?"

Carrick raised his head slowly and looked at her through narrowed eyes.

"Of course it was my ship. It was Marsh's ship, too. You know that, lass."

Faye went silent and her blood stilled. There was silence in the room, the same silence she'd heard before the storm.

She'd done it. She'd committed an error so egregious there would be no way to explain except with the truth.

"Carrick," Faye said, putting her hands over his on her hips. "I have to tell you something."

"You did hurt yourself that night, didn't you? When you fell off the pier? You've been different. I knew something was wrong. I should have hauled you to the doctor whether you wanted to go or not."

"That's not it, I swear."

"Was it Marsh? I told you my dad hit my mom so hard sometimes she forgot—"

"Carrick, stop. Listen to me, please."

"Talk," he said.

Faye was shaking. She had no idea how to explain it to him, how to make him believe her. "You promise you won't think I'm crazy?" she asked.

"I would never think that of you. The only crazy thing you've ever done is come to me when you could have gone anywhere."

"That's the least crazy part of all this. Carrick…"

She looked down into his eyes. There was no way to say it but to say it.

"I'm not Faith Morgan."

"Well, yes."

"That's not what I mean. I'm not Millie Scarborough, either, or Millie Carlyle."

Carrick looked at her but didn't seem to see her. Or perhaps he was seeing her, the real her, for the first time. Faye couldn't say, but he'd never looked at her quite like this before—with suspicious, searching eyes and his usually warm hands cold in her grasp. He looked afraid. Though she'd seen him scared before, she'd never seen him scared of her.

"Who are you, then?" he asked.

"Someone who loves you," she said. "And someone who came a long way to be with you."

Outside the house she heard the unmistakable whine of a motor boat coming into dock.

"Ignore him," Carrick said. "Tell me what's going on."

"I can't ignore him. I have his money. Dolly and I found it right before the storm."

"Money? What money?"

"Ten thousand dollars, all in cash. It was in a book under the dresser. That's why Hartwell broke in. I'm going to give it to him, and hopefully we'll never see him again."

Faye let go of his hands and started to leave.

"I'll be right back," she said. "When I come back, I'll tell you everything."

Faye fumed as she walked out the house to the dock. The sooner they were rid of Hartwell, the better. She didn't care at all that he was a bootlegger, but he knew too much about her real relationship with Carrick, and she hadn't come ninety-four years back in time just to let some Southern-dandy daddy's boy hurt the man she loved.

Hartwell had his back to her at the end of the pier where he'd tied off his boat. She wanted to walk right up behind him and kick him into the water.

"I found your money, Mr. Hartwell," she called out to him. "Come and get it. Then get the hell out of here for good."

Hartwell stood up and turned around. Though it was his boat, it was not Hartwell.

The man standing before her was tall and broad shouldered. He wore a light gray suit, a gray fedora with a black silk band. Everything about him looked imposing, from the too-jaunty tilt of his hat to the smile on his lips made sinister by his thin, impeccably groomed mustache. She didn't know him, but instantly she feared him.

"Now, now, Millie, my dear. Is that any way to greet your husband?"

21

Faye started to scream for Carrick, but Marshall took one step forward and slapped his hand over her mouth and grabbed her by the back of her hair.

"If you scream, I'll snap your pretty neck, sweetheart," he said. "You understand?"

Faye slowly nodded.

"Good girl. I'm glad I don't have to kill someone else today. It gets messy."

He dropped his hand from her mouth, though he still gripped her roughly by the back of her hair.

"Someone else?" Faye asked.

"Where do you think I got the boat?" He laughed and dragged her toward the end of the pier.

"You killed Hartwell?" Faye was horrified. She couldn't stand the man, but she'd never wished death on him.

"I killed my wife's kidnapper."

"Kidnapper? I wasn't—"

"Of course you've been kidnapped. After all, no woman in her right mind would run away from a loving husband

who dotes on her the way I dote on you." Marshall pulled
her into the boat and pushed her down onto the floor.

"You're a wife beater and a rapist," Faye said. "And you
should be in jail for the rest of your life."

"A rapist? A man can't rape his own wife," Marshall said
as he wrapped ropes around her ankles. "As for beating you,
well, I'm half tempted to beat you to death, but I've been
waiting on that baby two years. I'd hate have to start over
with a new wife."

"Baby? What baby?"

"Our baby, Millie, my love. That's how I found you. Your
friend Mr. Hartwell was digging around your bedroom for
some damn reason and found your note. Glad to know you
changed your mind about drowning yourself."

Marshall pulled a folded sheet of stationery from his
pocket, and Faye snatched it from his hand, opened it and
read it as Marshall started the engine and steered the boat
away from the pier, from the lighthouse, from everything
she loved.

Dear Carrick,
I don't know if you'll ever find this letter. I don't know
if I want you to, but for the sake of my conscience I
must write it. I thought I could be free of Marshall. I
thought I could start a new life, and I knew if anyone
could help me, it would be you. Marshall always said
you were the best of men. It is the rare thing my husband and I have ever agreed on. You are indeed the
best of men, but even you can't save me now. Today
was my seventh morning at the lighthouse, and the
third morning I woke up ill. No longer can I deny the
truth to myself. I am carrying his child. I cannot stay

with you and bring scandal to your good name, and I cannot return to my husband. There is only one place left for me and it is not in this world.

Please do not blame yourself for my death. I dreamt last night that I was reborn into another life where you were my husband and the child I carried was yours, but it was only a dream. Perhaps in another life. Perhaps in another time...

Forgive me, Carrick. Pray for me. I cannot be your Faith any longer, but in my heart you will always remain... My hero.
Millie

Faye gasped reading the letter, gasped and then wept. So that was why Faith had thrown herself into the ocean wearing a heavy coat although it was a summer night. She was pregnant with her abusive husband's child and was determined to drown herself. And if Faith/Millie was pregnant, then...

"I'm pregnant."

"About damn time, too," Marshall said, scoffing. They were speeding away from the lighthouse so fast the wind ripped the note from her shaking hand. "Apparently your friend Mr. Hartwell had been in Boston recently, heard about my wife's disappearance and put two and two together when he found your note. He sent me a telegram. I came right down and met him, and he made me a deal. For ten thousand dollars, he'd tell me where my wife was, and then he would conveniently forget to tell the whole wide world how my pregnant wife was giving up the goods to a Carolina lighthouse keeper. I gave your friend his ten thousand dollars and a bullet to the brain for his trouble. I took the money back. I let him keep the bullet. Would you like one, too?" He patted his pocket, where Faye saw the telltale bulge of a pistol. "I have five more."

Faye was going to be sick. She could hardly breathe, hardly speak.

"Don't worry, darling," he said. "I won't kill you until after the baby's born. Now I just have to figure out what to do about Carrick."

"I'll do anything you want, go anywhere with you. Just don't hurt Carrick."

He slapped her across the face, quick and hard. Faye gasped. She'd never been struck by anyone before.

"Don't you ever tell me what to do. I'll break that dumb mick's neck if I want. Jesus Christ, Millie Anne, do you have a single brain cell in your head? You really gave up everything I have for him?"

"Carrick would cut off his own arm before he raised his hand to me, or any woman."

"Well, I did my fair share of slumming while I was in the service. I suppose I shouldn't be surprised my wife wanted to do a little slumming herself. He's handsome enough. I'll still have him arrested and horsewhipped, but really, I can't blame either of you."

"You're a piece of shit," Faye said.

Marshall smiled.

"I just added another ten minutes to his whipping."

A popping sound exploded around them.

"What the hell?" Marshall said. Faye looked past him and saw Carrick standing on the pier with his shotgun aimed directly at Marshall. "Goddamn it, I wanted him to rot in prison. I suppose I'll have to kill him instead."

Marshall pulled his pistol out of his pocket. Faye instinctively lunged for the gun as it went off.

It was poorly planned on her part, but it did the trick. Splinters flew at Carrick's feet. His eyes grew wide, but he didn't back off. Instead, he raised the shotgun in the boat's direction again.

Marshall muttered to himself and pulled Faye close to him, using her as a shield. He raised the pistol over her shoulder and steadied his aim—

Not again. Faye would not lose the man she loved again. She would die first. She would die now if she had to. Anything to save Carrick. Anything.

Faye wriggled free of Marshall's grip and dived off the side of the boat.

Once in the water, Faye kicked the rope off her ankles. Her wrists, however, were bound tighter. She surfaced, and heard Marshall screaming. At her? Faye kicked hard and tried to swim away from him as fast as possible.

Swimming in the open water was harder than she'd ever dreamed. With her hands tied she couldn't do much more than tread water. Insane with fury, Marshall shot wildly in her direction.

Better he shoot at her than at Carrick. If she could only survive a few seconds more, then maybe it would be all right. Even now Faye felt the water churning around her like a pot on high heat starting to boil. It was happening again as she sensed it would. Time was coming for her. Better for her to live without him in 2015 than for him to die in 1921.

If she lived long enough to see 2015 again, that was…

Another shot hit the water near her head. She ducked under the water and when she resurfaced she saw Carrick dive off the pier. He was coming for her, but would he make it in time? Faye kicked harder, dived under the surface again and mermaid swam for as long as she could to escape the choppy waves and Marshall's bullets.

When she came up for air, a wave lifted her high and dropped her back into the water face-first. These waves seemed determined to kill her, and she couldn't use her hands to fight back. She paddled backward with her feet, hoping she was heading toward the pier, toward Carrick. Another wave lifted and dropped her, knocking the breath from her lungs and the fight from her body. It wasn't happening fast enough. She was still in 1921. It didn't matter anymore if Marshall shot her before she made it back to 2015. She would die from the waves before either could happen. The water pulled her down to her death, and as it took her, she gave her final thoughts to Carrick.

Carrick... I love you. I love you, and not because you look like my Will but because you look like my Carrick. If I can find a way back to you again, I will live in your light the rest of my life.

Carrick or Will or God must have heard her prayer, because just as Faye started to let go and give up, someone pulled her to the surface and into the light of day again. She howled, gulping air into her burning lungs. Hands yanked the rope free from her wrists. That same someone put her arm over two strong shoulders and paddled them toward the beach.

As she caught her breath, her vision slowly returned to her. She looked at her rescuer with confusion. Who was this man? He looked vaguely like a young Gregory Peck and he swam like a dolphin.

A young Gregory Peck?

"Pat?"

22

Pat, if it was him, didn't answer. Instead, he kept pushing them closer to the beach, cutting through the water with his powerful arms, a young man's arms. When they made it to within a couple hundred yards of the shore, Faye swam on her own until her feet touched the bottom and she could trudge through the water to the beach. Coughing and sputtering, Faye fell onto the ground, so grateful to be alive she'd almost forgotten about Marshall.

"Get up," Pat said. "We have to move. Right now."

Faye sat up and saw that a new storm was brewing. The sky turned purple as a bruise. The waves rose higher and higher, clawing up the beach with each crashing breaker. Pat took her by the arm and dragged her to the tree line. Faye clung to the trunk of a young oak out of harm's way. Out on the water Hartwell's boat pitched about like a plastic toy ship in a child's bathwater.

It seemed Marshall was attempting to run the boat aground on the beach. With the water so wild, there was no other way to escape the storm. Yet no matter what he did, he couldn't break free of the ocean's unrelenting grip. The wind whipped across the water, turning the surface white and foamy. Faye watched in silent horror as one wave flipped Marshall's boat on its side and the next wave capsized it completely. Water rushed over the hull. Wood crunched and splintered. And over the wind she heard a scream.

Instinctively, she started toward the water, but Pat stopped her with his hand on her arm.

"Stay here," he shouted. "I'll go."

He ran off without another word. Pat raced to the beach, stripping out of his shirt before diving into the ocean. How was Pat here? And why? And was it him? She knew it was. They had the same bright but pale blue eyes. The same distinct nose. The same voice. But all the signs of age were gone in this young man—no gray hair, no crow's-feet, no lines around the mouth, no loose skin at the neck. He had a young man's body, too—sleek and long and lean and terribly strong as he cut through the water with deceptive ease. Soon he was out so far Faye couldn't see him. All that she could see were the remains of the small motorboat bobbing in the water.

Waiting was hell. Faye could hardly catch her breath, and tears rolled down her face, hot against her cold skin. She shook and shivered in the rain and wind. She ached for Carrick's arms around her, for the warmth of his body and the safety of his love.

Had Carrick noticed they'd come ashore this far down the beach yet? Had Dolly? Had they called for help? Could they call for help or had the storm snapped the one phone line between the lighthouse and town? Faye couldn't wait anymore. She ran down to the beach and narrowed her eyes at the motorboat sinking fast. She searched for any signs of life, even Marshall's, but saw none.

The storm was subsiding now, blowing out as quickly as it had blown in. Two hundred yards or so out, she saw a man's face. He came in closer to shore. Thank God, it was Pat. He stood up when he reached shallow waters and walked tiredly toward her.

He shook his head before collapsing onto the sand.

"Gone," Pat said between rasping breaths. "Trapped… under the boat. Couldn't get him out. He's dead."

"You sure?"

Pat nodded.

Faye sank down into the sand next to him, relieved and yet ashamed of her relief.

"Him or you," Pat said, still panting hard.

"What do you mean, him or me?"

"It's why I came back." Pat rolled forward and grabbed his shirt off the beach. He yanked it on. "I couldn't sleep after you left. Bad feeling, like I had sand in my mind and it was shifting. I kept trying to remember how Faith Morgan died and I couldn't. The image kept changing. I got up and went to the lighthouse and saw the plaque on the side. You were still dead. Faith Morgan was still dead. But you didn't die June 10. You died June 17."

"That's today," Faye said.

"That's what I was afraid of. I waded into the water, and next thing I knew, there you were, drowning."

Faye stared at him, aghast, speechless. If Pat hadn't come back…she would have died in this time? Marshall would have shot her? It would have happened today, right now, but for Pat. She could almost see it happening, as if it had happened and she'd witnessed it with her own eyes. Marshall reaching over the side of the boat, fishing her out of the water before she could drown and return to her own time. They would have struggled over the gun, but it would have gone off in the struggle, shooting Faye in the stomach. It hadn't happened, and all because Pat had come back for her. They'd changed history again.

"Pat," Faye breathed. "Why am I here?"

"I don't know," Pat said. "But at least you're here a little longer."

Faye wrapped her arms around him, around this old priest in a young man's body who had traveled almost a century back in time to rescue her.

"Thank you," she whispered.

"Don't thank me," he said, patting her back. "Truth is, I just really missed being in this body."

Faye laughed and wiped the tears off her face.

"You look good," she said.

"You look a little different," he said, smiling. "But I'd know those violet eyes anywhere."

"Faith!"

Faye looked up. She could see Carrick down the beach jogging toward them. Pat turned his head to look.

"My God," Pat breathed. "Carrick. He's a baby."

"He's thirty-five," Faye said. "Big baby."

"He was my age when I saw him last. And I was... How old do I look?"

"Twenty-seven. Twenty-eight," she said.

"Twenty-seven. That's how old I was when I met Carrick the first time. How does this keep happening to us?" Pat asked.

"What?"

"Time."

"If I knew, I would tell you," Faye said. "Carrick's going to ask who you are. What do I tell him?"

"I'll tell him the truth," Pat said. "If you want me to."

"Why you?"

"Because he'll believe me."

Pat looked at her, and she understood. He'd been Carrick's confessor—he knew the secrets Carrick hadn't even told her yet and perhaps never would. If anyone could make Carrick believe the truth of this story, it was Pat. But that didn't mean Carrick would like what he heard.

"He thinks I'm a twenty-year-old girl who was a virgin until I married Marshall, not a woman of thirty who's been married twice, widowed and divorced. God, I'm divorced, Pat. Carrick will never forgive me."

"He'll forgive you," Pat said. "Carrick's more open-minded than you're giving him credit for. Have faith, *Faith*."

Faye set off running down the beach to meet Carrick. He grabbed her as soon as she was within grabbing distance.

"Oh, God," Carrick said, holding her so tightly it hurt. "I thought you were a goner. I thought Marshall did you in for good. I'll kill him. Where is he—"

"Dead," she said, looking up at Carrick's face. "He drowned when the boat turned over."

"Jesus..." Carrick pulled her even tighter to him. Faye rested her head on his chest and tried to make an impression of this moment deep in her mind in case this was the last time he held her. He was a wall to her, a warm wall of masculine strength and love. And that wall had a door and that was why she never got hurt running into the wall, because he always opened the door for her when she ran to him. "You're safe, sweet girl. That's all that matters."

But it wasn't all that mattered, no matter how much she wanted to believe that.

"Carrick, let me go."

"Never."

She laughed through her tears.

"I need you to meet someone," she said. "He saved me when I jumped out of the boat."

She pulled away from his rough embrace as Pat walked toward them.

"Chief Morgan," Pat said, extending his hand. "Pat."

Carrick shook it heartily. "I'm grateful to you, sir," he said. "Grateful beyond words. Pat, you said?"

The priest nodded. "Patrick Cahill."

Carrick's brow furrowed. He looked at Faye. "Patrick Cahill," he said to her. "Your...fiancé? I thought that was just a story."

"My..." Her voice trailed off. Of course. The fake fiancé she'd invented to keep Hartwell from sniffing around her.

"Carrick," Pat said, cutting in. "Forgive me for calling you by your first name, but we've actually met before."

"We have?" Carrick looked more confused than ever. "When? The war?"

"No, I'm not a sailor or a military man," Pat said. "I'm a priest. Your priest, actually."

"I'm afraid you're mistaken. A priest as young as you, I'd remember."

"I'm not your priest yet," Pat said. "I will be. We'll meet in 1965. So take a good look at me. This is exactly what I'll look like when we meet someday."

Carrick said nothing. He looked at Pat and then at her.

"What on earth are you saying to me?" Carrick said.

"Please listen to him," Faye said. "He has something to tell you. About me."

"I'm listening." Carrick raised his chin, his expression closed and carved out of granite.

Pat took a breath, glanced at the ocean, stared at it as if waiting for it to tell him a secret. He smiled like he remembered something, then looked back at Carrick.

"Do you believe in miracles, Carrick?"

Carrick narrowed his eyes at Pat, but nodded.

"Good," Pat said. "Because one just happened. And I can prove it."

23

It was the longest day of Faye's life. Pat and Carrick sequestered themselves in the watch room of the lighthouse to talk while Faye distracted herself by clearing storm debris from the yard. When her extreme exhaustion caught up with her, she finally slept. Even her sleep exhausted her as her dreams were plagued by images of Marshall and his gun, Marshall and his boat capsizing, Marshall and what could have been had Pat not come to save her.

And Faye? Would Pat save her now? Would Pat be able to convince Carrick of the truth about her identity? Would Carrick shrink from her in horror? Or accept her and love her for who she really was? Even then, he would have to grapple with the knowledge that Faith had drowned herself. Had Carrick loved Faith, or had he simply been offering her safe harbor from her abusive husband? Either way, Carrick would grieve her loss. Faye would respect that and keep her distance if need be. No one honored mourning more than a woman who'd lost her husband while she was still in love with him.

Faye's nap left her feeling more tired than before she let herself sleep. She hadn't been this tired in a long time. The last time she'd felt this sort of bone-deep exhaustion, she'd been pregnant with Will's baby.

And now she was pregnant with Marshall's.

She should have known that was what it was—the dizziness and the nausea and the tiredness, not to mention the weight gain Dolly had noticed when she'd measured Faye for trousers two weeks after measuring Faith for skirts. But how could Faye have known? Who wouldn't be dizzy and nauseous after being yanked decades years back in time? And who wouldn't be tired doing manual labor every day? And who wouldn't gain weight eating food cooked in lard? Even now Faye wished she could convince herself that it wasn't true, that it wasn't happening, but for one thing.

The pregnancy didn't matter.

How could it? Carrick would find out she wasn't the woman he'd known, and reject her. Then Faye would go back to her own time, where she wasn't pregnant. She should have known she couldn't simply slip on someone's life like borrowing someone's coat on a cold day. This journey had seemed like a gift, the rarest and most precious of gifts, but it was no gift. If Faye was to stay here in 1921, it would be at a great price. A price too high, since it would be Carrick paying it.

Despite her tiredness, she rose and dressed in her best black skirt, her prettiest white blouse—Faith's best skirt, Faith's prettiest blouse. Whatever happened with Carrick, at least Faye wouldn't feel like a fraud anymore, like a thief. Faye pinned up her hair as well as she could and washed her face, ready to meet her fate if her fate was ready to meet her.

A peaceful quiet pervaded the cottage, the calm after the

storm. Faye's footsteps echoed hollowly on the steps and the floor as she walked down to the kitchen. Dolly sat at the table reading a book. When she saw Faye, she pushed a piece of paper her way with a note already written on it.

"I have to stay the night again," it read. "Big boat came by and told the Chief it's too choppy still for little boats."

The big boat was likely a coast guard ship patrolling after the storm. She wondered if they'd found Hartwell's body yet or Marshall's.

"Stay as long as you need to," Faye wrote, grateful for her company.

"Hungry?" Dolly wrote.

Faye shook her head no. Nervousness tied her stomach in such knots no food could fit in it. She felt like a defendant in a court trial awaiting the jury's decision on her fate. Who could eat at a time like that?

"Who's that man?" Dolly asked, scribbling the question in her loopy, girlish handwriting.

"Friend of mine from home," Faye wrote. "Patrick Cahill."

Dolly tapped her pencil on the page before writing something with a grin on her face.

"He's handsome." Dolly's cheeks darkened in a blush.

Faye smiled. The knot of her stomach loosened slightly.

"Don't even think about it," Faye wrote. "He's going to be a Catholic priest."

Dolly's eyes widened with shock. Then she sighed. Twice.

"Don't worry," she wrote to Dolly. "You'll find true love someday and get married. If you want to get married, you will."

"I want to," Dolly wrote. Then she paused before writing something else. "Do you think a man will want me with my ears?"

Faye wrote, "Yes. Men like girls with ears."

Dolly pursed her lips at her. She clearly did not find Faye's joke amusing.

"YES," Faye wrote in all caps. "You're beautiful and smart and have lots of talents. A man will want you even if you can't hear. I promise. He'll be lucky to have you."

Dolly took the pencil from Faye's hand.

"You getting married to the Chief?"

"Should I?"

"Your bad husband is dead, right?" Dolly wrote. "Why not?"

Faye stared at the words. How did she know about Will? She didn't, of course. Dolly meant Marshall. Marshall was dead. Carrick must have told her what happened.

"Oh, my God," Faye said out loud. "I'm a widow again." And not just a widow again.

A *pregnant* widow again.

She groaned tiredly, drunkenly, and Dolly looked at her like she'd lost her mind. Maybe she had.

"Marry Chief," Dolly wrote. She underlined *marry* and *Chief* twice.

"I don't think that can happen," Faye wrote. Dolly looked at her with a question in her eyes. It wasn't enough of an answer for the girl. Faye sighed. "I may have to leave."

"Why?" Dolly wrote.

"Hard to explain."

"Because of the baby?" Dolly wrote.

Faye looked at her in shock. Dolly smiled and wrote something else.

"Only your belly is getting fat. I know what that means."

Well, Dolly did have five younger siblings. She knew what pregnancy looked like.

"Yes," Faye wrote. "The baby is my late husband's."

"Chief will marry you anyway," Dolly wrote.

"You sure about that?" Faye replied.

Dolly must have been very sure about it, because she wrote, "When you get married, I get to make your dress."

"You're not helping much here," Faye said but didn't write it. Dolly ignored her as she sketched the outline of a simple empire-waist wedding dress.

Faye left Dolly to her dress designing as she brewed a pot of tea. She took comfort in the routine of the act—in boiling water, in straining the leaves, in deciding between one lump of sugar or two. Her sweet tooth won. She carried her cup onto the front porch. A light wind kept the water awake and dancing in the fading sunlight. The cool breeze and Faye's hot tea did more to restore her than her nap had. The sun quickly dropped out of sight, and soon only pink light remained on the horizon. Pink turned to orange. Orange turned to red. Right as the last of the sunlight faded, the lighthouse came to life, and Faye took comfort in that, too.

Frogs and crickets started up a chorus of minor key singing as Faye sipped her tea. Her eyes followed the beam of light until it disappeared beyond human sight. The ocean was so vast it was a miracle anyone ever survived the crossing from one shore to the next. She wondered how her baby loggerhead turtles were doing out there in the deep blue ocean. She wondered what Carrick and Pat were talking about in the lighthouse. She wondered what she would have to do to get back to her time if Carrick sent her away. She wondered...

"Will, what's happening here? Why me? Do you know?"

"Do I know what?" Carrick said.

Faye turned around. Carrick stood in the open front doorway to the house. He looked tired, beat even. She wanted to run into his arms again, but she held back. It wasn't time for that. Maybe it would never be time for that again.

"Nothing," Faye said. "I'm talking to myself. I do that sometimes."

Carrick shut the door behind him and came to stand near her, not close but not far.

"I didn't know you talked to yourself."

"I'm lying to you," Faye said, shrugging. "I talk to Will sometimes. It helps to talk out loud. Makes it less like he's gone for good. Sometimes I can hear his voice in my mind."

"Will? He was the man you loved, the one I remind you of?"

She nodded. "You're learning a lot about me today," Faye said.

Carrick said nothing for a very long time, long enough for Faye's tea mug to cool in her hands.

"I don't talk about the war if I can help it," Carrick finally said. Faye looked at him wide-eyed. Of all the things she'd expected him to say, that hadn't even been in the top one hundred.

Carrick went on. "It's hard on a man, although we're not supposed to take it hard. They say words to us like *courage* and *valor* and *patriotism* and they're supposed to mean something. And they do, until that moment comes when words don't mean anything and it's all guts, smoke and terror like you can't believe… I hope you never know terror like I've known." He glanced up at the new night as if seeing something in the stars he wished he didn't see. "But maybe you do," he said.

"I saw your medals in the box in your closet."

"We were under attack, started taking on water. I pulled some men out of a room that was flooding, sealed that room off the best I could, got the old tub running again, and we managed to sink them before they sank us. That was what all those medals were for."

"Which I assume is Carrick-speak for 'I single-handedly saved the lives of every man on my ship.' Yes?"

Carrick only shrugged, but he didn't argue.

"Call it penance," he said.

"For what?"

"For what had happened a month before that. It was during a skirmish with a U-boat. We got the better of it, but it was a rough night. You learn to live with the fear, but it takes time. There were new kids aboard. And kids they were. Seventeen, eighteen. Boys so young you'd look at them and couldn't believe you were ever that young. One of them, Francis Walter... Why this kid joined the navy, I'll never know. From Iowa. I don't even know if they have rivers in Iowa, much less thirty thousand miles of ocean. I don't know if he had a screw loose or if being on the water for weeks on end loosened one of his screws, but he lost his mind one night and came at me with a knife."

"You? Why?"

"He wanted a 4-F discharge. Any kind of discharge. He'd rather wait out the war in a military prison than on the boat, he was that scared. Came at me from behind and sliced my whole side open."

The scar on Carrick's side. So that was where it had come from.

"I didn't think," he said. "I just reacted. I threw him into the wall, punched him so hard I killed him. Marshall found us in the engine room. He was my commanding officer. When I told him what happened, he said we should throw him over. No military court in the world would have convicted me, but it would still be a hell of a lot of paperwork, a trial, and during the war, no one wanted that. Marshall said the ship needed me. I was in too much shock to even argue with him. He tossed the boy in the water and I let him, praying for that kid's soul the whole time. I knew I shouldn't do it, but I let him. Everyone assumed he committed suicide. Nobody questioned it. That kid was a wreck from day one anyway. Marshall and I swore each other to secrecy, and we got on with the business of fighting the war."

"It was a war," Faye said, trying not to betray her horror at Marshall's act, what he'd made Carrick do, what he'd taken from that poor boy's family. "Terrible things happen in wars."

"After the war they started handing out medals. I felt like a fraud with every medal they gave me. No matter how much good I'd managed to do, that kid's blood is on me like a red shadow." Carrick shook his head, took a shuddering breath. "Seventeen years old. He should never have been on that boat."

"No, he shouldn't have. But he shouldn't have attacked you, either. I saw that scar. He could have killed you."

"His family had no body to bury because of us."

"I'm not saying what you did was right. I am saying it's forgivable."

"Pat says it's forgivable. He says he absolved me of the sin in 1965." Carrick turned and looked her in the eyes for the first time since coming out onto the porch. "I told Marshall I'd keep that secret until my deathbed. Turns out I did. But Pat remembers my confession. There's no way he could know the things he knows unless I told him myself. And I've never told anyone."

Carrick leaned back against the porch post and closed his eyes. With his arms crossed over his chest, he seemed like an impenetrable wall to her. No door opened to let her in.

"I have your prayer book," Faye said. "Pat gave it to me. In my time, I mean."

"Prayer book?"

"A red prayer book. There's a prayer in it you wrote asking for forgiveness for killing someone. Now I know what you were praying about."

Carrick pushed a hand through his hair. He looked as dazed as she'd felt when she'd woken up in this world. "To think I spent my whole life believing time only went in one direction," he said. "Thought it was a river. Turns out it's an ocean. Waves come in. Waves go out. Sometimes those waves take us with them."

"I didn't plan to come here, I promise. I got caught in one of those waves."

"Pat says you coming here was an accident—the first time. But the second time you came by choice. Why?"

Faye looked at him even though he couldn't seem to meet her eyes.

"Because I'm in love with you."

Carrick exhaled heavily. That wasn't the reaction she'd hoped for.

Faye wrapped both hands around her mug of tea, clinging to it for warmth.

"I should have told you," she said. "Told you who I really am. I was too cowardly to say, 'Hey, Carrick, I know I look exactly like Faith, but I'm not her. I'm from the future.'" Faye poured her cold tea out on the lawn. "I saw *Terminator 2* as a kid. I remember what they did to Sarah Connor in that mental hospital. And that was the early '90s. I don't want to know what they'd do to me in an insane asylum in 1921."

"You're speaking in tongues, love. Who's Sarah Connor?"

"If you live to be ninety-eight years old, I'll introduce you to her. She's a badass like you are. Except she kills robots, not alligators."

"Tell me about this Will of yours," Carrick said. "You were married to him?"

"Yes. We were together a year, a beautiful year. Then he was killed in 2011. I could tell you the exact date and the exact time they called it, but I'll spare you the details. I don't even want to know."

"That's ninety years from now."

"And four years in the past for me."

"You hope…" Carrick sighed. "I suppose everyone hopes that in the future that doesn't happen, that it's better, safer, that we finally start getting it right."

"The future isn't heaven, and it isn't utopia, either. It's just like now. Only, you know, with air-conditioning. Don't ask what it is. Just know I'd rather have you than it."

"Because I look like the man you were married to."

"You do look like Will. Enough that I mistook you for him that night you pulled me out of the water the first time. I wouldn't have…" She paused, rethought her words. "I thought I was dreaming. I thought I was dreaming of Will. It was the only explanation that made sense at the time. But that's not why I love you. I loved Will's face, but I didn't love him for his face. I don't love you for yours, either."

"Do you wish you hadn't come back here? Hadn't seen me?"

"Not at all. Not for one second. Not for ninety-four years

of seconds. But I do regret hurting you. I woke up in Faith's body, in her life. And you were in love with her, not me. Do you love me because I look like her?"

"Faith," Carrick said. "Before you…she…before she showed up here, she and I may have exchanged ten words. The day we met, and the day before the wedding when I saw her crying on the balcony of Marsh's house."

"They must have been ten damn good words."

"Let's see… It was 'Well, hello there.' That was me when she landed in front of me and I caught her. And she said—"

"'My hero.'"

"And when I saw her crying on her wedding day, I said, 'What's wrong, love?' She said, 'I've made a mistake.' And then I said, 'If you ever need me…'"

"What else?" Faye asked.

"That was it," Carrick said. "I said 'If you ever need me…' and Marshall's sister walked into the room to fetch you. Faith. To fetch Faith. I didn't even get to finish my last sentence. I was trying to say, 'If you ever need me, I'll help you. Find me. Write me. Come away with me.' I shouldn't have said that. You don't say that to a woman about to marry the man who used to be your closest friend. But I said it. And she must have believed me."

"She did. She came here because she believed you'd help her."

"Or she thought Marshall would never bother to look for her here. I don't fool myself for one second she was in love with me after those ten words."

"She was, though."

"How do you know?"

"Because she wrote you a letter. Hartwell found it, gave it to Marshall, and I read it. You want to know what it says?"

"It says she killed herself, didn't it?"

Faye nodded. "She did."

"Ah… I was afraid that was it." He looked up at the sky, and when he closed his eyes for a second two tears fell from his face to the floor.

"She killed herself because after she came here, she realized she was pregnant with his baby. And she couldn't be unmarried and living with you and pregnant if she was pretending to be your daughter. And she couldn't go back to Marshall. And she couldn't go anywhere else. In her letter she said she hoped she would be reborn in another life where you were her husband and it was your children she had."

Carrick looked at her in surprise. "She really wrote that?"

"She did."

Carrick leaned back against the porch post and crossed his arms over his chest.

"She's gone, isn't she?"

"Faith? Yes, she's gone somewhere," Faye said. "Who knows? Maybe she's living my old life. But I'd like to think she's with Will, wherever he is, since I'm with you."

"And the baby? Gone, too?"

Faye took a long, slow breath, shook her head no.

"Mother of God, you're pregnant," Carrick said.

"I can't say for certain. In 2015 we have these easy pregnancy tests. I'd know in ten minutes. But I think I am. Feels like I am."

They were silent for a long time. Faye knew what she had to say but didn't want to say it, but she loved Carrick enough to make the offer.

"I'll go back," Faye said. "I won't stay if you don't want me to. I'm not Faith, not really. I'm pregnant with another man's child. And God knows I'm not the girl you fell in love with—"

"I'm in love with you," Carrick said. His voice was stern and strong, unwavering, unflinching. He meant it. "I'm in love with the girl I pulled out of the water, the girl who kissed me and cried on my shoulder. I'm in love with the girl who can't milk a goat to save her life. I'm in love with the girl who didn't think to check for alligators before weeding her garden. I'm in love with the girl who put iodine on my cuts this morning. The girl who's making me quit smoking. The girl who brings me coffee before she goes to bed. The girl who says things that I didn't know girls knew how to say to a man. And I'm in love with the girl standing here, and Marshall's dead and gone, and good riddance. The baby you're carrying is yours, and since I love you, I love that baby. What I need to know is…are you really in love with me? Or are you in love with the man I happen to look like?"

Faye turned to Carrick, narrowed her eyes at him, smiled.

"Do you know what the infield fly rule is?" she asked.

Carrick shrugged and shook his head.

"Neither do I," Faye said. "But Will knew. If there's anything he knew, it was baseball. When Will was hanging out with his friends and they'd had one too many beers, they would fall all over themselves trying to explain it to me. One time they went into the backyard behind our apartment building and tried to act it out. I still didn't get it. But, God, we laughed so hard that evening I pulled a muscle in my stomach. So if you don't know what the infield fly rule is and you don't feel an overwhelming urge to explain it to me when you're drinking, then you aren't William Jacob Fielding."

"I guess I'm not William Jacob Fielding, then."

Faye took a step closer to Carrick, so close she could stand on her toes to kiss him if she wanted.

"I know you aren't," she said softly. "And yet...I love you."

"I want to believe that. But..."

Carrick stepped away from her and sat in the one rocking chair that she'd managed to put back into working order. Faye sat on the porch railing opposite the chair, the wind and the ocean at her back, her feet on Carrick's knees. He wrapped his hands around her ankles, held them gently.

"I can't ask you to stay here for me," he said. "I can't ask you and I can't let you. You tell me you were born in 1985... I won't even be alive anymore in 1985. How could you possibly be happy here? It must be like living... I don't know, on the moon?"

"I've never been to the moon," she said. "But humans do go to the moon. Not until 1969, though."

"Men on the moon. I can't..." Carrick glanced up at the sky. "It's too wonderful to believe. But I know you're telling me the truth."

"It's science fiction to you. It's just a chapter in a high school history book to me."

"So you weren't...you weren't happy in your time? Even with men on the moon?"

She shrugged. "Makes me sound like a terrible person, doesn't it? In 2015, women can hold any job men can. We still don't get paid quite as much, but we have access to a lot of power. Although men do still try to keep us out. Sexism is alive and well in 2015, but some things are better. Much better than they are now. The secretary of state was a woman for several years until she resigned. Now she's running for president."

"A woman president?" Carrick laughed heartily. "You're joking."

"Not joking, I swear. And this will blow your mind. Our current president? The man who is president in 2015 and has been for seven years? He's black."

Carrick's eyes nearly fell out of his head.

"That's..." he breathed. "Are you pulling my leg?"

Faye grinned. "No, I swear it's true. His father was a black man from Kenya who came to the United States for school, and he married a white woman and lived in Hawaii. And their only child is our president. Two-term president. Very popular, too, especially around the world. I voted for him twice."

Carrick rocked back in the chair, put his hands behind his head and interlocked his fingers. He looked utterly flabbergasted.

"It's not even legal," he said.

"What?" she asked. "A black president?"

"A black man and a white woman marrying."

"Not now," she said. In 1921 there were certainly laws against mixed-race marriages. She would hold off telling Carrick about same-sex marriage in 2015 lest he have a stroke. "But it's legal in 2015 and has been since the 1970s, I think. Maybe the 1960s. The laws varied by state. But in my time, there are a lot of interracial marriages. A lot of people don't even get married. They just live together. You know, like we're doing."

He ignored that comment.

"You know you couldn't be president if you stayed here," he said. "Maybe in your time, but now?"

"Honestly, I don't think I could be president in my time,"

she said. In 2015, Faye's own husband didn't want her working. "But I don't want to be president."

"What do you want to do, Faith?" He closed his eyes, wincing. "Faye," he said.

"Victoria Faye Barlow. That's my name. I always went by Faye since Vicky was my mom."

"Barlow? Not Fielding?"

"I didn't take Will's last name when we were married. Does that shock you?"

"Why wouldn't you take his name?"

"A lot of women don't anymore. I had already established a pretty successful freelance career as a photographer under my maiden name when Will and I got married. It would have been a pain to change it." She decided not to tell Carrick about websites. She wouldn't even know where to begin with the internet. "We'd decided our kids would be Fieldings. But we didn't have any kids."

"You would take my last name."

"Carrick, I already have. Remember?"

"Don't remind me," he said. He leaned forward and buried his head in his hands for a moment before looking up at her.

"There's something else you should know," Faye said.

"Please don't tell me you're from Mars."

She laughed. "No. We haven't sent people to Mars yet in 2015, only robots." Carrick started to open his mouth. She held up her hand to stop the question. She'd explain robots another day. "Did Pat tell you about Hagen?"

"No. He didn't tell me much about you, said he should leave it to you. Who's Hagen?"

"My other husband."

She had to give Carrick credit. He didn't gasp or swear or anything at all. He simply looked at her and waited.

Faye told Carrick everything—about Will, the baby, Hagen, the miscarriages, the failed infertility treatments, her divorce, everything. No more secrets. No more lies. She wanted him to love her, as Faye and not Faith, the way she loved him, as Carrick and not Will.

"You lost two?" Carrick asked, and the compassion in his voice nearly undid her.

Faye tried to answer but couldn't, not with the rock in her throat.

"I'm sorry," Carrick said. "Love, I'm so sorry."

She tried to smile as she wiped her tears.

"Anyway, that's it for my deep, dark secrets. Except for one—I'm thirty, not twenty. Although I like looking twenty again, and I'm shallow enough to admit that."

"Do you look like Faith? In your own time, I mean?"

"I do, a little. When I look in the mirror, I see me looking back. This body feels like my body. This life feels like my life. I feel like I belong here, which is why… I mean, I know I should have told you before this. I just didn't know how to tell you to make you believe me. I was terrified to tell you at first. I thought you'd haul me off to an asylum. Do you hate me yet? I wouldn't blame you if you did."

"No," he said simply. "Although I wouldn't mind going a couple rounds with your husband."

"Will or Hagen? Or Marshall? I have too many damn husbands."

"Hagen. God's already taken care of Marshall."

"Hagen's not an evil man. He just wanted something I couldn't give him."

"Children?"

"Love. I think he thought if I had his children, I would love him through them. But it wasn't meant to be."

"Is this meant to be?" Carrick asked. "You and me, I mean?"

"Seems like someone out there is trying very hard to get you and I together."

"If I didn't look like him...would you still want to stay?"

"If you didn't look like him, I wouldn't have stuck around long enough to find a reason to stay," she admitted. "If I'd woken up in this house with a total stranger, I would have run screaming from here as far and as fast as I could. And if I'd made it back to 2015, I would have stayed there and never looked back. That you looked like Will... It gave me a reason to stay until...you know. Until I had other reasons to want to stay. Now...that you look like Will is the least of those reasons."

"I must be bait, then," he said.

"What do you mean?"

"Bait. Bait on a fishhook. I look like the man you loved, and that got the hook in you. And now whoever wants you here is reeling you in."

"I'm hooked," she admitted. "Hooked so hard I don't even want to get unhooked."

"That's hooked, all right. But won't you miss your time? You can't say you won't miss something."

Would she miss anything? Cell phones? Netflix? Cars with seat belts? Air-conditioning? The Lilly Ledbetter Act? Fluoride?

"Penicillin, maybe?" Pat said.

Faye turned and saw Pat standing in the front yard looking up at the sky.

"Not this again," she said.

"What's peni…" Carrick asked.

"It's a drug," Faye said. "It hasn't been invented yet. But it's sort of a wonder drug. After it's discovered, it saves millions of lives. As many lives as lighthouses have saved. Maybe more."

Pat walked up the front porch steps.

"Millions and millions," Pat said. "Faye keeps forgetting what she'll be giving up if she decides to stay here. Access to modern medicine, for starters. In 2015 people can survive cancer, tuberculosis, scarlet fever. Vaccines eradicated polio and measles. Do you really want to live in a world with iron lungs and polio, Faye? Do you?"

"I guess I could go back to 2015 and live in a world with meth, heroin, terrorism, HIV and Ebola. Huge improvement, right? Sorry, Carrick," she said, giving him a wry smile. "We must be speaking a foreign language again."

"I don't know what you're talking about, but I know you need to talk about it," Carrick said. "So I will leave you two to talk it out. If you need me, I'll be up at the light."

Carrick started to leave, and then turned back and kissed her on the lips.

"I needed that," he said. "Sorry, Father." Carrick winked at Pat and then left them alone on the porch.

Pat exhaled heavily.

"You've decided to stay, then?"

"Carrick says he wants me to. And I want to."

"You're giving up an awful lot of modern conveniences."

"True. But gaining a lot in return. Carrick. Dolly. A baby."

"Baby?"

"Yeah," Faye said. "I'm pregnant."

"Carrick's?"

She shook her head no.

"I see," Pat said. "Carrick spent his whole life wondering if Faith killed herself—and if she did, why."

"I saw the note she left for Carrick. I guess she put it in her Bible."

"She was buried with her Bible," Pat said. "She was buried with the truth hidden inside, and Carrick never even knew..."

"He knows now. She couldn't go back to Marshall, couldn't stay with Carrick, couldn't have the baby of the man who'd beaten and raped her..."

"That poor girl," Pat said, gazing at the ocean with a faraway look in his eyes. "This is no time for fair and tender ladies."

"Good thing I'm not one, then," Faye said.

"Are you all right with this?" Pat asked.

"What? Being pregnant with the child of a man I don't love? Wouldn't be the first time."

"Faye, tell me the truth."

"You wouldn't understand," she said.

"Try me."

"I feel the same way I felt when I found out I was pregnant with Hagen's baby three years ago. Scared to death."

"Scared to have the baby of a man you don't love?"

"No." She put her hand on her stomach. "Scared I was going to lose it again."

Pat took one step forward and folded her into his strong, young arms.

"Unmarried and pregnant in South Carolina in 1921," Pat said as he rubbed her back, kindly as a priest, tender as a friend. "I'm half tempted to throw you over my shoulder and drag you back to our time kicking and screaming."

Faye pulled back and poked him in the chest with her finger.

"I'm staying, Pat. You could stay, too, you know," Faye said.

"I like penicillin too much."

"Nobody even prescribes that anymore."

"Fine," he said. "I like amoxicillin."

Faye reached out and took Pat by the hand. She lifted his arm into the air and straightened it. It stayed right.

"No tremor," she said. "Isn't that a reason to stay?"

"One reason, but not enough of a reason."

He lowered his arm again.

"I know," she said. "I just… If I'm here for a reason, I can't help but think you are, too."

"Maybe the only reason I'm here was to save you and convince Carrick of the truth. Maybe I should be getting back."

"And yet…here you are."

Faye stepped closer, searched Pat's face.

"Are you sure you don't want to stay?" she asked.

Pat laughed. "It was hard enough being a gay priest in the 1960s. And the 1970s. And the 1980s. At least gay people are allowed to exist in 2015. I don't get to exist in the 1920s. I like existing."

"Pat. Oh, my God, I'm sorry. I'm so clueless. I usually pick up on these things. You're such a flirt."

"Flirting with women is a gay priest's number one survival skill." He waved his hands dismissively. "And there's no reason to be sorry. You had no way of knowing."

"Does Carrick know?"

"He will in 1965," Pat said.

"You told him?"

"He was dying," Pat said. "You're never so close to anyone as you are when the Angel of Death is in the room with you. I'd visit Carrick at the hospital. At first it was just out of pity, visiting this old war hero, this old sailor dying alone. What I thought would be a ten-minute courtesy visit turned into an hour. I went back the next day and stayed two hours. One day I asked him why he never got married. He told me about the girl he'd loved, the girl we all know of as the Lady of the Light. He told me her real name and how she'd trusted him, and how she'd died and how Carrick had buried his heart in her grave. I mentioned someone to him I'd loved but couldn't be with when I was a very young man, another seminarian. I thought old Carrick would be shocked. He wasn't. You know what he said?"

"What?" Faye asked, smiling.

"He said it was hard to a shock a sailor."

"I can hear him saying that," Faye said.

"And I can still see that handsome weather-beaten old face of his smiling up at me from his hospital bed, the gleam in his eyes, though he was too sick to laugh by then," Pat said, grinning through his tears. "He said I was a good priest and a good man, and that's all that mattered to him, and he was damn sure that's all that mattered to God, too. His friendship was a beacon during a very dark time in my life."

"You could be friends with him here," she said.

Pat shook his head. "This time isn't for people like me."

"And it is for me?"

"You're white. You're straight. You're well educated, healthy and beautiful. Every time is for people like you."

"That's not fair," she said.

"Of course it's not fair. That's my point."

"I know," Faye said. "I know you're right. But I want to

help. If I stay, I can make things better. At least a little bit. Better than nothing, right?"

"You sound like the idealist I used to be."

"It's been a long time since I felt something like hope," Faye said. "Don't ask me to give it up for Netflix and a Prius."

"No priest worth his salt would tell you to abandon your hope. Hope is something God gives us. Hope is..." He turned his face toward the lighthouse beacon. "Hope is a bright light on a dark night. If your hope is guiding you into this shore, then this is where you should drop anchor. I only want you to understand what you're doing. I don't know what you'll do by staying to the timeline, but I do know this—Carrick will still die in a few decades, and so will you."

"I know," Faye said. "But for now we'll live."

"Then God bless you, Faye. I'll pray for you every single day."

"I'll need it," she said. "You know, in case I get polio."

"Stay out of public pools. And ponds. And rivers."

"I'll remember that."

Faye held out her hand. Pat took it, squeezed it, pulled her to him and held her again, held her like he knew he'd never see her again.

"Carrick won't get jealous if I hug you and kiss your cheek, will he?" Pat asked.

"He better not. You're my fiancé."

"If only my dearly departed mother could have met you. Wait."

"What?" Faye asked, stepping back.

"My mother is alive in 1921. Jesus Christ."

"I didn't think priests were supposed to swear like that."

"I wasn't swearing. I was praying. If I said Jesus H. Christ, then I'm swearing."

Faye laughed and kissed his cheek. "I'll miss you."

"I will miss you, too. You've given me quite an adventure. Try not to do that again. I don't want to hear any rumors about Faith Morgan managing to get herself kidnapped again or something. Once I go back home, I'm staying. This is my last trip."

"Mine, too. And I'll be careful, I promise."

"Faye, I mean it. This is a different world. I know you two are in love with each other, but this is an unforgiving time."

"I supposed we'll have to leave the island," Faye said, glancing around the island and loving everything she saw— the shimmering sand and the dancing waters, the cottage that was her home now, the lighthouse and Carrick and Dolly... She loved it all. "I hate to do it, but I guess we won't have much of a choice. Dolly can tell I'm already getting a baby belly."

Faye patted her round stomach. Pat patted his flat stomach.

"I will miss this young body," Pat said, smiling, and there wasn't a laugh line to be seen around his mouth.

"So will Dolly. She thinks you're very handsome."

"Did you tell her I was already taken by God?"

"I did. Broke her poor heart."

"She's too young to get married. Even in '21."

"I think she just really wants to make wedding dresses. She's been designing mine ever since she caught Carrick and I kissing. She thinks we need to get married. I told her I've been technically widowed for about twelve hours. She thinks that's long enough to grieve."

"I could marry you, you know," he said. "If you like. You and Carrick. It won't be a legal wedding, of course, but I know it would make Carrick feel better about being with you. And I am a priest no matter what year it is."

"You *could* marry me," Faye repeated.

"I could. But again, not a legal—"

"No, that's not what I mean. You could marry me. You and me—we could get married, here, in this time, in Beaufort."

Pat gaped at her.

"Faye."

Faye shook with excitement. The idea had come to her in a flash. Yes. Of course. It all made sense. The pieces were clicking into place. She, Faith Morgan, could marry the man the whole town already knew was engaged to— Patrick Cahill.

"Hear me out," she said. "You and I go into town and get married. I already said I was engaged to a sailor named Patrick Cahill. If Hartwell was as much of a gossip as he seemed, then the whole town knows the lighthouse keeper's daughter has a fiancé named Pat Cahill. You and I get married. Then you go home. You disappear. People will assume you shipped out again, because that's what sailors do. And when everyone finds out I'm pregnant, they'll think it's my husband's. Carrick and I wouldn't have to leave the lighthouse."

"You're asking me to marry you?"

"Can you think of a better idea?"

"Well…no."

"Do you have any moral objections to marrying me? I know priests aren't supposed to get married."

"I'm gay, retired, and seventy-seven years old."

"I don't expect you to consummate the marriage."

Pat dug his hands into his pockets and pulled the liner

out to show they were empty. "I don't have any papers on me, any identification. We can't just walk into town and get married."

"Yes, we can. It's 1921, Pat. Driver's licenses don't exist yet and neither does the Social Security Administration. Carrick will vouch for your identity. He's a war hero. He can get away with anything in this town."

"You mean this, don't you?"

"Will you?"

Pat raised his hands in surrender.

"Why not? Who knows? Maybe that's why God sent me back here anyway."

"You're the best priest ever," Faye said.

She grabbed Pat to her and hugged him. Dragging him by the hand, she pulled him into the house where Dolly still sat at the kitchen table.

Faye grabbed the paper and pencil.

"How long would it take you to make me a wedding dress?" Faye wrote. "A simple one, nothing fancy."

Dolly pulled her measuring tape out of her pocket and wrapped it around her neck like a jaunty scarf.

"Tonight," Dolly wrote. "If you're in a hurry. But it won't be perfect."

"Want to get married tomorrow?" she asked Pat.

"No time like the present."

"I always wanted a June wedding," she said. "Now I get to have two of them. I should probably tell Carrick."

"That we're getting married?"

"Yes. And that Carrick and I are getting married."

24

"By the powers vested in me by God and His Holy Church, I now pronounce you husband and wife. You may kiss the bride."

"That sounds really familiar," Faye said as Carrick took her face in his hands. "Where have I heard that before?"

"Your other wedding," Carrick said. "This morning."

"Oh, that's right." She glanced at Pat, who laughed and rolled his eyes at the absurdity of the situation. "I got married to that guy, too."

"You did, but this is the one that counts," Carrick said. "Now hush so I can kiss you."

"I'm hushing. Start kissing."

Carrick kissed her, or attempted to. She could hardly stop smiling long enough to make it a real kiss. But that was fine, as Dolly chose that moment to pelt them both with rice, which ruined the kiss even more than her semipermanent grin did.

Faye laughed as Carrick groaned, but he didn't give up. He tilted her head back, pulled her body flush with his and kissed her like he meant it, like every other kiss between them had been an ellipsis and this was the full-stop period.

The end.

Lips to tongue, tongue to lips... Carrick didn't seem to care they were being watched by both Pat and Dolly as he kissed her, and Faye couldn't care less, either. Only when Dolly hit them with another cup of rice did they finally stop. Carrick pressed his lips to her ear and whispered one more vow to her. "I'll will love you and take care of you for the rest of your life."

"Don't you mean *your* life?"

"I meant what I said."

She smiled, but didn't tell him Will would make the same vow decades from now. Why give the credit to Will when Carrick said it first? She tucked the vow in her heart, where she kept the vows Will had made to her. They glowed inside her like a beacon in the night, keeping watch over her.

Dolly took Faye and Carrick by the hands and dragged them to the porch, where she'd set up a wedding dinner. Marrying Pat had taken some doing. They'd had to register for a license and then had sit around for the two-day waiting period before they could get married. But Pat hadn't minded sticking around in 1921. Being in a body that didn't betray him with aches and pains and tremors was like being on vacation, he'd said. He slept in Carrick's bed at night while Carrick worked in the lighthouse. Then he and Faye and Dolly had gone into town during the day to fill out the marriage license and be seen by the fine people of Beaufort.

It had scared Faye to see the town finally, the people in their period clothes that weren't period clothes but simply their clothes. She'd passed a livery stable on the way to the justice of the peace. An actual livery stable. Carrick had pointed it out and said he'd kept a horse there for his once-a-month trips into town for supplies. A horse. Carrick owned a horse. For transportation. The way other people owned bikes in 2015. It amazed her, although it shouldn't have. Rural South Carolina had one foot in the nineteenth century and barely a toe in the twentieth. But she understood the temptation to live in the past better than anyone. When people lost hope, they looked in the last place they remembered having it, and it was always in the past. Maybe someday they'd stop looking to the past to find their hope and start looking at one another, where hope really lived. Pat had traveled back ninety-four years to rescue her. Carrick had carried Dolly 110 steps to protect her from a storm. Dolly had stayed up all night to sew Faye a wedding dress, and it was as lovely as anything she'd ever worn—a sleeveless ivory sheath dress made from the same fabric Dolly had used to make her baby sister's church dress. Hope was other people, no matter what the philosophers said.

And this was a time that needed hope. That morning in Beaufort, Faye had seen children sitting on house porches in the morning humidity looking unwashed and undernourished. She'd seen dogs roaming the streets snapping at one another and men kicking the dogs right in their skinny ribs. She'd smelled a fish plant on the water and gagged at the scent of rot and diesel. She'd seen an older white woman in a fine white dress being followed by a young black housemaid, who held a parasol over her head, a scene Faye found more noxious than the fish plant. These were ugly things, but she saw them with a photographer's eye that needed to see all, to record all, to hold a mirror up to the world so it could see itself—see the stark ugliness, yes, but all the beauty, too.

After her quick and perfunctory wedding in town to

Pat, they'd returned to the island by rowboat. Standing in the living room by the picture window, Pat became a priest again and performed a simple and lovely wedding ceremony with no one acting as witness but Dolly and God, which was more than good enough for Faye and Carrick.

By seven o'clock that evening, Faye had officially been married four times.

To which Faye could only say, "Give the lady a prize."

Not long after dinner, Dolly's father showed up in his little tin fishing boat. Dolly ran out to the dock to embrace her father. Faye followed and helped her into the boat.

"You're looking mighty fine today, Miss Morgan."

"I got married today, Mr. Rivers," she said.

"Then my heartiest best wishes to you, Miss Morgan. Who is the lucky man?"

"Patrick Cahill. A sailor."

"Well, I hope he's real good to you, Mrs. Cahill."

"He will be. And your lovely daughter made the dress. She's very gifted. She should sell the clothes she makes."

"That's a fine idea. We'll run that by her mama."

"Tell Dolly she has the day off tomorrow. She's more than earned it."

"I'll do that. You have a good night now," he said with a little knowing grin that wasn't quite a wink but served the same purpose.

She waved Dolly off and watched until she and her father were out of sight. She heard footsteps on the dock and turned to see Pat coming toward her, his hands in his pockets, a look on his face that told her it was time.

"Leaving so soon?" she asked.

"Carrick and I have said our goodbyes—for now. And I wouldn't want to overstay my welcome. You and Carrick should have the house to yourself. It is your wedding night, remember?"

"And Carrick is a lighthouse keeper, remember? He'll spend half the night in the watch room."

"And the other half with his new wife. I should be on my way before I get too used to this body. Wish I could take it with me."

"You are awfully handsome. Anyone ever told you that you look like Gregory Peck?"

"Once or twice. I never believed them."

He crossed his arms over his chest and looked out to the sea.

"It's just the damnedest thing, isn't it? Us being here?" he asked.

"That's one way to put it. You think this is God's doing?"

"I'd like to think it is." He stuck his foot out and toed a fishing net Carrick had left out to dry on the dock. "You know, I used to come out to the islands all the time to swim. I'd watch the fishermen mending their nets and I remember wondering if time was like that. They teach us in seminary that God is outside of time. He created it, knitted it, just like you knit a net. Sometimes you get a tear in that net and have to mend it. What Carrick lost, what you lost… That's a big tear. Maybe this is God mending that rend. Maybe He'll do it for all of us someday."

"Maybe He will," she said. "Maybe He is."

"Coming here was good for me. I feel His greatness again, His majesty and mysteriousness." Pat turned his face to the setting sun and smiled a beatific smile. "I'll take that back with me. It'll carry me to the end."

"What will you do when you get back? Will you tell anyone what happened?"

"No. Some secrets are too beautiful to tell. And too dangerous. We'd have to build a fortress to keep people from jumping into the waters around here, hoping to find a time machine. I'll paint my secrets instead. I'll paint the lighthouse keeper's daughter, and no one will know she's really my wife."

"You're going to paint me?"

"Someone has to paint the Lady of the Light."

"I hope they don't still call me that in the future. I don't want to be a ghost story."

"I'm sure they'll find something else to say about you now. Hopefully that you lived a long, happy life even though your bastard sailor husband knocked you up and abandoned you, never to return."

"Why did I marry that guy? What was I thinking?"

"Pretty girl like you could do a lot better. But it'll make for a good story, I imagine. Lighthouse keeper's daughter marries her sailor lover, and he ships out never to return. Or maybe he does return once or twice, depending on how many children you have. He loves her and leaves her, but our poor Lady of the Light is a constant lover and waits for him, never remarrying in the hopes he will come back to her someday for good."

"Nice story," she said. "Totally bullshit, but still very nice."

"The true story behind the legend is so much better."

"It always is," Faye said, reaching out for Pat's hand. She felt it shaking, but didn't know if that was her hand or his.

"I should go," he said.

She squeezed his hand and kissed his cheek. She would never see him again.

"Thank you," she whispered.

"Watch yourself. You're in deep waters here, remember?"

"It's okay," she said. "I have my own personal lighthouse."

Pat smiled and turned from her, turned toward the end of the dock. He slipped out of his shoes and took a step forward. He looked back at her one more time.

"What?" she asked.

"Nothing. Just trying to decide what color to use on your eyes when I paint you. Dioxazine violet, I think."

"Go," she said. "Go before I stop you."

"My wife is nagging me already. I'm out of here." He took one step forward and then stopped, turned around, looked at her without a smile, looked at her with a look that scared her.

"E. B. White once said—or maybe he'll say it someday—that the worst time to become a father is eighteen years before a war."

"Why are you telling me this?"

"Because it's 1921, Faye. In eighteen years and three months, Nazi Germany will invade Poland, and there is nothing you can do to stop it. Be safe, Faye. Keep your children safe."

"I will."

Pat looked out to the sea, back at her. "Let me know you're all right."

"How?"

He looked back at the house. "Put a note or something in a coffee can and bury it under the north end of the seawall. I'll dig up. I want to know how you're doing. Since you're my wife and all."

"I'll let you know." Because he was her husband and because he had saved her life and because she loved him as a friend and a priest, she kissed him on the lips.

"Safe travels," she said. "Husband."

With a last look back at her, back at the past, he took off running, bare feet slapping on the dock as he ran to the end and dived off into the water. Faye jogged after him and watched as he swam out deeper and deeper into the ocean. She saw waves rising higher and higher. One washed over Pat as he swam into the wave, and when the wind subsided, Pat was nowhere to be seen.

Faye watched the water until the waves subsided and the ocean quieted once more. She walked back to the cottage alone. Carrick stood on the porch waiting for her.

"He's gone, is he?" Carrick asked.

Faye nodded.

"You all right?" he asked.

"It's just strange knowing I'm never going to see him again. Or maybe I will…if I live long enough. But he won't know me. Isn't that weird?"

"Not homesick, are you?" Carrick searched her face.

She smiled. "Can't be homesick when you're home, right?" She leaned against him, and he held her in his arms and now…now she was home.

"Come inside," he said. "We should make this marriage official before I have to go to work."

"That's the most romantic thing anyone has ever said to me," she said, glaring at him.

Carrick grinned, and the grin was a warning. He swept her up in his arms, opened the door and carried her over the threshold into the house. Their house. Their home. Their wedding night.

"Okay, put me down now," she said. "I can walk the rest of the way."

"I carried a girl up the lighthouse. I can carry you up to the bedroom."

"I'd rather walk so you can save your strength and screw me longer."

Carrick put her flat on her feet.

"I'm never going to get used to hearing a woman talk like that," he said, shutting the door behind them.

"Shocking, is it?"

"Hard to shock an old sailor," he said. "But I'd love to see you try."

"Come upstairs," she said. "We'll see what I can do."

She started for the stairs, and Carrick grabbed her from behind, picked her up and carried her to the bedroom. He threw her down onto the bed before she could even get the lamp lit.

Screw it. Who needed light?

Carrick kissed her, his hands threading through her hair, his mouth to her mouth and his heart beating hard enough she felt it against her chest. Quickly, like he couldn't bear to wait a single second longer, he stripped her out of her clothes and took off his. As he entered her, Faye wrapped her arms around his shoulders and clung to him as he went deep, lifting her hips to take him deeper. He had his arms around her back, and he kissed her neck and collarbone, biting her bare shoulders. Later they would go slow, take their time with each other. But not now. Now it felt urgent, necessary. She needed it from him, and he gave it to her so hard he grunted with every thrust as she groaned with every withdrawal. It was hot in the room, and the sweat and her wetness sealed them together. Her hips pulsed against his. She couldn't get enough of him, no matter how hard he took her. The weight of him on top of her was the weight of her happiness. She'd die if she didn't come, but she needn't have worried. Carrick rolled her back on the bed and grabbed her by the backs of her knees, forcing her legs as wide as she'd ever opened them. God, they were married and this was missionary position, and yet it felt like the dirtiest sex she'd ever had. It was the sounds he made, and the bed made, and she made, and the sweat and the smell in the heat. All of it was so unbearably erotic and arousing, and when she couldn't bear any more of the overwhelming pleasure, she came with a cry that would have woken the neighbors if they'd had any. She lay back, spent, but still held on to Carrick as he moved inside her. When she came, he did, too, wrapped in the full embrace of her arms around his neck and her legs around his back and her heart around his heart.

For a long time afterward, they lay together on the bed, still entwined.

"This..." Faye said. "I remember this."

"What?" Carrick asked.

"Being happily married," she said. "I'd almost forgotten what that feels like. Are you happy?"

Carrick chuckled softly as he rolled off her and ran his hands through his sweat-soaked hair.

"Very. So happy you're not really a girl of twenty I could cry. There are things I want to do to you..."

Faye laughed, drunk on postcoital bliss.

"Do them," she said. "Do them all. But in a few minutes. I need to recover here. Been a long time?"

"Too long," Carrick said and laughed against her sweating skin. "Did I hurt you?"

"Only in the best ways."

Faye tried to sit up and promptly fell back on the bed. She was so raw inside she could barely close her legs. "I wish we had an ice maker."

"Ice maker?"

"One other thing I'll miss about my time. My ice maker. I could use an ice pack right about now and right about here." She pointed between her legs.

"I can't do that, I'm afraid. How about this instead?"

He dipped his head between her open legs and licked her gently. She twitched with pleasure, and Carrick groaned in annoyance.

"Hold still," he ordered. "I've been dreaming of this for days."

Faye laughed, but Carrick was serious. He took her thighs in his large strong hands and held her down in a death grip to keep her moving out of reach of his mouth. As he made love to her with his tongue and lips, Faye raised her head to see him. The last rays of evening sunlight spilled into the room, and in the shadows created by the dusk, Carrick looked nothing like Will at all. He looked only like Carrick; he looked like the man she loved.

"I'm so glad pussy-eating exists in 1921," she said.

Carrick looked up at her, one eyebrow cocked high.

"Pussy? That's what they call it in your time?"

"That's what they call it. Maybe because of the hair?"

"Really?" Carrick said. "How queer."

"We're going to have a long talk about that word. Later," she said. Carrick slid a finger into her and she collapsed back onto the bed. "Much later…"

Much later Faye lay on top of Carrick, listening to his heart beating and relishing the rise and fall of his broad chest with every breath.

"She gave you to me," Faye said.

"Maybe your Will gave you to me," Carrick said.

"Maybe he did. Will always said 'Give the lady a prize.'

You make a fine prize, Chief." Faye raised her head and met Carrick's eyes. "You miss her?"

"I'm at peace," he said. "I only hope she's as happy somewhere as I am here. You? You miss him?"

"Yes," she said. He wrapped his arms around her naked back and she turned her face to kiss the center of his chest. "I'll miss him a little later tonight. I'll miss him a little tomorrow. I'll always miss him a little." She smiled up at him. "I hope that doesn't hurt you. Does it? Tell me if it does."

"It's good you miss him. If you miss him, it's because you know he's not here."

"He's not here. He's not even born yet. I find that very comforting."

"And you'll be happy here with me?"

"I could die here a happy woman. I don't know if I could be any happier than I am now. I feel like I got everything back that I'd lost in my old life. Husband, baby on the way, a friend..."

"You're still missing something."

"I am? What?"

"Stay there," he said as he stood up and headed out the door.

"Thanks to you I can't walk," she called out after him. "Where would I go?"

"Just stay."

She stayed.

Carrick was gone only a minute before he walked into the room holding a leather case the size of a large book in his hands.

"You said the other day you wanted one of these."

Faye unfastened the leather straps on the case and pulled

out something she'd never seen before but recognized instantly.

She looked up at him in shock and joy.

"You got me a camera?"

"You said you missed having a camera."

"When... How?"

"Bought it from one of the keepers at Hunting. He wasn't using it. They say Kodak is pretty good. Hope so."

"Yes, Kodak is a good camera. A very good camera." She ran her fingers over the camera, turning knobs and adjusting the straps. She lifted the camera's viewfinder to her eye, aimed it in the direction of the lighthouse, and as soon as she saw it, she knew...

"You're smiling," Carrick said.

"I know what I'm here to do," she said, looking up at him, breathless with happiness and excitement. "I know exactly what I'm supposed to be doing with my life here. I should have known... I mean, it's what I was supposed to be doing in 2015."

"And what is that?"

"What I was hired to do. Take pictures of the islands."

25

Faye spent half the night with Carrick up in the lighthouse before coming back down to her bedroom. She woke up right after sunrise to find him in her bed, where he belonged, sound asleep. She kissed his forehead, and he didn't stir. She'd let him sleep. With Dolly gone they had all day to play honeymooners and half the night. And the rest of their lives. As quietly as she could, she slipped from the bed and went downstairs. The mantel clock revealed the time as half past seven. She'd slept late today. How decadent. When she was married to Hagen with no reason to get out of bed, she'd wake up around ten, and maybe by noon she'd be showered and dressed. But that was her old life, and she didn't miss any of it. Not even her ice maker.

Faye peeked out the front door at the ocean and saw an old friend of hers standing on the end of the pier. Wearing nothing but her slip, she walked out into the morning haze. The bit of grass between the porch and the seawall was cold and slick with dew. Her toes tingled, waking up the rest of her body.

"Hello, you," Faye said to the white wood stork perched on the very end of the pier.

The wood stork eyed her and said nothing.

"Don't worry. I won't take your picture. Not yet anyway. I have to get some film first."

The stork tilted its head sideways. Up close Faye was astonished by the sheer size of the bird. It must have been more than three feet tall. Perched as it was on top of the pier's post, they met eye to eye.

The stork didn't answer, but Faye hadn't truly expected it to talk.

"Was this your doing?" she asked. "Who do you work for?"

The stork dipped its head and dropped something onto the pier at Faye's feet.

It was golden and shining in the new morning light. Faye picked it up.

Will's championship ring.

Faye gasped, tears instantly springing to her eyes.

"Will..." she breathed.

I told you I'd love you and take care of you for as long as you lived.

"Yes, you did, babe," she whispered. "Thank you."

Faye slipped the ring onto her thumb and smiled at the sunrise, smiled at the ocean, smiled at the stork and the ocean and the waves, the blessed waves that had brought her here.

She smiled until a wave came from nowhere and slammed into the end of the dock, knocking her into the water and sweeping her out to sea.

26

He looked like an elderly Gregory Pack again. His hands trembled with the palsy that plagued him as he passed Faye a glass of red wine.

"I saw the stork I'd seen at the lighthouse standing on the pier. I walked out and the bird gave me the ring." Faye held up her hand to show off Will's ring on her thumb. "A wave came out of nowhere and hit me. When I woke up, I was on the beach and it was 2015 again."

Faye took a long sip of her wine. Pat said he'd had to drink at least two glasses a night or he couldn't fall asleep, his hands would shake so hard. Faye was drinking for other reasons tonight. She missed her husband. She missed her island. She missed her home. She missed the peace she'd had there, however brief.

"You didn't do anything at all?" Pat asked as he took a seat on the chair next to his sofa. "You didn't go in the water, touch the water, drop anything in the water?"

"No." She shook her head. "I was doing nothing but

standing there, and the wave came for me. I didn't see it coming, didn't hear it coming. It just came."

"You want to go back, I assume?"

"Of course I want to go back. My husband's there."

"I thought he was right here."

Faye laughed, but it wasn't a real laugh. There was no joy in it. In 2015 she wasn't pregnant, and she felt the loss of it as keenly as she missed Carrick and Dolly. She had to go back, no matter what.

"Pat, why am I here? I knew. I knew exactly what I was doing in 1921." She leaned back on the couch and stared at the ceiling. "I knew my purpose. I knew the plan. Everything I lost in this time I got back in the past. There's no reason for me to be here again. None."

"And yet here you are. Must be a reason. If there's a reason you went there, there must be a reason you came back."

"The hole," she said. "I think it's that hole."

"What?"

"The hole in the fishing net. Remember?" She lifted her head and looked at him. "You said you thought of time as a fishing net. God—or whoever—knits the net and sometimes that net gets a hole in it and God, or whoever, has to mend the net. I'm the patch in the hole in the net. I have to be. I'm back here to mend the hole."

"One more stitch in time?" Pat asked.

"Maybe. But I don't know what to do to make that last stitch." She couldn't keep going back and forth, one foot in the present and her heart in the past. She had to find a way to stay back and stay for good.

"There has to be something, Faye. Something that keeps dragging you back here. If you were a ghost I'd say unfinished business."

She shrugged, tears in her eyes.

"There's nothing," she said. "My father's dead. My mother might as well be. She's in good hands with her sister. I loved them. They were good parents but…it's not them. I have no brothers or sisters. I have no kids. I'm widowed. I'm divorced. I'm…"

Faye stopped. She looked into the deep red cave of her wineglass.

"I'm divorced," she said.

"Hagen?" Pat asked.

Faye nodded. "Hagen."

"Does Hagen still love you?"

Faye reached into her purse and pulled out her phone. She hit a few buttons and showed it to Pat.

"Ten missed calls while I was gone," Faye said. "And according to the clock and the calendar, I was gone twelve hours."

"Nobody calls a woman ten times in twelve hours if he doesn't care when she goes missing."

"You really think I was brought back here to 2015 just to talk to my ex-husband on the phone?"

Pat took a long, deep drink of his wine and then set the glass on his knee. It didn't shake.

"I told you. Ex-husbands are people, too."

"He played golf with his buddies the day after I had my second miscarriage."

"Well… I never said they were *good* people."

"I don't know," Faye said. "Compared to Marshall, Hagen's a saint. Low bar, right? But he did just what Carrick did—married a woman who was pregnant with someone else's baby."

"What do you think would have happened to you if you hadn't married Hagen?"

"Honestly?" Faye said. "I think I might have killed myself. Maybe I should tell him that."

"Maybe it wouldn't hurt."

Faye kissed Pat on the cheek—they'd said all their goodbyes to each other in 1921—and left her half-finished glass of red wine on his coffee table. She got into her Prius and cranked up the air-conditioning as she drove out to Bride Island. She knew she wouldn't find Carrick there. Or Dolly. Or her house or her porch or her garden. But she needed to be near the lighthouse if she was going to have this conversation. She felt naked in this time, stripped of herself, like she'd left most of Faye in 1921 and all that was here now was just fragments and pieces. If Hagen was the reason she kept coming back, there was nothing for it. She would have to call him.

But she didn't have to like it.

Faye made the call.

"Faye? Jesus Christ, I've called you a million times."

"I noticed," she said. "I'm sorry."

"Are you okay?" He sounded frantic.

"Of course I am."

"Of course? You had an MRI a couple of days ago, and you say 'of course,' like of course you're okay. I was afraid you'd passed out on the side of the road or something, gotten into a car wreck, I don't know."

"I didn't. I was just staying with some friends and didn't have my phone on me."

"Keep it on you, okay?" The anger in his voice was a mask for his relief. He should have taken the mask off more often.

"I will. I promise," she said, hoping that after today she'd never see her phone again.

"Good."

"Good."

Faye waited. Hagen would either give up and tell her goodbye or he'd start the third degree with her.

"Who are the friends you were with?" he finally asked. Third degree it was.

"Hagen."

"Sorry. Sorry. I know. None of my business anymore." Silence again. A long pause. Faye waited him out. "I hope you don't mind, I put something in the mail for you."

"What?" she asked.

"Your wedding album. Yours and Will's. I found it when I cleaned out the guest room closet. I know you hid it from yourself after we moved into the new house."

"I didn't hide it from myself—I hid it from you."

"From me? Why?"

"You hated when I talked about Will. I thought you'd…"

"You really thought I'd make you get rid of your wedding album? Seriously? You thought that of me?"

"It crossed my mind."

"I wouldn't have," Hagen said. "I swear to God I wouldn't have done that."

"I know that now. I just didn't know it then. Sorry."

"No, it's all right. I know I always shut you down when you tried to talk about him. I shouldn't have done that. We should have talked about him."

"I think that would have helped us both," she said.

"Looking at your wedding album brought everything back. You know in college, we joked that Will would make all his baseball money and I would take care of it for him so he wouldn't go bankrupt like a lot of professional athletes do. It was just a joke, but when you two got married, he asked me to promise to take care of you if anything happened to him. I'd forgotten about that until I looked at your pictures. There's a really good one of all three of us. I hope you don't mind, but I…I made a copy of that one to keep."

Faye lifted her hand to her forehead.

"No, I don't mind," she said. "Thank you for sending me the album."

"You're welcome."

She hadn't expected that Hagen would do that for her. She hadn't expected the apology, either.

"He looks so young in the pictures. And he's smiling like an idiot in every single one of them," Hagen said. "It was really tough to look at them, but I couldn't stop once I started."

"I keep forgetting…" she said, and swallowed. "I keep forgetting he was your best friend. Grief can make people selfish. It made me very selfish."

"Better selfish than bitter. That's what it did to me," Hagen said. "Bitter and stupid."

"You are not stupid."

"I was." Hagen laughed. "I mean, I asked you to marry me."

"Rude."

He laughed again. "You know what I mean. I asked you to marry me a month after Will was killed. That was pretty dumb, and we've both paid for that mistake." Hagen paused, and she knew he was wiping tears off his face. She knew that because she was doing the same thing. "The more I think about it, the more I wish I could go back and do everything different."

"Like when you went to play golf the day after my second miscarriage?" she teased.

"I didn't."

"You did, you jerk. You told me you did."

"I told you I did, but I didn't."

"Then where the hell did you go?"

"I went to Mom's and told her I was about ninety percent sure I'd ruined your life and I was about ninety-five percent sure I'd ruined mine, too. She talked me off the ledge and sent me home to you. Told me to take care of my wife. But you didn't want to be taken care of."

"I should have let you," she said. "I should have done a lot of things I didn't do. I should have seen a therapist. I should have grieved for Will like I needed to. I should have kept working even when you told me not to."

"We should never have gotten married," he said. "I could have helped you without marrying you. I guess I just thought it's what Will would have done. It wasn't meant to be, though. You and I."

"No, it wasn't meant to be. And I believe some things are meant to be."

"Can you forgive me?" he asked.

"For marrying me? I don't know. That's a pretty big sin."

"For hurting you," he said. "For being a bad husband."

"Trust me," Faye said. "I know bad husbands. After the first miscarriage, I don't know if I would have gone on if it hadn't been for you. I was drowning and you were the lifeboat. You saved me, put me in the boat, got me out of the rough waters. But then you and I, we never got out of the lifeboat. You were always trying to save me and I was always drowning. You can't live in a lifeboat. But I want you to know that you did save me. I don't think I would have survived losing Will if you hadn't been there for me in the beginning."

"Thank you, Faye. I needed to hear that."

"Will would have never wanted you and me to hate each other. He loved us both."

"He was better than both of us put together," Hagen said. "We almost deserved each other."

"Almost."

"Are you better now?" he asked. "You sound better. You sound... I don't know. Alive again?"

"I'm alive again. You were right. You really can't live in the past. So let's not. Let's move on. I forgive you, and you forgive me. And you find someone else to love, someone who can have your kids and who'll enjoy your big, pretty house. Someone who will let you take care of her. And I'll find someone who makes me as happy as Will did. And you and I will both be happy again. Fair enough?"

"I can live with that," Hagen said. He paused again, and Faye waited. "Is it okay... This is stupid."

"What? Ask it. Whatever it is, ask it."

"Would you care if... I mean, if I get remarried and if I have kids, would it be okay with you if I named one of my kids after Will?"

"He was your best friend."

"Yeah, but he was your husband."

With her fingertips, Faye brushed a new round of tears off her cheeks.

"So were you," she said. "And I would like it very much if you named your son after Will. Or daughter. Willa's a pretty name. I know Will would have gotten a kick out of that."

"Okay, good. I just... Do you think we should stop talking to each other? I mean, for a year or so or maybe more?"

"Yes," she said. "I think that would be good for the both of us to move on. Way on." About ninety-four years on, in Faye's case.

"I think so, too. And if this is the last time we talk, I wanted to make sure."

"You have my blessing. It would mean a lot to me," she said. "A lot to Will."

"Thank you. I'll let you go now."

"I'm glad we talked," Faye said. "You know, actually talked. Like human beings."

"Me, too. Take care, Faye. Thanks for…"

"For what?"

"Thanks for doing the best you could."

"You're going to be a great dad someday."

"Goodbye, Faye. I wish you all the happiness in the world."

"You, too. Goodbye, Hagen."

She let him do the honor of hanging up first. And when he did and the call died, Faye knew it was over. She'd done it. All loose ends tied up. The hole mended, but for one last little thing.

Faye took a deep long breath and waded into the ocean. The water was warm tonight, almost like bathwater.

"Please let this work," she said as she held out her hand and dropped her phone into the water. "I want to go home. I want to go home."

She heard in the distance the sound of a train, iron wheels on iron tracks.

Overhead the lighthouse lantern room winked into life. A beam of light flashed once and went dark.

Faye smiled.

Light.

Two. Three. Four.

And she could see the wave coming right for her.

Five.

"Wait up, Carrick. I'm coming back."

Six.

Just for fun, Faye kicked her heels together three times. "There's no place like home."

Seven.

Dark.

27

The pretty young guide hopped off the gray church bus first and ushered the group of a dozen or so tourists toward the telescope. Pat shook his head. Here they were again. Didn't that poor tour guide ever get sick of giving the same damn spiel every single day?

"This telescope is trained on the lighthouse at the Seaport Island, or what we locals call Bride Island. The island is privately owned, so this telescope is the best way to see it without chartering a boat…"

Pat picked up a clean brush and dipped it in his cup of water. He'd been painting nothing but the lighthouse for weeks now. Every night he dreamed of the lighthouse. Every morning he woke to the need to paint it again and again. He'd gotten pretty good at it. One of the better galleries in town had even offered him a show. This painting was shaping up to be the star of the show. It was the first one he'd ever done close-up of the lighthouse keeper's daughter. She stood at the end of the long pier, the lighthouse small behind her, and she was smiling toward the sun with a hand on her pregnant belly.

"The Bride Island Light is very special to us here in Low-country," the tour guide continued, and Pat still couldn't decide if her South Carolina drawl was real or put on to get better tips out of the tour group. "Dorothy Rivers Holt, the first African-American woman to be featured in *Architectural Digest* for her home designs, was housekeeper at the Bride Island Light in her teens. Her interior-design company was partly funded by the Morgan family, who gave her ten thousand dollars as a wedding gift in thanks for her service at the Bride Island Light. And of course, the light-house keeper himself, Chief Carrick Morgan, was a highly decorated war hero who worked as keeper of the light from 1921 until 1937. In 1926, a fishing boat broke apart during a storm, and, thanks to Chief Morgan's efforts, all fourteen lives were spared. He saved many lives during his tenure, including his own daughter, when she was swept out to sea by a rogue wave in June of '21, and we thank God for that around here. Faith Morgan is easily our most famous Bride Island resident. At age twenty, the lighthouse keeper's daughter married a sailor named Patrick Cahill, who promptly shipped out to sea, leaving her pregnant and alone."

"What a scoundrel," Pat said under his breath.

"This didn't deter Faith from following her dreams, how-ever. Her father gave her a camera as a wedding gift, and Faith used it to take pictures of the island, the island resi-dents, the lighthouse keepers and their families. Her pho-tographs are an indispensable resource. Not only did she preserve invaluable history with her pictures, but she helped raise awareness of the damage industrial pollution caused to the human and animal inhabitants of the island. In 1930, a photo series she did of factory pollution in the waters off the coast raised a national outcry. Laws were swiftly passed to protect and preserve Lowcountry's fragile coastline. Thanks to Faith Morgan our beaches are still the cleanest in the world, which is why to this day she's known as the patron saint of Lowcountry, or, as we like to call her 'The Lady of the Light.'"

"That's my wife," Pat muttered as he added silver shadows to the water.

"Another one of our local heroes is sitting right over there painting. That's Father Pat Cahill—no relation to Faith's husband, obviously. Everyone wave at Father Pat."

The tourists waved at Pat. Pat waved back.

"Father Pat was out painting the Bride Island lighthouse when he found a coffee can by the old seawall. In the can were ten rolls of Kodak film wrapped in oilskin. Those pictures, taken by Faith Morgan and never before published, show Bride Island and the lighthouse in all its original glory. This year the Preservation Society put together a very special calendar featuring those pictures. But not only those pictures. Faith Morgan's granddaughter, Dolly Morgan Bryant, a Hollywood cinematographer, has re-created the photographs Father Pat found. You can see what Lowcountry looked like in the 1920s and compare them to today's pictures. Thanks to those photographs, there's been renewed interest in the Bride Island lighthouse. Ms. Paris Shelby, owner of the island, has donated the original four acres of land leased by the government to the town. In spring 2017, restoration will begin on the light. By 2019, the lighthouse will be fully functional again, and the lighthouse cottage will have its first lighthouse keeper and lighthouse family living in it in eighty years. All proceeds from the sale of the calendar will go toward restoring the lighthouse and rebuilding the keeper's cottage, which will be furnished with much of the original furniture, donated by Dorothy Holt's granddaughter Elizabeth. The fund-raising calendars are available in the gift shop at the end of the tour."

"And my paintings!" Pat yelled to the tour guide.

"That's right," she said, laughing. "Father Pat's paintings of the lighthouse are also for sale in the gift shop, and all proceeds will go to the lighthouse restoration fund. We all need a little light, don't we?"

"Amen," Pat said.

The tour guide continued, "Lowcountry, as we say around here—"

"Lowcountry is God's country," Pat said under his breath, reciting along with the guide. "And Faith Morgan's photographs are proof God is keeping a close watch on us."

Pat rooted around in his art bag and found exactly what he was looking for. His painting was almost finished. All that was left was to give Faye Morgan her dress and her eyes.

There they were. Cadmium yellow and dioxazine violet.

Yellow for the dress and violet for the eyes, for her Elizabeth Taylor eyes.

★ ★ ★ ★ ★

Author's Note

This book is a work of fiction inspired by the real story of Florence Martus of Savannah, Georgia, a lighthouse keeper's sister. According to local lore, Florence fell in love with a sailor, became engaged to him and, after he shipped out, took it upon herself to greet every ship that came into the Port of Savannah in the hopes her lover was aboard. As far as I know, he never returned, but Florence is forever remembered as a symbol of Savannah's hospitality to visitors.

While there is no Bride Island in South Carolina, there is a Hunting Island, and several of the details about the Bride Island lighthouse were taken from the real Hunting Island lighthouse. It's worth visiting if you have the time and two dollars to spare.

This book was written with affection and admiration for the men and women of all nationalities, religions, and races who served in lighthouses all over the world, affection and admiration that only grew as I read their letters, diaries and memoirs. I am forever grateful to the keepers, their spouses and their children who wrote those records and published them for posterity. While most events in the book are pure fiction, one incident is taken from history's record. A South Carolina lighthouse keeper did once save his wife from an alligator attack with an ax. Faye is correct in her assessment that such a man is rightly to be called a "badass."

Also, thank you to Mary Herring Wright, author of the touching memoir *Sounds Like Home: Growing Up Black and Deaf in the South*, an invaluable resource while writing *The Night Mark*.

As always, thank you to my lovely readers.

Special thanks to the lovely people of Beaufort, South Carolina. Even without time travel, your town and its islands are a magical place.

Thank you to my amazing agent, Sara Megibow. And my deepest gratitude to my editor Susan Swinwood. It has been an honor and a joy working with you. I can never thank you enough for taking a chance on me and my weird *weird* books.

And endless thanks and love to my husband, author Andrew Shaffer.

My hero.